EZEKIEL

JOHN FANNING

Published by La Muse Books.

1, Rue de la Place, 11380, Labastide Esparbairenque, France.

Visit our website: lamusebooks.com

First Printing 2018.

Distributed to the trade by IngramSpark.

paperback ISBN: 979-10-97233-11-2

ebook ISBN: 979-10-97233-09-9

"Make for yourself a new heart and a new spirit."

Ezekiel, 18:31

CONTENTS

PART ONE
CARCASSONNE
FRANCE

SUNDAY, JANUARY 1, 2017

IN THE STREET

Ezekiel smiles. The sunlight shifts from his face. He opens his light blue eyes.

Behind the parasol pines across the street a floating white cloud covers the sun. His gaze travels over to the tan HLM buildings to the right, new BMWs, Audis, and two rusting Peugeot 205s parked below them. An elderly lady wearing a swollen black eye and a stained black headscarf hangs washing on the third floor terrace of one of the buildings. The paint peels like sunburnt skin from the worn wall behind her. A half-dressed child clings to her leg to fight the cold wind. A man screams from inside. The scream makes the lady drop a dark red sock. Ezekiel follows its fall onto the roof of one of the Peugeots, sees it finally slipping onto the bent handle of an overturned shopping trolley, the front left wheel of which is missing.

He sits back on the white plastic chair to the right of the main entrance to College Émile Alain, his smile gone. He remembers walking through that car park an hour earlier, with Pascale. How an overweight North African man, then a young lady with a headscarf, looked at them.

Pascale sits forward in the chair beside him, the rouge on her cheeks a fun flourish she's earned. "Where is that principal? Are we sure he's not Front National? *Renovations*. I don't care if a bomb fell on the place. They can't leave us parked out here like cars." She lights a roll-up, singeing some of her frizzy bobbed black hair in the process. "I'm getting too old for this, Zeke."

"Me too."

"So, are you going to stop teaching, then?"

"I can still walk. I can still talk."

Pascale laughs. "Ever the *Résistance* fighter." She wraps her arm around his back, holds him close for a moment. Her familiar smell, a combination of *Savon de Marseille*, cigarette smoke and lavender oil, mixes with the sea air from the *vent du Marin*.

"You know what they say, it takes one to know one."

They both laugh.

"How's your family, Zeke?"

"Well, you're here, aren't you? You and me are the only ones left."

"Not that family." She nods at a tall young man kicking small stones against the school gate, a cigarette dangling from his mouth, his hands thrust deep into his pockets. "Is Daniel not family?"

"Yes, he's family."

"You still get on with him?"

"Yes, we get on. He doesn't get on with himself though. You know his mother."

"Yes. Same genre as my sons' wives. They're all *porcs*."

Ezekiel laughs out loud, his thin hands holding onto his knees. "Oh, I've missed you, Pascale."

The cloud disappears. The sun shines on Pascale's lean face.

"And I you. And I you." She pulls on her cigarette. "Without a car, what am I to do? I'm not going to put up with this for much longer. If Daniel hadn't come, I'd have been stuck where I was."

Ezekiel fixes the gray *gardian casquette* on his head. "We never did get the *règlement de comptes* we always talked about, did we?"

"No. And now we're stuck with another stack of liars, political, familial, institutional, on the horizon. Did you hear Russia sent Le Pen twenty-five million?"

"You're surprised?"

"They're trying to get the Far Right into Germany too. It's working." She flicks some ash on the ground. "All the real revolutionaries are dead. You know that. We're left with the chaff."

"There's still a little wheat left in the world."

"Yes. In the silos of the elites."

A cock crows three times from the looming HLM behind them.

"Trump. Maybe now they'll listen to us?"

"No they won't, Zeke. We've been going into these schools for sixty years. The longer we go in the less they listen. You remember Lilly, the neighbor I used to have in Theziers?"

"Auschwitz?"

"Yes."

"She died?"

"Yes, but that's not why I mention her. You know who she voted for last time?"

"No, not Le Pen?"

"Yes. She had the number tattooed on her arm to remind her every day, and she voted for fascists. She hated *les Arabes* that much. They spray-painted *Fromage* and *Mort aux Français* on her car after smashing in its windows. That was after five of them molested her great-granddaughter in Beaucaire." She taps some more ash. "My own great-granddaughter was violated."

"What?" He pushes his *casquette* back from his brow. "You're talking to her now?"

"No. I had to find out from one of my old neighbors. She's even friends with the mayor of Beaucaire."

"Front National?"

"Yes." She stamps out her cigarette. "That's three times she's been abused. Is it any wonder they turn to Le Pen?"

Ezekiel pulls his *casquette* over his eyes. "Don't you also have family in the States?"

"Yes, my sister's daughter."

"Why don't you visit her for a break, a vacation?"

She laughs. "Visit Trumpland? I never wanted to go to that place before, but now!" She shakes her head from side to side. "She keeps threatening to send one of my grandnieces here. Can you imagine the conditioned young fool she'd send me?"

"She has children?"

"Two. One of them has a daughter with two girls, one black, one white."

"So, she's been married a few times?"

"Three times."

"Why don't they just have affairs? Why all this marrying?"

"How should I know."

"Maybe she'll come some day?"

"And maybe the stars'll fall from the sky."

"Maybe they will."

The cock crows again from the HLM.

Ezekiel takes off his *casquette,* massages his bald head. "I think I'm going to write it all down, Pascale."

"What?"

"What we've been trying to teach all these 12-year olds all these years. I don't think I'm going to be around for much longer. I'm nearly 99. If I don't write it down now it all dies with me."

"I've thought of doing the same thing, many times, but I'm no writer. You, though. You're different. You've always been a poet."

"I don't write poetry."

"You don't have to write it down to be one."

He smiles. "You could easily write it all down too, Pascale."

"No. Not any more. They say I have Alzheimer's. My short term memory is terrible. I was on my way back from the *source* two days ago. I got lost. I had no idea where I was. Yesterday, I was trying to talk to a neighbor about *Renoir, My Father* when I forgot the word."

"What word?"

"Book. I forgot the word book. You know me. All I do is read books, or crochet when I'm not in my garden. Book, Zeke. How could I forget the word book?"

"You see. That's why I have to write it all down."

"Will people ever learn though? Even survivors like Lilly forget because of new violence. Why can't human beings just accept difference?" She starts to roll another cigarette. "Everyone we knew is dead. Your Thérèse. Mathias. Raimond. Don't you get tired of it all, this life, this drama, this constant petty drama?"

"Of course I do. But I can't stop watching. Yes, it's boring, but then sometimes, someone like you says or does something beautiful and then, then it all makes sense, it all becomes meaningful for a moment, maybe a few. Then it's worth it. The flowers in the ditch on the side of the road. The slanted light on the parasol pines. The sound of that crazy cock in the high rise."

"See. Ever the poet, talking about beauty and meaning and flowers." She licks her roll-up. "When will the young people rise up like we did? When will they see this neo-liberalism for what it is: support for the elites? The pretend Left has killed the *real* Left. Now all we have are these extreme Right-wingers. Look at Hungary. Look at Trump. Look at the Front National. Where is the populist Left?"

The cock cries again.

"I'll be happy to be rid of all these horrible memories, Ezekiel. All of them."

"Even Raimond?"

"No. He's the only thing I need to remember." She hugs Ezekiel again. "And you too, of course."

Ezekiel laughs. She smiles as she lays her head on his shoulder.

A scream, from the other side of the school wall.

A young girl's voice. "Stop!"

Daniel looks at Ezekiel. His cigarette falls from his mouth onto the ground. He barges through the school gate.

Another scream. Ezekiel and Pascale stand up and walk as quickly as they can to the main gates. The gate screeches open. The red light stops the traffic to their right as they shuffle down the path. Pascale moves a little faster than Ezekiel. They turn the corner into the side street. Pascale coaxes a screaming little girl in off the street. Men and women are getting out of their cars, leaving them in front of a green light. Ezekiel arrives just in time to see six Maghrebian teenagers disappearing into a different HLM. He moves as quickly as he can to Daniel, lying in the street. He kneels down, puts his handkerchief against Daniel's temple to stay the blood.

The little girl, out in the street again as Pascale tries to revive an unconscious man, screams. "Papa. Papa, why are you sleeping on the ground?"

One of the women from the cars bends down to check the man's pulse. "He's OK. He's still alive." She looks at Pascale, then Ezekiel. "Don't let anybody move these bodies."

She opens her arms to the little girl. "It's OK, *petit.* Come here. Come off the street." The little girl goes into her arms. The woman stands up and walks down the street away from the bodies, rocking the little girl from side to side. "It's OK, *petit.* It's OK."

Pascale screams at a young man videoing the scene on his iPhone. "What are you doing? Are you insane? Call an ambulance! These people need to get to a hospital."

The young man touches his screen three times. "Yes, hello. Yes, it's an emergency. What? Le Viguier. Beside the school. In the street. No. It's not me. It's two men. They've been beaten, or maybe they've beaten each other."

Pascale glares at him. "Maybe if you hadn't been on your device you would have seen the gang of teenagers running off?"

The young man puts away his phone.

Pascale shouts at the crowd of ten to twelve people. "OK, all you people. Get into your cars, or there'll be a car accident too." The crowd doesn't move. "Didn't you hear me? Stop staring at me like a herd of sheep and get back in your cars. Now! How do you think the ambulance is going to get here if you people are blocking the road?"

They start to leave, slowly. The cars begin to move, unblocking the *bouchon.*

Ezekiel sits on the ground beside Daniel's head, his hand still staunching the blood. "In broad daylight. What next?"

"Le Pen. That's what." Pascale sits down beside the unconscious father. "You think she won't use this kind of thing to further her madness?"

They sit on the pavement beside each other, looking up into the HLM surrounding them. It starts to rain.

"Where's that ambulance? Where's the police?"

"Police? Ambulance, yes. Police? Just the other day, in Beaucaire, my friend's son Boris was beaten for looking at a group of Maghrebian teenagers. Looking at them, Zeke!"

"Did he report it?"

"Yes, but what did they do?"

"They arrested the teenagers."

"No. But it's even worse than that. The *commissariat de police* called Boris in the hospital and abused him. And he kept calling him. Threatening him. Telling him he had no right to criticize the way the police dealt with things. He had no right to get him in trouble with the *procurer*."

"The system is falling apart, just like it did when we were teenagers."

"I talked to a neighbor yesterday. Do you know what she said to me? Oh, the Front National isn't fascist any more. That's all in the past. I was shocked. This is an intelligent, kind woman. No. France isn't as violent as it was then, she said. It's more open now."

Pascale lights her roll-up. "People are so blind. What was this man doing? Walking with his child? And they beat him? I'll bet you it wasn't even over money. The children of North Africa, this generation, not the last one or even the one before that, they're just violent. It's what happens when people are uneducated, have no work, are treated as second-class citizens and treat women like animals. Oh, but we're not allowed to talk about this. They can't make arrests or the statistics go up for Maghrebian people arrested which they can use against the police."

She puts her hand on the unconscious man's shoulder. "This poor man's wife will contact the *commissariat de police* and be told there's nothing to be done. Sarkozy, Hollande and whatever fool that comes after him, are afraid to arrest them. So the man's wife will write a letter to the *procurer* explaining everything. How her husband had to be hospitalized. How their little daughter was left crying in the street with cars flying by, her father unconscious."

"You don't know that, Pascale."

"Don't be naive, Zeke. You know the truth better than any one I know. It's the same in the schools. The Maghrebian kids beat up the white kids and nothing happens. The schools allow an infraction and then another and another until all the kids see there are no limits. Violence is normal. We've normalized violence. But violence should never be the norm. This little girl is living beside that beautiful new *conservatoire* over there and the Maghrebian kids are probably sitting on their front lawn drinking beer and smashing the bottles in front of their door. Don't you remember the alto teacher in there telling us all about it last night at the end of the recital? When they have a barbecue the Maghrebian kids go in and take the meat off the spit and start eating it! If one of the white French kids so much as looks at one of those Viguier Maghrebians a knife slides out of their sleeve and they're beaten."

"They need to tell the police."

"Zeke, stop it. I know you're not that naive. One, it's too dangerous for them. And two, politically, nothing happens. My own son is a gendarme. When a woman calls him, a woman who's getting beaten by her husband, he listens, puts down the phone, and goes outside to have a cigarette. They wait fifteen minutes."

"What?"

"Then they go out to the place."

"Why? Because they don't care?"

"No. So that when they get there there's nothing to deal with. The violence is usually over. The husband is usually gone. Then there's no chance of them getting knifed."

She flicks ash on the pavement and puts her hand gently on the man again. "And this poor bastard can't even sell up and live somewhere else."

"Of course he can."

"Who do you think will buy his house?"

"Somebody will."

"Nobody from around here. They know what they're buying into. Look at Daniel. Look at this man. Look at that woman rocking that little girl down the street. The somebody who'll buy their house will be a Maghrebian."

"But they don't have money. They don't have the opportunities to work."

"They do when the house is priced at half its value. Those men with the BMWs and Audis have money. I don't know where they get it, but they'll buy those houses and rent them out to their own people."

"Where are the police?"

"They'll be here soon, Zeke. You'll see. It's nearly been fifteen minutes."

She stubs her roll-up out on the pavement. In the background, sirens.

"You see. They protect themselves, not us. You know the *gendarmerie nationale* is just here?"

"Where?"

"Just opposite the school."

"No."

"Oh, yes, right in the middle of this whole mess."

RÉSISTANCE FIGHTERS

Pascale opens the door into Daniel's hospital room. Ezekiel stands up. They hug, give each other *bisous*.

"Thanks for coming, Pascale."

"I would have been here earlier, but I only got your phone message this morning. You know SFR in the mountains. When did they move him out of the Intensive Care Unit?"

They both sit down.

"Late last night."

"Why didn't you call me?"

"It was too late."

"What did his doctor say?"

"He's stable. He's no longer in danger."

"That's wonderful. So what do they do now?"

"Well, usually they'll focus on maintaining his body. They'll want to protect him from pneumonias, decubitus ulcers, make sure he has balanced nutrition."

"Stop being a doctor for a moment will you. What ulcers?"

"Sorry. Force of habit. Bedsores. He can't move so he has to be moved."

"Are they moving him?"

"Yes. He has a lovely nurse. She's moved him once already. She should be coming back soon."

"That's great news, Zeke."

"Yes, it is. I'm very happy for him. Hopefully he'll come out of it sooner rather than later. The quicker he does the better for his brain. He hasn't been restless either, but they have the bars up just in case. Hopefully his body stays calm so they don't have to give him drugs, although he already had some in his body."

"What?"

"I didn't want to know. He parties a lot. It's like I told you before, he's really hyperactive. Feeds his high energy levels by doing drugs. It's always been hard for him. And his mother. You know what she said when I called to tell her what happened?"

"I can guess."

"*I'm busy.*"

"*Busy?* Busy doing what? Sleeping with another one of her neighbors?"

"You know, years ago they told Daniel he was schizophrenic, back in Avignon. I was in my garden when he told me."

"What did you say to him?"

"I told him nearly everyone is schizophrenic and kept weeding my tomatoes."

"Ezekiel Moran, the master of understatement." She smiles. "How is your insane garden?"

"I've been neglecting it, but it's been a bizarre year. Climate change."

"You're always out digging or meditating in that thing."

"You're as bad."

"I suppose that's why we're still alive. We garden every day. What did you tell him to do about the schizophrenia?"

"I said the diagnosis for most schizophrenics is so broad that it could be anything. I told him not to start taking the drugs they give him, to tell them he had and then throw them in the bin. If he starts taking them, he'll turn into the predictable schizophrenic for the years to come." He massages his temples. "Drugs only help you forget your misery for a period of time. They weaken you for the natural fight against misery. They're palliative treatments, not cures. The most important thing is to get him to see that schizophrenia is a madness that comes from starting on a spiritual path. And that drugs stop it, stop your inner growth."

"Does he hear voices?"

"Of course he hears voices, everyone does."

She laughs. "Yes, but most people chose to ignore them."

"He's different. He's like Thérèse was." He smiles. "She would have told him it's his body, images, emotions, sounds, trying to tell him his soul is suffering. The feeling he gets, that he can't breathe through his lungs, the thing that he was always showing with his asthma, comes from the fact he feels suffocated."

"That sounds a bit..."

"Does it? Did you know that schizophrenia comes from the word *phrenes* which means lungs, and the *schizo* part of it meaning *cut off* or *split from*. The metaphors of the body know no end, Pascale. They're contained in every organ, the stomach, the spleen, the intestines or guts, all of them. Each one has different emotions attached to it."

"Do you think it helped him?"

"What?"

"What you told him?"

"Yes. I gave him a homeopathic treatment too, but he still goes out and gets wasted now and again. He's nowhere as bad as he used to be, though."

"So the voices don't tell him to kill himself, or other people?"

"No, no. Not any more. When he hears them now he writes down what they're saying to him in a journal. He brings the journal to me and we read them out together sometimes. I gave him the journal. It's like this one here that I'm about to write in." He rests his hand on a large black journal. "As he's gotten older he doesn't get as freaked out by them as much. Now they actually help him. They tell him not to do cocaine when his friends offer it to him back in Avignon. They say it's a pollution of the soul. They say some really crazy things those voices of his."

Ezekiel laughs. Pascale puts her hand on his shoulder. "You really are crazy, you know that."

"It takes one to know one."

Ezekiel looks at Daniel.

"What's wrong, Zeke?"

"Oh, I don't know."

"It must be something. You were only laughing a second ago."

"Daniel. I worry about him. What will he do when I'm dead? Where will he go?"

"What, are you not leaving him your house and garden?"

"Yes, I am."

"Well, then. He'll always have his own home."

Ezekiel smiles. "You're right. He will. I'd forgotten about that. My head isn't really here any more. I've become obsessed with writing down what happened to us, before I die. Before Daniel dies."

"You'll be long dead before him."

"Yes, I know. It's illogical. I'll feel a lot better when I've got it all written down. I know it."

She points at the journal. "You sure it has enough pages? You've got a lot to tell."

"I can't tell everything, but like I said to you in the school yard, I feel like I need to write down what happened to us. Otherwise it'll all be lost. How many books have you seen on bookshelves written by actual *résistants*? How many accounts of resistance?"

"Hardly any."

"Now all they talk about is the rise of the Far Right. Why aren't they asking us what we think? We lived through it all before. It doesn't have to happen again. It doesn't."

"It's not what the elites would have us think, though."

"It's funny how it's only when we think we are about to lose somebody that we decide to tell them what we really want them to know. How many funerals have I been to where I found out things about people I thought I knew, things I never knew about them when they were alive. Kind things. Horrible things. I'm going to use this time waiting with Daniel, to write down what I can remember of this life, as best I can remember it, before I'm in a bed like he is. Perhaps in the future, he can give this journal to his children or grandchildren so that they can understand that the most creative thing we can do in this life is to resist and..."

A nurse comes in.

"Hello, Ezekiel."

"Hello, Pauline. Here to turn him again?"

"Yes. Yes, I am. Why don't we let some light in here? Daniel could use some light on his skin."

Pauline opens the curtains.

Ezekiel blinks. "I didn't realize it was light already."

Pauline turns to face him. "Winter's dying away. It's January already."

She moves Daniel onto his side, moves his arm up and down in the air.

"And how are you doing, Ezekiel? How are you feeling?"

"Good. I was a bit down, but it's passed."

"Well, you'd know all the emotional challenges this brings to a family." She starts on Daniel's other side. "I've been asking about you. They tell me you're no ordinary homeopath, that you're kind of famous."

She starts to move Daniel's leg back and forth.

"In my own mind."

Pauline laughs. "Ever the comedian."

"That's for sure." Pascale opens her tobacco pouch. "A lot of people'd be dead only for his sense of humor."

"You know you can't smoke in here, Madame."

"Yes, I know. It's just a force of habit."

"I'm sorry, Madame..."

"You can call me Pascale."

"Pascale. I hope you don't think me rude, but do you mind me asking you what age you are?"

"99."

"*Merde*! *Non*."

"Why? Did you think I was older?"

Ezekiel laughs.

"No. It's ... it's just you smoke. I would have thought..."

"That I'd be dead by now."

"No. Yes. It's ... how long have you been smoking?"

"Since the Nazis took Paris. I thought it was a good time to start."

Ezekiel laughs again, shakes his head.

"You have friends just as mad as you, Ezekiel."

"Just one. The rest of them are no longer here. This one," he nods to Pascale, "you can't kill this one. Even if you wanted to. Enough people have tried. She's immortal. She's like a gunslinger from one of those American movies. Bullets flying all over. She always comes out alive."

Pascale laughs.

Pauline stops moving Daniel. "Have you been shot at?"

Pascale looks at Ezekiel. They both start to laugh.

"What? What's so funny?"

"No. It's just..." She slaps Ezekiel on the lap. "It's just we spent so many years being shot at."

"What, were you soldiers?"

"No. We were resistance fighters. Big difference. Although, Zeke was a soldier for a while. All of five or six weeks, until we *lost* to the Nazis."

"*Merde*, I would have never guessed. It was..."

"All so long ago. Yes, we know." Pascale smiles at her. "What age are you?"

"Twenty-two."

"I'd already been in the *Résistance* for years by the time I was your age."

"That's unbelievable."

"Until you live it."

Pauline picks up a basin and walks over to Pascale with her other hand out. "Well, it's an honor to meet you, Pascale. I'm Pauline."

"Pleasure to meet you too, Pauline."

She turns. "Try to get some sleep, Ezekiel."

She closes the door behind her.

"You see. Lovely young woman, but she has absolutely no idea. Not because she's stupid, but because she's had no experience, no education. How could she know?" He looks at Daniel again. "That's why I have to write this book."

She presses his hand. "How long do you think he'll be like this?"

"Comas can last from days to weeks. If it is bad, it could last as long as five weeks. Some have lasted years. There've been cases who regained consciousness after decades."

"When he does come out of it, what will he be like? The same?"

"Physically, he'll be worse off from not moving about for so long. Intellectually, psychologically, nobody ever knows. Whatever it is it will be gradual, not like they show you in the movies. He'll become more and more responsive the more awake he becomes. In the first days, he'll probably only be awake for a few minutes. When that happens, I'll go back to the mountains. As time passes, his amount of time awake will gradually increase. He'll probably be confused when he first wakes. Perhaps have dysarthria."

"What's that?"

"He'll be unable to speak."

There are tears in Ezekiel's eyes as he looks at the tube going into Daniel's mouth, others coming out of his arms.

"You know, he first came to me when he ran away from home. He was barely a teenager. I gave him homeopathy. It made him feel better right away. When he had nowhere else to go, he always came to me."

"Like I did."

"Yes, like you did." Ezekiel smiles. "He used to tell me I was *hypercool*, that he couldn't understand why his mother, grandmother and great-aunt didn't talk to me anymore. He told me they say I'm crazy, but that's coming from two very crazy women, he said." Ezekiel laughs. "The first time he left the detention center in Montfavet – you know, the one for delinquents – he jumped out the window."

"He reminds me of someone, Zeke."

Ezekiel smiles again. "They call those places *Centre educatifs*. But he couldn't handle being around those other crazy teenagers anymore. He talked a lot about the boy in *The 400 Blows* back then. Said he didn't know what he wanted to be when he grew up, but that he wanted to be *free*, like the boy at the end of the movie."

"Did you ever talk to him about the war?"

"No. It just never seemed to come up. I can go into a school and talk to a pack of complete strangers but not to my own relatives. I suppose I've just gotten used to not being heard by own family. Maybe I can set it straight now?"

Pascale's phone rings.

"Sorry ... Hello. Yes. Yes. Who? Madeline? Madeline, who?" She stands up. "My, what? My great-grandniece...?"

She stares at Ezekiel, makes a face.

"Yes. We can meet. I have no car though, and I'm not in Provence any more. I've moved. Near Carcassonne. It's in the south-west. What? Yes. I can meet you at the train station here. No. I'm in a hospital. No, no. It's a friend. Yes. Call me when you get here. I have no car to collect you. Oh. That's good."

She puts her phone away.

"Looks like I've got a *chauffeur*." She smiles. "She says she's coming to take care of me."

Ezekiel laughs out loud. "Take care of you."

He keeps laughing.

PART TWO
RED

WEDNESDAY, JANUARY 4TH, 2017

CARCASSONNE HOSPITAL, FRANCE

A CROSSING OF SENSES

I was born in the Camargue, in this wonderful country we call France, at midnight, on the full moon of May 1918, and anointed, baptized if you will, Ezekiel Yusuf Moran, in the fortress church of Église des Stes-Maries on the twenty-fifth of that month. The celebratory gypsy festival of the three saints.

From what I remember it was a cold day in the village of Saintes Maries de la Mer, a distinctly red one. I don't mean in color, but in tone. Tonal color. You think I don't remember? I do. I don't remember all my days as a baby, but I remember that one. My brain wasn't fully developed so I hadn't perfected my gift yet. And no, before you think it, I'm not a medium, although I've known many good ones, and one great one.

I have fivefold synesthesia, so I perceive days as colors. That day, my baptism, was definitely a red one, so it was probably a Wednesday like today. I see the words as colors and "Wednesday" has always seemed red to me, just as Monday is orange, Tuesday yellow, Wednesday red almost going into a very light pink, but more of a rose like the flowers in my garden, Thursday a lapis lazuli blue, Friday indigo, Saturday, violet, and Sunday, a very dark red. I've used my synesthesia to remember many things over the years, such as mathematical formulae, poetry in foreign languages, the flight patterns of birds, practically every sailor's knot there is to tie, people's dates of birth, anniversaries, and later on, the numbers, coordinates and names of army bases, camps, *Résistance* fighters and allies, Vichy collaborators, 33rd Waffen Grenadier Division of the SS Charlemagne, and on and on *ad infinitum.* For mathematical formulae I see the letters of equations like Feynman did. I see them as colors. Functions take on colors and start to move around for me. Now, later in life, I am burdened, much like the Russian journalist and mnemonist Solomon Shereshevsky was, by this inability to forget even the most trivial details of anything that has happened to me. On a positive note, though, this bodes well for what I am now writing.

Dad once said to me about a piece of music: "In the beginning is the end. In the end is the color without beginning." We both laughed because it made *sense* to us. My Dad saw things synesthetically too, so he had a jumbled up way of looking at things as I do. I suppose it's genetic, as was the case with Nabokov. But where Nabokov used his gift for writing, I've used mine for music and in a different way for my profession as a doctor. Mr. Nabokov's wife, Véra, his mother, Elena Ivanova and his son, Dmitri, were all synesthetes. I think some of my Dad's brothers, especially his brother, Gabriel, were synesthetes too.

I see numbers, shapes and letters as colors too, not just music like Dad. Rimbaud saw colors in vowels.

> *"A noir, E blanc, I rouge, U vert, O bleu: voyelles,*
> *Je dirai quelque jour vos naissances latentes!"*

Five is green, four is gold, nine is vermillion and three is red to me. I've always seen the rhyme "five for silver, six for gold, seven for a story never to be told" as synesthetic.

When Dad and I played with Alphonse and Yusuf down the road in the local café, I used to get the same way Duke Ellington did. Like Ellington, any time I'm playing with a load of different people I hear each note someone plays as a color. I'd hear Dad playing a note on his alto and it was one color. I'd hear the same note played by Alphonse on the piano and I'd see it as a different color and then a different color again for Yusuf and his voice. When I hear a load of tones I see them in textures, what the Duke called "sustained musical tones". If Dad played a D, I'd see it as a coarse dark blue and if Alphonse played a G, I'd see that as a kind of silky light blue, almost glossy. I actually saw him play once with Ella Fitzgerald on the Cote d'Azur. It was in the town of Juan-les-Pins on the twenty-sixth of June, 1966. An amazing night. Wonderful!

Dad was so happy when he found out I could see colors. I suppose it took away a loneliness he'd always had, the way being different always makes you lonely until you find people on the same wavelength. Later on we'd play colored music, like blue music or purple music or green music. Yusuf understood us too, but for him it was more of a feeling. He felt the music instead of seeing the colors. He felt what purple was, and he could translate it into a chord or chords in his voice by mumbling it and then just stringing words and sounds together. Yusuf had an extraordinary voice.

"So, here's the way it is, Zeke." Dad and Yusuf always called me Zeke. Only my mother and people we didn't know called me Ezekiel. "The scale is a rainbow and every note is a different color. To me a C is red, but to you it might be something else. G is blue for me, and F yellow. Do you understand?"

"Yes, Dad."

I was five.

I can still remember him introducing me to Franz Liszt when I was eleven, staring at me, his light blue eyes widening, a huge smile on his face. He had done the same with Rimsky-Korsakov when I was younger.

"Well?" he said.

"What?" I said.

"Can you hear Liszt's colors?"

"Yes, I can see the color textures."

"But do you feel anything? Do you think you can feel anything from this composer, as if he saw things the way you do?"

"He heard colors too?"

"Exactly!"

Much later, how I wish I could have introduced Dad to Gyorgy Ligeti, Itzhak Perlman, Sibelius...

It was a secret Dad and I kept between us. When I was asked questions at school, I just kept my mouth shut instead of drawing attention to the fact that I found a lot of what we were learning boring and repetitive. Dad warned me when I was six not to let too many people know of our secret, not only because they wouldn't understand it, but because most people don't want to. Later he would tell me how powerful people especially don't like it when your difference is powerful. It makes them feel inferior, he said. Better to let people think they are superior and stick to doing what you love, whatever it is. Like Sibelius, he himself had endured enough people who were only too happy to make fun of what we saw as a gift and they saw as crazy. Mother thought I was crazy.

"Ezekiel, why don't you go and play ball with the other kids?" At the time we lived beside two different French families who had children the same age as me.

"I think balls are boring."

"What?"

"They're not fun."

My Dad had just got in from helping a friend with his *manade* of bulls in Saintes Maries de la Mer.

"James," my mother called him, "come here please."

"What?"

"Ezekiel, he says he doesn't like balls. How can a five-year old boy not like balls? Little boys love nothing more than throwing and catching things, and here we have one who sees colors and remembers the most inconsequential things, like how many flies have flown into the room in the last hour. Do you think that's normal, for Godsake?"

"Hannah, we should probably not talk about this in front of him?"

"What? He's not going to even remember this conversation tomorrow, never mind in a week or month or years from now. All that babble you talk about is just that, babble."

"Well, I think it's great that he can remember things so easily and that he can see things that other people can't. It'll serve him well as he gets older."

"Do you think it's normal, though, for him to sit there in his own little world all the time? I worry that they're all going to pick on him."

"Well, if they do, he'll adapt. Won't you, Zeke?" He picked me up and threw me in the air.

"Yes, Daddy."

"See, he understands! See how smart our little boy is?"

"Yes, that's what I'm worried about."

That was ninety-four years ago. I'd give you the month, day and minutes the conversation lasted as well, but I wouldn't want you to think I'm crazy.

So, you could say I was baptized, not on that violet day in that wonderful church in Saintes Maries de la Mer, but in the church of synesthesia by my father, in the fields of the Camargue but even more so underneath our apple and apricot trees and vineyards outside Aramon, near the mouth of the Petit-Rhône. I don't really see synesthesia as such a big deal. For me, it's normal, a crossing of senses, that's all, with the sensation of sound, of music, being the most important one to me.

My name, though, that was a big deal. Ezekiel Yusuf Moran. Why would two people ever think of putting something so Irish together with something so Jewish and something so Arabic?

Firstly, they didn't think. They let chance choose. My mother consulted her *Bible* with her eyes closed, drunk. The page she found herself on was the beginning of *The Book of Ezekiel.* When she opened her eyes there it was: "Ezekiel."

Secondly, Yusuf. This is the easy part. Yusuf was my other father. He witnessed my birth and stood for me as my godfather at my baptism much to the displeasure of the parish priest. He cared for me like his own son. I love this name, the way it rises out of your mouth as you say it. Uuuuuusoooof. I love it because of the love and nurture that man gave me as I grew up among the *salicornes* and *roseaux* of the large marshes, pools, dunes, salwort and wild plains of the Camargue. I plagued the poor man to find me elusive foxes or *coypu* or beaver. Later on, at our *mas*, a large stone farmhouse outside Aramon where the tamarisk trees were replaced by fig, apple, apricot, peach, pear, *mûrier*, olive, *cognassier*, cypress and *micocoulier* trees, Yusuf took me on "adventures" to find wild boars and fairies.

I always thought Ezekiel a foolish name, at least until later in life. But, then, isn't every name? I suppose if I was called John like my father's father I'd feel equally foolish and boring because everyone is called John, but then I'm not called John, am I? No. I'm named after a prophet from a different section of *The Bible*, the one who prophesied the fall of the temple at Jerusalem. The one who did or didn't resurrect three youths from the dead or whom the Muslims still can't decide is or isn't their prophet Zul-Kifl...

The reason I used to think it was a foolish name? Because it has consistently earned me either confused reactions, sneering, or gotten me into trouble when I meet people, at school and especially during the war. The school bully, Maurice Jalabert, started teasing me about it so much every day that by the end of a year of *maternelle*, I had punched him, giving him a ballooning black eye. Of course when my mother, the one who had conjured up my name I might add, found out, she was disgusted and beat me. Dad was off at the time, taking care of his black bulls outside Saintes Maries de la Mer with Yusuf. Her weapon of choice, the belt Dad used to clean his shaving blade on. I suppose she thought it ironic to hit me with his shaving belt because he never so much as gave me a *fese*, a slap on the backside.

When I got to London to train with the British SIS before the Allied Invasion, it was the same. Instead of French people sneering at me, it was now the English calling me a "Paddy Frenchman Arab Jew". When I parachuted back into France ahead of the invasion, the Gestapo didn't like it either. Do you think they believed me when I told them my name?

Yes, we all need a name. And yes, I am proud of mine, not

because of anything I did, but because of what it represents, so perfectly, the many different parts of me that helped me to grow into the individual I am today. Yes, a Paddy Frenchman Arab Jew, but one who is aware that none of that really matters.

THE WANDERING JEWS

Our tribe, not the larger Jewish one, but my immediate family, James Moran, my father, and Hannah Stein, my mother, met in Avignon quite by chance, as such things happen, at a gallery in the center of town at a time when they were both feeling like what they were, outcasts. What I've always found intriguing, never mind the fact that they were both lapsed Jews, is that each of them came from a country not usually associated with migratory patterns of Europeans to France. Dad arrived from Ireland, most of his fellow countrymen having chosen America, Australia or England. My mother fled Germany, a nation which, historically, only seems to migrate when trying to conquer its neighbors.

They fell in love because of this primary bond of foreignness before they had a chance to get to know each other. Dad would later tell me it happened as quick as your first try at sex, in a flash, and then it was all over, leaving you to wonder how you ever got yourself so worked up in the first place and into the messy predicament you now found yourself in. He never regretted marrying my mother, though. He respected the love they had created together when they met and never stopped respecting her because of what they'd achieved together, the farm, a family. Still, it didn't stop him from falling apart when her drinking became too much. He'd take off into the orchards and get drunk and, when she was drunk for weeks on end, he'd stay on after the market, visiting bars and brothels. This didn't happen very often, but it happened enough for the guilt to eat away at him.

The southern France we come from has people from every country, but only one type of person, the Provençal. You could be Irish like my father, you could be German like my mother, but you were really French and nothing else, to the French. You loved wine more than Guinness, garlic more than potatoes and *terroir* more than any country. Until I was six Dad was a *gardian*, taking care of the small horned black bulls they have in the Camargue, much like he and his family had taken care that the Irish Moiled cows didn't go extinct back in Limerick. The cattle were the same kind of animal, capable of eating poor quality grass and being very hardy. It was then that Dad became a thoroughbred Provençal, speaking Provençal as well as the locals and drinking pastis like it was water, although he later gave this up when my mother's alcoholism knew staggering levels of escalation. We lived in a *gardian*'s house, the Provençal cross with its heart and anchor proudly standing on the front white triangle of the house, the roof being changed every three years for new *roseaux*, what we called *sagne*, from the nearby marshes.

Of course the irony of France, especially where I find myself now in the Aude region of Occitanie, is that the vast majority of individuals down here who have a penchant for Le Pen and her personal form of madness, the *Front National*, are the progeny of emigrants. You only have to ask a lot of the new immigrants how they would vote in the next election. Bear in mind that a lot of these people from the Maghreb are the very people the *Front National* wants out of France, and during the war, worse. How can this be? Don't they understand where the *Front National* comes from, that they are part of that dark anti-Semitic side of the Catholic church which gave birth to Le Pen's organization as well as the Arch-confraternity of the Holy Family in Ireland that spawned the Redemptorist priest Creagh's pogrom of our family in the Limerick of 1904?

The southern Frenchman's Pope supported social nationalism, a phrase which eventually became synonymous with fascism. To the end of World War II, Pope Pius XII never condemned Nazi war crimes, the Final Solution, or Nazi Germany, even when the world begged him to do so. Even Roosevelt wrote to him, asking him to speak out, but the Pope, irrespective of all his personal good works, remained silent, allowing Nazi supporters such as Cardinal Baudrillat, Cardinal Suhard in Paris and Cardinal Garlier in Lyon to hamper all the courageous priests like Father Victor Dillard in Vichy who was killed in Dachau, or Father Pascale Chaillet in Lyon, men who merely wanted to help their people. Instead, priests like Monseigneur Mayol de Lupe, the chaplain of the Légion des volontaires français, was able to say "Heil Hitler!" at the end of every mass.

It was Dad who explained to me how our country's embrace of the cliché of the perfidious Jew as the corrupting influence of Catholicism, murderer of Jesus and usurer who wants to take over the world arose in earnest: it was because of Alfred Dreyfus' case in 1894. That last point, Jews taking over the world, is anything but true if one looks to the facts. In the Aude region alone, where I live, Vichy documented the number of Jews they found here. There were a meagre 765, and of these the "rulers of the world" were soldiers, hospital workers, traveling hosiers, salesmen, shopkeepers and prisoners of war.

Two months after Hitler was put in jail for his failed Beer Hall Putsch of 1923 my parents bought the farm, our sun-bleached stone *mas* outside Aramon, midway between Beaucaire and Avignon, with the money they'd saved after ten years as *manadiers* to the Camargue bulls. I was a year old, the same year Hitler was writing *Mein Kampf.* We stayed in the Camargue until I was nearly six so Dad could make more money to invest in the farm as it was a completely run down. Dad sold his beautiful white horses and stake in Camargue bulls to buy the old *mas* and land around it for planting trees and melon fields. We moved to the Gard, but Aramon is still Provençal, even if the only horse Dad ever owned after that wasn't a noble-headed white Camarguaise but a mule, our big-eared, coal-black, pig-headed Moses.

By then, seven years into their marriage, after three too many miscarriages and far too much alcohol my mother went Cathoholic as my Dad playfully put it, or became what the locals call churchy women: *une punaise de sacriste*, a sacristy bug, or a *grenouille de bénitier*, a frog of the stoup. Her churchiness extended to crocheting lace for the priest's albs as well as the church altarpieces, visiting the sick at Beaucaire Hospital and making me an *enfant du choeur*. What she didn't realize was that her little altar boy was stealing from the collection basket any chance I got. The way I saw it I was doing a job I was being forced to do and, at the very least, they were going to pay me for it.

My mother was an oddity, a Jew who had escaped her homeland and insane family only to arrive in France and convert to Catholicism. As Dad often said, she was more Catholic than the Catholics, a distinct group of Cathoholic individuals who go to Mass nearly every day and drink every night to make up for the time they lost during the day at Mass or tending to the poor and having their confessions heard.

On the *mas*, Dad, Yusuf and I planted fruit trees. Since the age of seven I've planted thousands of trees. If you ever drive around the niggard land of Aramon, Theziers or Montfrin and see some old battered apple trees chances are it was either me, Dad or Yusuf who planted them. But we didn't just plant fruit trees. With the help of our neighbors, Yvette and Henri, we learned about local trees, a lot of which have sadly disappeared from the Gard and Provence. They showed us how to use the fleshy fruits of one of my favorite trees the *micocoulier*, what the English call a nettle tree, to make aperitifs and how to fashion whips, handles, sticks and canes from its remarkably flexible branches, as well as yellow dye from its leaves which you can also feed to livestock. What I love most about the *micocoulier* is that its dainty leaves are always vibrating, always moving, as if frightened by its own immense height.

Even today, in Sauve in the Gard, they still use *micocoulier* to fashion forks. Indeed, a neighbor here in Lastours told me recently that they're still working the wood the way they used to in the thirteenth century in a factory in the village of *Sorède* near the Spanish border. All the way up our drive to the *mas* we planted *micocouliers* and *mûriers*, or mulberries in English. It was also Henri and Yvette who advised us to plant *cognassiers* all around our property to protect us from the *Mistral*. They preferred the *cognassier* to the allergy-generating *Piboule*. Not only is it prettier and gives more protection from the wind, but it also gives you *coings*. My mother opened this fruit with the neighboring women every November to make the *gelées*, jams, cakes and *pâtes de coings* which were served at Christmas. The women also had the same tradition of breaking open the almonds from their trees together. For a whole night in winter they'd assemble to break the shells as the men played *belote,* which Dad said is a version of what they call the card game Twenty-Five in Ireland. The women then mixed the almonds with local honey to make real *nougat* for Christmas, not the white stuff one sees in the tourist shops today.

These were the years following the Great War when there was a lot of land for sale because so many of the sons and fathers never came home. The first years were the most difficult because there was hardly any income from the vegetables we planted and my father in his compassion always blamed those first years, along with the three miscarriages, for my mother's increase in drinking. The real reason went far deeper.

But when the trees started bearing fruit, Dad started making money. He built a huge barn which my mother saw as folly but which made them even more money because he now had somewhere to store all his fruit and keep his dry stock when we had our few months of bad weather. We had chickens, cows, sheep, geese, turkeys, pigs, dogs, all manner of pigboars – pigs crossed with wild boar – which the locals loved to buy from us along with the honey from Dad's thirty *ruches* of bees which he took care of as if they were his children, often laughing about his love for them by quoting *The Qur'an*: *From its belly come forth a syrup of different hues,* Zeke, *a cure for men. Surely in this there is a sign for those who would give thought!* Dad could pick the bees up in his hands and all they would do was flutter their wings. Because of the wild vegetation and fruit trees around the *mas*, we collected many different types of honey, my favorite being rosemary. By spring, in addition to all the fruit trees and rosemary, the bees would be carrying nectar from the thyme and acacia flowers to the hives all over the different parts of the *mas*.

Another outcast on the *mas* was our mule, Moses, one of the most intelligent and stubborn animals you could ever imagine. He was beautiful for a mule, even though the locals thought he was a profound misfit. Dad loved and hated him. Maybe it was that outsider thing which Yusuf talked about, or maybe it was because he was just so damn predictable. He could pull anything that any workhorse could. And what a jumper! But if you tried to jump something Moses thought it impossible to clear there was no second shot. He simply refused, and that was it. You could have whipped him until he was dead but he wouldn't make that jump. We knew this for a fact because the man Dad bought him from had done just that. When Dad rescued him, he was covered in cuts he'd been whipped so many times.

He'd show the same refusal with a load of hay. If Moses thought it was too heavy, he wouldn't move. He wouldn't budge until you'd taken just the right amount of hay off the load. The few times I ever saw Dad angry were usually in connection with Moses. It was a comical thing to watch him try to cajole that animal to pull a train of hay he didn't want to. He'd start by whispering gently to Moses and stroking his hind quarters and then his forelocks. Moses wouldn't move. Dad would raise his voice a bit and even offer him a carrot or an apple. He still wouldn't move. In the end Moses always won. Dad would fling the apple or carrot into the ditch cursing "that animal" to hell and then he'd go and take the extra hay off. When he'd taken enough off, Moses would start moving of his own volition, sometimes making Dad fall off the back of the trailer into the road. Yusuf and I would have to sit down because of the tears of laughter that overcame us. Of course, this would make Dad even angrier and he would storm off into his apple or peach orchards to smoke a roll-up and regain his composure.

When Dad met my mother she was a young and vivacious

woman discovering a new country, but at the same time stymied by her own lack of confidence in herself and her still nascent belief in Catholicism. As her Catholicism worsened, so did her alcoholism. The more pious she became, the more she drank at night. Because he had grown up in Ireland, Dad didn't mind so much. He'd witnessed what he used to call Crosshumpers all his younger life. He'd lived beside his grandfather, a belligerent alcoholic, for many years. He explained to me that you are only considered an alcoholic in Ireland when you wake up in the morning and start drinking out of your bottle of whiskey, as his grandfather did. Five to ten pints at least three days a week, while the odd one or two each day the rest of the week is deemed normal. In the same conversation he told me how his grandmother used to go out and buy her husband his whiskey after he'd lost his two feet and most of his fingers to the drink. He sat in his chair all day smoking and spitting into the fire, drinking his whiskey from a small white teacup.

My mother's brand of Catholicism says if you go to church, give them money, don't question their dogma, and beg Christ to do all the work for you, then you can live in perpetual bliss when you die and go to heaven. She had me kneeling on our terracotta tiled floor saying decades of the rosary as soon as I could walk, whacking me with a stick if I didn't kneel correctly. Dad was always either gone to town or in the fields or vineyards working when she had me say the decades. It took him until I was five to discover her beating me with a stick as I faced the black shiny cross on the wall. By chance he'd come back early because he'd cut his hand badly, branding cattle at the *ferrade*.

"What are you doing to the child?" he screamed. He threw his coat and gloves on a nearby chair and picked me up in his arms. I was crying at this stage, even though I'd learned by then to keep it in because tears meant more beatings. He held me close to him, his eyes watering.

"I ... he wasn't ... kneeling correctly..." she said, falling in a defeated heap into her armchair, the stick still in her hand. "You don't understand. You're a sinner. Men who frequent brothels have no right to judge others. You've never understood me or the Lord Jesus, our Savior."

I can still remember his face looking down at her when she said this, a red rage in his eyes I never saw again. He put me down gently in his armchair, caressing my cheek softly with his bloody hand.

"There's no hope for you!" She started crying. "Atheists go straight to hell and you know it, which makes it all the worse!"

He went up to her and reefed the stick out of her hand.

"Shut up, do you hear? For once in your life shut up!"

"You can't speak to me..."

"You lost all rights to be talked to as a human being when you hit that defenseless little boy!"

"Don't you speak to me like that in front of him!"

"I want him here. I want him to witness what I have to say to you." He raised the stick, stood directly in front of her and broke it into pieces, bit by bit, drops of blood from his already cut hand dropping onto her clean white dress. He took all the pieces and threw them into the fire. "And so help me God, if you ever so much as touch this child again, I'll kill you. Do you hear me? I'll kill you. And not even the Lord your Savior will save you then!"

"You'll go to hell."

"Well then I'll pull you down there with me!"

He came over to me and picked me up gently. He grabbed his coat and mine, his wallet from the dresser, and he left, slamming the door behind him.

She flew out the door after us.

"Where are you taking him? Where are you going?"

Without turning back, he said: "You'll know, if we ever come back."

For five weeks myself and Dad stayed with the Garcias in Aramon. Henri Garcia had been a mentor to my father when he first arrived in Provence, getting him his first job on a *mas* in the Camargue. He and his wife Yvette, a magical woman who became a mentor to me throughout my life, moved to Aramon when he'd found a ruined *mas* for sale. Henri farmed geese and ducks for *foie gras* and sold their eggs, and the ones from his countless chickens, to the same buyer from Avignon who would later buy our apples, apricots and pears. It was during those five weeks that Dad decided he wanted to try and find a ruined old *mas* near Henri. Four years later we owned the one beside theirs, Henri having ridden all the way down to the Camargue to tell Dad about it the very day the old owner died.

Yvette, the village *magnetiseur*, helped heal Dad's bloody hand and minded me while Dad helped Henri on their farm. They were a wonderful five weeks for me with Yvette and her funny daughters, blue-eyed, flaxen-haired wisps of things, who were always busy making things with flour or dirt or paints, all the time tittering away at me for no apparent reason. Yvette paid so much attention to her girls, something I wasn't used to with my own mother, that it seemed unnatural to me in the beginning. As the weeks disappeared, it felt like the most natural thing in the world to give your child love like that. We never talked about my mother while we were there and it wasn't until my mother appeared at the front door, Dad beside her, that I started to think about her again.

We went out amidst an avenue of cypress trees, planted fifteen years before to keep the mistral from driving Henri and Yvette crazy, and talked. We sat down on the bank of a ditch and, in tears, my mother apologized to me for beating me and promised me that she would never hit me again and that if she ever did that she would leave. I looked at her and then to Dad, not knowing what I was supposed to do. "You can hug your mother if you want," he said. She hugged me so hard I couldn't breathe. I thought she'd never let me go. We went back to the Camargue and talked about nothing but the *mas* we were going to buy somewhere near Henri and Yvette and about all the fruit trees we were going to plant.

MUSIC THAT WILL MOVE THE STARS

We were grading the apples by the light of the full moon, sorting the good from the rotten, throwing the bad ones in a pile to use for seeds to grow new saplings. The rest, the flesh and skin, would go to my mother to cook the good pieces in Dad's favorite dessert a *tarte tatin* or mine, apple *compote*. Everything else would go to Moses to be added in with some grain and hot water as a treat.

"Dad, why do you have to chose a *métier* in life?"

It was 1933. I was fifteen at the time. Hitler had begun to assert dictatorial powers over the *Reichstag* and Jews were being attacked in the streets of Berlin. Soon afterwards Goebbels was burning books and Dachau concentration camp was imprisoning Jews, communists and socialists. Over in the United States Roosevelt had been inaugurated president and here on the front page of *Action Française* Anatole de Monzie, Charles Maurras and Leon "*le gros Leon*" Daudet were busy writing about the funerals and deaths of royalty around Europe, in addition to spouting poisonous anti-Semitic vitriol.

"Who says?"

"The teachers at school. Everyone."

"Did I?"

"No."

"Well then that's not everyone is it? What's the problem?"

"I don't know. What if I don't get the farm?"

"Of course you'll inherit the farm. I don't have any other kids, do I? But you know, you don't have to be a farmer if you don't want to. You can be anything you want to be. The world is right outside that gate. You know that."

"I don't want to go anywhere. This is my home. I love it here. I love working in the fields, harvesting and planting and taking care of our animals. I'll never leave."

"Never say never. I said the same thing and ended up here. And anyway, there's a tradition in our family of leaving to see the world especially all the places our family was forced to leave."

A *moineau* was picking away at one of the apples furthest away from us, twitching her head towards us after each peck, pretending to not be there.

"Anyway," he said, throwing another rotten apple on the pile, the sparrow flying away now that her cover was blown, "I wouldn't worry about it all, Zeke. And if you never inherited it, you'd always be able to get a job in an orchestra! They always need alto players. Violinists are as common as piano players, not alto players."

"Did you ever want to play in an orchestra, Dad?"

"I did once, in Cork. You know the way I used to teach French and music?"

"Yes."

"Well, a load of us music teachers in Cork decided to set up an orchestra for the laugh. It was a lot of fun, but it was a nightmare. We had two concerts and it all fell apart."

"Why?"

"People never turned up on time for rehearsals. Others were always squabbling about how a certain piece of a symphony was supposed to be played. People. You put a load of them in a room and they start behaving like chickens, clucking and pecking each other's heads off for want of a simple silly morsel of understanding. Everyone wants to be heard but everyone else is always misunderstanding them because they want to be heard too. And we all go around like chickens not understanding this simple truth, blaming our language instead of ourselves."

He laughed and looked up at the stars, two good apples still in his hand. "You know, Flaubert said it a lot better: *Human speech is like a cracked kettle on which we tap crude rhythms for bears to dance to, while we long to make music that will move the stars."* After a moment, he turned to me. "Moral of the story: Don't ever set up an orchestra, else you're in for it!"

We started laughing and he lobbed the two good apples into the wooden crate that was now full. I went around him and lifted the crate down off the grading table and walked it over to the long trailer which had about twenty boxes of *chanteclers* already on it, nearly enough for the apple buyer that was coming the next morning.

When I came back to the grading table, Dad was down. Only my mother could bring him down like that. I followed his eyes. She was getting sick out the kitchen door into the geraniums, what she would later say was gastro, like she always did, when we both knew it was because she was on another of her binges. It was useless for either of us to go over to try to help her. It only made things worse.

For days, weeks, sometimes months, she wouldn't drink and then, for two or three days, she was gone, sleeping it off only to start again the next day when she came out of her stupor. Countless times Dad had tried to stop her, to speak some sense to her, but it never worked. Even our local priest, a likeable old man from Normandy who loved our apples, would come to try and help, but again it was futile. When she drank, we lost her, but when she was sober she worked, and tried to love as hard as she worked.

"Dad," he had already filled another quarter of a box, "do you think she'll ever get better?"

He stopped what he was doing and looked at me. "Your mother?"

I nodded.

"My father gave me this answer when I asked him about your great-grandfather: *Alcoholics are like the blind leading the blind into a ditch, except it's themselves that are leading themselves. They have to open their own eyes. You can't do it for them. You can try, but you'll only make things far worse.* Does that help?"

"I don't know."

He took an empty wooden crate and put it on the ground and said, "Here, sit on that. I suppose now's as good a time as any." He took another box from the pile behind us and sat on it across from me, taking out his pouch of tobacco and papers from his inside pocket.

"For what?"

"To tell you about your mother."

"What about her?"

"Why she is the way she is. I'm not saying I'm an authority on human nature or anything. I'm no doctor, but it seems pretty clear to me where a lot of it comes from."

He started to roll a cigarette. "It all started when she was seven, when her parents and brothers and sisters moved to Berlin from Eastern Europe. It was a very difficult time for them. There were five of them, your mother being the eldest, and then her brother and sister who were four and three. Anyway, her parents weren't able to make enough money to support them. There was hardly any food. So, your mother got a job in a grocery store, stacking the shelves with fruits and vegetables and everyone was really happy because every bit of extra money went a long way."

He lit his cigarette. "You have to promise me you'll never tell her I told you any of this."

"Why?"

"Because it'd destroy her. The only reason she told me was so I'd allow her back into our lives after she beat you."

"Oh," I said.

"Well?"

"I promise, Dad."

He flicked the ash on the grass and took a deep breath. "The owner of the grocery store was a very unhealthy man. He started to make ... advances to your mother."

"What? But she was seven?"

"I know."

"So he was a pedophile?"

"Jesus, Zeke, do you always have to be so blunt?"

"I'm sorry."

"No, I'm sorry. It's just difficult to talk to you about this."

He smoked some more of his roll-up and put it out. "So the owner made your mother keep what he called their 'secret'. Over the months..."

"Didn't she tell her parents?"

"I'm getting there."

"I'm sorry."

"Well, your mother saw that her family had become dependent on the extra money she was bringing home every week. She also knew that what was happening to her wasn't right so she told her mother but she was warned not to talk about it to her again and that the family was depending on the money she was earning."

"God," I said, getting up and walking about, "How long did she stay there?"

"Until she was fourteen."

"What?" I sat down, shocked.

"After she left her job there she soon left school too. She was about fifteen. She got another job working in a clothes store and that's when she started to drink, every night, to try and block out all the nightmares and trauma she was going through. The family tried to stop her from drinking but couldn't. She would scream at them saying it was because she was forced to work for that grocery owner. She knew that her mother had told her father because her brother and sister were forbidden to ever go near the store. Later on, she realized even her brother and sister knew. Her brother would sneer her and say she had enjoyed it."

"God..."

"So, when she was twenty she left Germany and vowed to never go back. That's when I met her in Avignon, about six months after she'd left Berlin."

"So that's why she never talks about Germany!"

"Would you?"

"No. So, so how can we help her?"

"Oh, Zeke, I've tried. I've tried for years to get her help. There's no organization to help people stay sober. If only there was. But then she resists any kind of help."

"But there must be some way to help her?"

"It's like my father said about his father. You can't do it for them. It has to be their choice. The first step would be to stop drinking, but that's like chopping back a tree that has a disease at its roots. The branches'll keep growing back."

"You mean she'll keep getting drunk?"

"The root of her disease is not the alcohol, it's the sexual abuse. And even then I don't think that's the root of her disease. I think the fact that her family never tried to help her hurts her far more than all the physical abuse she endured. She said as much to me that time she begged me to forgive her for hitting you, but I don't think she's ever realized that that is the real root of her problem, as opposed to just alcohol."

"Did her family not support her later on though?"

"No. They told her she was a drunk and a failure for dropping out of school and wanting to be an artist."

"She wanted to be an artist?"

Dad rolled another cigarette, spitting out some tobacco that had got caught on the tip of his tongue. "Of course. Sure didn't we meet in an art gallery? She's a bloody good painter too. The thing is she has no confidence in herself, that's all. That's why she pours so much of her energy into an all powerful God. She wasn't like that when I met her. She was as free as the wind. She wore all these colorful clothes that she made herself. She was extraordinarily creative back then."

"Do you think she'll ever go back to Germany, Dad?"

"I hope so, for her sake. I'm not saying that what they did was right. To me it was immoral, more than wrong. But somewhere in there I think she has to find the courage to forgive them. Forgiveness is a very powerful thing, Zeke. Don't ever forget that. There are things in my past, in Ireland, that I forgave, that lifted a great burden from my soul. I've told you of these experiences before."

"When you forgave your father for beating you, you mean?"

"Yes. There were other things, but family is always the biggest one to overcome. That's why I say I think if Hannah tried to forgive them and confront them she would be able to clean out her soul. Clear away the betrayal, that loss of power she feels she endured because of them."

"They should be in jail!"

"For what? It doesn't work that way, Zeke, and anyway, forgiveness is far more powerful than any jail. It is a part of the hidden power within humans. Pain can be turned into something meaningful with forgiveness. Punishment never gets a person to grow, forgiveness does. The whole of creation is full of one person doing something another sees as abominable. Saying yes to forgiveness, forgiving them, or their actions, is what releases you back into living. Otherwise you sink into your pain, into ugliness."

Standing up, he put his cigarette out with the tips of his fingers, pocketing the butt into his *bleu du travail.* "Here, give us a hug!" He opened his long arms and I walked into them. We held each other for a long time.

"There, now you know it all! Jesus, am I glad to finally get that off my chest!" He turned to the grading table and picking up some apples said, "And remember, not a word of this to her. Compassion deems it so. It's up to Hannah to talk about it to you some day if she wishes, not for you or I to force it out of her. We can only be here for her in loving kindness."

"Yes, Dad."

"Good lad. Now, let's get these apples done or we'll be hearing it from that buyer tomorrow morning."

I took a bad *chantecler* out of the pile and threw it on top of the other heap, frightening away the nonchalant *moineau* who'd come back again to feed. She flew up into the night sky through an olive tree towards the stars.

BLUE PEOPLE AND THE DESERT

It was mid January 1936. Yusuf and I had stopped chopping wood for a lunch of bread, dry *Cantal entre deux,* local *chèvre* and one of the many bottles of *jus de raisin* our neighbor Henri Garcia gave us ever year. In addition to his many other talents, Henri was a *maitre de chais* of *Côtes du Rhône.* The taste of this prized first press *jus* straight from the *cuve* was a wonder to drink under the January sun in addition to our simple meal of bread and cheese. We needed our *midi* lunch more than usual. We were exhausted after enduring rain continuously from December 28th to January 11th, on the heels of a biblical flood in November that had drowned the majority of our animals and destroyed a lot of our trees. We were still trying to salvage and clean up after it.

People who live between the Rhône and the Gardon rivers are used to this kind of destruction. We see flash floods as a way of life. When I was even younger I remember going to school in a boat with the neighboring children. This is why the houses in Aramon and the villages that surround it are constructed the way they are, out of local beige stone, so that you can climb to the second floor with any belongings you can grab, and wait out the flood, sometimes for up to five or six days, watching everything pass by outside until the Rhône leaves. Only recently, in September of 2002, the *digue* burst in the village, the wall of water from the Gardon killing eleven villagers, leaving police to pluck people from rooftops and balconies in little boats.

As we ate, Dad was in Beaucaire trying to sell the fruit that hadn't floated away with the flood. It was important that he went to the market, not because it meant money but because it gave him a break from the difficult months we'd just endured, in addition to the fact that he loved Beaucaire. He often talked to me about the history of the town, how it was designed by the same architect who did Versailles, but he especially loved to talk of the time after the Hundred Years War when Charles the VII pronounced that the Foire de la Madeleine would take place there, allowing the tax-free trade of goods from all the Mediterranean basin countries. It had been the largest commercial fair in the Mediterranean region, doing more trade in six days than Marseilles did in a year and only ended when Napoleon stopped the tax-free trading.

Every 21st of July Dad would be invited by his friends in the Camargue to help run the bulls through the streets of Beaucaire for what is still celebrated today as a six-day festival commemoration of the Foire de la Madeleine. Dad also loved Raimond VI of Toulouse whom he often referred to as a closet Essene, even if he did have an over exploitative sexual urge. He admired Count Raimond's defense of Beaucaire against Simon de Montfort during the Albigensian Crusade, and lauded his defiance of Pope Innocent III who ordered the genocide of the Cathars.

"Where do you come from, Yusuf?"

He drank some *jus*. "Ah, not even your father has ever asked me that question."

"Why?"

"Because he knows what it is to live through a war."

"What war were you in?"

"It wasn't really a war, it was more like a massacre. You're too young to know about things like war, Zeke."

"I'm nearly eighteen. Is that not old enough? When we

slaughter one of our pigs or chickens, is that not murder? Is that not like war?"

"No. War is when everything dies."

"Did everything die on you, Yusuf?"

"You are too young to talk about these things."

"What age is the right age, then?"

"That is a good question. I don't know."

He invited me to sit beside him by patting his huge hand on the *mauvais herbes*.

"Your mother must not learn of this, Zeke. Most people would think it is wrong for me to talk to a boy about war."

"I told you already, I'm not a boy! I'm almost eighteen."

He laughed. "Okay, okay!"

"I've asked you of my own free will, Yusuf. My mother lost hers to the Catholic church and you know the church is about as religious as an empty tin can."

"You are wise for your age, Zeke, but you must still respect your mother. She is your mother. She gave you life and all things are one. We must have compassion for all people, all beings, even the pigs and chickens you talk of. We are all religious. Even your father is a religious man, but not the way the Mohammedans, Christians, Jews and Hindus are. He sees the potential inside himself, the God hidden inside us all."

"Did everything die on you, Yusuf?"

He laughed again. "You are as your father says you are, relentless." He looked at me seriously. "No and yes is my answer. Yes, they were all taken from me. My children. My wife. My parents. My three brothers. My two sisters. They are all gone now. The only reason I survived was because I was covered, covered by many, many bodies ... When I first met your father I had barely escaped."

He closed his eyes and took a deep breath. He opened his eyes and exhaled. "I have stolen, I have ... I have killed ... many times." He closed his eyes again and after a moment opened them. "I did everything I had to do to escape that place. Then, in the desert, I really escaped. For days and days, maybe weeks. I moved through the harshness of sandstorms, dehydration, freezing nights. It nearly killed me, but it also freed me, liberated me from my suffering. The qualities people criticize the desert for became my liberation."

"Why do you never talk about where you come from or where you met Dad?"

"I didn't meet your Dad. I was saved by him, near Saintes Maries de la Mer, where the black Sara is, just before you were born."

"What? Where the gypsies go every year to celebrate the Marys?"

"Yes. He was a *gardian* then. He was respected. After a day of raking salt, a *saunier* had found me in one of the *salins*, a salt marsh near one of their salt 'mountains.' They called at your father's house for him to come carry me away because he had a horse. They left me with him. Your mother cared for me while he worked and they brought me back to life with their love."

It made me think of all the ways my mother cared for Yusuf without ever saying anything, in the way she gave him extra of the food he loved at the table, or mended his shirt without his asking, or cared for his cuts from the vines and the orchards the same way she did for Dad and me. It also made me think of how today's mayor of Saintes Maries de la Mer would welcome Yusuf, him being a *Front National* supporter who does everything he can to keep the gypsies from celebrating their festival and traditions there.

"They never told me any of this."

"There is a reason for everything. There is a reason it was your father who was the nearest one with a horse. He was an outcast too. If it had been any of the locals they would have helped perhaps, but not like your father. He found me work. He took care of the paper-work with the mayor. He was respected in the community. He didn't have to do what he did."

"Yes, but why did they never tell me about any of this?"

"To protect you. Since you were a little boy I have been here. You don't see this big black man like other people do. You see Yusuf. A child's eyes see more clearly than an adult's. Children are mystics until we put them in schools and civilize them."

He touched me gently on the face with his massive right hand.

"There is a reason I am here having this conversation with you, Zeke, at this time. Only Allah knows the reason. There are no coincidences in life. I see that now. Your father saving me on his beautiful white horse was like a dream, but it was real. There are miracles happening every day to all of us and we choose not to see them. There is a reason your mother is your mother and your father is your father, just as there is a reason why the leaves fall from the tree. All is connected. It is for us to follow our destiny and leave our family behind some day, to leave our tribal ways of thinking and become ourselves, respecting that all is one. The leaves are, they change, they fall from the trees. The tree is, it changes, but its change does not change the One, because how could the One's existence be changed when it *is* change?"

"Where do you get all this from, Yusuf?"

"From here," and he placed his hand on his immense chest, a smile on his face. "I had to leave my home. Your mother and father left theirs too. We all had different reasons, but we broke from our tribes because we had to become who we are, become what our destiny has laid out for us."

"Do you think my mother is herself, even with all her Catholicism?"

"She's trying, in her way. Everyone is different, Zeke. And sadly, not everyone fulfills their destiny. Some of us have a harder time accepting the things that happened to us and some of us don't. Not everyone can let go of the things that happened to them."

"Do you think my mother has things to let go of, things she doesn't talk about?"

"Oh, Allah, you are relentless!" He laughed. "A real seeker. We all have things to let go of, my little friend!"

He stretched up and touched a low-hanging branch of the cherry tree we were sitting under.

"People are like trees, Zeke. They have roots. That is their family. There is a place that they live and they are rooted, but a tree is not just its roots. If it grows, if it evolves like this cherry tree, it will have a large trunk with long branches and beautiful leaves. It is not only the ground it has grown from. People forget that they are not just their roots. They also have a trunk, and long lovely branches that shoot out into the sky in search of the sun, new ones growing all the time."

"But the roots, Yusuf. Without the roots, the trees..."

"Of course, there are people who forget their roots completely. They do not respect their roots and that they are one with everything. They leave their home and concentrate on pretty leaves, not the branches and trunk and roots. They only see what changes with the seasons. This they can understand, but seasons pass so quickly, and they haven't paid attention to their branches and roots and a lot of the time it is too late. They have rotted at their roots. They have drunk too much, eaten too much, had too much sex or too much need for power over others and they realize later on in life that it was all just an illusion, what we call a mirage in the desert."

"What are you saying? I don't understand."

He laughed out loud. "If there is one thing nobody will ever accuse you of Ezekiel Yusuf Moran it is not speaking your truth." He continued laughing. "We're humans. We're not made to understand everything. That is Allah's job!"

"You still haven't told me where you come from yet."

He shook his head from side to side, smiling, and stretched out his long black legs. Their sheen in the sun reminded me of what Dad told me the Irish call black people, *"na daoine gorm,"* the blue people. As I looked at Yusuf's legs I understood why. They were so black they almost shone blue.

"I come from the desert, a desert that stretches bigger than the Aude, even bigger than Occitanie, even bigger than France!"

"No, that can't be!"

"I will bring you there one day if you like."

"I'd love that!"

"So would I, so would I. You would love the desert because you love trees. The desert is like these trees, it speaks to you if you listen to it. You just have to close your eyes and listen."

"And what does the desert say?"

He smiled, lifted up the half-eaten *baguette* of bread. "The sand always remains the same, Zeke. Yes, it may move and change and get smaller but it is always the sands, like this tree. It is the seed, the tree, the seed, the tree and on and on."

"So how do we become like the desert then? We're not trees or sand."

"To be wide open. To see reality as she does. Throw off all the rubbish and sermons people give you. Unburden yourself."

"But you could say what you're saying to me is a sermon?"

"Yes, you could, but am I asking you for donations? Do I tell you to go to a church or a temple or a mosque or a university to be talked at by a priest or academic? Do I force you to do anything?"

"No."

"This is the desert. She will not burden your mind like a camel with its load."

Yusuf broke off some of the bread to accompany the *chèvre* he'd just cut with his *opinel*. I reached for the *jus de raisin* and drank it down even though the sun had made it warm. The heat helped the *Cantal* though, it tasted moist and soft in my mouth as I ate it after the *jus*.

Yusuf lay down on his side and smiled at me after finishing his cheese and bread.

"You're lucky, Zeke. You have a father who understands this, and you live in a place close to nature. I grew up like this too, in an oasis. The desert was all around us, her power was everywhere. Pure. Uncontaminated by priests, politicians and academics ... all who try to tell you how to live your life. Who to trust. Who not to. Which people are bad, which are not. The older we grow, the more this insanity grows."

Yusuf sat up and stretched out his hands toward the sun in a long yawn. I yawned too and closed my eyes to rest a while after eating. A few crows were making a lot of noise in some cypress trees in the distance and I could hear the wind like a stream in the cherry trees, running through the leaves in little waves.

"This is why I love poetry, Zeke." His voice was beside me now on the ground. "This is why I sing songs. Poetry is the opposite of philosophy. There is no truth other than poetic beauty. It sings of love and compassion, the birds singing in the trees, the wind sweeping across the desert. When you lie under a tree like this, or out in the desert the way I did when I was your age, you see this beauty. You don't have to do anything! The birds sing, the leaves move, the sands shift. All is one."

Yusuf yawned again and grew silent, like me. A silence fell around us that was wonderful and we would have slept beneath the cherry trees if I hadn't wanted to know more.

I sat up and drank some more *jus*. "Yusuf, I don't understand. What's enlightenment?"

He opened his eyes and sat up. "In the desert they say it is like the sand moving across the sand. The Buddhists and the Indians would say enlightenment happens by meditating."

"Like we do in the mornings and evenings?"

"Yes and no."

"Why?"

"Because they say it takes many lifetimes to happen. Everything becomes one. *Satori. Samadhi.* Satori is the harmony inside you and *samadhi* is the harmony with all of this," he raised his hand in an arc, "with everything. Conflict goes and then you disappear, you bloom like the cherry blossoms."

"And this is what happens to saints and Sufis and holy people?"

"Yes, but Sufis are not serious. Saints are serious. I don't understand saints. They seem very miserable to me. Mystics laugh. We laugh. This is just the way things are. I sing and laugh, like you. Even sinners can laugh! Not those who want to be saints. I'd rather joke and sing and dance and recite poetry than be in their heaven. I think they'd make me very unhappy, all those saints. I think it's better that they're up there in their heaven. Let them stay up there. I'm happy right here being ordinary, a human, not superhuman!"

We started to laugh.

"When will you go back to the desert, Yusuf?"

"When it is time."

THE FINEST SCHOOL IN FRANCE

I got into the *Ecole Normale Superieure* in Paris when I was eighteen but refused to go. Needless to say my mother went ballistic. It also confirmed to the locals that I was stupid: how could I refuse such an opportunity? Ever afterwards the locals considered it a clerical error on the part of the *Ecole*.

"It's the best school in France."

"I don't care," I told her.

My father sat in his chair rolling a cigarette beside the fire.

"What do you mean you don't care? Over half the government and nearly all the intellectuals in France come out of that place every year. It's an honor to be accepted!"

"I don't want to be a politician or an intellectual."

Dad started choking on his cigarette, trying to hide a laugh behind his cough. This made her even angrier.

"What, do you want to be, a farmer like your father? You see how hard he works. Every day he's out in those fields from sunup to sundown."

I stopped myself from asking her why he was out in the fields every day. Not because he had to work, I wanted to say, but because he didn't want to have to be near her. Of course, that wasn't why he was always outside. Dad was always in the fields because he felt at one with everything out there. He loved my mother, even if I couldn't understand why. It was me who needed the distance from her. It was me that needed to forgive her.

"Is that what you really want for yourself?"

"If it's good enough for Dad, it's good enough for me."

She looked at Dad, blowing his smoke up the chimney so it wouldn't enter into her living room.

"You see? Do you see what you've done? You've ruined him!"

Dad said nothing, as was his habit. He knew better.

"Aren't you going to say anything? Your only son is about to make the biggest mistake of his life and you just sit there puffing away."

Dad threw his cigarette into the fire and rocked his head up and down in his signature yes and no response that said neither.

"Oh, you're both pathetic! Out there playing your violins..."

"Altos," I said.

That did it.

"I don't care if they're oboes! You two out there under the apple trees every night with Yusuf or out in that damn barn playing every day of the week. And then to think you have the chance and luck to get into the finest school in France and you throw it away? No wonder they call you the idiot savant in the village. No wonder they..."

"Ah, now Hannah, there's no reason to..."

"No reason to what? Be mean? Is it not meanness and disrespect to refuse this offer? I don't see you telling him to go to Paris."

"It's his choice. "

"His choice? He's only eighteen years old! What does he know about choice?"

"Well, you chose to get married at about the same age."

"You're pathetic! Do you hear me, pathetic! After all our hard work and effort for that boy he just throws it all away, just like that. Well, he'll see. Mark my words! Years from now he'll look back on this day and remember the wisdom of his mother!"

She stormed out of the room, crying, my father following

quickly behind her. In my teenage eyes his following her was some sycophantic way of coddling her, the same way he did every time she exploded into one of her fits of rage. Now, I know he followed her because he loved her, because he cared for her, and who can ever understand love and lovers, why they love and why they love certain people and not others. Back then, love was beyond my comprehension. Compassion was just a word my father used. It is only now that I understand my father's love for my mother. There was really nothing to understand, save the fact that love is, nothing else. We love who we think we've chosen to love but oftentimes we aren't really choosing the people we love, more like life is choosing them for us. It is only afterwards that we understand.

Looking back on that day, I see it as one of the best decisions I ever made. If I hadn't stayed, I would never have had the opportunity to meet Mathias and Thérèse, or spend those last few wonderful years with a father I will always remember as my first and most precious of friends.

IRELAND ON A RED DAY

It was raining when I arrived at Hanratty's Hotel on Glentworth Street, in the center of Limerick, on the evening of March 13, 1965, a few days shy of St. Patrick's day and six months after my marriage had fallen apart. For obvious reasons I needed to get out of France. I had just come to that painful point in everyone's life where I had to accept my life as it was, or else lose even more energy focusing on what was missing from it. Instead of seeing my life as empty and meaningless, I had started to accept my personal responsibility for the failure of our marriage. I had created it. I had allowed her physical abuse. None of it was anyone's fault except my own. What was the use of blaming Julie? What was the use of blaming anyone anymore?

It was what jazz and blues players would call a blue day, but in my world it was a distinctly dark red one, a Sunday, like today. As I looked up at the gunmetal gray sky, I remembered what Dad used to say about Ireland and its rain.

"The Eskimos have their countless different words for snow, Zeke. Well, it's the same with the Irish and rain. It can be soft, hard, drizzly, even wet if that makes any sense, but it's never the same.

You know, in the nearly three decades I lived there I can't remember a day without a cloud up there somewhere in the sky threatening rain."

Ireland. I wanted to see where Dad and his family had lived in Limerick, as well as the farm they settled on afterwards outside Cork. I also wanted to visit Canfea Stone Circle to the southwest of the village of Ardgroom on the Beara peninsula, where my grandfather initiated my Dad into the Essene tradition when he was fourteen.

Now, looking back, I see that day as another example of how everything in my life has followed the design of what Yusuf used to say is already written, that there is no such thing as luck or coincidence, only what your destiny holds for you, and whether you choose to react or respond to it.

In front of me in the hotel was an omen, a Dublin man, a Redemptorist priest, talking to the receptionist. I didn't get the significance until later, of course.

"Yes, Father."

He left with his keys, his tall frame limping down the corridor to his room.

"Hello," said the receptionist, a tiny piece of toilet paper covering the part of his jaw he'd cut shaving.

"Hello. My name's Moran. Ezekiel Yusuf Moran. I have a reservation."

He looked at his ledger. "Ah yes, here you are Mr. Moran. Room 47. Can you sign this please?"

"Of course."

"So you're here for the symposium are you?"

"Pardon?" I handed him back his book.

"With a name like Ezekiel you must be Jewish, no?"

"Yes, but..."

"The symposium on the 1904 pogrom."

"What?"

"Sorry, I got it wrong. Well, here's your keys."

"Thank you."

I took my keys and walked into the bar with my bags, what the locals call the Gluepot, to enjoy a pint of Guinness, something I'd never tasted before. As I drank I read the Cyclops chapter of *Ulysses.* I found myself drifting away from the words as the Citizen was about to attack Bloom, wishing Dad were in front of me to enjoy the moment of Guinness and Limerick and Joyce, when a bearded man with a black beret asked whether he and his three companions could sit down at my large table. I said yes. I was sitting at the only empty table in the place.

As the man took his first sip of Guinness, I recognized him and, without interrupting his conversation with his friends, I waited for an opportunity to shake his hand. It was a long wait, as at the bar there were a number of what could only be called fervent Irish nationalists, more "citizens," who kept sending emissaries and pints of Guinness and whiskey to the table. One man, a tall, overweight red-faced Goliath wearing some form of football jersey, offered his hand after slapping Che on the back as if he were an old friend. He continued by thanking Che for his example as a revolutionary, praising his achievements and offering shamrocks to him and Dr. Osmani Cienfuegos, the Cuban Minister for Construction, as well as to his other Cuban friends, both government officials.

When the citizens had finished I put my book away in the outside pocket of one of my travel bags. On the way by, I offered my hand to Che. He smiled and shook it firmly, a welcome smile on his face.

It was immediately after that trip to Ireland that Che Guevera went back to Cuba, met Castro and decided to become a traveling revolutionary, even though it would mean death. Two years later he was captured by the Bolivian government with the help of the CIA and their recruit, the "Butcher of Lyon", Klaus Barbie, the man responsible for sending 44 Jewish children to Auschwitz and Jean Moulin to his grave. They ordered Che's immediate execution. I've often wondered since what we might have talked about, given the chance. Medicine? Or warfare? Or just the weather, as I often find myself doing when I meet old veterans.

Sitting at the foot of my hotel bed with my bags still packed and my coat on, still in shock from the surreal experience of meeting one of the most well known revolutionaries of our time, I remembered Dad under our apple trees, talking. I smiled.

"Cork was a new start for the family, Zeke. We were all very excited. Unlike the others in our community we didn't get into law or medicine or politics. Dad and my brothers loved the land. Yes, it was hard to leave Limerick, but not that hard. We had joined with the locals after the uprising and the Civil War. We became revolutionaries. We, my father and brothers, fought the Black and Tans. My brothers, Solomon and Leo, died. That was enough proof for them of our loyalty. Why they couldn't see us as human beings before those atrocities I'll never know. I suppose sometimes it takes horror to make a man wake up."

He took out his papers and tobacco.

"Then why did you leave Limerick?"

He smiled. "Because we were still outcasts. After the deaths of Sol and Leo, Dad became sickened by our treatment as outsiders. When we moved to Cork he changed his name to Moran. He wanted to be shut of them all. The Jews and the Irish. He wanted to be himself. Have a fresh start. And we did."

He lit up his roll-up. "Still, I'll never forget that mad, bad fool Father John Creagh."

"A priest?"

"Yes, the worst kind. He was a Redemptorist. Tried to redeem his parishioners with clichés of hate."

"What age were you, Dad?"

"Thirteen."

"What were the clichés?"

"Oh, you don't want to know. People just look for the outcast to project their jealousies, Zeke. It's just their own lack of confidence in themselves."

"I want to know, Dad. I'm a Jew too you know."

He slapped me on the side of the arm. "I know, I know. But none of that matters now. This is a new country. All that's dead and gone now."

"You once told me people don't change Dad. You said it takes too much effort. Maybe people are just the same now, they just haven't had the opportunity to show who they really are yet?"

"You're too smart for your own good you know that, Zeke?"

"What did they say, Dad?"

"And relentless too. I've never met someone so relentless. You just have to know everything, don't you? You have to play that alto every day and pick those apples until there's not one hanging from a branch."

"What did they say, Dad?"

He stamped out his cigarette. "The first is the obvious one, that the Jews rejected Christ. That one we'll always be to blame for, that we put Jesus up on his cross. Second, even though we lived on a farm we were usurers sucking the hard earned money out of the poor, selling shitty goods at hiked prices, paid for in installments, taking over the local economy, oh, and in league with the Freemasons who were persecuting the Church in France at the time. The only thing Creagh didn't accuse us of was kidnapping and murdering Christian children, but it didn't stop him howling that we'd taken the food out of their mouths and the clothes off their backs."

"He was crazy."

"Of course he was crazy. Oh, and then there was the wedding. That sent him over the edge. He started comparing the rags of the locals with the silks and satins of a Jewish wedding."

"And nobody said he was crazy?"

"Michael Davitt, the Protestant bishop of Limerick and other political leaders denounced him alright, but he had six thousand Limerick men behind him, the Arch-confraternity of the Holy Family. They listened to him. He was a clever madman. He turned people's hatred of the Protestant ruling class with all its power over us onto a weaker minority. The Jews became the new exploiters. So they boycotted us. They didn't pay us anything they owed us. There were anti-Semitic riots all over the city and even though Creagh said later that he was disgusted by violence, he still battered us with the "I don't hate Jews, just your business practices". We were beaten in the streets and the boycott went on. As I said, our family was lucky in that we had our own farm. It didn't mean we were paid, but at least we had cows and pigs and fields. We were self-sustaining. But the lawyers and doctors and businessmen, they had no choice, they had to leave. Everything was taken from them."

"Didn't the police do anything?"

"What could they do? They would've charged Creagh with incitement to violence but you have to remember the time. They were the Royal Irish Constabulary, representatives of the Queen of England. If they'd done anything, those six thousand men would have been after them. It would have made that madman Creagh a martyr, and not just a Catholic one, but a nationalist one."

"So what happened?"

"The church did what it always does when it has a problem priest. They sent him away. They sent him to Belfast. When he got back he kept his mouth shut, simply blathering on about indecent literature and alcohol. They finally shipped him off to the Philippines. A few years after that, the Pope, in his wisdom, promoting him to Vicar Apostolic of Kimberley, Western Australia, where he stayed until 1922."

"But why didn't you leave Limerick earlier?"

"My father. He wasn't going to let anyone kick us off our land." He laughed. "He was like you, Zeke, relentless!"

"Then how did you end up in Cork?"

"We migrated to Cork after the Civil War."

"But why? I thought you said grandfather wouldn't move."

"Oh, my father'd had enough of Limerick by then, especially after Sol and Leo died, and even though we'd broken with our religious traditions, my mother was still very much a part of them, even if my father wasn't."

"So what did you do there?"

"We bought another farm. And it was beautiful there. And as I said before, that's where our people were."

He lit another roll-up. "Why don't you go get our instruments, Zeke? These apples can wait. I think some Mozart quintets would go down well right now, even if there's only two of us, don't you?"

I ran through the orchard towards the house.

"And try not to let your mother see you!"

THE SYMPOSIUM

On my way to meet my cousin, the grandchild of my uncle Gabriel, I looked out the taxi window onto the green fields of Cork flowing by and thought of the symposium the previous night in Limerick.

The limpy Redemptorist priest sat in front of me, a chewed pen between his bony fingers, a notebook on his lap. He scribbled down everything Gerald Goldberg had to say. He stopped writing at one important juncture though, when Goldberg recited Father Creagh's first sermon. In fact, the whole audience went silent. Local opposition to the symposium, which had threatened to disrupt the meeting, found its intimidating energy dissolve as Goldberg read aloud the sermon. People were disgusted that something so peculiarly hateful could have been delivered from a pulpit in their city. The silence alone said it all. The opposition in the form of skinhead youths and serious-headed soccer fans slithered out the doors. When the sermon ended, I left and walked through the streets, thinking of Dad.

Yes, it's sad to me today to think the Jewish community is gone from Cork. Its last synagogue is not closed, but it's unable to achieve a *minyan* and although the Herzog Center for Jewish Studies at

Trinity College Dublin is a good thing, it's still no substitute for a living Jewish community that contributed to Ireland in so many ways. To its politics, law, medicine and freedom.

My father never complained about the anti-Semitism he grew up with, but I found out later how difficult it must have been for him. Even United Irishmen like Arthur Griffith were anti-Semites. How Griffith could be so hostile to the most vulnerable minority in Ireland, and at the same time talk of the inequalities of Britain to their small neighbor, goes beyond my comprehension. Later on, this type of disregard for human suffering became even more apparent with the signing of the Condolence Book by the Irish prime minister, De Valera, and the Irish President's visit to the home of Hitler's diplomat, Hempel, in Dun Laoghaire. De Valera actually said that to refuse condolences *would have been an act of unpardonable discourtesy to the German nation and to Dr. Hempel. During the whole of the war, Dr. Hempel's conduct was irreproachable ... I certainly was not going to add to his humiliation in the hour of defeat.*

I wonder would he have cared about Hempel's "defeat" if he'd visited Buchenwald or Belsen-Belsen or Dachau or Auschwitz. De Valera was a devious man. He survived the 1916 Rising even though he was sentenced to death. He did what he did for Ireland in the way that he could, and he helped Allies who landed in Ireland while interning Germans, but he did nothing proactive to save Jews from the camps. He only made reactive gestures that never came to anything, even though one of his friends, a man who hid De Valera in his own house when he was a fugitive from British and Free State police, was Isaac Herzog, the Chief Rabbi of Ireland at the time, who became the Chief Rabbi of Palestine in 1937.

The family farm near Clonakilty had been transformed by one of my cousins into strawberry fields, acres and acres of them, covered by polythene tunnels that gave the land an almost extraterrestrial white gleam, a silver sea of light. I had always imagined it as some kind of bucolic oasis of verdant green, not an alien seascape.

My cousin's name was James, like Dad's. He came out to meet me on the steps of the old house. He was a tall man with a good smile and hands like shovels, as they say in Ireland. We sat in his kitchen and he smoked his cigarettes, his wife, Finnoula, a strawberry blonde lady who was pregnant with their third child, constantly asking me would I like another cup of tea.

"Granddad died of the cancer. It was in his lungs," James said.

"I'm sorry," I said.

"Oh, it was alright. It only lasted a few days, not like some who suffer for months. These things happen. He lasted to a great age. He was an amazing man. Do anything with his hands he could."

I looked up over the fireplace at the antiquated clock which had just tolled the hour, only to see some writing in a frame above it. By the form of the sentences I guessed it to be Psalm 23. I asked him whether my guess was right.

"How'd you know that? You'd have to be an eagle to be able to read that from where you're sitting there."

"Just a hunch. Your grandfather gave it to my father before he left for France."

"Granddad loved that Psalm. It's a tradition in our family, along with many others, as you probably know," he smiled, knowingly. "I know it by heart, as will all my kids. Say it every day I do. He used to say it protects you."

"It does."

"He says it was what protected him during the War."

"Oh, in the Civil War?"

"No. In World War II."

"But Ireland was neutral during the war?"

"Not for my granddad it wasn't. At the time he was in the Irish army, stationed at the Curragh. He joined to make extra money so that we wouldn't lose this land." He looked out the window onto the sea of silver.

"What? Who did he fight with?"

"The British of course and boy did he suffer for it when he came home. You know the bastards took away his old age pension, any kind of social welfare and banned him from ever working for the government again. The fuckers. Went over there and fought the fuckin Nazis and they took away his fuckin pension!"

I sat across from him, shocked. First, this man across from me was an Essene like me, initiated in the same tradition as me, and second, Dad's brother had fought with the British while Dad had fought for the French.

"They arrested him when he came back too, the fuckers. They arrested hundreds of them."

"What?"

"That fucker Traynor called himself the Minister for Defense, more like the Minister for fuckin Stupidity. He said they were worthy of very little consideration! Jesus, only in fuckin Ireland I tellya would they have a defense force cutting peat for power stations when the rest of the world is trying to stop that psycho Hitler! That madman De Valera and his cold comfort, or, as my grandfather used to describe him, *that bitter, bad man, rotten from the roots to the crown by his buckled understanding of this world.*"

Finnoula, another tea in her hand, placed her hand on my cousin's shoulder. "Ah Jim, don't be getting all riled up now. That's all in the past."

"Like fuck it is! Granddad went to his grave without a penny and if it wasn't for men like him, you and me'd have been shot because we weren't fuckin Aryan enough!"

He nestled his two dirty hands over his tea for a few moments and then smiled at me after he'd settled himself. "Sorry about that. It's just despicable, so it is. It's fuckin 1965 and the bastards still haven't given them an amnesty. The whole fuckin world and their mother agrees with me, but the government won't budge. Everyone knows how just their cause was and how bravely the Irish fought for the freedom of Europe. Jesus, no war is just, but if there was ever a just one to fight in, it was that one. They gave granddad and sixty-two others from the so-called neutral fuckin Ireland the Military Cross!"

He looked up at the Psalm above the fireplace. "They deserved better treatment when they came home. They deserved the same treatment the British got, that the French and Americans got. They were heroes and they were treated like second class citizens."

Later that night, after drinking in the local pub until it was closed and we were, to use Jim's description, "polluted drunk", we staggered back to the house in the dark, the stars smiling down on us as we talked about the surreal reality of us both being Essenes, a Frenchman and an Irishman from the same Jewish family. Near the house Jim climbed, or more fell, over a big red gate into a field. I followed him, falling into a hedge for a while before I crossed the happy grass to a giant oak by a small stream. Jim was sitting underneath the tree in a half lotus position, smiling as he patted the hearts above his head, carved into the bark many years before.

"You know, I'm fierce glad you came, Zeke."

I sat down beside him. "I am too, Jim."

He put his wide arm around me. "You know, it used to be that I thought we were the only ones left. It's a joy to me to know our family's *Tree of Life* continues in France and elsewhere." I could feel the big man's loving kindness and gratitude. "It really is a great joy to me."

"It's a great joy to me too, Jim."

THE FRUIT BUYER FROM AVIGNON

Monsieur Ducon, the very overweight, balding fruit buyer from Avignon, our biggest buyer, wouldn't eat at the table with us because Yusuf was present. He didn't say it out loud. He whispered it to my father, but I could hear it. I knew my mother could hear it too. Yusuf was washing his hands at the kitchen sink.

In the past Monsieur Ducon had always refused to eat with us due to his rounds. He usually ate later than *midi*, he'd told us, with Madame Ducon back in Avignon.

"She doesn't like nature, Madame Ducon. It disagrees with her. She prefers the shops and people and going to see other cities in France and abroad. She does like the sea, though. We go to the sea often for her lungs as the sea air helps her. I tried to buy a little house in Lunel years ago to be nearer the sea but she was having none of it. She said, does Lunel have the festivals? Does Lunel have the shops and culture and distinction and refined people that Avignon does? No, I think not, she said. So, there we are. In Avignon." He laughed. "I grew up in Remoulins! *Avignon*. Never would I have thought that I'd live there. But she is right. There's a certain class of people there whom we enjoy. And the city, it conforms to a certain cultural context that is very agreeable!"

Any time someone visited us it was Dad's custom to invite them to eat if we were eating. His invitation to Monsieur Ducon was an easy one to make as Monsieur Ducon was a jolly man who had praised our apples and apricots as the best in Provence and paid us handsomely for years for the opportunity to have them, even when we all knew he could buy cheaper ones from our neighbors. Even though Henri next door told us Ducon was racist, Dad still invited him to eat with us.

"Quality, Monsieur Moran!" he would say. "You have to give people quality, otherwise they will not come back! I didn't get where I am in this business by dealing in inferior quality! Those *chanteclers* of yours are the same ones my grandmother used to grow, sweet but not too sweet and dependable for freshness to the touch, not flaccid and insubstantial around the skin like these other fools try to pawn off on me! I can see that you grade and care for your apples better than anyone else!"

"Thank you, Monsieur Ducon."

"The truth! I only speak the truth. And you are right. A *chantecler* is a *chantecler*, not an attempt at one, the epitome of the variety, not something inferior, some mixture of the variety, but a true French apple in all its perfection!"

Dad didn't shout or scream when Monsieur Ducon waited for him to send Yusuf away. Instead, he politely asked Monsieur Ducon outside for a moment. A few minutes later Dad came back in. Alone. Monsieur Ducon apologized, but he had to leave unexpectedly, Dad said. He had a meeting he'd forgotten about. We never saw Monsieur Ducon again.

I doubt I'd have ever known a thing about it if, two weeks later, I hadn't gotten into a fight at school with that fool Maurice Jalabert.

"It's not right having a black man in France. He's not French! Well, all the better for us. Ducon came and bought our apples instead of yours. He said yours were of an 'inferior quality'!"

"What, are you saying Dad didn't sell his apples to him because of Yusuf?"

"Of course. Your idiot father told him he wasn't going to sell to him anymore so he came to us."

"What?"

"And he gave him his money back too! Do you think my father'd be that stupid? You Jews think you're so smart and good with money but you're all idiots!"

When I told Dad what had happened at school, he hugged me and walked me to the outside tap beside the barn. He cleaned the blood stains from my face with the cool water so my mother wouldn't get upset. Maurice Jalabert's mother was another churchy Catholic. Dad told me about the fights he'd been in for the same kind of thing in Limerick. He said fighting wasn't the answer, but that sometimes hatred and the destructive tendencies of people had to be stopped. He was proud, but sad and though he didn't say it, I knew what the sadness was, not pity or shame, but disappointment. He was disappointed that people behave the way they do.

PART THREE
ORANGE

THURSDAY, JANUARY 5TH, 2017

CARCASSONNE HOSPITAL, FRANCE

MATHIAS

Mathias was a black belt in judo and a dressage champion before the age of seventeen. He could speak German and French fluently by eighteen and could read English better than most people who grew up speaking the language. When I first met him, the day before his eighteenth birthday, at the Saturday market in Avignon, he was a man. It was hard not to notice how different he was from the other people around him. Where I am of average height, Mathias was tall, his muscles showing through his summer shirt, his clothes clean as snow, his walk reminiscent of some regal stallion that didn't have to prove anything to anyone. I remember thinking when I first saw him how great it would be to look like him. Later, even when his ego would take over and he would show off, I still kept this reverential feeling for him because he had this lovely way of asking you to forgive him when he became insufferable.

The next time I met him was at our *mas*. His mother wanted a dog and our Mayor had told her we had Britney pups. There was only one left and we'd all become attached to him, even my mother. He was the smallest, the runt. We were out in the fields when their fancypants, Dad's words, 1936 burgundy and gray Delahaye 135

Figoni and Falaschi Torpedo Cabriolet, came up our driveway and parked beside the apple cart at the front of our house.

"Who's that, Dad?"

"I don't know. Let's go see."

Mathias' mother was tall and beautiful in a very lithe way. I think she was the first woman I ever really wanted to get into bed with, her long nails painted pink, her skinny fingers I imagined playing gently on my skin like some piano until I ... Her fragility was fascinating to me.

My mother rubbed the goose blood from her hands onto her apron, her face brightening into a rich red of jealousy and humiliation. She was unprepared to meet a lady. Later, when she found out what a Crosshumper Madame Kreutzmann was, there was nothing the woman could do wrong. She was to become the personification of the perfect Catholic, capital C, the Virgin reborn.

We went to the house and my mother made them tea with the fine bone china reserved for the parish priest, baptisms and communions. Dad went to get the runt. Mathias' mother stood in the middle of the kitchen staring around like some lost parrot transported in a cage from a jungle somewhere in South America. Mathias smiled at me, embarrassed by her. I immediately liked him. I knew full well what a mother can do to your self-esteem through dogmatic attachment to mores that nobody really cared about save fools and sycophants, least of all the postman, the mayor, the banker, the neighbors.

She turned to my smiling mother and took her *tisane,* sitting down opposite her after adjusting her whimsical dress. Mathias, having already refused, very politely, his *tisane,* told my mother he was allergic to *verveine* – a lie.

I offered Mathias a seat and he sat on it before his mother could tell him not to. I sat beside him and asked him in French did he speak the language. He replied yes. So I asked him where he was from, and he told me Heidelberg.

"Heidelberg?" I'd never heard of it.

"Oh, it's just a city, a pretty boring one at that. It has some lovely architecture, but it's as boring as a brothel."

"Mathias..."

She tried to scold him in German, but his smile defeated her. He shook his head up and down as if she was some fly he was trying to push off his clothing, with about fifteen to twenty *Ya Mamas* coming mechanically out of his mouth. Ya, Mama. Ya, Mama. Ya, Mama. I was in awe of him. Here he was giving it right back to her without so much as raising his voice. He was in complete control. He even fixed his collar in between a Ya Mama, straightening it out to the sides.

While they sat at the table talking about Jesus and the good news and life, how one lives it, etc., we were left the other side of the room looking out the window at one of our sheep, Judas, trying to escape through a fence.

"Do you speak English?" I said absentmindedly.

"Yes."

"Does your mother?"

"No. She can't stand English or English people. She and my father hate all minorities, especially Jews, something I will never understand. However, they have a particularly ingenious hatred for the English."

"Do you hate minorities?"

"Why should I? Do you?"

"No. I just..."

"Well, then, can we speak candidly?"

"What's *candidly* mean exactly?"

It was the first of many English words I learned from Mathias in the years to come.

"Freely."

"Why not?"

"Great. To tell you the truth I'm bored out of my mind. She," pointing with his head towards his mother, who was politely pontificating on something liturgical, "has me cooped up in that monstrosity of a house all day playing solitaire and reading books. It's not that I don't love books but you know there's got to be other stuff to do." Mathias moved closer to me and whispered, "Are there any easy girls about?"

"Easy? What do you mean, *easy*?"

"You know." And he smiled that mischievous smile I came to adore.

"Know what?"

"Sex."

The conversation at the other table stopped again. Mathias' mother was the same as mine: if swans didn't deliver your children, then boys came from the *choux*, cabbage patch, and girls from under the rose bush. His mother turned around. He spoke to her in French.

"What, mother? Can't I tell Ezekiel here about my sextant and all those beautiful navigational maps uncle Hermann gave me?"

"What?"

"You remember, for my birthday. Going where you need to go by the stars."

"Oh, yes, dear." She blushed. "I'm sorry, I thought you were asking about the ... sex of the dog."

"No, no." And he laughed from his stomach for no apparent reason, but it was obvious that he was so used to stuffing her with subterfuge that by now it felt more ridiculous the more he did it.

She turned back to her new Crosshumper friend and Mathias stared at me, his playful smile broadening.

"Well?"

"Well what?"

"Christ!"

His mother turned around again. "Mathias, you will not take the name of our Lord in vain."

"Yes, Mama. I apologize," he responded in French with faux sincerity. He knew as well as I did not to mess with the holy of holies.

He looked at me again. "Are you really that naïve?"

"Look, ever since I left school I don't get off the *mas* much, save for the village *fêtes* or mass."

"Mass? God! You don't go to that, do you?"

"I've tried to stop." I looked at my mother, defeated.

"We can fix that."

"How?"

"You have to slowly inculcate your absence so that your presence is no longer needed."

"What?"

"Act sick every Sunday morning."

"But she'll know."

"Have you ever put a thermometer over a candle flame?"

"No."

"Have you ever made yourself get sick?"

"No."

"So you've never invested in making yourself absent. You'll see, it'll be easy. It just takes time."

"How long did it take you?"

"Six months."

"Holy fuck!"

"Ezekiel!"

"Sorry, Mother."

"Go find your father," she said. "I can't imagine where's he's got himself to."

"Yes, Mother."

"Can I go, Mama?"

"Do you mind if my son goes with him, Madame Moran?"

"No, not at all," she responded, happy that she'd been asked another innocuous and unnecessary question.

Mathias prodded me ever so gently in the back as I walked down the dark hallway out into the orange light of our kitchen garden.

"So, do you know any hot women?"

"Hot?"

"Have you been living in a monastery all your life?"

"You could say that. My mother has her ways."

"So does mine, I just don't let them interfere with mine!"

"Well, I don't have the same amount of time and money as you."

We stopped outside our back door. I was waiting for him to react to my cut, but he didn't and that was when I first understood what a generous person Mathias was.

"Well, we'll just have to help you find the time to spend my money!" He clapped me lightheartedly on the back and ran down to my father who was playing with the runt in the potato patch.

"Oh, he's beautiful!" cried Mathias in English.

"I thought you were German?"

"He is Dad, but he speaks English and French too."

"Well imagine that. That's great." I knew by the way that he looked at Mathias turning the little pup around in his hands that he liked him straight away, not because he loved the least lovable of all the pups, but because he could speak our secret language, my father's mother tongue, the one we used against my mother when she became insufferable.

"How long are you staying in France?"

"Papa has to totally refurbish the family hotel. The place is in ruins since the Great War. The Germans, irony of all ironies, destroyed the place because the French were using it as a headquarters. He was too disgusted to ever come back, until now. Greed's always stronger than shame, for him." Mathias started pushing the little pup into the potato patch laughing another of his amazingly deep stomach-tightening laughs, infecting Dad and me. "Isn't he lovely?"

As we looked at him playing with the runt, I knew Dad was wondering the same thing as me: where does someone like Mathias come from?

JUDO AND THE ALTO

It was three months later, a Sunday. My mother had just gone to Mass on her own. Mathias and I were in a field harvested of wheat, the stubble of stalks sticking into our backs like needles as we lay watching the clouds float by.

"I'm never getting married," Mathias said.

"Yes you will."

"I promise you I won't, Zeke. Never. Look at how unhappy our parents are. If I ever get married, shoot me."

I started laughing.

"I mean it. If I ever marry anyone, it'll be because I've completely lost my mind."

He pushed himself up and lay on his side, a long piece of straw sticking out the side of his mouth. "Marriage is an institution..."

"Yeah, yeah, and you don't want to be put in an institution. You're worse than Dad with your old jokes."

He took off his left shoe and threw it at me. "This coming from the comedian of the south of France!"

"It wouldn't be hard to be funnier than you!"

He took off his other shoe and threw it at me, this time

connecting with my head. I jumped up from the grass but Mathias was already up. Any chance I had was gone.

"If you're ever going to surprise me, Frenchman, you'll have to be quicker than that!"

"Oh, this is useless. I can't even jump on you and play fight, what with you and your fancypants black belt."

He sat up beside me and smiled. "I'll teach you if you like."

"Would you?"

"On one condition."

"What?"

"That you teach me the alto."

"Playing music is not like judo, Mathias."

"Yes it is. Judo is a science and an art, my friend, just like music. It has a flow and a movement to it just like your chords and tones or whatever you call them. When I spar with someone, I never remember how I threw them on the ground."

"Of course you do."

"No, I don't. One moment we're in front of one another and the next he's on the ground, pinned. It just happens. I become inspired, like you when you play Handel or Mozart."

"You're not talking shite, are you?"

"Talking shite? What kind of English is that?"

"Dad's."

"I wish my Dad was like yours. My father talks true shite all day. Business, business, business. Either that or prejudice and racism. He's probably the most boring and stupid man on the planet..." He bent down to pick up a stone, "... about as inspired as this pebble!"

The first time I met Mathias' father, Carl Hans Kreutzmann, in the hallway of their immense *maison de maître*, he looked down on me much like Thérèse's mother did the first day I met her. His ridiculous monocle blinded me as the sun glanced off it into my eyes, making him ever after into a tall, skinny, flour-faced Cyclops. This image turned out to be very close to the truth. Mathias was Kreutzmann's first victim, but the camps during World War II gave him ample opportunity to show everyone just how big a monster he really was as *Commandant* at Natzweiler-Struthof concentration camp.

The camp lay about thirty miles south of Strasbourg in the Vosges Mountains, but of course, you will not find a record of Carl Hans Kreutzmann ever having been there. Like so many others after the war, he was too smart to officially exist. Instead, in this period from 1942 to 1944 you will only come across commandants Egon Zill, Hans Huettig, Freidrich Hartjenstein, Heinrich Schwarz and Josef Kramer, not one Carl Hans Kreutzmann. At the end of the war, I met one of Kreutzmann's prisoners liberated by the American 42nd Rainbow Division. He was one of what the Germans called the *Nacht und Nebel,* Night and Fog prisoners, chosen by the SS to build roads and quarry in the nearby mines.

I was interviewing him about French *Résistance* fighters he had witnessed entering the camp. After the Liberation, my job was to assess whether any of our compatriots had survived these camps. Most *Résistance* fighters were killed on arrival at Natzweiler-Struthof. He recounted vividly the last day he ever saw Commandant Kreutzmann. I told him there was no Commandant Kreutzmann in the official paperwork. He said it didn't surprise him, as Kreutzmann was by far the smartest of them all. Kreutzmann, he told me, was not the kind of man you could forget. He liked to kill defiant prisoners himself. The last day he saw Kreutzmann he marched him and 2,000 other prisoners down the mountain to take the cattle train for Dachau. It was the 31st of August, 1944. D-Day had happened two months before, so the Nazis were trying to cover up their genocide by shipping prisoners from small concentration camps to larger ones. The train wasn't there. From his big car, Kreutzmann ordered the prisoners to march back up the mountain again, barefoot, with no food or water. Then, at five the next morning, he marched them all the way back down the mountain barefoot again and with no food or water, and forced them to wait in the cattle wagons for hours in the August heat until they left at ten.

He went on to tell me how this same man was the one who ordered the construction of the Natzweiler-Struthof gas chamber the previous August. Ever the business man, Mathias' father charged the Strasbourg University Institute of Anatomy 236.08 Reichsmarks for the construction of the gas chamber so that the Director of the Institute, Professor August Hirt, could have his murdered prisoners to dissect. His colleague, Professor Otto Bickenbach, also conducted failed experiments on antidotes for the poisonous gas, phosgene. It was when I asked him for a description of the Commandant that I finally realized who he was. How it took me so long to make the connection still surprises me today, but then again, it was war and your ability to connect your life before the war with the world of war is never easy. Very tall, he said. Very white, almost milky complexion. Monocle in his right eye and a tiny scar above his left eye. I asked him whether he knew anything else about him and he said no, only that he came from Heidelberg.

"Can you really show me how to spar, Mathias?"

"I've told you already, as long as you show me how to play the alto. I love the harmonica but I think it'd be a lot more fun to play strings. You'll love judo. It really is an art. There's no winner. The only winner is the judo. Like the way philosophy used to be. The truth should win. It doesn't matter which person wins, which one's defeated. Philosophy today seems to be mostly a battle, a contest. When I'm beaten in judo I love it! Then I can learn. I can see how judo has beaten me again. That's why we bow to each other at the beginning and at the end. We respect the art of judo more than our egos!"

"I'm not too small?"

"Not at all. You're the exact right height for sparring. If you had as much technique as me, you'd probably beat me every time. You see, the lower your center of gravity, the easier it is for you to keep your balance. Everything has its positive angle."

"Even marriage?"

He tossed the pebble from one hand to the other. "Do you want me to throw this at you?"

"He that is without sin..."

"You and your *Bible*." He jumped up. "Come on, let's go see if we can find a *maison close* in Avignon!"

"I thought you said you would never see a prostitute there

because there was too much of a chance of getting a disease in a city?"

"Diseases are not only found in cities, my friend. Let us go forth and procreate!" And he started marching down the side of the ditch with his shoes swinging from side to side in his hands, his legs taking great forward steps, his deep voice screaming, "Onetwothree march! Onetwothree march!"

I ran after him and jumped on him from behind pulling him down to the ground. The two of us rolled one over the other into the ditch of nettles and briars.

"You see! Lower center of gravity!" he screamed out, laughing, even though nettles stung his face and arms, and thorns plunged into his bare feet.

SHAKESPEARE AND MARCUS AURELIUS

That summer I grew up in more ways than one. Mathias taught me judo nearly every day just as I taught him the alto. He also lent me his books. Soon I was reading Hegel, Sartre and Proust. *Nausea*, *Being and Nothingness*, *The Wall*, *Remembrance of Things Past*. Dad left me alone to read and train. When my mother asked him where I was, he'd make up some excuse when most of the time I was in the barn reading. He and Yusuf did the work. My mother considered all 'modern' books to be filth for the mind, all that is save *The Bible*, St. John of the Cross' *Spiritual Canticle* and *The Story of a Soul*. To my amazement Dad would later tell me that he had read Sartre, Proust and Hegel, which of course endeared him to me even more, and more again when he said he'd forgotten everything Hegel and the rest of them ever said. Except for Nietzsche. He loved Nietzsche. Dad was the one that introduced Mathias and myself to *Thus Spoke Zarathustra*, which we loved reading aloud to one another, laughing out loud at how hilarious *The Awakening*, *The Ass Festival* and *The Sublime Man* are.

Mathias was reading all of Shakespeare, chronologically, in English, and having a hard time of it because he spoke French a lot better than English, especially Elizabethan English. But when he came across a passage that, blew him away, we'd all hear about it. One I especially remember was the passage in Macbeth that goes:

But 'tis strange;
And oftentimes, to win us to our harm,
The instruments of darkness tell us truths,
Win us with honest trifles, to betray us
In deepest consequence.

Though he loved *Macbeth* the most, his favorite quote came from *Hamlet*:

This above all – to thine own self be true;
And it must follow, as the night the day,
Thou canst not then be false to any man.

And yes, we had our to be or not to be philosophical questions, but Mathias was obsessed with *Macbeth*, even demanding that we go to Scotland and Dunsinane "at our earliest convenience". We had great fun quoting stuff to each other in the barn, seeing who could discover something even better than the last quote or passage. We were like little boys finding seashells on the beach, shrieking and running up to one another to show some new treasure.

Thanks to Yusuf I was obsessed with Sufi poetry. I have so much of the stuff in my head that it probably takes up about an eighth of my mental hard-drive. All my life I have loved poetry, those poems that lift you up the way Sufi poetry does! Indeed, it is poetry that has always sustained me, always raising me up when I am down.

We were in the café in Theziers one Saturday when I discovered one of my all-time favorites. I interrupted Mathias who was half way through *Titus Andronicus*.

"Mathias, you have to hear this. It's astounding. Listen!"

"Oh please stop bugging me will you? This *Andronicus* play is terrible. I've got to get to the end of it as soon as possible."

"Why not stop reading it?"

"I can't. I have to get through it. I've read all the comedies and histories and this and *Timon of Athens* are the only tragedies I have left. I'm not going to let one bad apple ruin the whole bunch for me."

"Listen:

They're not Hindu or Muslim.
They don't pray in mosque or temple.
Yet they receive the Light of God
And are immersed in beautiful visions.
These madmen are truly insane.
They're lost in God's domain.
I would give my life for these
Who are blessed with Love's disease!

"That's brilliant! I love *These madmen are truly insane*. Who is it?"

"Sultan Bahu."

"Is he the one Yusuf was twirling about once?"

"No, but he was one of the ones he's talked about."

"Well, here's a promise. When you fall foul to this ridiculous romanticism of yours and find some poor unfortunate to marry I promise to read it at the ceremony!"

"Could you imagine my mother?"

"*Love's disease* would have her screaming in the aisle."

"Hearing you reading would have anyone screaming in the aisle."

"Leave me to my *Andronicus* before I throw it at you!"

That summer I found someone else besides the Sufis: Marcus Aurelius. If there are three things I'm mad about they are: music, poetry and Marcus Aurelius, in that order. There is not a day that goes by that I don't read something from his *Meditations*. It used to drive Mathias crazy because I was forever quoting him aloud. It was Dad who got me addicted to him.

One Sunday Mathias and I were eating apples under our old olive tree beside the stream while our mothers went to Mass in Aramon.

"Why don't you read Marcus Aurelius, Mathias?"

"I don't have to. You've practically quoted the whole thing to me! I have Shakespeare to finish first anyway. I'll start reading the stuff from over a thousand years ago when I've caught up with the last five hundred!"

"But Marcus Aurelius is one of the most modern of writers there is."

"He was an emperor. Emperors are not modern. They're not even semi-modern. They're ancient history."

"So you don't care about Socrates or Plato or Epicurus? How could you not love Epicurus?

If there is a God, why is there evil?
And if there is no God, how can there be good?

"I never said that! I just said I haven't got the time for it all right now."

"But that's like saying you haven't got time to taste an apple pie because you're tasting a *croissant*. There's always time to take little bits of everything at the same time. Life is everything!"

"You're mad. Who wants to eat an apple pie with his croissant? One thing at a time, my friend."

"You're avoiding my question."

He laughed. "You see. You're completely crazy. You have to argue with me until you have me exhausted in a corner for no apparent reason save to drive me crazier. Take that, foul knave!" He threw his book at me. "Don't shake thy gory books at me again!"

"*The lady doth protest too much, methinks!*"

"For the time being, then, *I shall use more gentle treatment, so that your hardened and excited condition may be softened by gentle handling and thus prepared for more potent remedies.*"

He jumped on top of me and we wrestled about on the ground for a few moments until he had me pinned, his knees on my arms, his hands on my face.

"Now, you *foul and pestilent congregation of vapors...*"

"Unhand me, I say. Unhand me now! Unhand me now I say!"

Mathias fell off me onto the ground to my right, lying on his back, watching some *hirondelles* pass by. "Isn't the world a marvelous place, Zeke?"

"Yes, amazing," I said. "What was that you quoted me before about gentle treatment?"

"Boethius. He's a bit late for you though. Five hundred years give or take."

I elbowed him. "Just when I think I know you, you surprise me, again."

"And just when I think I know me, I surprise me, too!"

I laughed. "Promise me you'll never turn into your father, Mathias."

"That's easy. I promise. Now. You the same. Promise me you'll never turn into my father!"

"I promise."

He laughed and then his face grew serious. "Zeke, what are you going to be when you grow up?"

"Aren't we grown up already?"

"You know what I mean."

"A musician. A farmer. What I am right now. I'm happy being who I am right now. And you?"

"I don't know. Maybe a jockey?"

"You'd need to lose half your height!"

He laughed. "I really don't know," he said. "When I read Shakespeare, I want to be a playwright. When I read Nietzsche and Boethius, I want to be a philosopher. Now that I've seen Dali's work, I want to be a painter. Who knows? Maybe tomorrow I'll want to be a farmer!"

"Does it really matter as long as you're happy?"

"That's the thing, to do something that doesn't make your head big. The head and happiness don't make good partners. Seems to me that all the miserable people are the ones with the most money, and the happiest ones are the ones that don't have any, or least don't obsess over it."

"Isn't it weird that people define themselves by how miserable they are? If someone says they're happy, people think they're strange. It's as if the misery makes them feel special but also the same as everyone else. Yusuf would say trees are happy and birds and animals are happy, everything except humans."

"Exactly! People think they're being extraordinary by being miserable. The more hotels my father owns, the more miserable he gets. The more things he gets, the more distant he becomes. It's as if he wants attention and because he's not getting it then he becomes more miserable, because everyone understands a miserable rich man, not a happy one. His mind, like everyone else's, wants the attention, the love, the sympathy. Everyone's sympathetic to the miserable man. Who's going to give you sympathy, if you say you're happy? Also, people don't get jealous of miserable people. The fascists don't want to hurt a poor Jew, only the rich ones, because it's their fault that others are miserable and poor."

He took an apple seed from the tip of his tongue and sighed. "You know, I think my mother is just like my father. She's only miserable all the time so that she'll get some attention from him. She has everything she needs but she's still miserable. She wants him to worry about her. That way she doesn't feel lonely. So, she invents all these illnesses for his attention. The doctors give her medicine, even though they know there's nothing wrong with her. She gives them no choice. If they don't give her pills, then that means she's healthy and healthiness doesn't get her attention. If she were happy, he wouldn't pay any attention to her whatsoever. I'm sure of it. She enjoys her misery, it gives her pleasure."

"I think that's why my mother has such a hard time with Dad. He's a generally happy man and that drives her crazy."

"Exactly! She's in the darkness of her alcoholism and misery and he's playing his alto and enjoying his trees and work and you. The way she sees it is: how can he be so happy, when I'm so miserable?"

"I think that's what makes Dad such an individual. He doesn't have to look to other people to reflect his misery like they do. I think that's why your mother and mine need to be a part of groups like the church, so that they can be miserable with other people who have chosen to be miserable too. They can all get God to take care of things. That's why they kneel in front of miserable saints. They respect, even adore the misery of saints, these people who have lived whole lives of misery, instead of learning from the joy and ecstasy you get by letting go of misery."

Mathias sat up and looked at me. "You know, Zeke, I'm so grateful to have you as a friend."

"Why?"

"Because you're not miserable! I doubt I'll have many friends like you. It's not out of any desire to be lonely or estranged from people. I doubt there'll be many people out there like you that will agree with me when I say that most people are miserable."

"Yusuf gave me an example of what we're talking about once. He started by saying, Imagine dancing down the main street of Avignon, laughing, asking people to smile and laugh with you. What would their reaction be?"

"What did you say to him?"

"That they'd think I was crazy."

"That's what I'd think."

"You see, that's how miserable people are. And you know why he told me that?"

"Why?"

"Because once, after he and Dad had made a delivery of apples and pears in Avignon, they went up the rue de la République, Dad playing his alto and Yusuf singing and dancing. It was summer, they'd worked hard and sold a huge part of our crop in one go. They were happy and they wanted to have some fun."

"That's great!"

"Yes, but what happened?"

"They got drunk?"

"No. Two gendarmes at the top of the rue de la République warned them they'd arrest them for *trouble à l'ordre public.* And the only reason they didn't arrest them was because they had their papers on them."

"How sad! You can't even smile without people thinking there's something wrong with you. My father asked me at dinner a few nights ago why I was smiling? I told him I was smiling because I was happy. Then he asked me why I was so happy and I told him I didn't know. I told him, I'm just being happy. He thought there was something wrong with me because I was happy! It's insane! If I was sitting eating my lentil soup with a grimace on my face being miserable he would have said nothing. He would have thought it was natural! Since when did being blissful become unnatural?"

"It's crazy!"

"I know. Insane. No wonder humanity is so crazy. They need proof to be happy, but how can you prove happiness? You're either happy or you're not. No wonder crazy people like Hitler are becoming powerful. They're appealing to the same insane logic. Oh, it's these Jews over here that are causing all the misery. They're taking all our money and power. That's crazy! But people like my father, who are so crazy about being miserable believe a Hitler because they have to blame someone else for their misery, not themselves. Doesn't he realize that our basic nature is to be happy? We are born with it. We didn't lose it in a ditch! The Jews or the communists didn't take it away from us! *We* did. But this is the thing, just as you can choose misery over happiness, you can choose the opposite. You can choose to be happy!"

"Yes, but if you don't, then you constantly look to other people to make you happy which is completely irresponsible. How can you be free, if you don't respect your own freedom?"

"Exactly!" he shouted, sitting up. "Nobody's going to save you. Isn't it enough to save yourself?"

"Yes!" I said. "You can't blame someone else for your misery if it was you who started it by doing something wrong. That's ridiculous."

"Mistakes are inevitable. If we were all perfect, then we would never make a mistake and if we never make a mistake, then how are we to learn anything? Mistakes make us more intelligent, not more stupid. In judo, when you throw me wrong, I show you where you made your mistake. When I play a piece incorrectly, you show me where I went wrong. Sick people like my father and Hitler never make mistakes because they are robots, not human beings. They can't accept responsibility for their own misery, and so they blame others. They are the cause of their own misery not someone else.

That's where the madness of this war that's beginning is coming from, blaming others for recession and economic failure, not their own mistakes. Sartre got it wrong. Hell is not other people, hell is yourself!"

He jumped up, flinging his apple core into the stream. "Come on, enough of this misery talk. Time for my alto lesson!"

YUSUF AND THE WALLED GARDEN OF TRUTH

Yusuf was at the top of a cherry tree, the summer sun casting a sheen on his broad black back as he fished the cherries into his wicker basket from the branches. Mathias had just finished reading the last of Shakespeare's plays and was delighting in saying with confidence that Shakespeare was unparalleled in technique, beauty, insight and wonder.

"You know, Mathias, your Shakespeare may have been a great poet but there are many poets," Yusuf said.

"Such as?"

"There are so many. One example would be Hakim Abdul Majdud Adam Sanai Ghazanavi."

Mathias laughed. "Are you sure that's his full name?"

We all laughed.

"He spoke of a garden wall like your Shakespeare in his *Romeo and Juliet.* Shakespeare's was a wall that divided lovers, Sanai Ghazani's *The Walled Garden of Truth* revealed it."

"But Shakespeare wrote works of genius around love," shouted Mathias from the foot of the tree. "He reinvented the English language! He created a whole new form of sonnet."

"I don't know much about the sonnet, but I know Sanai Ghaznavi was probably the first one to use the *qasidah* and the *ghazal* and the *masnavi* in Sufi mysticism.

Attar was the spirit and Sanai its two eyes –
We come after Sanai and Attar.

"How can you sit up there picking your cherries and say Shakespeare is not the greatest poet who ever lived?"

"Have you read all the poets?"

Mathias kicked the tree. "No!"

"Then how do you know he was the greatest poet that ever lived? Am I the greatest cherry picker that has ever lived? Have you witnessed all the other cherry pickers?"

The tree picked, Yusuf gently handed me the wicker basket and climbed down. "Sanai Ghaznavi's *The Walled Garden of Truth* is 11,000 verses long and his *divan* is 30,000 verses long and then there is Fariduddin Atar and Jalaluddin Rumi and they are better known than Sanai Ghaznavi. And what about our great mystic martyr Mansur Hallaj who memorized *The Qur'an* before he was your age or Sultan Bahu whose verses are sung all over Pakistan and India by the *qawali* and *kafi* singers and whose shrine is still visited every year when they have a huge festival and celebrations? Do the English jump and dance and celebrate in joy every year for Shakespeare in England with euphoric spiritual festivals of singing and dancing?"

Yusuf started to dance, twirling around and around in a circle around the tree, singing. I sat down and listened because when Yusuf danced and sang it was like birdsong in your heart, like a sun in summer when you've just made love in a field.

I am no accomplished scholar,
Nor a judge, nor doctor of law –
My heart neither hell desires,
Nor my soul to heaven aspires!
I do not fast as required,
Nor am I the pure, praying kind.
All I want is union with God,

I care not for the false or true!

And he twirled again and again and again repeating the last two lines, absorbed, lost in God, his sense of being lost, what he called *zikr*, remembering the name of God,

All I want is union with God,
I care not for the false or true!

After a few minutes he turned and fell down into a sitting position and laughed, out of breath, his eyes closed for a long time. When he opened them again, he smiled at Mathias.

"Oh, Mathias..."

"You're crazy, Yusuf."

"Yes," he said, "we all are."

We all laughed again.

Still, that afternoon I found myself wanting to ask this man, this second father of mine, this man who had entered into my life like something out of Homer, how he had read so much, how he knew so much so deeply, who his family were, how many children he had, how many wives, how he managed to be always calm, laughing when someone tried to get a reaction out of him, smiling or simply not responding when someone inadvertently insulted the color of his skin or took him for an idiot when he had read and knew more than most scholars.

Only once did I ever ask him about where he came from and that was the last time for I felt I had betrayed a hidden trust, a walled garden of truth that Yusuf didn't talk of. It wasn't out of a sense of empathy for his pain and suffering but out of respect for the grace he had achieved by forgiving those who had made his family and friends disappear. Yusuf's walled garden of truth was his overwhelming forgiveness and to enjoy the fruits of his growth all I had to do was listen and experience the man, his dancing, his joy in the now, his love and rapture for the divine all around us.

COMMUNION AND THE WIND

After my confirmation, Dad brought me into the olive grove behind our house telling my mother he had a job for me, his code that he had something he needed to talk to me about. The mistral was driving hard through the trees but the sun was high and it felt good upon my face, the wind and the sun together. Henri's seven white doves were playing on the gusts above us, falling and climbing.

"Zeke, I want to talk to you about something."

"I thought you might."

He smiled. "You know this whole communion business..."

"I had my confirmation, Dad, not my first communion."

"Don't mind confirmation. I'm talking about communion. You were too young for me to talk to you about it before. Well, you know it's all just symbolic, don't you?'

"Yes, kind of like *The Tree of Life*?"

"Well, yes and no." He lit the cigarette he'd just finished rolling. "You know in the *Tree of Life* the way you feel energy going up and down your body?"

"Yes, the rush of energy. It's wonderful."

"Yes, well, a long time ago communion would have been a ritual that was the same way. It would have had more than a symbolic meaning: an actual physical experience to it. In some traditions, such as in India, it's called *satsang. Communion* in that sense means to have a meeting with a mystic or master as well as communal assimilation of the Truth."

"Like Yusuf's Sufis?"

"Yes." He smoked a bit and kept walking. "So when you receive the sacrament of communion what it represents is giving to others, honoring others in a communion, a communal understanding. My father told me that thousands of years ago this meant breaking bread, hence the communion wafer, because you were celebrating this communal sharing. It's when you start becoming a man or woman, when you have to come to terms with the fact that you are part of a larger world community of human beings, not just your family, and that you have to honor that community as an individual man or woman."

He smoked some more and stopped for a moment. "Which makes sense when you think of the meeting of the master and the disciple. You would meet someone outside of the people you knew, an authority figure, an elder, like the Catholic bishop, who would come and accept you into the wider community by breaking bread with you. *Community* sounds very like communion, doesn't it?"

"Yes, but why don't the Essenes have a communion ritual?"

"They do, but we haven't done it yet. We do it when you are fourteen. We see seven as a sacred number."

He started to walk again.

"Ah, so that's why I was initiated into the *Tree of Life* when I was seven."

"Yes, that was your initiation into our spiritual family."

He blew some smoke into the wind. It disappeared as soon as it left his mouth. "You know the most important communion though, Zeke?" He stopped again and put his hand on my shoulder, the other one on his chest. "It's here." He patted his chest. "This is the real communion, the communion with the inside, the spirit inside of you. When you commune with your soul, with yourself, then you have real communion. Then you can commune with the trees, the birds, others, everything around you!"

We kept walking though the grove, saying nothing for a long time.

"Dad, I need to ask you something."

"What?"

"It's about..."

"Yes."

"Well, at school, they're saying that she's a..."

"A *pute* or a *cocotte* or maybe even a *putain*?"

He kept walking. I stopped. "But Dad..."

"Is that why you've been getting into fights at school?"

"How'd you know?"

"Your ripped clothes, your face. Black eyes don't come from falls, Zeke. You're a bad liar."

He smoked the last of his roll-up and put it out with his fingers.

"But how'd you know they were calling her those names?"

"Because your mother has had lovers."

"Dad!"

He stopped walking. "What, do you think those young men that visit our house from the church come to crochet for the altar?"

"But, Dad, why do you allow it? It's disgraceful. It's..."

"What, disgraceful to be a cuckold and not do anything about it?"

"Yes. She's an adulterer."

"In the eyes of her church. Yes. From my perspective, no. Your mother is entitled to do whatever she wants. I don't own her. Just because we're married, just because society has given us a contract of marriage, doesn't mean I have to hold her to it. That's ridiculous. It's like saying you own the wind if you have a contract that says so. The wind changes every second and people are no different. Your mother is a very beautiful woman. A young man falls in love with her and wants to consummate that love. Who am I to stop him, if she wants to make love to him too? We are all free to make whatever choices we want in this life, Zeke. We are all free to commune with whatever we want to. I've seen prostitutes. I'm not proud of it, but then we all have desires and sometimes they overwhelm us."

He started walking again. "That's what real communion is, Zeke, not judging, not condemning others for their actions. If we call your mother a sinner, as her church would, then we would be sinners too for judging her. When you judge you judge yourself, not others, even though it seems like the opposite."

"You know, sometimes I feel like just shaking you and Yusuf up, Dad. Why do you both always have to be so fucking calm about everything!"

He grabbed my shoulders lightly in his hands and looked into my eyes. "Zeke, I understand your anger. You idealized our relationship. I used to be like that too when I was your age. I wanted everyone to be true and faithful and good, but that's not nature's way. The wind is true and faithful and good but it changes direction and sensation every second. It is faithful to change and nothing else. It is good and true to change and it tears up crops, brings down rains and cools the hot air. We are the same. We change. Our feelings and sensations change. We tear things up and bring things down all around us. It's natural, natural as the wind."

I was crying. "But I thought she loved you?"

"She does."

"But how can she have affairs, if she loves you? Stop talking about the fucking wind! I want to know why!"

"Why? I don't know, Zeke. Maybe she needs to take lovers to fill that emptiness she can't fill. I tried to help her fill it but never could."

"But she drinks and fucks..."

"Zeke. She's your mother and a human being. That language makes you as low as those teenagers at school."

"Oh, Dad, I'm sorry. I just can't understand your patience and understanding. How can you put up with it? How can you get into the same bed as her knowing that she shares it with a man ten years younger than you?"

He sat down, his spine in line with the olive tree behind him and lit another cigarette. "Oh, Zeke. It just doesn't seem so complicated to me anymore. Look at Yusuf. He lost everything. His wife, his children, his whole village, his country. Here I am sitting under an olive tree in the sun with a son I love with all my heart, in a country that gives me a wonderful life. I appreciate everything in my life. I am full. I don't need to love other women. I used to have sex with other women, but if I do it again it will be the same for me as in the past, I'll do it joyfully. I am full of life. I love my life. I love everything about it. Why would I judge my friend, your mother, for her actions? She's as free as the wind as far as I'm concerned. What violence is there in making love if it's done with love? She makes love and it makes her happy. It makes her feel beautiful. If I can't make her feel beautiful anymore, because I am no longer a young man, then isn't it wonderful that a younger man can?"

"But the neighbors are all laughing at you!"

"Great! It gives them something to talk about. They are so bored out of their minds that they need gossip to while away their days. I don't need gossip. I enjoy my work. I enjoy Yusuf and Henri and Yvette next door. I enjoy you. And as hard as it may be for you to understand, I enjoy your mother too. I enjoy her singing and generosity. I enjoy what we have created here together."

"But it's you and Yusuf that have created this place, Dad."

"Be fair, Zeke. When your mother is not at church or drinking, she's working harder than any of us. Who minds the chickens and kitchen garden? Who washes all our clothes and linen? Who makes most of the meals? Who cleans the house? Who helps us pick the fruit when she can, or load the carts?"

"I don't know if I could ever..."

"Share your woman with someone else?"

"I didn't mean that. I..."

"You have to understand my perspective, Zeke. I am grateful to have your mother in my life. If she were to walk out the door tomorrow, I would be sad, but I would move on because I'm detached. I love her but I don't own her. She's an individual, as I am. She can do whatever she wants and if she choses to leave with one of her lovers, I'll be sad but I'm not attached to keeping her. I'll respect her choice because it's her choice. For example, some day you'll want to leave this place. Do you think I'm going to keep you here?"

"No. But I'll never leave."

He smiled and put out his cigarette. "Look, just because you're my son doesn't mean I can keep you here. Like your mother, I don't own you, Zeke. You are free to do whatever you want to do. Everyone is. It's society and religion that would have you think otherwise. You have a choice, and choice is freedom. Do you think I should take away your mother's freedom to be who she wants to be?"

"No, but aren't you angry?"

"Not anymore. In the beginning I was angry. I got drunk and went to brothels. Then I talked to Yusuf about it and calmed down. Nobody's perfect. How can we be? We're human. Not machines. Yusuf helped me understand more deeply something my father used to say: "There is an old Essene saying from Avalon and Glastonbury: *We are as free as the wind, we only have to chose freedom.*"

"How do you know that?"

"Because my father told me it, and his father told him and his father him and, you know, aren't all fathers right? Sure, isn't that wisdom as old as the wind!"

He laughed, and so did I.

"Dad, why did you marry her?"

"Because I loved her. Why else?"

"But shouldn't you have loved someone more spiritual, someone more like Mary Magdalene or one of the many Marys in the Essene tradition?"

"Your mother is a very spiritual person. When I met her she was the last person you would ever have thought would knit an alb for a Catholic priest. She was as free..."

"No, don't tell me! As the wind?"

He laughed. "Exactly! She was as Essene a woman as you could find. Creative, meditative, loving, open."

"Then what happened?"

"She changed. The more she poured her astounding creative potential into the church, the more she changed."

"So she lost her freedom?"

"That's one way of looking at it, yes."

"But have you ever told her about our tradition, about the *Tree of Life*?"

"Yes, of course. After a year and a day, it is our custom to let your partner begin to understand some of our tradition, if they are open to receiving the information. As I said, Hannah was open to it all. We would meditate and fast together. We went far along the path of light, but we were never twin flames like my parents and grandparents."

"But why did she get involved with the church?"

"She was brought up as a lapsed Jew, but she felt she had to chose between the Essene way and the Catholic one. Soon after you were born, she went to confession and after that she started to go to church more and more regularly. She preferred to pray in a church instead of meditating at home. When I would talk of celebrating the new moon or the full moon she would grow silent and say she had something she had to do. She would say she was tired or too busy planning something for the church. Maybe she liked the community. She slowly grew away from the Essene way. It saddened me but, as I said before, we are all free to chose whichever path we choose since the paths to God are many."

"But didn't you see it as a betrayal?"

"In a way, yes, but mostly, no. It is difficult to follow the Essene way unless you have gone through the initiations. Hannah already had two decades of the Catholic tradition behind her. I had grown up in a family that practiced the Essene way in all we did. We meditated every morning and evening together. We gave thanks to the great being of Divine Mother Earth and to the greater universe itself at every meal. We lived in a community of love and sharing. What did Hannah live in? She worked for a horrible man as a child and went to church every Sunday to listen to sermons about a God of damnation and purgatory."

"Do you think our tradition will last, Dad?"

"It's lasted over two thousand years. It'll last as long as people like you and I are here to pass it on."

"Do you ever wonder if you're the last, though? How many of us can there be out there?"

"I don't know. We no longer stay in contact. It is a part of our covenant, to keep the tradition a secret so that it continues to grow and help people to evolve. I think there are plenty of Essenes out there right now having this same conversation in different languages in different time zones. The Great Gathering seeds of light were sown across the whole known world. And you know what a seed does. It grows into a great tree like this olive tree and it produces many fruits with many, many more new seeds that will be planted to grow new trees. All the seed needs is a little nurture at the beginning of its life and then it can pretty much survive on its own, no matter which way the wind may blow!"

He laughed and wrapped his arm around my shoulders. We got up and swayed playfully back through the olive grove the way we always had when I was a child, the sun high in the sky as the leaves gossiped and the branches chattered in the wind.

SEX

The most important thing I learned from Mathias in the summer of '36 wasn't judo, it was sex. How we didn't get any diseases still amazes me.

It was delicious! Our sexual organs moving about inside all those lovely ladies, beside their large intestine, the lower vertebrae, our pelvi pulsating, the appendix and bladder and whole hip area a symphony of movement. Oh, how fun and full it all was! There were no ethics and honor in our young minds, just the sex. No blame or guilt, just the sex. Yes, there was money involved, but it was for fun that we went, not for punishment and pain. We didn't think of the repercussions. We were young and full of life and living and it just seemed like the natural thing to do, as if we were laying a foundation to the world, our worlds at the very least.

I snuck out as many nights as possible. Mathias and I would cycle to cafés far away from where we lived and drink and talk and talk until some of the cafés closed, sneaking back into our beds by scaling the drainpipes and trellises of our houses.

At least once a week we would visit a *maison close* to have sex with prostitutes, but after a time I started to understand what Mathias had said that first day when he used the simile *as boring as a brothel.*

We tired of the *maisons closes*. Of course we'd go further afield and we'd find new ones, and over the weeks we'd run through all the women in them too.

But there was the depressing aspect of being with prostitutes, or *morues*, as their clients and pimps call them. Their pimps, *macqueraux*, make their young women "work" by *coeur et peur.* They get these young girls and women to fall in love with them: the heart first, with presents and time and then make them "work" to support them, then threatening them with violence; the fear, afterwards, when they eventually try to stop working. Back then, with the war on, it wouldn't have been a choice for the girls, though, as a lot of them were Roma or African and had little or no education. *Maisons closes* and *raccolage,* talking to potential clients, can get a prostitute arrested, but being a working prostitute can't. Of course today there are countless contemporary *salons de massages*, and *maisons closes*. The *macqueraux arrose les flics,* pay the police with sex to stay quiet, so that clients, never mind spouses and lovers, never find out that most of the girls are trafficked from countries economically devastated after leaving the Soviet Union, Moldova, Bulgaria, Transnistria, Belarus and Romania.

We had started to feel bored and then depressed by our antics when one of the girls, "Marie," told us how she had been trafficked when she was fifteen years old. We went back the following week with a plan to rescue her. Mathias had hijacked his father's car and we were going to drive her to the Spanish border. When we asked for Marie the two *macqueraux* smiled at us. They knew. They led us to a different girl we'd never met before.

"Girls come and go," said the tall one with a tiny blue tattoo above his right eye.

Then the older one spoke. "There are always more girls, no matter how many leave."

They laughed as they left us with the new girl. They'd named her Marie too. We paid her, and never went back.

We were so young, and talked as if we were men, but we both knew we were acting out parts. Then we met Madame Forte.

It was late, about eleven at night, in a café far from Aramon, when we met Madame Elisabeth Forte, her wonderful body a silhouette in the corner. Her forest green, a-line skirt, went down to her knees, accentuating her tiny waist, full hips. She was smoking and drinking her wine alone, the smoke floating up into the broken light fixture, clothing its cracks in a fog for a few moments only to disappear. Mathias asked whether we might join her. I was shocked. Mathias looked like a man. I did not. I could tell Mathias was nervous by the way he flicked his curls out of his eyes, but this was like a poker weakness, something I'd gathered over months of watching him. Madame Forte picked up on it immediately.

"Why are you both so nervous?"

"We're not nervous," said Mathias.

I kept my mouth shut, terrified. This was the first woman we'd actually sat down with in all our trips to the cafés that summer.

"Don't play games young man. I am delighted to meet you, but at the very least let us be honest with each other."

"I'm sorry. I'm Mathias, this is Ezekiel."

"Strange names for strangers. I'm intrigued. Are they real?"

Mathias produced his German driver's license and I my French one.

She smiled. "I see you're both teenagers."

We were mortified.

"Why are you both so embarrassed? It's a blessing to be a teenager! To have your whole life ahead of you. To have an exotic friend who will sit with you in a café and talk to strangers like me. Isn't it wonderful?"

We both smiled, and Mathias responded. "Yes, it is wonderful!"

She put out her cigarette in the ashtray and looked at us through the smoke coming out of her mouth.

"I have a proposition for you two men."

I was getting worried. Did she want us to kill her husband? Was she a drug dealer? Every ridiculous proposition addled my brain except the one she offered.

"You know, I've had a difficult marriage. I'm 35. He's 45. My husband married me when we were so much younger and we tried for a decade to have children. Now, he has left me for his secretary.

He's a commercial lawyer. I can understand him in a way and I forgive him his infidelity, but after all these years I really just want to have some fun. I feel claustrophobic nearly all the time from this *ennui*. When we first met I was twenty-two. We had fun every time we met. We went out to restaurants and dances in Avignon. We went to Paris. We went to London and Berlin. And after all that we came back here to where we were born. Anyway..."

She lit another cigarette and looked at us again. "When I saw you both walking in that door I thought to myself: How wonderful youth is with all its verve and optimism. They can do anything they want with their lives. They are alive!"

Mathias smiled at her. "Thank you."

"No, thank you, Mathias, for having the courage to sit down beside a lonely woman with so much money and time on her hands that she drinks in a decrepit café far away from Avignon and Paris."

"Why are you bored?" I asked.

"Good question. And you know, I think I finally have an answer to it. I am bored because society is nothing but these dead patterns created by others, society, the state, family, not me. I am bored because I've been living the life of The Divorcée. How ridiculous! That's why I sit in these cafés. I am waiting for a transformation to happen. That's why I'm not doing what society requires of me. The way I was living was wrong. You know all the men are afraid of me? I still have my looks. I'm rich. They don't know what to do with me. Women are not supposed to have that kind of power in our day and age, but I do. I could buy this café if I wanted. I could transport the whole damn thing to the grounds of my chateau!"

We all laughed.

"But ... I suppose what I'm trying to say is: Thank you for making me feel like a woman again. For six months I've been going into cafés in the hopes that some man, any man would have the courage to sit with me. And here you are! Not one, but two. A Frenchman and a German! How lucky am I? And it is your nervousness that has won me over. Your nervousness shows me how honest you both are. You admire me but are still interested in me. It is not a question of prestige or power or money to you. You sat down beside me for fun, not any of those other *boring* things! You are interested in something more than those *maisons closes*, no?"

"We never meant to..."

"What, to want to have sex with me?"

We all stared blankly at each other until it came up and out of Mathias like a river breaking its banks, laughter, loud, long and infectious. We all laughed until tears came into our eyes, a hysterical laughter that gave me a pain in the back of my head.

We wiped our tears away. Madame Forte's mascara was running. She started laughing again and so did we. She took off her black hat and flung her coal black hair into the air behind her back so that she could look into her pocket mirror. When she finished she slipped the mirror back into her slim silk bag and looked at us with a happy smile spread across her face.

"Well, shall we do it then? My car is just outside."

I was about to say Do what? when I remembered Mathias' words from our first meeting: Are you really that naïve?

We walked out the door leaving our glasses full.

That spring Madame Forte introduced us to some of her friends. Their husbands had mistresses and left them in their big houses with their maids. We went to the Île de Porquerolles with them every weekend save one: Madame Noez, Madame Pages, and Madame Forte. Madame Noez had the most wonderful breasts imaginable and Madame Pages was as light as a leaf. She jumped up and down on you like a little girl playing on a ball. The sun and food and sea and sex was euphoric. The house we stayed in had so many different trees out front that to name them would be like creating some kind of encyclopedia. We had sex, myself and Madame Noez, countless times against the Eucalyptus trees, the apples of her breasts rubbing up and down against the bark as we let go of ourselves.

They were all called Madame, though. This was something we all agreed upon from the beginning. We would all remain detached, attachment being the thing all these women told us they were trying to escape. This was supposed to be fun, a ride. It was supposed to liberate these cuckolded women from their overbearing, controlling and macho husbands. And it did. It freed them to such an extent that Madame Noez asked for a divorce, this being a time when divorce was just not the done thing in Catholic France. Surprisingly, Madame Pages' husband, the meanest and most patriarchal of the three husbands, actually changed. He left his mistress and implored his wife to stay with him, giving up his golf and club to spend time with her and the children, even going away on weekends alone with her to Italy and Spain. It was beautiful.

When the end of July came we would go to see Madame Forte on the weekends, but it was never really the same. The sex became anterior to our meetings and then we never really had much to speak about when we weren't planning where to go on the next weekend and what to eat. It was a natural breaking away and, over the months that followed, our friendship receded. She would tell us how Madame Noez had gotten remarried to a man her own age and how Madame Pages had become a *punaise de sacriste*, meeting up with women like my mother when their mutual organizations had charity drives for the poor, knitting and crocheting with these other ladies for the local babies of unmarried mothers and charity sales.

Later on, after the war, I found out what happened to Madame Forte. Like Berthe Fraser and many others, Madame Forte was tortured for helping Allied fliers get back to England from the south of France. Every day for 25 weeks they beat her and threatened to kill her. She was stripped and flogged publicly in front of the Nazi soldiers, but nothing broke her determination to protect her *Résistance* fighters and contacts in the British army. She spent twenty-four hours a day in solitary confinement for over 8 months and still refused to betray her contacts. Finally, condemned to death, Elisabeth was shot on the tenth of June, 1944, four days after D-Day. They gave her George Medal, her Legion of Honor, her American Freedom Medal and her Croix de Guerre to her ex-husband. It was his former secretary and lover who handed him the letter of commiseration and thanks from Eisenhower.

So, at the end of July we found ourselves bored with brothels again, visiting cafés to see if we could find another Madame Forte to take us out of our lethargy. We didn't have long to wait.

PART FOUR
YELLOW

FRIDAY, JANUARY 6TH, 2017

CARCASSONNE HOSPITAL, FRANCE

THÉRÈSE

She was nineteen when we first saw her, walking into the *boulangerie* in Aramon. Mathias dropped his book, *Love's Labor's Lost.* I tripped over him and fell onto the ground. I was ready to write love songs to her right there and then. Instead, I looked back up at Mathias from the ground and we both started laughing. From that day until she became our friend, Mathias and I became, what they call today, stalkers.

Thérèse Marie Francoise Alençon was born on the Rue de la Libération in Lisieux on the second of January 1918, not ten minutes from the Basilique Sainte-Thérèse de Lisieux. Her father, a drab man with a limp and a habit of twisting the ends of his long mustache between his girlish fingers, inherited a hotel, *Le Grand Hotel de l'Espérance* on 16, boulevard Sainte-Anne in Lisieux and sold it for a fortune when Thérèse was fifteen. After that M. Alençon moved himself and his family to Provence and spent the remainder of his life buying houses that took his fancy and renting them out to those he called "good" Catholics for income. The rest of the time he maneuvered his mustache, read *Le Pelerin* and *La Croix,* railed about the *étrangères* ruining France and had lunches with people like Mathias' father, either after Mass in Beaucaire every Sunday or when their wives had to meet to talk about crocheting an altarpiece, or organize an outing to the Beaucaire hospital to talk to the patients about Jesus and their religious health. Thérèse's father was an avid supporter of Charles Maurras' *Action Française*, believing that the German occupation was a "divine surprise" that would re-establish the *Ancien Régime.* We would often overhear him complaining to Mathias' father about the failure of the fascists of 1934 to launch a successful *coup d'état* during the 6th of February crisis on the *Place de la Concorde.* From 1941 until the end of the war M. Alençon became one of the men behind the *Camp des Milles* internment, or "transit" camp near Aix. About 2,000 inmates were shipped from Les Milles to Drancy and on to Auschwitz under M. Alençon's "efficient management." He would order his guards and *Milice* to make sure that all the windows, shutters and businesses in the town were closed when a deportation wagon was leaving the camp. M. Alençon did so so that there were "no annoyances from the public".

Thérèse was the first girl, woman, we'd met our own age who wasn't married, remarkably plain, or working in a brothel. Here was an angel, a woman who held her head high and let her blond hair flow in the air behind her instead of, as was the custom back then, tying it up into ridiculous buns or pushing it under some lacy, dreary hat even when it was roasting outside. She wore men's pants before it became fashionable, much to the disgust of her father. They were mostly cotton and denim and were very high-waisted, with buttons or a zipper down the side, and full legs, usually with wide cuffs at the bottom. Her absolute favorite was a pair of blue denim overalls that later became known as Rosie the Riveter overalls.

We sat outside the *boulangerie* on a green bench pretending to read, waiting for her to come out. My stomach was on fire. I had started to sweat involuntarily. It felt like I was no longer responsible for my upper intestines, liver, kidneys, middle spine. My trust in myself disappeared. I fainted.

When I awoke Mathias was standing over me, his face worried, his shouting like a trumpet in my ears. The clouds moving by above him made me remember I was alive. I thought I'd died.

"Are you alright?"

"What?"

"You just keeled over. Right there. Tipped off the bench."

"I had this ... mad rush of ... energy ... in my guts." I took in a deep breath. "It was ... like I was frightened ... and intimidated ... at the same time ... yet confident ... I think ... Jesus ... I think I fainted..."

"Oh, no. You've gone and fallen in love you fool! Christ, you're as bad as Dante!"

Then I heard the bell of the door from the *boulangerie*. I tried to rise but couldn't, my head still swimming.

"Jesus, get up! She's coming."

"I know ... I can't seem to..."

"Here, I'll lift you." Mathias lifted me up and propped me on the bench, but the mother had already seen my little drama.

She came toward us, a monument to everything her daughter was not, prim, proper, beleaguered by a gait that made you think she had something very painful and hard rammed up her posterior, her imperious nose making her head tilt back, and her gloved hands in a little pouch in front of her. She was, to use a turn of phrase my mentor, Yvette, used when she first experienced her, *Elle pet plus haut que le cul!* She farts higher than her own ass.

She looked down upon us from her height, blocking out the sun like some Alexander the Great, and said, in polished Parisian French: "Is there something wrong with the boy?"

"No, he just tripped over that step there, Madame," said Mathias.

"Oh?" She said. Thérèse was now behind her, and clearly wondering what was going on. Still stunned from my first fainting spell I became even more speechless when I saw her wonderful face. It seemed to shine, but as if the sun had nothing to do with the glow coming out of her.

"What's wrong, Maman?"

"Oh, it's nothing. This boy has fallen and this man has picked him up."

Boy. I disliked her even more.

Mathias stood up, never one to miss out on an opportunity.

"Allow me to introduce myself. My name is Mathias Kreutzmann and this is my good friend, Ezekiel Moran."

"What? Are you German?"

"Yes."

"My husband has a lot of German business associates. Are you holidaying here?"

"No, my father is renovating one of our hotels in Avignon and investing in other properties. We have been here nearly a year now and will probably be here a few more."

"Really. How interesting."

Thérèse smiled at me, totally uninterested in what her mother was saying. I smiled back at her and blushed. My abdomen started to get that rush of energy and I was terrified of fainting again.

"And you, Monsieur Moran, where does a name like Ezekiel come from?"

Distracted, I said the first thing that came into my mouth. "*The Bible*."

Stung, she turned to Thérèse and said, "We must go. Luncheon will be ready. We mustn't keep your father waiting."

"Yes, Maman."

She smiled at us both as she followed her mother, arm in arm, down the street to their car.

"Well, that went really well."

"Yes, for you."

"Well, what did you want me to do? Leave you on the pavement?"

"I'm sorry. I'm nineteen years old and this, this fainting business has never happened to me before."

"Oh, I wouldn't worry about it, Zeke. My mother faints all the time. The next time you meet her you'll charm her into submission. You'll see. You won't faint again anytime soon. Unless of course she just passes by!"

"Stop. I feel bad enough as it is. Jesus, fainting? What next?"

"Lunch, that's what. Let's go! The *boulangerie*'s going to close any minute now."

THE RAPTURE

Mathias and I started going to church. Our mothers nearly had heart failures and my Dad and Yusuf smiled shrewd grins at me as I left each Sunday. They knew there was only one thing that could make me go to church. Love, and not for a Catholic God. They knew the damnation story was the last thing I would ever be afraid of. Yes, our stalking knew no bounds. As the man in the shawl behind the altar droned on about some epistle to the apostles we pagans, wrapped in a rapture his sermons would never understand, stared at our prey, Thérèse. She had elevated us to unparalleled heights of desire.

She sat looking at the architecture of the church, the floor, the ceilings. She studied her nails and at intervals leaned her head back with her mouth slightly open looking down the runway of her nose at the priest in an obvious stupor of boredom. Her mother would nudge her ever so slightly with the side of her arm and Thérèse would make a slight grimace, right her posture and sigh, pretending to listen to the sermon like the rest of the congregation.

Mathias would open his eyes into ridiculous owl stares, or suck his cheeks in to make a little puckered circle of his mouth any time I looked at him. Of course this meant I had to cover up my laughter with bouts of coughing. I'd try to make faces at him too, but he would always beat me to it, causing me to spurt out another wave of coughing.

And so it was, on our third Sunday of grinding boredom, we finally got our opportunity. Thérèse was a yard or two away from us, uncharacteristically apart from her imperious mother who was solemnly listening to the priest, a very fat man with the silly habit of holding his chin with his right hand. I nudged Mathias and we sidled over to her. We didn't have to say anything. Thérèse, as always, took control.

"You seem to have a bad cough."

"Oh ... oh it's nothing."

She smiled. "You know, it almost sounded as if you were laughing."

I went red. "I..."

"I know," she said. "You think it's as boring as I do, don't you?"

"I..."

Mathias jumped in. "Of course he does. I was making faces at him."

"Ah, that explains the muffled laughter."

I smiled at her. "I'm Ezekiel."

"Yes, I remember, from the *boulangerie*. What a wonderful name. More Jewish than Catholic I would have thought."

"My parents are Jewish, well, were."

"Really. How interesting. You must tell me more about them. Where are they from?"

"Ireland and Germany."

Before we could go any further her mother was amidst us. "Oh, it's the German man from the *boulangerie* and," dismissively, "his friend. What were you talking about?"

"About Ezekiel's parents. They're from Ireland and Germany."

"How intriguing," she said, actually interested.

"They're Jewish," said Thérèse.

"Oh..." she said, in a completely different tone. "Well, we had better be going, Thérèse. Your father has a business luncheon."

"But Maman, it's Sunday."

“Thérèse.”
“Well, see you next week then.”
Mathias and I smiled. We couldn't wait.

THE DIVINE DESIGN

In the weeks that followed we found out Thérèse went to double bass lessons every Friday afternoon in Aramon. We made a point of just so happening to be in the vicinity on every occasion. She would arrive on her great bay horse and tie him to a lamppost outside the old man's house where she had her lessons. He was a lovely old man, Monsieur Moffre, his skinny little fingers and huge paunch a delight to witness as he held his bow like a conductor's wand in one hand, and his double bass in the other as if it were the neck of a swan singing. He invited myself and Mathias into his house to listen to them play when he found out we played the alto.

Since leaving school at the age of eighteen, Thérèse had refused an offer of marriage her parents had arranged with a man twenty years her senior. Even the mere thought that they would go behind her back and arrange a marriage with a man she, one, disliked, and two, barely knew, was, as she put it, Neanderthal. From then on she did everything in her power not to do anything they desired. She went to Mass only to annoy her mother with her blasphemous yawning and impious slouching. She did everything that her mother and father saw as unbecoming in a lady. She rode her horse everywhere alone, swam in the river naked, never wore skirts or dresses, and smoked roll-up cigarettes like my Dad. She also took up the double bass because it seemed to her the most unladylike instrument she could find. She started to wear trousers and hunted on her horse through the local farms for *morilles*, skinny wild asparagus and truffles, anything in season, stopping often by the river to swim, or by an old ruin to read one of her many mystical books.

Thérèse called herself a Catholic, but that was it. After the appellation, the church lost her to mysticism and anything she herself could channel, for she was as free as the wind, something she and Dad never stopped saying, Thérèse identifying with Joan of Arc's wind epiphanies, Dad with my grandfather's Essene saying. Thérèse would quote us Saint Clare of Assisi, Julian of Norwich, Saint Teresa of Avila, Saint Francis of Assisi, Saint Catherine of Siena and St. Thérèse of Lisieux as if she'd written the words herself. She talked of worlds behind our eyes, not the one in front of them.

On the terrace of the café in Aramon after one of her lessons, her horse tied to a lamppost and her double bass tipped into a corner inside, she gave us one of her first sermons.

"I'm in the world, Zeke, but I'm not of it. I'm not letting it enter into me anymore! Do you understand?"

"Not really, but I've heard that before."

"Stop being so scientific, Zeke. This is not about spouting syllogisms or mystical clichés!"

She started twirling around and around on the street like a dervish, her eyes closed and her words still coming. "Don't you see that all this is an illusion! You have to wake up from all this material madness! A Buddha means someone who is awake!"

She fell onto one of the chairs at someone else's table with a smile and a huge sigh. Mathias looked at me as if to say she was mad.

"But how do you know when what you're hearing isn't just what you call an *illusion*, and not the voice of one of your spirit guides?"

"Easy," she responded, springing up. "When there's no emotion attached to the voice it's positive. When I have no emotion, just the voice, then that is my soul or another one speaking. If I get emotional about what I'm hearing then it's poisoned and useless. It's for the person I'm saying it to to get emotional. It's for them to hear, not me. I'm just the conduit, the messenger."

"You're mad," said Mathias, "you know that?"

"Isn't it great?

She started to twirl again. I could see that Mathias was warming to her even though he was trying to hide it.

Then, she fell on the ground hitting her head on the edge of a table. We ran over to her immediately and knelt down. The owner, our friend Alphonse the piano player, a slim man with a permanent Gauloises on his lips, rushed out from behind the zinc bar. A little blood trickled from the side of her head.

"Thérèse, are you alright?" It was Mathias.

She started laughing when she saw the blood, wiping it away with the back of her hand.

"Look at it this way, Zeke. We are not human. We are beings. We are energy beings who are living this human experience. We were created by the Divine. So our biology is not us. It's part of the divine design. We are Divine beings living a human experience. Do you understand?"

Alphonse looked at us. "What's she talking about?"

I handed her a yellow tissue and she wiped the rest of the blood away as she spoke to Alphonse. "I'm so sorry. I'll stop dancing. I was just having some fun." She got up, put her arm under his and brought him back to the bar. "Can I buy you a drink?" she said.

Alphonse looked at her as if she was crazy, but then he melted. "I'll have a pastis," he said.

"We all will," she said. "One for everyone!"

From then on every time she came into the café she would buy Alphonse a pastis. She could have danced on his zinc bar for all he cared after that. As was Thérèse's habit, she had a way of imbuing joy and fun in nearly everyone she came in contact with. Indeed, this is what she always said joy was, other people, laughing with them, dancing with them, having fun and sharing with them. She hated to spend too much time alone because she said misery is separation from other people, in loneliness the ego strengthened, and that laughing and dancing made the ego disappear.

Alphonse served us our pastis and we all drank them in one go, like shots. Thérèse's idea. And then we left, Thérèse on her horse and Mathias and I walking beside her, alternating the carrying of her double bass.

"So, to return to our conversation before my fall: the divine design."

"What?" I said.

"I was saying our biology is not us."

"Oh..."

"It's part of the divine design. We are Divine beings living a human experience. Do you know what I mean?"

"I think so."

I hiked the double bass further up on my back and looked up at her. She was pointing up at the clouds moving across the afternoon sky.

"Energy comes from up there, we only have to ask for it. It's the most powerful creative force there is. When you ask for that energy with a clear mind it comes down to you, but people don't want to ask for it, they prefer to have some *man* with a big white beard control it all. That's what the church wants us to think. It's in their interest. Who would give them money if people like our mothers didn't go to Mass every Sunday? It's all about intention, personal intention, not the attention we give to some God someone made up for us! As Blake once wrote, *I must create my own system, else be enslav'd by another man's.*"

Mathias smiled at her. "*The Marriage of Heaven and Hell*!"

"Well done!" she said "To the top of the class, Mathias!"

I handed him the infernal double bass.

"How do you manage to get this thing onto your back?" he asked.

"With a great deal of difficulty, but I do! I wear it sideways. We don't live far from the village."

"You're crazy."

"Exactly. I would rather be crazy than sane in this insane world.

So. To continue..." She leaned her body down on the mane of her beautiful horse and massaged his muscular neck as she spoke. "Other people, mostly men, enslave us with their made-up dogmas. They don't want us to grow up and away from religion. Become adults. If we do, then we leave home, the house of God, and build our own houses out here in the fields! In the beginning, you had many gods, the earth Goddess being one of them. Then *The Bible* came along and God in *The Bible* became the biggest god of all, the one who became a world savior to the Jews in Babylon. It is this judgmental god that is the craziest thing of the lot!"

"Why?"

"Because this God has already judged us, Zeke! You don't need to wait until you get to the pearly gates. There's no reason to be frightened of Judgment Day on your last day because he's already judged you on your first day! And why? Because *he* is responsible!"

"How?"

"Because he knows you. He created you. If you do something wrong, then it's his responsibility. It's not yours! You didn't create yourself. He did. If I play you a bad piece of music on my double bass it's me that's responsible, not the music! It's my fault, not the instrument's. Yes, maybe you have done something wrong, but *you* are not wrong! Your being cannot do anything wrong. Your being is always in the right. It is always *becoming*. Don't you see, we are free to be whatever we want to become!"

"Jesus, I thought Ezekiel was *The Bible* madman. It looks like he may have a contender for the title!"

"Have you read *The Bible*, Mathias?" she said.

"No. I have other things to read first."

"Oh, you should. It's wonderful and horrible all in one book. For instance, you know one of the ten commandments in *The Bible* is 'Thou shalt not kill.'"

"Yes."

"Well, in the very next chapter what does it say? Go into Canaan and kill everything in it! I told that to my mother the other day, and she nearly threw me out the window. She was having some *ladies* from Avignon over for tea and superiority."

"You see! And you're encouraging me to read it."

"Yes. It's important to know it so that you can understand that its madness, written by men." She sat up on her horse. "Is there a female gospel? No! Where's Mary Magdalene's gospel? Don't you think Mary, the mother of Jesus, would have something to say too? I don't believe any of it. Yes, there are beautiful myths out there but when society creates them to keep you in line with a *Bible,* then Nature becomes the enemy. And why has Nature become the fallen and the corrupt? That's a murderous idea! There is no fallen Nature. It's still here, all around us. Where has it fallen to? Do you know that in Japan they have never heard of the Garden of Eden or the Fall? The law of Nature lives in Japan!"

"Where do you get all this stuff from?" I said.

"I read. When you're rich you can buy lots of books. I order books. I've been reading Blake since I was a child. I've read a lot of the three big Western religions, Christianity, Judaism and Islam, but the most wonderful of all are the jewels of the East that don't care what religion you are! *In any way that men love me in the same way they find my love: for many are the paths of men, but they all in the end come to me.*" She righted herself in her saddle. "And the rest..."

Mathias' eyes were falling out of his head. "You're as crazy as Ezekiel with your memory! What's that from?"

She smiled at him and said: "It's the 'Song of God' from the *Bhagavad Gita.*"

"You'll have to give that to me," he said.

"Aren't you re-reading Shakespeare?" I said. "And anyway, isn't the *Bhagavad Gita* too old for you?"

He nudged me off the road into the ditch and then pulled me out of it again, laughing.

"What are you two doing?"

"Oh, just being modern," I said.

"What?"

"Sorry, Thérèse. Try to ignore my uncouth friend. I interrupted you. You were saying, And the rest..."

"Oh ... just that the rest is from experience. Power. You have to watch it when your power is lost. That's why I like being around you two. You always make me feel more powerful. You see, you always have to ask yourself: am I losing my power in this situation? Why? Is it because I'm beside this negative person? Am I in a negative situation? That's even more important! It's not even who is sucking my energy from me, but *what* is doing it! It's because of something in me, like a mirror, that the other person is reflecting back on me. Everyone is a lesson. We just have to want to be taught the lesson instead of resisting it by saying the other person is the problem!"

"So how do we learn about this power stuff?"

"You have to practice every day. It's like exercise. If you want the muscle to grow you have to lift the weights every day. If you want your awareness to grow, you have to be aware every day. Then with each day your awareness gets stronger and stronger. Its roots are in divinity, not this!" She grabbed her cheek and squeezed it hard. "The truth is that simple. You have to trust as if what you are, or want to be, is right now. Look at me. I trusted that I would meet lovers because that's what I put out into the universe, and here you are. Instead of one I got two. It just shows you, you have to be specific about what you want!"

And she started laughing out loud, falling forwards onto her horse.

"Well, what am I here for then?" I said. "You know what you're here for, but what about me?"

She stopped her horse and closed her eyes. After a few moments a slight shiver passed through her whole body and she opened her eyes again, except this time there was a great peace in them, a silence.

"Someday you'll write a great book, Zeke. That's your gift."

"A book? A book about what?"

"I don't know, but they say it will help many people."

"Many people do what? Who's 'they'?"

She smiled. "Be at peace to change the world. To create a new world from being more aware."

"What? That makes no sense."

"It will when you sit down to write it."

"Tell me something I can understand now."

"I just did, it's just you won't completely understand it until you write your book."

Her horse started moving again. I looked at Mathias. He was looking up at her, in awe of her.

Years later, after the war, I wrote many books on homeopathy. I even self-published an encyclopedia of homeopathy so everyone could get the information instead of just us few doctors trained in it. Nobody read it. Today I still get kind letters from doctors in the United States and elsewhere, but mostly the States, inviting me to come over and give lectures and speeches at their colleges because they say I was a pioneer in the field.

This is good for my ego, or my *atta* as the Buddha calls it, but not my heart. Yes, it would be nice to talk about Paracelsus and Hippocrates and repeat what they have already said, how the doctor is but a servant of Nature not Her master and that wisdom suggests we follow the will of Nature. However, I still feel that I never wrote the book Thérèse always talked to me about. It is only now, as I muddle through these pages, that I am beginning to understand what she said to me all those years ago. Be at peace to change the world. Create a new world out of being more aware. Yes. Now, that makes perfect sense to me, Thérèse.

THE MUSIC OF THE SPHERES

"Man killing man killing man killing man killing man. Why? Do we have to say yes to so much pain in order to have a life?" said Thérèse.

We were in the barn sitting on bales of hay, our instruments on the floor.

"Why are you talking about killing?"

"My parents were talking about it last night."

"Father was talking about it the other day too," Mathias said. "He says we have to go back to Germany soon, irrespective of our investments here. He says I have to join the cavalry."

"But why? Why does man always have to kill and kill and kill over nothing, over bits of land that nobody can ever really own anyway?" she said.

"Because men are sick in the head," I said.

"My father fought in the Great War," Mathias said. "His brother died in it. He refuses to talk about it, but then he refuses to talk about anything except money and business and how inept the French are at everything they do. I don't understand him at all. Yes, the Germans never forgave the French for defeating them in World War 1, but does that mean they have to sympathize with an obvious madman like Hitler? What do you think makes my father just switch off like that from life? What do you think makes my brother Peter switch off too? He's had exactly the same upbringing as me, yet he seems to hate anyone or anything different."

"Fear," said Thérèse. "It's simple. They're exactly like my Papa, they're terrified of change. We might both be rich but we don't have what you have, Zeke, a father who talks to you like an individual, like a human being, one who doesn't cower to money and prejudice. Ours are surrounded by death but they fill their lives with money and prejudice to pretend it doesn't exist. Your father has accepted that death is all around us. He's not as frightened. It's impossible not to see it. The difference between our fathers is that ours are terrified of death and yours accepts it. That's why he hardly has any ego, because there's no point to the ego when someone accepts fear. It doesn't mean it won't always be there, but with acceptance it disappears more and more."

Every time she spoke she made me want to make love to her. It was like a wave, no, a tide that just kept coming in, hitting off the shore of my consciousness.

"So you're saying we invent our fears?" Mathias said.

"No. We invent about ninety percent of them. It's the other ten percent that we need to accept, death being one of that ten percent."

We all went silent. In the background our randy cock was singing the one note he knew.

"COCORICOCOCOOOOOOO!"

Thérèse got up and looked out the barn door. Turning around she locked it from the inside.

"Let's play some music together, naked."

"What?" I said.

"You heard me. Let's play something, anything, anything that comes to mind completely naked and when we've finished ... Let's make love and when we're finished that we can play music again!"

Mathias looked at me as if someone had stolen his head. We both waited for the other one to respond.

"Well?" But Thérèse didn't wait for a response. Instead she

started to take off her shoes. She threw the first one at me and the second one at Mathias.

"What, are you two going to let a lady get undressed on her own? Now that would be indecent, like going to some *maison close* to pay for sex!"

I looked at Mathias. Had he told her? His face said no. So how did she know?

She smiled at us and took off her long silk stockings, again throwing one at me and the other at Mathias.

I fumbled my right shoe off, then my left. I glanced over at Mathias again. He was as still as a Buddhist monk.

"Mathias," I said. "Are you okay? You look like you're going to faint."

He looked at me and then at my shoes and then stood up, grabbed his left shoe off and threw it at me, laughing.

Thérèse already had her Rosie the Riveter overalls off before our socks were on the floor. Before we had our tops off she was already behind her double bass plucking at the strings without her bow. I was naked before Mathias and I took up my alto and tried to tune it but my fingers wouldn't do what I wanted them to.

Mathias tripped over the leg of his trousers and fell on his face on Thérèse's overalls.

"Hey, don't dirty that! Not that I care, but Mother just got that from Paris and she'll kill me if I bring it home dirty."

Mathias looked up at her, his legs tangled in his trousers and burst out laughing. I laughed too and the stress release helped me get control of my fingers and forget the pounding of my heart.

Eventually Mathias found his harmonica and started to clean it.

Thérèse started to move her bow and play. But just as Mathias started to play his harmonica there was a knock on the door. Thérèse opened her eyes and stopped playing. Mathias' harmonica went flying.

"Hello? Ezekiel? Why's this door locked?"

I looked at Thérèse. She raised her arms in a "Don't look at me! I don't know" way.

"The dogs. We ... they kept coming in and bugging us, so I had to lock the door."

"Alright. Your dinner'll be ready in half an hour. If Thérèse and Mathias are there you can invite them too."

"Ok."

She walked away into the evening.

We waited. I had my alto blocking my crotch. Mathias had Thérèse's overalls over his and Thérèse was simply standing beside her double bass smiling.

We all started to laugh.

"Well, shall we try again, then?" Thérèse said. "We only have half an hour!"

Mathias dropped the overalls and picked up his harmonica. Thérèse closed her eyes and started to play something red. I tried to join in, but it didn't work because she kept changing colors so I played counterpoint to everything she'd just played. Thérèse was already lost to the music, now playing some black music and then some blue and some red again until, suddenly, Mathias blending in with his harmonica, everything started to become orange and red and sensual and I closed my eyes and for almost fifteen minutes we played, completely forgetting that we were naked. All there was was the music and it was divine, above the banal pleasantries of rehearsed rubbish, soaring, then coming down and coming back up again, and down and up and down again into a climax of sound that was spherical, a music of spheres, spherical sounds of violet flying around and around, and in and out and into one another until they all sublimated in a silence that stayed with us for over five minutes.

Then, then I felt the touch, her warm, thin hand in mine. I opened my eyes and there were her smiling eyes, alive with enthusiasm and grace, her other hand in Mathias'. We touched each other and touched each other again and again until passion overtook us.

We didn't pick up our instruments again that night and were very late sitting down to eat our meal.

In the days and weeks that followed we made love and talked of love together nearly daily in the barn or in the fields after riding to some abandoned *garrigue*.

When one of us would finish the other would continue. When we were both spent, Thérèse would dance naked and twirl and sing at the top of her voice the most wonderfully whimsical songs of joy that would send us all into hysterical, cathartic fits of laughter as she continued twirling and twirling until she collapsed lightly onto the ground like a sycamore seed swaying from side to side before it lands.

BLACK HOLES AND DOGMEN

Of course Thérèse's gift came at a price. Transforming one's consciousness has risks, risks most people prefer to leave to mystics and artists. Alongside her heightened states of physical and transcendental eroticism, were severe states of what she called her *black holes* – depression, hallucinations, general despair, especially for the rest of the world. She despaired for a world that didn't really want to be happy. She also suffered from what she called *confused emotional states* which she blamed on the fact that she had nobody to teach her how to come down from such great heights of joy.

"In the past there was always the master and the disciple. You were taught how to raise *kundalini* energy in you. You were physically shown and placed in safe environments like the temples to Isis or sacred caves."

I was sitting by her bed with the *Bhagavad Gita* open on my lap, her favorite book. I had been reading it to her to calm her down. The previous week she had tried to commit suicide, and both myself and Mathias had taken turns every day since to visit her and read to her when she didn't feel like talking.

"Now, what do we have? The church and its dogmen."

Thérèse called all priests *dogmen* for several reasons. They teach dogma not the truth, she said. They convert your freedom into imprisonment by making you unaware and asleep, making you obsess over the past which is no longer, and the future which doesn't exist. And lastly, she said, dogmen were like trained dogs, using violence to protect themselves and to force their religion onto frightened people as they did with the Cathars in Occitanie. She liked the way "dogmen" represented dog – the dogs of the Church, but also because the word was *God* spelled backwards and a play on the word dogma. She called St. Peter the first dogman, saying Jesus had to tell him to put down his sword in the garden of Gethsemane. And who became the first pope? she always asked. Peter, the rock, the man who chops off ears with his sword and makes priests celibate with the result that they become sexually aberrant with young children!

She often talked of the Roman Catholic Corporation and how it makes its priests celibate for economic reasons. How would the Church be able to inherit the wealth of its priests if they had children? How would the church be able to continue getting away with not paying their employees, priests, if they had children to feed and care for? Can you imagine the cost, she would ask. Can you imagine the amount of poverty and starvation the Church could eradicate if they sold even a fraction of their worldwide real estate? Do they really need all those empty churches when children are starving? And then she would point out what the Church is actually doing: sending missionaries to the poorest parts of the world to get the poor to build new churches.

"And to think she sent one of her dogmen to come and see me. Did Mathias tell you?"

"Yes."

"It was disgusting. We were having a lovely time. I was starting to come out of my blackness when in she walks with her dogman and his sanctimonious smile. Jesus, it was disgusting. You know, I wouldn't have minded if he was a nice priest. They're just like anything, like horses for instance, you can have good ones and you can have downright devils that'll bolt and leave you in a ditch, blinded by *ronces* and mud."

She started laughing. "Oh, I quite like that. Blinded in a ditch.

You know the quote in *The Bible*? What is it again? You know, Zeke. You're a fiend for remembering everything."

Let them alone: they are blind leaders of the blind.
And if the blind lead the blind, both shall fall into the ditch.

"Yes, that's it! Someone should have pushed that priest into a ditch!" She laughed. "I knew you'd know it. Anyway, she had no right to bring that man into my bedroom. He actually started quoting *The Bible* to me. Can you believe it? It took all of my will not to throw him out. Of course my mother stood behind him like a stuffed chicken, looming, pecking up his every dismal, dead word."

She made a silly clucking sound with her tongue and we both started laughing.

"Do you want me to keep reading?"

"No. I just had an inspiration."

An *inspiration* to Thérèse was her code for her voices, her angels, her guides, talking to her. "Did you ever think about words, Zeke?"

"What do you mean?"

"Look, I know they are not a bridge, if anything they are a damn impediment to communicating, a kind of barrier or lexical prison. Yes. Did, you ever think about them?"

"What about them?"

"Well, they have a dictionary meaning but they mean more than that. They're all sitting right in front of us waiting to wake us up if we only take the time to look at them for what they really are."

"How do you mean?"

"Take *intuition*, the little voice in my head, as clear as yours." She smiled. "But what is intuition? In-tuition, a *teaching* from inside us, or in-sight, what we *see* from inside. You never hear someone use outsight or outuition do you? No, because they're useless to us! And what about inspiration, the opposite of expiration, from *in spirito*, when *spirit* is *inside* us? Or enthusiasm, from the Greek, when *God* is *in* us! It's never *exthusiasm*? These are..."

I sat, wondering would I ever meet another person like this again.

She sat up in her bed. "Yes! These ones are the ... the most important ones, and when people use them, I know they're speaking from their hearts. If you were to say to me that a poem inspires you or something makes you enthusiastic to write poetry I know in my head that you have spirit inside you, you have God inside you, and that reading or writing is something you need to do. Or if you said to me you had an intuition about something then I'd know to listen because it's a lesson that's coming from inside you!"

"That's beautiful, Thérèse."

"Words are powerful, Zeke. Not as powerful as images, but still very powerful. We don't even know what we are saying half the time. Like *transformation* for example. It's trans and formation."

"Yes, but *trans* isn't a word."

"Yes, it is. Trans means to move, and forms are things that we see, the shapes all around us. So if you want to trans-form, you have to move beyond forms, shapes, this illusion of reality, the forms all the philosophers and mystics talk about. But the mind doesn't want to trans-form. It's too happy where it is, in control, like my father, always in control of everything, my mother, the house, everything. He has chosen not to trans-form. I have chosen the opposite. And that's why I'm in this bed, because how are you supposed to be sane, trans-form, in an insane world, where doing anything different than the way you've been conditioned to is seen as narcissistic or crazy?"

"Yes, but if you're trying to trans-form, what are you trying to trans-form from?"

"This rubbish reality. This dimension of reality, this banal three-dimensional reality." She picked up the blanket and her pillow. "This, this is all three dimensional. You think this is all there is? Things? Forms?"

"No. But if this three dimensional reality isn't reality, then what is?"

"Magic, that's what. Alchemy. Pure sound when we play certain pieces of music. You know. You can hear it in certain pieces. All the great composers knew those special notes and movements."

"I know that time is said to be a fourth dimension of reality."

"But linear time is an illusion, Zeke. Time isn't horizontal, it's parallel. How could it be any other way?"

"You lost me. What are you talking about?"

"Time is what you could call the fourth dimensional reality, but that's made up too. What's actually real is when you get to the next dimension of reality, the fifth. That's when things happen outside this," she lifted the pillow again, "three dimensional reality, and this," she showed me the watch on her wrist, "fourth dimensional reality." She put down her pillow and took off her watch. "When you get rid of the pillow, the object, and the watch, Time, you are left with the fifth dimension. It is outside time and space, outside birth and death and the body. And by going there, like your Essenes did, like the Egyptians did, like the Celts did, like the Mayans did, like shamans and healers and saints and visionaries today do, well then, you can change this third dimensional reality."

The *Bhagavad Gita* slipped out of my hand onto the floor and I just stared at her, speechless.

"Are you alright, Zeke?"

I came out of my mental stupor. "Yes, I just..."

Her eyes opened wider than I'd ever seen them before in an almost violent enthusiasm. "I know, it exploded my mind too when I finally grasped it!"

Her ecstasy spent, she leaned her back against her headboard and took an immense breath in and then let out a long sigh. She smiled at me. "Oh, Zeke, thank you so much for listening to me. If you only knew how important it is that you listen to me!"

"Isn't that what friends do?"

"No. You're more than a friend. You're a soul friend." She took my hands in hers. "I thought I would never be able to tell anyone of what I've just told you. You've both been coming here for days and not once have you asked me why I tried to kill myself. Not once. And I know you've done it out of your love for me and that is why up until now I was unable to even talk about all this dimensional reality stuff because I didn't want to lose your love. I didn't want you to think I was crazy."

"I respect you too much to ever think you are crazy. You just intuitively know things that other people don't. People need to see that as a gift, not an illness."

"Oh, that's so lovely of you to say, Zeke!"

"It's the truth. It's easy to speak the truth."

"Not for everyone it's not," she said. "Look where it got me. I tried to tell my mother about my visions and she got the doctor to the house to see what was wrong with me. They'd have me in an insane asylum if they had their way."

"No they wouldn't."

"They would, and you know it. That's why you're the only one I've told all this to. What do you think the priest would have done? He would have said I had the devil or some such rubbish in me. The doctor said I was completely normal. But I know he and my mother think I'm losing my mind. But none of that matters. What matters is that you understand me."

She took a deep breath and leaned forward to take my hands again in hers. "That's why I tried to take my own life. It just became too much, the joy, the blissfulness. I entered into that dimension for an hour and it seemed like a lifetime. When I came back to reality I was standing on the balcony ready to jump and I didn't care because I knew that all this is an illusion, so I just dropped into the rose bushes below my window thinking I would just float down like a feather, onto and into the red and orange petals below me. When they found me I was unconscious in my nightgown with the bedroom window open onto my balcony, the curtains blowing in the wind. What was I supposed to tell them? That I fell because I'd just been in another dimension, another reality, that I wanted to dive into those rose petals?"

"I think that's what Dad calls *samadhi*."

"Oh, what a wonderful man! How lucky I am to have you and him in my life. Of course it's no coincidence is it? There's no such thing as coincidence in life ... well, now that you know my whole story, do you think I'm mad?"

"Why would I think that?"

"You know why."

"Well, yes, I do think you're crazy, and that's why I trust you.

Look at Yusuf the way he dances spontaneously under the trees singing Sufi poetry? Do I think he's crazy? I think he's beautiful. Look at Mathias reading his damn Shakespeare to me from the apple trees in the loudest voice you've ever heard. Do you think I think that's crazy? No. Just as with Yusuf, I think it's beautiful. Do I think Dad is crazy when he starts chanting the *Tree of Life* to me when I'm seven and fourteen and any time there's a major event in our lives? No. Why? Why do I love all these things? Why do I trust these people even though they are playful and irrational? Why? *Because* they are crazy. *Because* they sing a song that your father and my mother and the fruit buyer from Avignon and the politicians and priests that cause pogroms and suffering will never sing because they choose not to lose their minds, because they choose not to love life and dance and sing to all that is crazy and beautiful!"

She jumped out of her bed and wrapped me in her arms.

"Oh, Zeke, how I love love love you!"

GERMAN STALLIONS

Our sexual escapades were not long in falling foul of jealousy and competition. Fear and intimidation have their way of working their way into everything fun and free.

Where I made love in slow rhythmic movements, Mathias thrust into Thérèse as if he was trying to go through her. In the beginning it was fun to watch as I lay fatigued from my own climax, but as I saw that Thérèse was enjoying it, my mind started to compel me to think that his way was better than mine. At first, it was nothing. A passing idea at the back of my head. When he had finished, I would be ready to go again and Thérèse would welcome me again with the same smile and open arms with which she had received Mathias. But as the days and weeks passed, sexual inadequacy became a refrain inside my mind. Then one day I went into Thérèse the way Mathias did, forcefully, and of course, she reacted.

"Hey, Zeke, what's gotten into you?"

"Nothing. What do you mean?"

"Well, you know, I'm just not used to you being so, well, forceful."

"Why, are you saying you don't like it when I'm forceful?"

"No, I was just surprised."

Mathias, spent on the hay, opened his eyes and said, “Hey, relax, Zeke. We can’t all be German stallions you know!” and he and Thérèse laughed.

I turned, looked at him with what he would later call daggers in my eyes and started to put on my trousers.

“Zeke, what are you doing? We were only getting started.”

“I’m finished. You two can ... I have to go.”

“Zeke, it was only a joke. Mathias didn’t mean anything by it. Please! Don’t go. We’re having so much fun.”

Mathias jumped up. “I’m sorry, Zeke. I didn’t mean any harm.”

I knew immediately that he hadn’t, but that made my sense of shame even more unbearable. “Look, I’m sorry too. But I have to go. I just need some time to myself. I’m sorry.”

I left the two of them standing there, naked in the loft. For years afterwards I couldn't forgive myself for my stupid pride.

PART FIVE
GREEN

SATURDAY, JANUARY 7TH, 2017

CARCASSONNE HOSPITAL, FRANCE

THE MYSTERIUM

It was the first night of a full moon in August. The sky was so clear it felt like you could reach up and take down the stars one by one in your hands.

Thérèse rode up our laneway with her double bass slung around her back, singing and swaying to the movement of her horse's haunches.

"*Au clair de la lune...*"

I ran down to meet her and gave her *bisous* when she dismounted. As we walked towards the barn I tried to ask her but I stopped myself, questioning myself again whether I should or shouldn't for about the thousandth time. When she closed the old door behind us, I got down on my knees in front of her and she looked down at me.

"What are you doing, Zeke? Come on, I want to show you something I made up today. It's like a twist of Bach and..."

"Thérèse, please stop and listen."

"What, what's wrong, Zeke? You look so sad."

She knelt down in front of me.

"There's nothing wrong, in fact everything could be all right.

Everything could be..." I looked into her light green eyes and smiled. "Thérèse, will you marry me?"

The smile left her face like the speed of some falling star. "Oh, Zeke."

"What?"

"I can't."

"Why not?"

"I've already..."

She didn't have to say another word. Mathias. She and Mathias.

I fell back on my heels, my shoulders slumping.

"I was going to tell you, Zeke. Mathias only asked me two days ago and..."

"Please, you don't have to say anything else. I just need to get my bearings a bit. I know this is a good thing. It just has to settle in my mind, or something. I..."

She grabbed my face gently with both her soft, thin hands. "Make love to me, Zeke."

"What, are you crazy?"

"Yes! Isn't that why you asked to marry me?"

"No. I asked because I..."

"And I love you too. But what does love matter! I'm getting married for the experience. I want to experience everything life has to offer. Do you understand? What's marriage got to do with love? Come. Let's make love right now while the moon is full. It'll be wonderful. It'll be beautiful."

She took off her top and put my hands on her breasts. "See, doesn't this feel wonderful?"

"He's my ... our friend!"

"Yes, I know. Stop talking, Zeke. Make love to me."

She kissed me and I kissed her back. We made love until I couldn't keep it in me any longer. I went to pull out of her but she stopped me.

"No, please. Don't stop."

"But..."

"Don't stop. Don't talk anymore, Zeke. Just be love, not the beloved. Just be love."

I moved in her and she moved in me. An energy flowed between us that I cannot explain, an orchestra played inside us, an inner phenomenon, a celebration, as if we were twin souls created for each other. It wasn't just orgasm because we were pulsating, totally participating in existence together. There are some things that are not explainable. Like those words in the *Song of Songs* that they can't translate, the *hapax legomena*, magical, alchemical words that change you inside because their meaning doesn't have to mean anything, because it's the experience of saying them aloud that matters, the experience being the *mysterium*, the mysterious sameness the Tao talks of:

Those who know do not say;
Those who say do not know.
Close the senses,
Shut the doors;
Blunt the sharpness,
Resolve the implications;
Harmonize the light,
Assimilate to the world.
This is called mysterious sameness.
It cannot be made familiar,
Yet cannot be estranged;
It cannot be profited,
Yet it cannot be harmed;
It cannot be valued,
Yet it cannot be demeaned.
Therefore it is precious for the world.

I opened the wooden *volets* of the window at the top of the barn through which we pulleyed the hay in through in the summer and we dangled our naked legs out the window into the darkness, our heads looking up to the stars, her right hand in my left hand. Instead of facing each other in loneliness we faced the moon, both of us alone and together, completely present, absorbed by the moon, our common awareness drawing us even closer into what I can only call a higher harmonic happening, happiness happening again and again and again in each common moment together with the moon.

THE FÊTE

In 1939 the talk of war was a threatening black cloud on the horizon of every conversation. It wouldn't be long before young men like myself, and middle-aged ones like Dad, were conscripted to fight in the Battle of France. As was Dad's way, even with the negativity of oncoming war all around us, he wanted to continue tradition. So, at the end of the harvest we had our annual mini *fête*, as always, with *vin nouveau*, barbecued vegetables and one of our pigs turning on a spit we had dug out from the ground not too far from the kitchen door.

Alphonse from the café was sitting up on our long hay trailer in front of the makeshift dance floor playing Chopin's *Nocturnes in B flat minor* on his prized piano forte which Moses had just finished pulling from Aramon. All around him were chairs and lanterns the Mayor had lent us from the municipality, and surrounding the dance floor were wild flowers and bouquets of fruits that Thérèse, Mathias and I had arranged that morning. My alto and Thérèse's double bass were on the trailer under the piano, away from the young village girls who were laughing and pretending to dance, while the boys rooted about, digging holes in the dance floor looking for ants.

How wonderful an experience that drive with the piano was,

watching the fields and animals go by as Alphonse played the first third of *The Well-Tempered Clavier*. Myself and Dad talked up front as Alphonse played. As with everything, I remember every detail of that, our last real conversation.

"Before you go I want to tell you a story, Zeke. Here, take this first."

He handed me an old piece of paper. "What is it?"

"Something my brother gave me before I left Cork."

"Which one?"

"Gabriel."

Gabriel was the youngest son in my Dad's family, the baby, the seventh son of my grandfather, also a seventh son. Dad always talked about Gabriel as the gifted one. He would tell me stories of how he could do anything with his hands, carpentry, drawing. He could fix anything. And though he never said it, I knew there was something else to Gabriel, something even more different, something he never mentioned.

"You know, when I left Ireland after the Civil War I thought I'd never have to endure that kind of pain again, Zeke. There is a horror you are going into now that you need to brace yourself for, because if you survive you're going to need a lot more than bullets to get through so-called normal life again."

I read the handwritten paper. "A psalm? You've always told me *The Bible* is bad journalism, Dad. Why would you..."

"Just because it's a work of fiction doesn't mean it doesn't hold some very deep truths, Zeke. There are passages in *The Bible* like the *Song of Songs* or what you have there, *Psalm 23*, that far surpass any of your Hegel or Sartre. There's a spiritual poetry to those passages, an alchemical nature to them."

"Jesus, I never knew you were into *The Bible*."

"How could I not be? Isn't it a great read, except for all that business about women being unclean and God being the boss and ... There, you see, you always get me going."

He laughed and then his face changed as he looked at the paper in my hand. "During World War 1 there was an infantry troop that went through the war without a single soldier getting wounded.

Seems this particular platoon sat down every morning and read Psalm 23 aloud together before they went back out to fight."

"What, so you're saying if I say this every morning I'll be protected?"

"I'm not saying anything, Zeke. I'm just telling you the story the mayor told me."

I moved some dirt around on the wooden floor with the butt of my boot, holding the psalm in my hand. Dad shifted the reins in his hands to roll a cigarette.

"Thanks, Dad."

"Ah, sure, I was tired of carrying it around. It was about time someone else had it."

"Won't you be needing it though?"

"I have it in here." He tapped his right hand off his head. "And in here." He let his hand fall to his heart and smiled. He took two pulls from his roll-up and exhaled. "There's something I've been meaning to ask you, Zeke."

"What, whether I want to emigrate back to Ireland with you?"

He laughed and nudged me on the shoulder. "You know, conscription hasn't happened yet and you've never been a violent macho kind of man, so I was just wondering whether there was another reason besides getting rid of that psycho Hitler that made you so eager to join up."

"You mean Thérèse, don't you?"

"Yes, I do."

"In the beginning, yes, I was angry with her for choosing him over me, but in the end what are you going to do, kill yourself?"

Dad laughed and coughed up smoke as he put his roll-up out in the palm of his hand. His face became serious. "I'm worried that's exactly what you're doing by signing up."

I said nothing.

"When you say him, I'm presuming you mean Mathias?"

"Yes."

"It's just you remind me a bit of me, that's all."

"How?"

"Well, before your mother, there was..." He moved about in his seat. We were entering our driveway, moving past the olive tree we had planted together when I was seven, in celebration of my *Tree of Life* initiation.

"Do you remember planting that tree?"

"Of course! I can still remember you laughing when I jumped into its hole as you were trying to lower its old roots into the ground."

He laughed again.

"Dad, there was what before?"

"Ah, you let me away with nothing!"

"No."

"Well, you know the story of *Her Mantle so Green*?"

"Yes."

"Well, you could say I had a friend very much like William O'Reilly, but he died in the Civil War."

"So you had a Nancy in Ireland?"

"Here, let's sing it the way we always do when we're bringing fruit in. We'll be at the house any minute now." He closed his eyes and sat up straight and we sang his favorite song:

As I went out walking one morning in June,
To view the fair fields and the valleys in bloom,
I spied a pretty fair maid she appeared like a queen
With her costly fine robes and her mantle so green.

Says I, "My pretty fair maid, won't you come with me
We'll both join in wedlock, and married we'll be,
I'll dress you in fine linen, you'll appear like a queen,
With your costly fine robes and your mantle so green."

Says she now, "My Young man, you must be excused,
For I'll wed with no man, so you must be refused;
To the green woods I will wander and shun all men's view,
For the boy that I love dearly lies in famed Waterloo."

"Well if you are not married, say your lover's name,

I fought in the battle so I might know the same."
"Draw near to my garment and there you will see,
His name is embroidered on my mantle so green."

In the ribbon of her mantle there I did behold
His name and his surname in letters of gold;
Young William O'Reilly appeared in my view
He was my chief comrade back in famed Waterloo.

And as he lay dying I heard his last cry
'If you were here, Lovely Nancy, I'd be willing to die;'
And as I told her this story, in anguish she flew.
And the more that I told her the paler she grew.

So I smiled on my Nancy, twas I broke your heart,
In your father's garden that day we did part.
And this is a truth and the truth I declare,
Well here's your love token, the gold ring I wear."

There were tears on Dad's face. I knew he was crying for his Nancy but even more so for us. He knew that day would probably be the last one we would spend together under the Provence sun beneath our trees.

We had arrived at the house and he jumped down, wiping his face with the back of his hands.

"Did I ever tell you that my mother used to sing that to me as a child?"

"No."

He started to make another roll-up to hide his tears.

"What was her name Dad?"

"You know my mother's name was Mary!"

"No. Your Nancy."

He raised his head and smiled. "Róisín. Róisín was her name. It means little rose. There's a great old Irish song of the same name called *Róisín Dubh.* One of the verses has always stayed with me,

Shiubhalfainn féin an drúcht leat is fásaigh ghuirt,
Mar shúil go bhfaighinn rún uait nó páirt dem thoil.
A chraoibhín chumhra, gheallais domhsa go raibh grá agat dom –
'S gurab í fíor-scoth na Mumhan í, mo Róisín Dubh.

"What does it mean, Dad?"

"It means different things to different people. To some it represents Ireland, but to me it talks of love. This would be a rough translation:

I would walk in the dew and meadowy wastes with you,
In hope of receiving love from you, or part of my desire,
Fragrant branch, you promised me you had love for me –
The flower of all Munster, my Little Dark Rose!

"Was she beautiful?"

"As fair as a summer's day."

"And what happened to her?"

"She married a rich man, a lawyer. He was a nice fella all the same."

He finished his roll-up and placed it in his mouth.

"What, so she married him because she didn't love him?"

"Yes, I think so. It's very easy to love all this, the whole world, everyone in it. The problems come when it's one human being you want to love. Humanity and God are easy to love, one person is a different story altogether. She felt marrying someone else for love would dirty the love she'd had for Patrick."

"Patrick?"

"Patrick O'Malley. We grew up together. He was mad. Kind of like your friend Mathias. Full of piss and vinegar, but with a very gentle touch when needed, like the way Mathias handled that pup the first time we met him. He was amazing at everything he did. Football, school, everything."

He lit his roll-up and looked through me. "The Black and Tans. They took him out in the dead of night. We found him in a ditch a week later."

"I'm sorry, Dad."

"Don't be sorry, Zeke, just be careful! They were bad times and I only mention them now because these are bad times too." His face turned into a smile as he looked behind me. "And would you look at what's coming up the lane!"

"Mathias!" I shouted.

A few moments later his horse stopped in front of me and he jumped down.

"Couldn't Alphonse play something a little more fun than Chopin? Isn't this supposed to be a party?"

"Are you ever content?" I said.

"Yes, but only when I'm around you, Horatio!"

"Here, let me help you put your nag in the stable."

"Nag? Has your vision failed you as well as your mental capacity, sir?"

"Moses could..."

"Oh stop. Where's Thérèse?"

"She's out back with your parents and the other cathoholics and collaborators. She's probably bored out of her mind by now with their talk of business ventures and the necessity to welcome fascism into France, while us peasants prepare the vitals in our uncouth, outdoor, provincial manner!"

Dad walked over to the spit to give Yusuf a break from turning the pig, shaking his head and smiling. I took Mathias' horse by the reins as he opened the barn doors, hardly able to contain himself for all the dancing he was planning on doing that night. As with all things, Mathias was a great dancer.

THE HEART OF THE TREE

Yusuf knelt down on the ground beside the front door of his house at the end of our lane. He planted two seeds from the apple he'd just eaten, one either side of his door, then got up to close the door of his house for the last time.

Dad had helped him build his house when I was child, just as Yusuf had helped Dad rebuild our run-down *mas* and later, our barn. He'd also helped build our farm into one of the most successful in the region through his intelligence and hard work. Where once there was nothing but weeds and briars, now you looked out on vineyards, fields of melons, asparagus, beans, salads, eggplant, zucchini, pumpkins, squash and our version of the sweet Cevennes onion, the *Vers-Pont-du-Gard.* Beyond the vegetables were our orchards of cherry, fig, peach, apricot, pear, olive, and apple trees with local *Côtes du Rhône* vineyards surrounding them.

Dad gave Yusuf the value of his house before he left. They both knew he would never have sold it before the war came, and it wasn't as if Dad wasn't well off by then. Yusuf didn't really need the money. As we guessed, he'd saved a small fortune because he never spent any of his pay in over two decades with us. To Dad, it was another way of showing Yusuf how much he loved him without telling him.

Yusuf was finally going to Mecca and back to the desert before the war came. A week before, in the apple orchard picking apples, he had told Dad that he was leaving, that he would rather leave now than live through another war. When Dad asked why he was embarrassed, he said he felt like he was abandoning us. Dad told him his life was his own to live and that only an idiot would think that over twenty years of hard work was abandonment. It's abundance, Dad said. I'm just surprised you didn't leave us earlier, he said. Most men would have run for the hills if they'd had to work the way you have, he said.

"Why'd you do that, Yusuf?" Dad asked.

"In the desert, every time we leave the oasis on a journey we plant something, because we never know if we'll be back."

"That's beautiful," I said.

"Here, follow me," Dad said. "We have a tradition like that too."

Yusuf put down his bags beside the fresh earth and we followed Dad through the orchards to the ancient olive tree by the stream. When we got there Dad took out his old knife, an *opinel* Yvette had given him years before. He started to carve away the bark from the center of the tree.

"Dad, what are you doing? If you take away the bark, you'll kill it!"

"It'll be fine, Zeke. Wait."

We waited, but I couldn't understand why he, of all people, would cut into such a tree.

He turned to face us. "When someone in our family leaves," he smiled at Yusuf standing tall beside us, "we always leave a remembrance of them somewhere sacred." He touched the tree. "This bark will heal, just like we will, and by the time it has Yusuf will have found a new home in the desert."

Yusuf smiled and Dad handed me his *opinel.* "It's for you to finish." I looked at Yusuf and carved the rest of the heart out. When I finished Yusuf opened his arms and I went into them for the last time. It was the first and only time I ever saw that great man cry.

THE THIRD FORCE

On the train to the Maginot Line in 1940 we stopped in a village outside Nancy. I was at the back of the train and I could see down into the valley because my carriage wasn't inside the station proper as yet. Most of the other soldiers were asleep except for a man with a ginger mustache and an indolent air, about my Dad's age, his sad eyes reading.

There was a wedding going on down in the valley. The bride and groom were in the middle of a huge open space with people all around them, watching the couple have their first dance. The bride had on a long white dress, with lilies of the valley in her hands and hair, the same ones Thérèse wore at her wedding. As the train moved out of the station and the countryside started to speed up outside my window, I thought of that day a few weeks before Mathias and Thérèse left for Germany.

Thérèse wanted to have nothing to do with tradition. So, they were secretly but legally married by the Mayor of Saintes Maries de la Mer in the town hall, myself acting as best man and Alphonse from the café being the other witness. My hands trembling, I handed Mathias, then Thérèse, their rings engraved inside the band with the words *Amor Vincit Omnia*.

The wedding ceremony itself, which couldn't be stopped now by either family since they were already legally married, took place on the beach of Saintes Maries de la Mer, immediately in front of the stretch of water where the horses and gypsies bring Saint Sara every year. The "congregation" looked out to the Mediterranean, much to the disgust of all our mothers.

I can still remember Mathias pretending to be profound when we went to clean the beach of driftwood and seaweed to prepare the aisle and altar of rocks. He was bending down to pick up more driftwood when he fell under the weight he already had. Laughing, he shouted:

"Oh, you skeletons of trees scattered in this sand like the remnants of ancient animals abandoned before the time of man and his madness! Oh, poor trees, decapitated and desolate, let us be fast friends on this most joyous of days!"

"Mathias, come on. We'll never get this aisle and altar built if you keep finding damn Yoricks all over the beach!" I said. "Here, help me with this rock. It could be part of the altar."

"Capital idea, old fellow!" he said.

"Hope your mother doesn't forget the flowers."

"Oh, if she does, it doesn't matter! Not flowers, not storms, not the folly of family could ruin this day!" he said.

I gave Thérèse a *coing* from the *mas* as a ritual wedding gift, as Paris did for Aphrodite centuries before, and then played the alto to start the ceremony, while a yacht passed by out at sea. Some birds sang in the *roseaux* above the beach as I played one of Thérèse's favorite pieces, the third movement from Berlioz's *Harold in Italy*, "Serenade." They had asked me to read something after I'd played, but I didn't have to read a thing. I knew every word by heart, the passages being some of the things we'd often quoted to each other over our few years together in France.

Some pink flamingoes took flight over our heads as I started *The Song of Songs*:

Come, my beloved, let us go forth into the field;
Let us lodge in the villages.

Let us get up early in the vineyards;
Let us see if the vine flourish,
Whether the tender grape appear.
And the pomegranates bud forth:
There will I give thee my loves.
The mandrakes give a smell,
And at our gates are all manner of pleasant fruits,
New and old,
Which I have laid up for thee, my beloved!

I raised thee under the apple tree:
There my Mother brought thee forth:
There She brought thee forth that bare thee.
Set me as a seal upon thine arm:
For love is strong as death;
Jealousy is cruel as the grave:
The coals thereof are coals of fire,
Which hath a most vehement flame.
Many waters cannot quench love,
Neither can the floods drown it:
If a man would give
All the substance of his house for love,
It would utterly be contemned.

When I'd finished I realized I'd been crying. I wiped away the tears and looked out to sea past Mathias and Thérèse. There were two cranes playing on the wind like some kind of natural epiphany. I looked at Mathias and then at Thérèse and quoted St. John of the Cross from his *Spiritual Canticle*, as remembered from *The Story of a Soul*, where I'd first read it.

Love is repaid by Love alone.

Then I recited what I knew would make Mathias smile:

They're not Hindu or Muslim.

They don't pray in mosque or temple.
Yet they receive the Light of God
And are immersed in beautiful visions.
These madmen are truly insane.
They're lost in God's domain.
I would give my life for these
Who are blessed with Love's disease!

Thérèse was crying, tears falling onto her white dress. I looked at Mathias. He was crying too. We smiled at one another and I remembered sighing very deeply before I stepped over the makeshift aisle of rocks into the sand. As the ceremony continued, I recalled Mathias quoting me the beginning of *Macbeth* from what seemed like years ago:

"When shall we three meet again?
In thunder, lightning, or in rain?
When the hurlyburly's done,
When the battle's lost and won."

I waited, the rest of the ceremony passing by like the tide on the beach, flowing in a movement that all sounded the same to me until they both arrived at the words "I do" and I started to cry.

Now, in my old age, I sometimes think about marriage and although a beautiful thing I don't really know if it works any longer in our society. I don't merely say this because I had an abusive wife. Thérèse used to say the same thing. She said marriage was madness. Of course, Thérèse was so far ahead of us all then. She got married anyway to make sure she wasn't missing out on a beautiful experience, experience always being her litmus test for her every action.

This is not to say marriage can't work. But if the old system continues, where the man continues to try to control the woman, or, as in my case, the woman tries to control the man, then where's the balance? Where do the children come into the equation anymore? Do they all have to suffer like my Rose and Celine did and then, as with Rose and Celine, continue that same suffering into their own marriages? Where have the individuals gone? Where has, as Yvette always used to say, that third force in marriage gone?

We were in Yvette's house, in front of her huge fireplace drinking *tisane*, preparing the *midi* meal, cutting the tomatoes from her garden, still warm from the sun they'd been sitting in outside not ten minutes before. It was a Friday. Every Friday I took off early from my medical practice and spent from midday well into the night with Yvette, learning all she had to teach me. In the past in France there was nearly always a person in every village who would *prendre le feu* when someone was burned. When I was sixteen I got a really bad burn from some *chaux vive* we were using to paint the exterior walls of our house to make it look clean and new, but also to keep infection away.

Usually you're meant to leave the lime to rest for at least twenty-four hours before you start using it. I didn't. I started painting our house with the roiling white solution a few minutes after the lime had been mixed with the water. After fifteen minutes I started to burn and the burning didn't stop even after the doctor in Aramon had given my mother a *pommade* to put on my arms. So Dad brought me to Yvette, who laid her hands over the burns on my arms. She started to sweat as she took the fire, finally washing her hands in running water until the sweating stopped. As soon as she laid her hands on the burn it had stopped hurting and about five minutes later it had started to clot where before it had been continuously weeping.

I had just told Yvette that Julie had asked me for a divorce.

"A marriage is not a union of two people, Zeke. It's three." She drank some of her *tisane*. "Relationships are spiritual opportunities. We forget this truth every day. Even science tells us this: oppositely charged objects attract, cause and effect. We are those objects too. Every action we cause creates an equal and opposite reaction. This is the law of cause and effect, the law of magnetism. Why do we forget it in our relationships?"

She put down her *tisane* and raised her hands. "This is one individual." She made a fist of her right hand. "And this is another individual." She clenched her other hand into a fist. "Each individual must be allowed their individuality. They must be allowed to grow independently of the other." She moved each hand up slowly, bit by bit and stopped. "Then, when this happens, something magical also happens. Another thing begins to grow, a new individual, a spiritual one, a force, one you can't see, but Lord can you feel it! The couple. It's like hydrogen and oxygen when they come together to create water, something that takes away your thirst. But if you take a load of oxygen or a load of hydrogen, your thirstiness will not go away. You feel this third force when you meet a couple that has allowed it to grow. Myself and Henri had it in our way."

Yvette had been married to Henri for decades, until the Milice tortured him to death, in front of her.

"This third force is created inside, in our intention toward that communion with the other individual, that mirror of ourselves. It creates a new thing, the water, love."

She tied both her hands together in a knot of fingers. "This is not individuality. This is patriarchy. This is control. This is clinging to habit, what Julie wanted from her marriage to you. She didn't want you to evolve as an individual. She wanted to maintain the status quo. She wanted you to remain the "normal," accepted, allopathic doctor she married, not the homeopath you've become. She was unable to accept your growth. This sort of resistance squashes the soul, the flow of change, starving reality and bloating unreality. What is needed is more openness, more of the feminine, the lack of a need for control over the other individual. This is another fundamental law of life, like magnetism and cause and effect: even the things we hide keep on growing, but if we let them reveal themselves, if you allow them openness, space, and they are negative, then they will disappear. If they are good and right they will be nourished."

She pointed at the tomatoes on the table. "The tomatoes, they die on the vine when there's no sun. The third individual, the third force, is the same. It will die on the vine, it will never grow unless it has its time in the sun and that sun will never shine unless each individual is allowed to shine, unless each individual is given their time to evolve into the kind of human they are meant to be."

THE BATTLE OF FRANCE

He lay dying beside me in the ditch. The blood had passed through his jacket, staining the hand he couldn't use anymore.

In his other hand was a photograph of a young woman. Her features, the small pointed nose and sly smile, reminded me of Thérèse. He had asked me to fish it out of his chest pocket only moments before. I read the inscription on the back before I gave it to him: "Je t'aime toujours! Veronique."

My wife, he said, in perfect Parisian French. I smiled.

Above us you could still hear the sound of bullets and screams. Beside us, on top of each other, were two other German officers I had shot.

He reached his hand out to mine, the photo now submerged in blood on his chest. I took his hand in mine. I could feel his fear. We looked into each other's eyes. Then, as I was to experience so many times in the future when people died in my care, a peace came over him, as if he were bathed in silence. The fear had gone. All that was left was innocence, the miracle of the human being, a deep thankfulness in his eyes, a gratitude. He smiled and said, "Merci, Ezekiel Moran."

I smiled at him, and then he died.

I closed my eyes and quietly recited Psalm 23, his hand still warm in mine. After a few moments I lifted his hand and rested it on her photograph.

In my other hand was Dad's *opinel*, a gift before I had left the *mas*. Only a minute before I had thought I would have to use it if my last bullet hadn't done its work on Veronique's husband. Her husband's name was Hermann, Hermann Schmidt. He was the last man I killed, in the Battle of France, as a regular soldier.

PART SIX
BLUE

SUNDAY, JANUARY 8TH, 2017

CARCASSONNE HOSPITAL, FRANCE

VICHY

I had signed up in August 1939, nearly two weeks before England and France declared war on Germany, having completed my training in Saint-Cyr just outside Paris. After nine months they promoted me and sent me to the Maginot Line. A month later I was captured and sent to a German POW camp.

I arrived in Oflag II D Gross-Born in Pomerania, Poland, what was then Northern Germany, on the 20th of June 1940, two days before *Pétain et Compagnie* surrendered to the Nazis. They had just changed the camp's status from a Stalag to an Oflag to house French officers and orderlies. By February 1941 there were 3,166 officers and 565 orderlies there. We were packed into wooden huts, frozen in the winter and roasted in the summer, bored out of our minds, eating soup and dried bread while the lice ate us. But this was nothing compared with what was happening at the same time to the people being transported to concentration camps.

When I was younger I used to play rugby, every weekend training or playing a match. Dad and Yusuf would always come to watch me from the sidelines, while Maurice Jalabert's father, Ernest, would accuse every referee we played under of blindness, homosexual persuasions, stupidity or a problem with the vicinity of

Provence they came from. We found this all the more amusing when one considered his son was one of the dirtiest rugby players you could imagine. He played hooker. In the scrum he would bite, head-butt, knee, kick and curse as if he were possessed. The whole village knew Maurice was demented. Maurice was the same child who put diesel on cats' tails and posteriors then lit a match to revel in their flights of terror, the same child who blew up frogs and tortured dogs by hanging them with fishing wire from trees for days.

Another thing Ernest Jalabert was famous for was his phrase "the second half nightmare." His contention was that our national team had the most beautiful and brave players of rugby in the world. He would use the word "poetic" a lot, or, "it's like watching poetry when they pass"! But if they weren't winning, or had a marginal lead when they went into the dressing room after the first half, he would start cursing and kicking inanimate objects. Now he would have to endure "the second half nightmare." This meant watching his team give up in the second half, demoralized for not being as he put it *"le Coq"* when they went into the dressing room.

Pascale sees this second half nightmare as an expression of the psyche of our country, one that is proud and courageous until we get a whiff of defeat. Jung said the psyche of the English will always be to be superior and distant, the stiff upper lip, because for countless centuries they have been the colonizers, and if a colonizer wants to keep their power they can never show empathy while the natives are murdered in front of them. It would be a sign of weakness. My Irish cousin, Jim, in the sixties, had much the same thing to say about what he called Ireland's servile psyche. He said it was the reason the older generation mumble and keep their heads down to avoid eye contact, as the colonized have always done if they don't want to be punished for impertinence.

I mention Maurice Jalabert's father because his feelings strangely became my own and that of over one and a half million other Prisoners of War after our government cowered before the Nazis in 1940, bringing us the second half nightmare of *les Années Noires*, the Dark Years, from 1940 to 1944 of *Pétain et Compagnie.* When Pétain came to power, our country had another propaganda campaign to contend with, a very Catholic one, one that talked of "sacrifice" instead of the sin of "pleasure," and finding "atonement" for these sins by working hard under a reinvention of the old nationalistic, agrarian and obedient French ideal of *Travail, Famille, Patrie* instead of our nation's revolutionary nature: *Liberté, Egalité, Fraternité.*

From September 1940, Pétain's "National Revolution" made the world a desperate place for Jews, Gypsies, communists, socialists and Masons, but the "normal" French people suffered too. Dancing was banned. There were blackouts at night. Meat was very scarce, and tobacco, wine, butter, clothes, petrol, coffee, even salt were rationed. The children in schools were taught to write: "If your bread is grey and your piece of it smaller, it is not the fault of Marshal Pétain." Pétain, the womanizer, the man who had married a divorcee in 1920, and was secretly re-married by the Archbishop of Paris without even attending his own ceremony, had the audacity to adopt the Catholic idea of the family, giving greater civil rights to men who had more than five children, childless men not being able to get a job as easily. And if you were a woman, you got medals for having children, a woman with ten getting a gold.

Because of Pétain's decision to surrender, we had to endure POW camps when we were willing to die to protect our country from fascism. Instead, we were separated into the *German Occupied Zone* and Vichy's useless *Zone Libre*, which we had to pay for, something the Germans never mentioned in the Armistice Agreement. How was Vichy supposed to be able to achieve anything with an army of 100,000 men, especially when Hitler had fifteen times that number of us in POW camps? De Gaulle saw it from the beginning. He went against the national psyche, broadcasting as much in his famous *L'appel du 18 juin* on the BBC. He knew we'd become subjects, not citizens.

Oftentimes it is only after a tragedy that we see the truth. When everything is taken away from you, then you see what is important. The Buddha left his palace behind, Jesus his atelier. I left my home just like many millions to fight in a war to defend our right to have a home. We left everything we loved behind only to find ourselves in

POW camps, but some of us contrived to escape and somehow defeat the Nazis, especially when we witnessed the many ways they broke the Geneva conventions and basic human rights, never mind what we found out about after the war: executions of prisoners like the Australian Sergeant Leonard Siffleet by beheading on the orders of the Vice-Admiral of the Imperial Japanese Navy.

And of course it all continued after the war, each country keeping soldiers as forced labor, many dying from exhaustion or from clearing land mines. And what happened to Thérèse's parents? They moved to Madrid like Mathias' parents, meeting up every Sunday with the other *Maquis blancs* at the French church of St-Louis des Français, moving back to France in the fifties to reclaim vast quantities of land her father had received through "economic Aryanization," much like Paul Touvier in the seventies. Pétain and Hitler's people also went to the Middle East and Australia. And Mathias' parents? Where did they go after Madrid? Who knows. Maybe like Klaus Barbie they went to South America, to Bolivia or Buenos Aires.

When I went back to Poland in the nineties to visit the pretty town of Borne Sulinowo, I discovered nothing of our POW existence there except the steps to the entrance of the Oflag chapel. I found out later that a memorial to the French and Polish officers who died there was erected at the site of the camp, but even today nothing has been done by Russian authorities for the thousands of Red Army soldiers that were buried in mass graves beside what Oflag II D became, Stalag 302. Like the Japanese, the rules of the Third Geneva Convention were ignored for Soviet prisoners. What was even sadder was that their own government saw anyone who retreated or was captured as a traitor to their country.

At Oflag II D we found out that General de Gaulle was continuing a "foolish" war alongside the British. At least that's what the propaganda they handed out to us said. Most of the officers there thought Pétain would be able to resist the Germans, even in defeat. After all, they would always say, Pétain was the Victor of Verdun and England will never last. But then England showed they could withstand the constant bombing, and even though most of the officers felt the war was over, myself and others disagreed. When I fully realized what de Gaulle and the British were doing I became hopeful, then excited, about escaping in order to help.

One man who was not excited about de Gaulle and the British was officer number 1294/9, Louis Darquier, a man who was born and raised not too far from where I am writing this, in Cahors, in the Lot. From my first meeting with the man, I found him insufferable, a buffoon, but one of the most dangerous ones you could encounter. As my mother used to say, you can't argue with an idiot and that's why they're so dangerous. Darquier was one of the most dangerous idiots to come out of the Vichy years, eventually becoming head of the infamous CGQJ, the *Commissariat General aux Questions Juives*. He arrived a few days after me and immediately started peddling his anti-Semitic bile at lectures on the "Jewish question," where he advocated a *total solution*, that is, appropriate everything the Jews owned, what Hermann Goering would later call *Gesamtlosung*, to stop them from taking over the world. Immediately after his "lectures," he would boast about his many extramarital sexual escapades in Paris.

Darquier also delighted in the fact that the internment camps, housing thousands of communists, refugees from Italian and German fascism, political refugees, and foreigners in general ("undesirable aliens"), had become as bad, if not worse than concentration camps. Today as I write this, I am aware of the fact that I live only a little over half an hour from one of these camps, Bram, just outside Carcassonne. If I were to go spend the day on the Mediterranean in, let's say, Saint-Cyprien or Agde or Argelès, it would be hard for even me to imagine the beach teeming with thousands of prisoners surrounded by barbed wire. In Saint-Cyprien alone there were 90,000 refugees, in Argeles 77,000. They were treated, especially in places like Gurs, to use the title of Arthur Koestler's book of that time, like the "scum of the earth".

As the war went on, Vichy cherry-picked Jews from these camps but, more importantly, used the camps as transport hubs for their raids on Jewish households before they sent them to Drancy in cattle trains, thirty to a car, with one bucket as a toilet, and then on to the concentration camps and the Final Solution, or *Endlösung*, in the East. Between the 17th and 31st of August, 1942, 7,000 were sent, half of them children, the youngest being Solomon Brojman. He was nine months old. In the same year 1,000 children under the age of two were sent to Auschwitz from France. None of them ever came back.

Later on in Britain, I would give snippets of things I remembered about Darquier in the camp to add to Jean-Louis Cremieux-Brilhac's attacks on him for the BBC show, *Les Français parlent aux Français*. Myself and Jean-Louis escaped. Darquier was released. The Germans had never let anyone out before. When the other prisoners begged him to send them a compass or civilian hat to escape, he told them to wait, to be patient. He had better things to do, such as getting the French police and the CGQJ to hunt Jews, enabling Hitler to utilize his troops to wage war.

They were trying to transfer me to Oflag II-C in Woldenberg, Germany, now Dobiegniew in western Poland, when I escaped. I was one of the lucky eleven to escape from Oflag II D. The officer in charge in Woldenberg needed musicians to play for his drunken orgies. Myself and Jean Vialette, a wonderful gypsy guitar player from Perpignan, escaped together. I would never have been able to escape without Jean. As the proverb goes, *A brother who is helped by a brother is like a strong city.* Jean was that city. He was a rugby player, but where I was a runner, a winger, Jean was a Colossus of the first row, built like a human flying buttress. But for Jean, I would have been strangled to death by a guard a foot taller than me.

After the war, I was blessed to meet Jean again at a Nina Simone concert in Brittany. It was 1982, in the town of Morlaix. After the show we went back to his hotel for more drinks. When he was drunk, he told me. Told me what the Gestapo had done to him in the Hotel du Portugal, which is still open to this day, in Vichy. He was recaptured just after D-Day. I thought I'd had it bad. First they submitted Jean to the *baignoire*, what some people have recently compared to water-boarding, as witnessed under the Bush administration in the United States. After countless *baignoires* Jean still wouldn't talk. So they nailed Jean's feet to the hotel room floor. They made him stand nailed to that floor for two days, eating and drinking their meals in front of him. The Gestapo captain then told him he was shipping him to Bergen-Belsen, near Hanover, in north-west Germany. Bergen-Belsen started as a POW camp but it ended up serving as a concentration camp, a death camp, from 1943 onwards. You'll be dead before you get there, he told Jean. Because of the confusion of German losses from the invading Allied forces Jean ended up in Oflag VIE due to the fact that he was a Lieutenant. Even today it astounds me that he not only made it to Dorsten Oflag but that he survived it.

Every year after the war, on the twenty-fifth of May until his death in 1992, Jean and I would meet in Saintes Maries de la Mer to celebrate the festival of the Marys. I'll be there again this year. Pascale has driven me every year since I moved to the Black Mountains. I know what Jean would have thought of our previous President, Monsieur Nicolas Sarkozy, evicting a lot of his people, both Jean's parents being Roma people, from France. Every two months or so, Jean's son, Charles, comes up to the mountains from Perpignan to see me. Apart from his rugby fanaticism, Charles, like his father before him, is an amazing guitarist and is very much involved in keeping gypsy music alive. He plays every year at the end of August in the *Guitares au Palais Festival* in Perpignan, as well as other festivals all over Europe. His regional cultural leanings extend further when he puts on a pointed *caparutxa* for the Procession of the Sanch every Easter, chanting the *misere des pendus* to celebrate the passion and agony of Christ, but also the lives of those who were condemned to death and torture.

Myself and Jean escaped into Lithuania. At the time, it was occupied by the Soviets. When we arrived we were arrested by Red guards. They accused us of illegally crossing the border. This meant they could put us away for four years in a Soviet POW camp. We served eight months. I didn't get out of the gulag until the 30th of August, 1941 when I was transferred to a Canadian cargo ship in the White Sea, way to the North, with 185 others.

In September 1941, I finally arrived in London and joined our band of Free French *résistants.* While there, I tried to find out about

Thérèse, Dad and Mathias. They knew nothing about Dad. I tried to find out as much as I could about where Mathias and Thérèse were in Heidelberg but, because of its strategic location on the Neckar, British intelligence information was limited. It wasn't until after the 63rd Infantry Division captured the city in April of 1945 that I could even think about trying to find them. And anyway, talking about German friends was not the kind of conversation my comrades cared for. Instead, they wanted to talk about who had been in my Oflag, especially Louis Darquier "de Pellepoix" and other collaborators.

Information British Intelligence could give us was what *Pétain et Compagnie* were doing, or more, not doing. Pétain's policy of collaboration with the Germans, as distinct from Darquier and the collaborationists or *collabos* of Paris, disgusted me the more I learned. The Wannsee plan, arrived at on the 20th of January 1942, when I was doing specialist training with the *Action militaire* section of the *Bureau Central de Renseignements et d'Action*, brought my disgust to a whole new level. There, beside Lake Wannsee, Reinheard Heydrich, his deputy Adolf Eichmann, and fifteen Nazi civil servants conferred about how to put into effect the murder of eleven million Jews.

While they plotted, I was probably parachuting, night training on the southeast coast of Britain, or doing reconnaissance raids somewhere on French beaches from the Loire-Atlantique to Normandy. They never used the word "murder". Jews were to be eliminated, exported to the East, resettled, migrated, evacuated. This "work" was never referred to as murder. Had it been, the administrators and civil servants of the occupied countries would never have cooperated the way the Nazis needed them to, the way Karl-Albrecht Oberg's Gestapo operated in France, with efficiency, as Vichy did under Rene Bousquet, Louis Darquier and the French Gestapo – the *Milice* – by sending thousands of Jews to Auschwitz in Poland.

Dad had often talked to me of how the Maurice Jalaberts of the world could easily turn into the same kind of enemy the English had become to the Irish, when they killed them for speaking their own language. It wouldn't be the first time cultural cleansing of Jews would occur. Dad never forgot what had happened to his family in Limerick when a single Redemptorist priest recited clichés of hate from a church podium. Before the war he used to read me Joseph Roth's essays citing criticism of Jewish immigration into France as the "threat from the East." The irony was that the real threat from the East were the Nazis of whom the French Right of the time actually approved. The same kind of intellectual still exists in 2017. One only has to read the newspapers, which I no longer do. Pascale tells me what these "intellectuals" are up to, criticizing the working classes and sneering at foreigners when all one has to do is look at the names around us to see that we are a nation of foreigners who started off with working class roots. Is *Sarkozy* a French name? Is *Bruni* a French name? Hypocrisy knows no reason, only its own blind opinion.

THE BATH

I finished training my last British intelligence officers on May 28th, a little over a week before the Allied invasion of 1944. My own English training had taken six months, before I joined the RF Section of SOE. For the next year and a half, my main work was to liaise with our four hundred agents in France. After shaking hands with de Gaulle at 4 Carlton Gardens, I parachuted into France to help organize the various *Résistance* groups scattered across the country into the French Forces of the Interior.

I landed in a field of grass just outside Chartres. I felt blessed, being that close to its wonderful cathedral. It was my task to brief my contacts in the FFI and FTP to outline for them the parts of Plan Vert and Plan Bleu. This was the central and only official purpose of my journey. But once I'd achieved that, I went to visit the cathedral. I was unable to resist, no matter how hazardous and foolhardy it was. I just had to see it. I had to see the *Tree of Jess* above the Royal Portal, beneath the western rose window. I wasn't sure if I'd ever get the chance again. Dad had always told me it was one of the many hidden representations of the Essene *Tree of Life*. I sat in front of it, reciting the *Tree of Life* for about an hour, only leaving when Christian, a little red-headed *résistant* alerted me to three Germans waiting to have their confessions heard on the other side of the church. This same boy, seven years old, used to bicycle by German checkpoints with bread every day. He never knew until after the war that the frame of his bicycle held secret communications between the villages where he lived.

Two weeks later, on my way to meet with people from the Parisian resistance, I was discovered hiding in a barn by the Gestapo.

The *Obersturmführer* offered me a cigarette. I refused. The cigarette and soft words were a short reprieve to make the water more painful the next time they plunged me in.

"How did you learn to speak German?"

"I had a German friend before the war."

A mistake. The ice cold water had me exhausted. Interrogation protocol. Keep repeating the same thing. Never change your pattern. But how many days, weeks was I in that cellar?

"What was his name?"

I combined Mathias' favorite writer and composer together. If they had gotten his name from me he would have become a Jew lover, no matter how high up his father was in Hitler's army.

"Herman Holst."

"Where did he come from?"

"Berlin."

"What did he do?"

"He was a student."

"What did his father do?"

"He was a doctor."

"What kind of doctor?"

"A specialist. He was doing research. I can't remember in what."

They put me under again. When I came up they started on me again, immediately.

"What was his research?"

"Plants ... Medicinal plants," I said, gasping for breath.

"You are a good liar."

"I'm not lying."

"Anyone that says he is not lying is always lying. It seems you have decided not to be helpful in the slightest, *Ezekiel*. And you think I will believe that that is your real name? Ezekiel? Is that from *The Bible*?"

"Yes."

"You see! Finally, you are telling me the truth. You know, your name sounds like Zek Heil. The Führer would be very happy. However, I am not. Goodbye, Zek Heil."

He strutted out the door, his despicable, shiny, black boots ludicrous in my foggy mind. Some time later, they transported me to Auschwitz for cleansing.

THE DYING AND THE DEAD

Two days later, I arrived at Auschwitz II-Birkenau and became a “nurse”.

Birkenau was one of the three big camps, the extermination camp, claiming more lives than any other, even though it came into use well after all the others. Its easy access by train and its sheer size were exactly what the Germans needed to ensure isolation and perform *Die Endlösung*. In the beginning, this was primarily executed with Zyklon-B gas in two brick cottages called "The Little White House" and "The Little Red House." The gas chambers lost all euphemisms after that. The others were named Crematorium III, IV and V. The staggering total of the dead weren't believed by the Allies. They saw it as an exaggeration even when the amazing Polish Army Captain Witold Pileck, who actually volunteered to go into the camp, sent them information documenting the facts. They couldn't and wouldn't believe him, even after he escaped.

On the train, I took the identity of a gentle psychiatric nurse from Bordeaux named Claude Huc. He’d been in the *Güterwagen* for two weeks. He died of exhaustion and starvation from the transport. The beating he'd endured beforehand resulted in one broken arm and a smashed face. The heat of the summer sun, in addition to all the bodies piled together, had dehydrated him completely. Claude was a gift from God, or as Yusuf used to say, *It is written.*

At some stage in your life you have to surrender your will to divine will, or whatever you want to call it. The man above, as Dad used to call Him, had given me the opportunity to save myself again. I didn't need a second offer. In those years you learned how to do things incredibly quickly. When it's the difference between living and dying you have no choice. I stole Claude's papers from him like a professional pickpocket. Not a soul on the wagon saw me. I tore out the photographs and put my papers into the outside pocket of his jacket.

After I passed under the iron gate – *Arbeit macht Frei* – they took all my papers anyway. They told me to go to the right, "Rechts!" I had been "selected" to work in the camp. Later, forced to play in the orchestra that "welcomed" the new inmates, I found out what happened to those who went to the left, "Links!" Claude Huc, nurse, alto player, not Ezekiel Yusuf Moran, the *résistant* the Gestapo wanted dead, had a hard time not wanting to kill himself playing that cheerful music to the "selection" process. I am reminded of the line from *The Revenger's Tragedy*: *Is there a hell besides this, villains?*

I can still remember the dark inside the car when we arrived, then the light blinding us when they opened the doors. It was then that I heard the music while all around me people were screaming and shouting. They were playing merry classical music, but I could hear the reds and blacks, the sorrow and pain, in what they were playing, even though it was orchestrated to make us feel at ease.

Of all the things I've endured, watching *Selektion* is the worst thing I have ever experienced. I'm sure that being forced to play to the new arrivals is what gave musicians the highest suicide rate in the camp. Only the *Sonderkommandos* killed themselves more, for obvious reasons. While playing monstrously lighthearted music in the "orchestra," we witnessed what the SS did to men, women and children. I was playing my alto in the background on this day, the day Oscar Groning, the bookkeeper of Auschwitz, described this scene in recent years:

... a baby crying. The child was lying on the ramp, wrapped in rags. A

mother had left it behind, perhaps because she knew that women with infants were sent to the gas chambers immediately. I saw another SS soldier grab the baby by the legs. The crying had bothered him. He smashed the baby's head against the iron side of a truck until it was silent.

Gifts from God, miracles, always work on more than one level. First, those papers saved me from immediate extermination because, while Ezekiel Moran was on the Gestapo list, Claude Huc was not. Second, in addition to being a member of the orchestra, they now made me a nurse, a useful tool in a concentration camp when Germans need Jews to tend to Jews. The last thing they would do would be to give a German soldier the job. We were beneath them, subhuman, "pigs".

However, a miracle, or more specifically, fate, was one of the most difficult things to get used to. If you volunteered for a hard-working group with the idea of making life easier for yourself, then you could find yourself in the gas chambers. If you were in one selection where you thought you were going to die, you found out later that it was the other group that had died. Each day you waited for fate to tell you what was going to happen to you. When you thought you were escaping, fate would be there again, taking a friend to the gas chamber, or transferring you into another work party where you were "rented out" as slave labor to a daily twelve-hour work day with hardly any food. Being put on a work party could mean certain death in a week, two weeks, three weeks. Yes, we were killed by gassing, but so many of us were also exterminated by labor. The more miracles happened, the more immune you became to them. You never knew whether today would be the day you were selected as a *Muselmann* for the gas chamber.

I am reminded of Job being tested by God when he said, *Once have I spoken; but I will not answer: yea, twice; but I will proceed no further.* He wasn't giving up, he was giving in, surrendering. He chose not to reject fate a third time. He was letting go. He was letting God. I think I survived those *selektions*, those work details, the beatings and starvation, because I had made the choice to let go of my will and let something greater be present, a greater Will, allowing existence to use me in whatever way it wanted to use me, as Krishna advised

Arjuna in the *Bhagavad Gita*. If I hadn't, I know I wouldn't be writing this right now. It was by giving up my will to the Will of existence that everything became authentic, intense, deep. I saw too many fight fate and die. I chose to see everything as having the eternal about it, preferring to be last than first as Jesus once said.

"Do you think this is ever going to end, Claude?"

My friends knew me as Claude. The Capos, officers and foremen only knew me as a number. Not a soul in the place knew me as Ezekiel. Sadly, even in the camps there were informants, people who would do anything for an extra piece of bread, an extra day of life.

I looked at Emil and didn't know what to reply. Here was a man who had been in the camp as a nurse from the very start, watching people disappear like shadows every day. Here was a man who had the audacity to tell jokes and riddles, childish jokes and riddles that lifted your soul in their simplicity. One I loved: What falls but never falls? The night.

"Of course this'll end, Emil." I didn't tell him the rest of my sentence. Death ends everything, eventually. "Doesn't everything end, Emil?"

"Yes, it does. Yes."

I looked at him and knew he'd given up. I wanted to give him some scrap of hope, but hope in a camp has to come from you, from inside. It can't come from anyone else. Hope for that loved one you wanted to see again. Hope for anything, anything that could keep you alive and give meaning to your life. For me, I thought of Aramon. The apple trees. The olive trees. The light moving through the leaves. Thérèse. Dad. Mathias.

When the Capos came to wake us to work the next day, Emil stayed in bed. I pulled at him, but it was no use. Emil took the cigarette from deep inside his clothes and lit it. This would be his last whimsical flourish of resistance, of freedom, to smoke, to choose not to go on, to choose not to wait any longer. As he lay there staring through the smoke at the wooden ceiling, I knew that the light of his mind had gone out. *SS-Obersturmführer* Franz Hössler was delighted. He broke Emil's nose, shot off his ears. He beat him for fifteen minutes. He left him to bleed and starve to death in the rain where everyone could see.

Emil is just one example of the many people who slipped through my fingers each day. I didn't have time to think of how inadequate a job I was doing to care for people, but it didn't matter. They gave us so little in the form of medication or tools that it was a twisted joke to use what you had, like putting a bandage on a heart attack. Mostly, bandages were made of bits of toilet paper. Supplies were in Block 10, the hospital, also known as the human experimentation center, where people like Dr. Carl Clauberg and Josef Mengele did their "research". It was not a place to visit looking for bandages. Clauberg, Mengele and the others weren't alone. Bayer, a subsidiary of IG Farben at the time, bought our prisoners to use as human guinea pigs for their drugs. After the war, some of the IG Farben war criminals were sent to jail. All those who were sentenced received early releases, most of them quickly restored to their directorships, some of them even being awarded the Federal Cross of Merit.

We needed bandages most after food distribution. Prisoners beat each other for the daily ration of a cup of turnip soup. Anything we did to help broken ribs and wounds was hopeless, because the next day the fights would start all over again. If you went to the hospital you were inviting an experience much like, if not worse than, the gas chamber. When you went to the gas chamber, you died. When you went to the "hospital", you were experimented on first. In the end, the only way I had to treat my patients was with my voice, by telling them stories, by telling them that one bright blue day they would be able to have a birthday again, that one day they would be able to sing again and celebrate *Rosh ha-Shanah.*

Another man I remember very vividly was a Pole who refused to tell me his name. He said it didn't matter. Names don't matter to me anymore, he said, smiling. He had edema and had given up eating as did so many when they'd had enough. I remember him the most because of what he said to me before he died.

"Remember, our darkest hour always comes just before the light."

People like him made me never forget the light inside. That man's one line of defiance against the darkness reminded me, as I held his limp tepid hand, of the day I'd gone with Mathias to Madame Noez's house in Les Baux de Provence. Near where she lived was a sixteenth century Protestant temple with the words of Jean Calvin inscribed on it: *Post tenebras lux*, "after the shadows, light," something I read again later in Victor Frankl's book.

Back then, each new day I saw a different way to seek meaning. I was not on this planet accidentally. There was a purpose within me. Everything around me was trying to work through me. This was not narcissism, this was respecting the fact that each person on this planet has a purpose, a gift, something to share with the rest of the world.

Yes, I knew the next day would be darker than the day before it, but I also knew that even in that darkness there was a light waiting for me. Yes, I was numb, like everyone else. Yes, apathy would crawl under my skin and make me want to end my life, but when this would happen, I would look to those solitary birds on the barbed wire singing over the mayhem and murder, to the clouds passing overhead the way they always do, to the wind in the trees in the distance, as sentinels of that light. I felt lucky to be in my body no matter how much of it disappeared each day. I also remembered precious pieces of poetry, or words like those of Marcus Aurelius, as I stared from my bunk at a shaft of light coming into our block:

To see the nature of a sunbeam, look at the light as it falls through a narrow opening into a dark room. It extends in a straight line, striking any solid object that stands in its way and blocks the space beyond it. There it remains – not vanishing, or falling away.

His words made me think about the light coming into my block, how I didn't have to push the darkness out for it to enter. The light was enough. Its presence was enough. The darkness was but an absence of light, only appearing to exist. I couldn't remove the darkness, but I could block out the light! And this is the truth I realized on that bunk. I could do nothing with darkness, but I could let in the light. Marcus Aurelius and many others made me understand that I needed to stand my ground, not in violence or action, to just be accepting and aware, for that which doesn't allow or accept the light can only create darkness.

Love is absent in darkness. The heart's eyes are absent. The darkness of the camps opened my heart's eyes to the light of love and its absence, darkness and fear. For this I will always be very grateful. Thanks to the camps, I try to love more. The more I love the less I fear, because fear disappears when the light of love is present. Intellectuals all over the world refuse to see the light. They are basically saying life is meaningless because their intellect is blinded by the impossible. They don't look to the heart inside themselves to see. This heart doesn't have physical eyes, but it sees, it feels. It is always waiting for you to be aware enough to listen to it. The heart's eyes are a ghost to intellectuals, one they flirt with and try to understand by reading what they call *esoteric* books or trying to analyze healers and mystics. They are frightened. Darkness is fear.

Much has been written about those days in the camps, a fact I am very happy to record here, especially when one considers all the deluded people out there who still say it never happened. So many, like Victor Frankl and Elie Wiesel, have written it down. Their words speak for us all, but especially that great unnamed devastation of people that disappeared into the "baths," "ran into the wire" or merely dissolved because they were selected as *"Muselmanns"*.

Now, as an old man looking back, my strongest memories from that time appear like a lethargic black and white movie. People like Emil and the Pole without a name stay with me, but there were so many other Emils and Poles. The details have fallen away perhaps because there were none of the trappings of the outside world inside the camp. Inside. The survivors will always call it *inside*. Outside's a world of pretty, pleasing details. Inside is an unexplainable horror. The experiences inside cannot be understood by the outside because out here, with our TVs and jobs and three meals a day, inside is unimaginable, unless you were there. This is one reason details are hard to come by. They are hard to come by when you strip a person, not just of their clothes and shave their heads, but when you brand them the way Dad used to brand the bulls of the Camargue, or tattoo them with numbers and sew the same number on their coat, jacket or trousers, the same coat, jacket or trousers everyone else is wearing.

Today when people talk to me about survival of the fittest, I completely disagree with them because of my experiences in the camps. After the camps I know for a fact that there is an intelligent design, as Thérèse called it all those years ago. To demean the whole of Nature to a failed fish flopping onto the ferns in pre-human times to escape a far superior species is not only far-fetched to me but ignorant of the facts. You only have to look at men arriving at the camps to see this. I remember one large, physically robust lawyer and one small, scrawny postman who came in on the same day at Auschwitz. If you were a betting man you would have put all your money on the lawyer. He definitely had his wits about him and he had a relatively good attitude to life. The postman seemed morose and unsettled. Which one lasted three weeks and which one was still alive when I left Auschwitz?

The fittest do not always survive. The individual with a reason to live does. Then there's also the fact that fate has something to do with it. The large lion stalking the gazelle may fend off and kill other lions, but when you turn to humans, large humans, the fittest, can somehow go off the hunt, leaving the scrawnier ones to survive. And you may see this all the way through our society. How did that "nerd" do that? What, one young man created Facebook in his dorm room? Another young man helped create Microsoft in a garage? Why didn't a good-looking, well-connected, rich young man do that?

What sets them apart? Survival of the fittest? No. Having a meaning, a passion to live and create something? Yes. One tied with intelligent design or, if you want to call it by another name, coincidence, luck, fate. Yes, we see it every day. The biggest sycamore seed doesn't always find the best soil. Its flight pattern all depends on which way the wind is blowing. It depends on where it lands. It depends on whether it's lucky enough to have a human or other animal crush it into the ground so that it's covered in sufficient soil to be reborn as a new tree.

What I remember the most from those days is something even

more lacking in detail than our similar clothing and shaved heads: the spiritual power of love, the love inside ourselves for ourselves, those places and palaces inside us for lovers and loved ones. Even while on work duty, even while cleaning out the latrines those first few weeks after I arrived, even while trying to recover from being beaten to the ground again for no reason save the other's malice, even while enduring the wait for the day's ration of a paltry piece of bread you mightn't even get, even through all these and many other illnesses and deprivations, there was always that night making love to Thérèse under that full moon or Mathias quoting me Shakespeare for the thousandth time or Dad singing *Her Mantle So Green* or the orchards in summer or the ancient olive tree beside the stream and that dream, that vision of walking down our lane-way under the *micocoulier* and *mûrier* trees and into our barn to fall onto the hay with my alto and play and play and play until the strings flew off.

LIBERATION

At the end of 1944 the SS staff forced us to dismantle and dynamite the remaining gas chambers, to destroy the evidence of mass killings. Sixty thousand prisoners went out of the camp into Germany on death marches, leaving the sick in the infirmary to die.

Before leaving our *Blockaelteste,* the psychopath in charge of our barrack, came in to make sure nobody was left behind. I was hiding on my back in the barrack bread box. He rifled through the bunks, flinging things off the walls. As he left, he kicked the box I was in. If I hadn't been so skeletal the box would never have caved in. He would have found me. An hour later I got out of the box and shuffled about the camp.

As the Soviet forces advanced toward Auschwitz in January 1945, I hid among the dead bodies by night and roamed the camp by day. The Ukrainians and Poles wouldn't let me into the barracks in case I was a German. I hid amongst the piles of dead bodies at night, like them, expecting the Germans to come back at any moment.

When the Soviet troops came into the camp I was too weak to stand up. I had found some potato peelings and had been eating them for days to stay alive. When a soldier came to help me up I still didn't believe what was happening, that I was being liberated. He helped me to a truck where other inmates were sitting. They brought us to a field hospital where I collapsed and lost three days of my life to delirium and fatigue, finally allowing the starvation and exhaustion to take its toll. When I woke, there was a woman in the bed beside me, Helen, Helen Wiesenthal. They had just transferred her back from the hospital in Oświęcim because the German nurses paid no attention to her, calling her a "sick Jew." Because of these nurses, after surviving three years in Auschwitz, Helen died half an hour after our first and only conversation.

Three weeks later, I left the hospital with the accordion, mandolin, sitar and alto I'd stolen from Auschwitz. I played for food as I walked the 1,700 kms home through Poland, the Czech Republic, Austria, Italy and finally France, in less than two months.

Of the 2,819 of us liberated from Auschwitz, there were 180 children, 52 of them under the age of eight years of age. How had they survived? Because "doctors" Mengele and Schmidt hadn't had the the time to perform human experimentation on them.

Over 1.1 million Jews, tens of thousands of Roma people, Christian Poles and Soviet POWs died at Auschwitz. But I had been given the gift of survival.

MOTHER

She held out her arms and I went into them, crying. This surprised me as much as it did her and she started to cry too, which surprised me even more. We stood there, two broken people, holding onto each other like twisted branches of the same tree. When we finally let go and sat opposite each other, everything returned to the way it had always been. After worrying over my health and talking about the weather, she asked me if I needed somewhere to stay. I said no. I was staying at a *chambre d'hôte* in Theziers. Then she said what she knew she had to say in order to put an end to any talk of the past.

"As you probably know from the locals, I sold the *mas* when myself and Philippe got married." She bent her head over, twisting her gold cross in circles in her left hand. "I thought you were, well, that ... that you were never coming back."

Silence.

She raised her head again. "There's not much money left after renovating this huge place, but I do have something to give you."

She handed me a check and I absentmindedly put it in my pocket without even looking at the numbers.

"Thank you. That's very generous, Mother."

"You're welcome."

Silence again.

Our whole past erased and invested in a new life with a vague man who appeared to despise living. Home was gone. So was I. I was gone. Still, that check allowed me the freedom I needed for the next few years to go on the odyssey I had no idea I was about to take.

We sat in silence in the sitting room of her new house, an old *maison de maître* in Aramon, its perfectly coiffed front garden standing out on the street as a perfect testament to how things should be done. I wondered what form of *Catholic Action* she was involved with now, whether she sewed for the clergy still and helped the poor.

She fixed an irritating wrinkle on her spotless white dress. The cross hanging over her chest swayed from side to side like the pendulum in the old hall clock.

Jesus, I thought, I have been born into a time that detests its most beautiful creations and rewards brutes and cowards. Of all the millions who died, it was my mother and I who survived? Why? She was an *enfant non juif* under the Vichy state. Her father's parents were not Jewish, even though both her mother's parents were. I was the opposite, an *enfant juif* because both my parents were Jewish, not pure Aryan like Thérèse or Mathias. Of course, there was Yusuf rambling around somewhere on the planet after his pilgrimage to Mecca, but where was Alphonse from the café and all the others I loved? Even that bully Maurice Jalabert was dead, shot in the first week of the Battle of France. And where were Thérèse and Mathias?

I began to sweat. All the questions distressed me, depressed me. They still do.

Why, why have people like Thérèse's family got even more money and power today than they did before the war, when they were the ones that ardently supported Vichy France? What about all the other businessmen collaborators like Taittinger. The only punishment he received was to never be allowed to hold public office. Then there's Eugene Schueller's *l'Oreal*: the fascist Cagoule leader Eugene Deloncle's men, Jacques Correze and Jean Filliol, became the bosses of the company's subsidiaries in Spain and America. Francois Mitterrand also worked for *l'Oreal* after the war and was still doing so when he ran for office in 1946. His sister was mistress to Jean Bouvyer, CGQJ senior official and Cagoulard. His brother married Deloncle's niece.

And what of René Bousquet, chief of police under Vichy, friend of Francois Mitterrand, who ordered and organized the Vel' d'Hiv Roundup of 13,152 Jews? Why did Mitterrand never apologize for the use of French police and officials at the Vel' d'Hiv? But then why would he, when it was one of his friends who ordered it? It took until 1995 for one of our Presidents to apologize. Fifty-three years? And what happened to Bousquet over the decades? Well, he led a comfortable life working first for the Banque de l'Indochine, then in newspapers, supported and helped finance Mitterrand's presidential foray in the seventies and after Mitterrand was elected in the early eighties went to the Élysée Palace to "talk about politics". Mitterrand publicly admitted to their friendship on television in 1994. And then people wonder why Bousquet was shot before he could talk about his views and the views of his friends? It wasn't until 1964 that we changed our laws to allow retroactive trials for crimes against humanity. Twenty years later?

She sat, silent in her chair. She was still in shock at how emaciated I was, even though I'd been eating well for three weeks. I watched her eyes examining me. It would take years for my body to regain its weight.

Moments before, reminiscent of an episode from the *Wife of Bath*, she introduced me to her new husband, a harmless man, a lawyer, whose bad eyes had allowed him to escape the war. I started to wonder whether he'd been a part of the Vichy regime and then quickly dismissed the idea from my brain, trying not to judge a man I barely knew. He seemed a pale reflection of Dad, but also very much like him in that he did everything she asked, never questioning her demands. He lurched out of the room in his impeccable suit, the back of his head shining from all the *pommade* in his hair, a piece of toilet paper sticking to the heel of his right shoe. I didn't have the heart to tell him about it. It must've been embarrassing enough for him to have to meet a grown man his wife called son. To his credit he never showed his embarrassment, a gift he was going to need, being married to my mother.

She handed me the letter, her hand trembling. It said he died honorably on the eleventh of May 1940, the day after the German invasion of France. Finally, I knew.

The letter slipped out of my hand and onto the floor. I was too shocked to even notice. I found myself thinking rationally instead of emotionally. I was grateful, grateful that he never had to spend years in some POW camp. I knew he would have tried to escape. Dad was not the kind of man you could have kept behind a barbed-wire fence.

As she touched and twisted the cross around her neck, trying to think of something to say, her eyes beginning to fill with tears, I found myself wondering what Dad would've been thinking of as he died. The *mas*? Yes. Me? Oh, yes. My mother and Yusuf? Of course. I wondered whether he had thought of his mother and father or his brothers. And it was then that I knew I had to go to Ireland. I had to see whether Gabriel was still alive. I had to tell him what a wonderful brother he'd had, how brave and loving and full of life and love and music.

I shifted the chocolates I'd given her from side to side on the nearby table. She looked out the window behind me after briefly dabbing her eyes with a white handkerchief. I stared into the mirror above the marble fireplace at the reflection of the light coming in through the window from outside. It was a beautiful day outside, the kind Provence is known for, blue skies, sun, but in the distance you could see an *orage* coming, the dark clouds nearing. The silence started to become unbearable. Then, all of a sudden a bird smashed off the windowpane. The glass was so meticulously cleaned that you barely knew it was there. I got up and ran to the window. The bird, lying on the ground beside some purple and pink geraniums, writhed on the ground for a moment, righted itself and flew away.

I turned around. She was standing beside the fireplace, her hands moving about unconsciously, not knowing what to do with themselves as they tried to rest on her immaculate white apron.

"Oh, I wouldn't worry about that. They're always crashing against the window. They always seem to pick themselves up and fly away though."

"I'd better go, Mother. I was supposed to meet some people in Avignon."

"Oh, okay then. When will you be coming back for your things? I have everything boxed and labeled in the attic."

I wanted to tell her to give it all to the *Secours populaire* but could see how proud she was to have kept it, proof she'd loved me once upon a time. She was happy it was now ready to give to me on my return, a return everyone had advised her would never happen.

"I'll come back for it another day, if you don't mind."

"Not at all. It's not going anywhere. It's been up there for years."

I went out of the room and she followed me into the huge hallway festooned with paintings of a hunt and the head of bored boar, obviously killed by her husband's father or grandfather.

"I'll call again in a little while, then," I said, knowing I'd never see her again.

"Oh yes, that would be nice."

I opened the main door. It had started to rain outside.

"Oh, Ezekiel, wait! I nearly forgot."

She went back into the house and returned a few minutes later, out of breath.

"Sorry it took me so long. I had left it in the attic with all your other things."

She passed me a large manila envelope. Inside it were letters held together by an elastic band.

"They're from your friend, Thérèse."

I could see from the handwriting that they were from Thérèse.

"Thank you, Mother."

"Don't you want an umbrella?"

"No, I enjoy a storm."

"See you soon!"

"Yes, see you soon."

We kissed and hugged each other again, not so tight this time or for so long.

She died of cervical cancer while I was in India. I found out from her husband's new wife in the same huge hallway I'd said goodbye to her in, the paintings of the hunt and the boar replaced by a copy of the famous Fragonard painting with the lady on the swing and an immense reproduction of Renoir's last painting, *The Bathers*.

About ten yards from her huge house, I stopped and slumped onto a small wall. The weight of his death had finally started to slowly register inside. Dad was dead. The rain hid my tears. I sat there until the storm passed.

CONFESSION

When I got home from the war, all I had wanted to do was to return to our *mas* and my music. I wanted to recognize my own nature again. No more deceptions, lying to enemies and informers, but more importantly, no more lying to myself about the world I lived in. After the war I wanted to become a different man, more of a human being. I wanted absolute honesty.

With the farm sold, I thought of trying to buy a small rundown *mas* with the money my mother had given me, but every time I went out to look at one I found myself getting more and more depressed. It didn't have this. It didn't have that. I found myself asking: Where's Moses? Where are all the apple trees and the barn? I tried to be positive, even thinking I could build my own *mas*, but my heart wasn't in it. I felt lost. In the camps it was one of the images, the image of our farm with its trees and animals and so many memories of joy, happiness, and bliss that had kept me alive. Now I realized that I didn't have a home in Provence anymore and I wasn't emotionally evolved enough yet to understand that home wasn't where the hearth is, but where the heart is, inside me, not outside on some land I'd gotten attached to, not a place name with fields, but that place inside. It took many more decades for me to finally realize this.

Unlike Thérèse, I had never completely allowed some kind of divine authority into my life, allowing my weaknesses to be strengths, my scars to be successes. As soon as I let go of my ego and understood that everything was as it was supposed to be, because it couldn't be any other way, I started to feel more free. My first step was to seek through what I knew, what my mother made me know. So after my meeting with her, while walking back to my *chambre d'hôte,* I stopped in front of the village church on Avenue de la Liberation to look at the Madonna, then at the little *affiche* to the right of the door. The priest was holding confessions. I smiled, took a deep breath and went in. I needed to talk, to someone, anyone.

"Have you ever heard the expression, let go and let God, my son."

"Yes, Father."

"Well, have you ever tried it?"

"What do you mean, Father?"

"From my experience, and the experiences of my parishioners, any time one lets go and lets God then extraordinary things happen. People walk into their lives, who they haven't met for years. They get offered a job in a field they never would have thought of exploring. Anyone I have ever met, who has given over the reins to God, has never regretted it, my son. It's liberating."

"How do you do it, then?"

"It's simply admitting that there is a power far greater than you or I, and that it is against our natural design to deny that truth. A simple example would be lying. Do you lie, my son?"

"Yes. A lot. When someone is about to kill you, it's hard not to."

"I am not here to judge you, my son. I am here to help you through this spiritual crisis."

"I'm not having a spiritual crisis."

"Then why are you here? You just told me you haven't been to confession in years."

"I'm sorry, Father. My ego takes over. I'm in such a crisis I don't even know what kind it is."

"Look, what I'm trying to say to you is that even lying is a violation of that trust in God. There is no reason to lie. Everything that is has been laid in your path for a reason. That's why you are in here, to purge yourself of any spiritual distortions you have created in your life to deny that truth. You could just as easily speak your truth to the Lord by sitting at home and meditating to him through prayer. I am merely here to facilitate the Lord, my son."

"I think I understand what you mean, Father."

"All it means is that you respect the precept of speaking the truth. Your power comes from judging all that is around you from that perspective, truth. And to know truth it is better that I give you what John of the Cross wrote once: *Never fail, whatever may befall you, be it good or evil, to keep your heart quiet and calm in the tenderness of love.*"

I could hear him taking a deep breath and sighing.

"Thank you, Father."

"Don't thank me, my son, thank God. He's the one that gives me my faith so that I can strengthen yours. It's a mutually beneficial cycle."

He took another deep breath, and on the out breath said, "May the Lord grant you forgiveness of your sins. May you go in peace to love and serve the Lord. Amen."

"No prayers, Father?"

"No, my son. Where you've come from you've said more than enough prayers. Just concentrate on the ones you have for Him every morning and evening."

The grille closed.

THE ANGEL OF DEATH AND TRANSFORMATION

I walked out of the church into the sun, the large brown envelope under my coat, and walked out to our old *mas* outside Aramon. It was a wonderful walk. Memories of walking along the same road with Mathias and Thérèse came back to me as I passed familiar trees, houses, gates and signposts. The road was like a necklace, each memory attached to it like beads on a string, all coming together into one beautiful new experience.

I knocked on our front door and a young woman about the same age as me opened it, her long hazel-colored cords of hair flying over her shoulders from the sudden draft of wind. A little girl held onto her dress behind her as if it were a life-raft and a voice hollered out from what must have been our old kitchen.

"Who is it, Anna?"

The woman smiled at me, pushing her little girl in behind her.

"Sorry to disturb you. My name is Moran. Ezekiel Yusuf Moran."

"Yes."

"I used to live here when I was your daughter's age, and older."

Her face whitened. "You're the one, the one from the war."

"Yes."

She smiled at me. "Would you like to come in for some coffee? My husband was in the war too."

"No thank you. That's very generous of you, though. I was just wondering whether it would be alright for me to walk around the land a little and maybe go spend some time in the old barn? It holds a lot of good memories for me."

"Did you want to see your old room?"

"No, no. It's the land and the barn that I would love to see. Do you mind?"

"No, no, not at all. Take all the time you want."

I walked toward the barn and already tears of joy started to form as I remembered the three of us, naked in the loft, trying to stifle each other's laughter as my mother came in to collect eggs from the hay below us.

It was the same door, made from the huge pine trees Dad had cut from the base of the Cevennes. It creaked open with the same noise that always warned us someone was coming. I started to wonder where all the carpentry tools Dad loved so much had gone. She must have sold them when she got the news of his death. And how could I blame her? How was she to manage a farm on her own? She wasn't the only woman to sell up because of the war.

I went through the second door and climbed the old ladder that led up to the loft. When I reached the top the memories overwhelmed me and I cried at having the opportunity to be able to come back to such a place of joy and fun. I remembered Thérèse swinging from a chevron above us as she talked to Mathias.

"But why worry about our relationship, Mathias! Can't we just enjoy it? Love is not a relationship! It's a state, one of being, of becoming, a flowing river. When you start worrying about our relationship then you're being fear, the very opposite of love. We need to become great lovers of life, not of each other, but of ourselves and thereby lovers of all that life gives us because all of it is a gift, especially the part of it that makes us suffer the most!"

"What, where's the joy in suffering?" he said.

"A broken heart is open. Don't you want a broken heart? Don't you want it open so that it can receive all the love of the world!

Don't you want to explore your world, not only the world? Don't you want to explore your nature?"

"But then you're saying we should all suffer so that we can experience love? That's crazy!"

"Do you really think love is between you and me, or between me and Zeke?"

"Of course. It's not as if I'm making love to this straw!"

"I'm not talking about making love, I'm talking about love, the love inside you and in the sky above you. But what I'm really talking about is the sky inside you. That's the greatest love. To dance, to sing, to go deeper and deeper inside yourself, to hear the music of love inside you without putting names on things. The dance is the dance. The song is the song, not the type of songbird singing it. We don't have to categorize love. It isn't this or that. There is no relationship. Love is the energy we create together, the energy the flower gives you as it smiles and laughs at you."

"But what about your parents? Are you saying they didn't love each other at some stage because they don't appreciate this bigger love?"

"Their marriage is like any marriage. The fear is always in the room with them. My father's afraid of my mother and she's afraid of him."

"No he's not! She's just like my mother, a doormat to my father!"

"You're not listening. I agree with you. Our mothers are passive and closed, almost ghosts. But what's important is to understand that their relationship is based on fear and fear is the opposite of love. Their relationships are just arrangements. They're the arrangements of frightened people dominating, possessing, fighting, manipulating and depending on each other because of this flawed idea of love."

She fell down on the hay beside Mathias and kissed him.

"Then how does a relationship last?" he said.

"Is it supposed to?" she said. "Love happens. It just is. It's not something you agree upon by signing a contract. It flows from the dance, the flower, the music! When it happens, it doesn't need a temple or church or prayer or meditation because it is everything, it is God."

"So can we be in love then?"

"We aren't! We're being love. Be love. That's it! We are love, not the beloved. The Beloved is love, not the beloved! You don't have to go searching for love in a temple. You *are* God making love to God. Then you don't need to search for God because love is there!"

"You're not making any sense."

"It's perfect sense," she laughed and grabbed him in her arms and kissed him.

Now, decades on, I understand what Thérèse meant. The subtlety of what she said was hidden by our lack of awareness of how she was using words. She had let go of fear where we hadn't. She'd had nothing to lose because she'd let go of being frightened. It was as if she had left us standing on the side of a river wanting to jump in because of the heat of the summer sun when she had already stripped and taken the plunge. There was no reason for us not to jump in. In fact, everything was pushing us to, but we still stood on the banks, frightened someone would see us naked in the river.

I leaned back onto a bale of hay behind me and opened the letters by date, the oldest first.

LETTER I

HEIDELBERG, 1939

Dearest Zeke!

It's finally happened! I've heard an angel. The Archangel Ezekiel. His energy is so powerful! Beyond anything we ever talked about before. I channeled him and I wrote it all down, word for word! It's all just too exciting for me and yet it has made me suspicious of myself. I don't know if you remember me singing Hildegard of Bingen's *"O frondens virga"* to you from her *Ordo Virtutum?* I think she describes best how I felt, before writing her *Scivias*:

But I, thought I saw and heard these things, refused to write for a long time through doubt and bad opinion and the diversity of human words, not with stubbornness but in the exercise of humility, until, laid low by the scourge of God, I fell upon a bed of sickness; then, compelled at last by many illnesses ... I set my hand to the writing. While I was doing it, I sensed, as I mentioned before, the deep profundity of scriptural exposition; and, raising myself from illness by the strength I received, I brought this work to a close – though just barely.

Just read what follows. His words are more important than mine or any explanation I might offer. Read. Read. Read. I wait for your response, immediately! I do pray you are not fighting in this horrible war...

LOVE LOVE LOVE

Yours,

Thérèse

LETTER II

HEIDELBERG, 1939

Dearest Zeke!

It's happened again! The last time it happened I slept for forty-eight hours. Can you believe it? Me sleeping for more than eight hours!

Mathias was really worried. He said he kept coming in to see if I still had a pulse. He even brought in a doctor who said I was just in a very, very deep sleep. Me in a deep sleep! Oh the dreams I had, Zeke. No, but they weren't dreams, they were visions! His energy is so powerful. Beyond anything we ever talked about. The things he showed me. Other planets! Other beings of light! The Ancient Ones. I wrote it all down, word for word. It's all just too exciting. I've added it to this letter. Again, his words are more important than mine, or any explanation I might write. Read. Read. Read.

I wait for your response, immediately!

I so really pray you are not in this war, Zeke. Mathias has been constantly training in the cavalry for months now. He hates it. All he wants to do is paint and be with me. How I wish we'd never left France!

LOVE LOVE LOVE

Yours,

Thérèse

LETTER III

HEIDELBERG, 1939

Dearest Zeke,

For two days I didn't get out of bed after what I can only call my "experience." I slept for 36 hours this time! It was wonderful. I know I'm repeating myself, but what dreams I had. I can tell you of them when we see each other next.

Wasn't my revelation, his message, amazing! Oh, all the things I want to talk to you about!

Please God, I pray that you have not written me because you have been conscripted into this despicable war. I cannot bear even thinking for a moment that the two people I love most on this planet will be fighting each other! Horrible. Disgusting. Men are such animals! For what? This madman Hitler? Does he actually think he'll win?

There is something else I need to tell you. How do I say this to you? Oh, how I wish I could say it to you in person not through words on a page so that you could share our joy.

I AM PREGNANT! Isn't that wonderful? If it's a boy, we have chosen a name for him. Do you know what it is? Yes: Ezekiel! You see, I keep my promises. And if it's a girl, we do not know what we will call her.

You see, even amidst all this warmongering and horribleness there are little souls wanting to be born back into this world. Isn't it wonderful?

Please write me soon! How I wish I could hug you. Soon!

LOVE LOVE LOVE

Yours,

Thérèse

LETTER IV

HEIDELBERG, 1939

Dearest Zeke,

Mathias has gone to war. His superiors say he should be able to get back to see our little baby when it is born. As you know, his father is a very powerful man here in Heidelberg. They've made him a *Festungswerkmeister* in the army because of his engineering background, but I think it's got more to do with his family's vast wealth. We are very lucky that way, although I have never liked the man or the way he treats Mathias. You know how difficult he has made it for Mathias to be a painter and sculptor – he created a wondrous statue before he left that he called *The Venus of Heidelberg*. It looks like a huge *Venus of Willendorf*! You would think his father would be enthusiastic and happy and supportive for his show in this great gallery in Heidelberg, but he hasn't said a word. The local paper even ran a story about his paintings saying they're like Jack B. Yeats' work.

Have you ever seen his paintings? Mathias and I hadn't even heard of him before we read the review. We went out and got copies of his work immediately. We were so happy. Yeats' work is brilliant. But still, not one word from his father! Poor Mathias. He excels at so much and yet he is given a father who only wants him to excel at one thing, money! Some day when his paintings make us loads of money I'm sure his father will be the same. If the money is not earned from being an architect or a doctor or a businessman (his dream job for Mathias, any kind of business), then it will not be real. But we do not care, do we, Zeke? Artists and musicians and inventors and healers are always the new Gnostics, keeping alive the revolution the priests and businessmen think they have under control!

I know, I know. Here I am going on about his parents again. I don't even mention his mother. She is barely there, a slave to his father. It is so sad to watch.

Oh, Zeke, how I wish we could have one of our conversations! This city is SOOO boring and German people are so boring I find. I don't mean to generalize but, my god, do they ever laugh, like really laugh? I'm sure it's just because I haven't met some funny ones yet, but still, the more time I spend here the more amazed I am by Mathias and his exceptional attitude to reality, how enthusiastic and free-flowing he is and how he laughs! Of course I have you to thank for a lot of that, Zeke! The time he spent with you and me in Aramon really opened his heart to life, allowed him to bloom, as it did me. Oh, thank you, Zeke! How grateful I am to have had that time with you.

By the way, my Angel of Death and Transformation has left. He said he has said what he has to say for now. He did say that one day his words would be in a book and that the whole world would read it. Isn't that marvelous? Who knows when that will be, though? It doesn't matter. What matters is that now you have a copy of his words and so do I. That way if mine are ever blown up by some plane or tank or grenade, then you'll always have them safely over there in our wonderful France!

Sometimes I hope you've gone to war already so that you don't have to read my sad letters to you! Just think, in a few months when all this horror is over with we'll be able to be together again in Provence singing and dancing and playing music naked – why not! – with our little girl or boy playing underneath the apple trees. Oh, how wonderful it will be, away from this dreary too well made city!

LOVE LOVE LOVE!

YOURS!

Thérèse

LETTER V

HEIDELBERG, 1940

Dear Zeke,

This is a letter I do not want to write, least of all to you, my friend.

My tears are falling on the page as I try to control myself in the writing. I pray that you are still alive and that you are somewhere safe. The Battle of France does not look well for you, Hitler's army spreading like a cancer across Europe.

I will get straight to it then, because if I spend too much time on this I know I will not write it, as I have been putting it off now these two days and as I have to go back to the front, I will have to send this to you immediately. There is a friend of my father's who has ways of getting the letter through to you quickly. I am grateful to my father for that at least, even if he shouts at me that he cannot understand me when we are at war with France. It saddens me that he forgets so quickly all those good friends we made in France or that his daughter-in-law is French and...

Again, I have stopped myself from writing what I wanted to write.

After two days of agony from the childbirth, Thérèse passed

away on the 30th of September at around 7:20 pm. She was buried on October 1st, in the old cemetery in Heidelberg, Steigerweg.

I pray to God that you somehow do not receive this letter until after the war. From your last letter to us, I am sure you are deployed in this madness, and if you are I am glad for one reason only, that you do not have to read the words I have written above.

If for whatever reason we ever do meet in this sickness of war, please know that there is no one on this planet I hold more dear to my heart than you and my little daughter.

In loving kindness,

Yours, as ever,

Mathias.

THE HUMAN AVALANCHE

I left the barn in tears, my newfound joy now knowing new depths of despair and sadness.

The farm. Dad. Now Thérèse?

I walked down our old lane remembering the time she had talked to us about how heroic women are and how badly men have treated them, men like her father and Mathias', men like those who wrote in *The Bible* that women are unclean. Men don't give birth, she said. How heroic is giving birth! And now it's taken as commonplace? Why? And then she told us about the ancient Aztecs and how they had all these different heavens. How you died meant which heaven you went to. And which one do you think women who die in childbirth go to? she said. We had no idea. The heaven where all the great warriors who were killed in battle went, that's where! she said.

For years I tried to get Thérèse's Archangel Ezekiel channeling published by big houses and then smaller presses. I even vanity published it, but nobody wanted it, not even little bookstores in Paris well-known for what was called *arcana*. Looking back on it now, I see that it was to be expected. Even today, people still think it's crazy, even if they do say it's very inspired. I suppose now that Trump is in power and the end and the beginning of a new cycle is starting, people will be more interested in what Ezekiel had to say through Thérèse all those years ago.

As to me: what do I think? After over nine decades of living on this planet I trust that anything can happen, at any time, in any way imaginable. The fact that over sixty years ago Thérèse wrote about solar winds, computers, neuroscience, the magnetosphere and megalithic tombs like the ones found at Gobekli Tepe in the 90s, as well as dictators who appeared long after she was gone, such as Mugabe and Amin, not only boggles my mind, it simply goes beyond it, way beyond it.

There was an absolute genius in that young woman. How I miss her! She was like a human avalanche. Sadly, avalanches finally fade away. But, oh, how beautiful they are to experience as they dis-assemble all in front of them, including themselves! How magnificent!

I left Aramon on the next train, broken, for Germany. I was going to find Mathias.

HEIDELBERG

Heidelberg could have been a nice city, but then what city is a happy place after a war, especially a defeated one? I should have felt good about it. We had beaten them. But I felt nothing of the sort. Instead, I only felt sadness and compassion for all the mothers and fathers I passed on the streets who had lost sons and daughters, for all the spouses who'd lost husbands and wives, and for all the children, the children left with one parent or none in a country with a battered and defeated psyche. Even the ones who had come home came back from fighting in an army that had committed genocide.

Why did I go there? I suppose I was searching for myself, anywhere I could find myself. I still clung onto a vague hope that I would find Mathias amidst the rubble and desolation of that place. I was trying to cling onto my old life, but it was like trying to cling onto a cloud.

I found his parents' house. It reminded me of a German version of my mother's house, but even more proper, which I had previously thought impossible.

His shadow of a mother met me in her drawing room. His father had escaped to Franco's Spain, leaving her in Germany to trawl for as much cash as possible before she met up with him in Madrid. Agitated, she stood and sat, sat and stood, the whole time I stood in the doorway of her drawing room asking her questions.

She faltered in her speech as she told me where I could find Thérèse's grave.

Then she finally sat down, stricken by what she was about to say. Mathias deserted from the army, she said. His father had forced him to serve in Buchenwald, to toughen him up, she said. When Mathias got there he found out first-hand what they were doing to the prisoners. His father was specific about where he should serve there: the pathology block. He would not receive his commission as a captain in the cavalry until he had shown that he could be of assistance in the camp. His father knew.

He knew Mathias would never endure being introduced to a place where lamps were made from human skin and inmates were killed for fun. When he tried to get transferred, they wouldn't allow him, even after he explained that he was in the cavalry. His father had left orders that he would not be allowed to leave Buchenwald for three months. Some of the soldiers tried to talk sense to him, she said, but he escaped on his white horse, Victory, the name Mathias had given to all his horses, by paying the SS adjutants Blank and Hinkelmann for safe passage. The horse had come with him to Buchenwald. They shot it first from under him. Then they shot him in the back as he tried to run into the woods that surrounded Buchenwald.

I went to comfort her, but for the second time in my life I felt an energy inside me fill me up with an all consuming fire, deep in the heart of me. Place, time, circumstance disappeared. Her mouth moved but I heard nothing. I sat down on a nearby chair, as light as a leaf in the wind. If I hadn't sat, I would have surely fainted.

Mathias came to me, the image of him leaning with his back against an old plough, reading *Hamlet* aloud to me as I smoked Dad's beloved hives to harvest the honey:

Since my dear soul was mistress of her choice,
And could of men distinguish, her election

Hath seal'd thee for herself: for thou has been
As one, in suffering all, that suffers nothing;
A man that fortune's buffets and rewards
Hast ta'en with equal thanks: and blest are those
Whose blood and judgment are so well commingled,
That they are not a pipe for fortune's finger
To sound what stop she please. Give me that man
That is not passion's slave, and I will wear him
In my heart's core, ay, in my heart of heart,
As I do thee.

My mind was a fog of confusion and pain. As the tears fell down my face, I found myself wondering whether he had suffered and was grateful to understand that he had been shot, not tortured or starved. Out of the fog came another image of Mathias sitting under the ancient olive tree beside the stream reciting Whitman to me:

Word over all, beautiful as the sky,
Beautiful that war and all its deeds of carnage must in time be utterly lost,
That the hands of the sisters Death and Night incessantly softly wash again,
and ever again, this soiled world;
For my enemy is dead, a man divine as myself is dead.

Her voice pulled me back into that dour room. She was asking me whether I was okay. She said I looked as white as chalk and whether I would like her to call for some water. I said no thank you and surreptitiously pinched my right hand with my left to try to get the feeling back into my body.

After a few moments, I asked her about their child. She said it was a girl and that she was taking care of her now. The poor child I thought. Cared for by a ghost in a ghost town.

She told me she was asleep for her nap and asked me if I wanted to see her. I said no, it'd be a pity to wake her. The real reason was, I couldn't. My heart had been broken so many different ways, I couldn't even imagine going through that.

I tried to leave, but she asked me if I wanted to see Mathias' paintings.

There was one of Thérèse, a full portrait of her standing in profile looking out a window. Beautiful. The other paintings were beautiful too, landscapes and cityscapes, but I couldn't take my eyes off the one of Thérèse. I must have stood there for a long time, lost in it, staring.

She gave the painting to me. A gift, she said, because I had always been so good to her son. Good to her son I thought. Her son, my brother, my friend.

I have the painting hanging in my little living room. Even now, when I look at it, it makes me smile and frown at the same time, the two of them, gone into forever.

PART SEVEN
INDIGO

MONDAY, JANUARY 9TH, 2017

CARCASSONNE HOSPITAL, FRANCE

SCOTLAND

After meeting Mathias' mother, I wanted to get as far away from Germany as possible. I got on a train west to Brussels and when I got there took another train to Calais. I kept taking trains so I wouldn't have to settle anywhere for too long. After more than a week, I ended up in Scotland looking down through the rain from Dunsinane Hill outside Perth thinking about the over 34,000 Scottish soldiers and nearly 6,000 civilians killed during the war. Mathias would never get to see the place, its wonderful views and wind-swept rains.

I had hired a car in Perth to get to Dunsinane, so I got back in and drove the hour and a half to Fortingall. The sun was setting when I got there and I was tired from all the travel. In seven months I had gone to seven countries, a reverse odyssey. I was exhausted, but instead of trying to get home, having so recently went back, I'd run away from it.

Dad had overheard myself and Mathias talking about going to Macbeth country one day when we were playing chess in our kitchen. Mathias was saying that as soon as he escaped his parents and got a job, other than his full-time one of working at not working, he was going to go to Dunsinane. He made me promise to go there with him. After Mathias had left and my mother went to bed, Dad talked to me about Scotland beside our huge stone Provençal fire.

"If you ever go to Scotland with Mathias, Zeke, you have to go to Fortingall. It's a very special place."

By the way Dad had said special I knew it had to be a place sacred to the Essenes.

"There's a yew tree there that's one of the oldest in the world. Beautiful beyond description."

"When were you there, Dad?"

"Just after I left Ireland. I made a pilgrimage of the cairns and megalithic tombs from Canfea on the Beara peninsula all the way up to the sixty-six sites in Donegal. I stopped at Newgrange, Knowth and Dowth towards the end, before I got the ferry over to Holyhead. Holyhead is on an island that used to be one of the most powerful places for the Druids. They called it Avalon. Avalon and Glastonbury were very sacred places until the Romans came and cut down all the sacred groves. I went to a lot of places before I landed in Provence, and I'm sure you and Mathias'll be as bad!"

"But why Fortingall?"

"Well, for a start, your great-grandfather was initiated there. But before that, and before our family was truly scattered to the ends of the world by the Church and its fanatical ferrets, there was one last meeting of all our family members at Fortingall. It was called the Great Gathering. It's a magical story. Not *Le Petit Prince* magical, but even more wonderful, alchemical."

"The Great Gathering?"

Dad paused so long I thought he wasn't going to continue. "It seems it is time that I pass it on to you then. Today is the Vernal Equinox and it has come to us naturally to talk of it. It is the time."

"Pass on what, Dad?"

"The tradition of our family, who you are, a seed of light. Those seeds of light were sown that day at the Great Gathering."

"What day?"

"The Summer Solstice of 55 AD."

"What? But that's nearly 2000 years ago, Dad? Are you trying to tell me our family tradition goes back nearly 2000 years?"

"Longer."

"But that's not possible."

"Everything is possible, Zeke. Anything impossible is just an imagining or illness of the minds of men."

"But..."

"Let me tell you about it all before you give me any more of your buts."

He lit a cigarette he had been rolling and threw the match into the fire. "Fortingall is a sacred place although not many people see it as such today. It's located in the very heart of Scotland, in Perthshire. The Fortingall yew itself is planted beside a modern day church, but as with most churches, the yew came first, planted on a sacred site of the Druids. The church masons knew these holy places and so built their churches beside them or on them."

He flicked some ash from his cigarette into the fire. "It was the return of the full moon and they came from everywhere, the Himalayas in India, Egypt, Palestine, Bugarach in France, Glastonbury in England, from all the Essene communities and monasteries all over the world. At Fortingall, the ways of the Essenes, the wisdom of the Druids and the Goddess all came together. They all met beyond the three rings of Fortingall in a pitched arbor attached to the long boughs of the great yew, living in a tented village with hundreds of fires around the great arbor, waiting for everyone to arrive. The unmarried ones used this waiting time to meet spouses from other communities and a lot of them were bound to each other in the Celtic tradition."

"What, they got married?"

"No, their hands were wrapped in tartan and scarves and cords, ceremonially bound for a year and a day. If, after that time had passed, the couple chose to continue being bound, then they had a hand-fasting for life. Alternatively, if they didn't, then the bond was broken, and they were free to find another spouse."

"But why did they go all the way to Scotland? Couldn't they have found somewhere more central?"

"No. The Romans were everywhere else."

Dad tossed the butt of his cigarette into the fire.

"And who were all these ancestors?"

He started to roll another cigarette. "All the Marys. Joseph of Arimathea. Jesus' grandmother. Yeshua himself."

"Yeshua?"

"That was what they called Jesus then. It was only later that he became known as the Christ, after the drama of his ritual crucifixion and resurrection, the repetition of the drama of Osiris and Isis, and before them of Mithras or Mithra."

"What? Jesus? What drama? You've never talked to me about a Jesus drama, Dad?"

He lit his cigarette and smiled. "That's because you weren't twenty-one. Let me finish and then we can talk about the Mithraic and Egyptian mysteries as well as other resurrections such as Puhua's in China."

He flicked some more ash in the fire. "Myriam of Tyana, Mahavatar Babaji and the then future Buddha, Maitreya, were also at the Great Gathering."

"But Dad, this isn't possible. This is..."

"Impossible?"

"Yes."

"As I said before, and as my father said to me, like I am saying to you today, everything is possible. Anything impossible is just an imagining of the minds of men."

He looked into the fire. "For three days they waited in meditation for Yeshua to arrive, fasting in silence. When he arrived our ancestors all filed into the arbor one by one, receiving blessings from Yeshua and the others, then taking their seats. Later they met the Sacred Ones, Babaji, Yeshua's guru, and Maitreya and experienced the opening of their energies to the Infinite Light."

"Jesus, Dad, this is all a bit, you know..."

"Crazy?"

"Yes."

"Well, many crazy things seem crazy at first until they become what we call normal. The first time you realized there were stars in the sky, you ran to me frightened that they were going to fall. The first time you saw a car you ran to me too, screaming. I could have told you what a car was before you saw it, and you would have thought I was crazy. Yet they exist. A hundred years ago they were an impossibility. We think everything we have never witnessed or seen with our own eyes is an imagining or madness of someone else, when in reality the stars sit in the skies and the cars pass by on the road."

"Yes, but to say we're the descendants of Jesus Christ is like saying we came from Mars. We can never know who we are descended from that far back. It's ridiculous."

He smiled. "That's exactly what I said to my father when I was your age. Look, the point is that whether you trust me or not, I am passing on to you what has been passed on to me. It's your choice to pass it on in the future, whether you trust it or not. All I can do is pass on to you the events as they were given to me. If you want me to tell you about Yeshua's drama and what happened to our family after the Romans set them adrift on the Mediterranean without an oar, then I can tell you, but if you don't, then so be it. None in our family has ever forced the information upon another, and indeed that is why I think it has lasted this long."

"But two thousand years, Dad? Wouldn't they think of writing it down at least?"

"They have and they have hidden the scrolls in monasteries and mountains, their whereabouts hidden and a lot of the time forgotten. But not even Peter's Catholic Church will stop them seeing the light of day. The seeds of light are many and their representatives in many forms."

"Where do you get these sayings from Dad?"

"I'm repeating them. The same way Homer recited *The Odyssey*. The same way the Druids could recite poetry and laws for days. The same way a *seanachai* could recite. The same way contemporary Serbian *guslars* such as Filip Višnjić could recite. It is an oral tradition. I tell you and you tell me until you know it by heart. Do you not find it unusual that you have this amazing gift to remember things, Zeke?"

"Yes, but that's just synesthesia."

"You can belittle your gift by trying to label it, but it's there and it's there for a reason. Yes, you will use it for music and you will use it to be of service in the future, but did you ever think it could have another use?"

"Well, no."

"Neither did I until my father asked me the same question."

"So tell me the story of Yeshua then."

"It's late. We have work in the morning. I'll tell you about Yeshua as we work tomorrow in the olive groves."

ROME

Postwar was a difficult time in Rome. I'm reminded of Roberto Rossellini's *Paisan*, because its six different parts really give you an idea of the Italy I arrived in with its destruction and bleakness, the exact opposite of what I had hoped to find after getting out of active service. I had hoped everyone would be feeling better because everywhere was liberated, but being liberated didn't mean everyone felt liberated, especially when nearly everything they'd ever owned or loved was gone.

I had gone to Scotland and Spain for Mathias, to see Dunsinane and Port Lligat, Lligat being where Dali created the paintings Mathias adored. Mathias had always wanted to see both places. He called Dali his inspired madman and Shakespeare his replacement for God. It was a good trip because on the way I got to stay in Collioure where Thérèse lived for a few years before her father moved them to Provence. Mathias and Thérèse spent their brief honeymoon there in *Les Templiers* hotel. As I walked on the street outside *Les Templiers*, I wondered whether Mathias would have ever become someone, like Matisse or Derain or Dali, and then I realized how pathetic the thought was. Mathias already was someone.

Why Rome? I wanted to go somewhere that had nothing to do

with anyone except me. I wanted to eat and eat and eat. I wanted to feed my soul with *carbonara* and pizza and homemade *fettuccine, gelato* and *biscoti.* I wanted to enjoy myself and, of course, I also wanted to visit the tomb of Marcus Aurelius. Dunsinane was Mathias' tomb to Shakespeare, mine was Hadrian's Mausoleum, or Castel Sant'Angelo as they call it now. It was the last place Marcus Aurelius' ashes rested before Alaric and his Visigoths scattered them to the wind. The Catholic Church owned the Mausoleum for centuries, changing its name to Castel Sant'Angelo, indeed using a lot of the Mausoleum's pillaged pillars to build St. Peter's.

Of course the Papal state also used Sant'Angelo as a prison for such "heretics" as Giordano Bruno who was imprisoned there for six years until they martyred him to the ideas of free thought and critical inquiry. The Church performed his and many other executions in the small interior square. The Castel is also where Mario Cavaradossi was imprisoned in Puccini's *Tosca,* Thérèse's favorite opera. It was while sitting in the *Caffetteria* of the modern day *Museo Nazionale di Castel Sant'Angelo* that I remembered Thérèse singing to myself and Mathias Cavaradossi's romanza *"E lucevan le stelle"* one summer night in the barn after making love:

The stars were shining,
And the earth was scented.
The gate of the garden creaked
And a footstep touched the sand...
Fragrant, she entered
And fell into my arms.

I thought of Mathias and Thérèse as I slowly stirred my coffee. It all felt like a dream from a long time ago.

Before I left Rome I hoped to find something wonderful in the church of Santa Maria Maddalena on the Via della Maddalena, some Essene clues to the tradition hidden in the architecture or statues. All I discovered was a weird Rococo facade and relics of Saint Camillus. Where was the joy of Mary Magdalene, the love, the compassion? Donatello's carved wooden statute of her as a penitent whore in Florence is anything but joyous and at the church of Santa Maria Maddalena she lewdly extends her leg, holding a giant cross as if it's a baby. It disgusted me. Where were all the great statutes to her as a woman instead of as a whore the scriptures have made her out to be? Where is the vision of God in all the things that Michelangelo reproduced in his David, or what Dante wrote about in his poetry:

Within its deep infinity I saw ingathered,
and bound by love in one volume,
the scattered leaves of all the universe.
The universal form of this complex whole I think that I saw,
Because as I say this I feel my joy increasing.

Her treatment reminds me of a simple, dilapidated statue in the old Cité of Carcassonne, the smiling Madonna. Not the one they call *The Smiling Madonna*, but the one in the same great room not too far away from it, the one that used to sit above the gates of the drawbridge into the Cité. I must have stood transfixed by joy in front of that statue for ten minutes. If the little town of Carcassonne can have a divine statue to the Madonna, then where are all the divine statues of Mary Magdalene, Jesus's first disciple, in Rome? A special woman so close to Jesus' whole ministry nowhere to be seen? But then, what can one expect, isn't this the case for his Mother, too? Didn't it take the Holy Catholic Church nearly five hundred years to facilitate a specific Marian liturgical system? Women have never been powerful players in Peter the Rock's church.

I left Rome disappointed and, frankly, bored by the grandiosity. I went there seeking some form of spiritual uplift, from the food, architecture and history, only to leave a little bit more depressed than when I'd arrived. Maybe this was because of the feeling that was in the city at the time, the same kind of feeling I'd experienced in Heidelberg, one of loneliness and sadness, a defeated city trying to raise its head from a recent ugly past.

DELOS AND MILOS

Dad used to tell me about the Greeks, how they believed Delos to be the center of the universe. He also said the temple of Isis was a place of pilgrimage for Essenes, that Isis rebalanced people's bad health. I sat in front of her temple meditating and reciting the *Tree of Life* for an hour, until I was interrupted by a rude Englishman who wanted to know whether I worked there. How he thought a strange man with his eyes closed, quietly chanting Hebrew on a Greek island in the middle of the Aegean, would be a tour guide goes beyond me.

Standing in front of the temple of Apollo, I imagined the *Know Thyself* inscription that used to be in the *pronaos* or forecourt of Delphi. It would have been just above my head. I tried to meditate on what it really meant to me, wishing that it and the island would somehow wake me up from my sadness. They didn't. What did I know about this Knower? How could the Knower be known to a man broken and botched by loss and depression? Was the psychologist James Hillman right when he said, it is impossible reflectively to know ourselves, that only God knows our real names. No, I thought, it couldn't be right, for aren't we all looking for the name we had before the world was made? And isn't that what keeps us going, trying to find out who we are? Isn't this what the Essene tradition teaches, what Jesus taught, what all the Buddhas have taught?

Even with all this existential anguish swirling around inside my head, I was relatively happy in Greece for, ever since reading *The Iliad* and *The Odyssey* as a teenager, I'd always wanted to visit. The names of the places and people and the marvelous feats long gone still fascinate me. The Spartans at the hot gates of Thermopylae. Pericles and Athens. The Parthenon with its crazy nine-is-to-four ratios that even explosives couldn't destroy. The many amazing oracles. The Agora. Diogenes in his bath telling Alexander the Great to get out of his sun. Phidias and all those statues. The Venus de Milo. Oh, how the list goes on.

After Delos I went to Milos to see where they'd found the Venus de Milo. Even though nearly all of Greece was evacuated in 1944, a few German units remained on Milos. They didn't surrender to the Greek Sacred Band until May 1945.

When I visited the little hidden fishing village of Klima, I fell in love. She was tall like Thérèse, but where Thérèse's hair was straw-colored, hers was as black as night. Her body seemed to flow through the street as if she'd stepped out of a different time. I wanted to hold her, touch her, tell her about everything I'd experienced. We never even talked, but we smiled at each other as she passed by on her way to her washing line overhanging the sea. She was singing what I found out later was a song called *Tzivaeri*, or *Τζιβαέρι:*

Ah! foreign lands enjoy
my treasure
My fragrant flower,
softly, softly, softly and humbly.
Ah! it was I who sent him,
my treasure,
of my own free will;
softly, softly, softly I tread the earth.
Ah! damn you foreign lands,
my treasure,

you, and your good things.
Softly, softly, softly and humbly.
Ah! you took my child,
my treasure
and you made him your own;
softly, softly, softly I tread the earth.

I felt like Odysseus, an interloper in that wonderful little village where it seemed no foreigners had been for decades, listening to a Nausicaa, a woman I would never know except for those few minutes of song.

When she left and went into one of the colorful little houses, I watched her washing waving in the wind and remembered Mathias reading me Keats in Alphonse's café:

O Attic shape! Fair attitude! With breed
Of marble men and maidens overwrought,
With forest branches and the trodden weed;
Thou silent form, dost tease us out of thought
As doth eternity. Cold Pastoral!
When old age shall this generation waste,
Thou shalt remain in midst of other woe
Than ours, a friend of man to whom thou say'st
'Beauty is truth, truth beauty, – that is all
Ye know on earth, and all ye need to know.'

I remember wondering if those isolated villagers even knew about the war we'd waged all over the rest of Europe. And if they did, I doubted very much if they thought about it then, as they hauled their tiny boats out the little doors of their colorful houses and into the wine dark sea.

MECCA

Italy and Greece were dreams of mine. Mecca was Yusuf's. The way my mind was working at the time I thought it only natural to go there next. It was the *Hajj* or pilgrimage period, the twelfth Muslim lunar month of *Dhu al-Hijjah*. Yes, I knew that it was an imitation by Mohammedans of the pilgrimages of the Ishmaelites, but that didn't make it any less significant to me. The way I saw it, pilgrimages had their way of purifying the soul which therapists never could. I had seen enough of them after the war to know. Also, what if Yusuf had never made it even though I was sure he had? No. Marcus Aurelius, Delos and Fortingall had had their day. Now it was time to pay respect to the divine love of all the Sufis and the man I'd loved like a father.

When I arrived in Mecca they questioned me about my faith. My face is as white as snow and I have never worn a beard. When they asked me was I Muslim, I said yes. Non-Muslims are banned and I can understand why. First, it is written in *The Qur'an* that only believers can enter. Secondly, over the years they must have had any number of crazy people pointing fingers and ogling the believers. More importantly, Mecca was desecrated at one stage. And yes, numbers are a problem too. Most Saudis who live in or near

Mecca sublet their homes for the month to get away from the crowds.

I wasn't a believer, but I respected the believers and the sanctuary. I had a father who had taught me everything one needed to know about being a good Muslim. I quoted them their doctrine in Arabic and asked them whether they wanted the verse and chapter or perhaps a translation into English. The old bearded man with twisted toes who was questioning me was more confused than shocked. He was unable to understand how I could quote him obscure sections of *The Qur'an* he probably didn't know himself. I confused him even more by informing him that you don't have to be Jewish to visit the Western Wall, Catholic to go to the Vatican, Buddhist to attend a gathering with the Dalai Lama. I also asked him why the house of Abu Jahal, one of Islam's great defenders, had been demolished and replaced by public toilets? Why has the house where Muhammad was probably born been demolished and made into a library? He said nothing. He let me pass, a meek smile on his face.

I walked around the *Kaaba* seven times, the sun making me sweat as I'd never done before, the immense throng of people in the Al-Masjid al-Harām creating a sauna-esque experience. I did what Yusuf had explained was to be done, but instead of praying I remembered. I remembered one of the many special moments with Yusuf. We were lying on our backs on a jostling trailer-full of hay, Dad up front leading Moses home.

"You know, Montaigne had a very good way of explaining it. He said: *The world always looks outward, I turn my gaze inward; there I fix it, and there I keep it busy. Everyone looks before him; I look within. I have no business but with myself.* He knew. That is knowing, not knowledge, not the *Tree of Knowledge* with its poisonous apples of philosophy that turned Adam from a mystic into a scientist."

"When did you read Montaigne, Yusuf?"

"The same time you read. When I wasn't working."

"Yes, but where did you get it from?"

"Your father of course. We swap books with each other in the evenings."

"But I thought..."

"Just because a man comes from the desert doesn't mean he only reads things from the desert, Zeke. There is more to the world than deserts. There is more to a man than his country or religion. Just because I come from a Muslim country doesn't mean I'm a Muslim. Just because..."

"Yes, yes, I know! I just always thought you were reading Sufi poetry and *The Qur'an*."

He laughed. "And so, do you only read Marcus Aurelius?"

"No."

"And why?"

"Because I love lots of different types of books."

"Well, I am the same. I love lots of different types of books too. I have read *The Bible* and the *Tao Te Ching* and the *Upanishads* and *The Bhagavad Gita*. I am not shackled by one tradition! Oh, no! I love life too much for that! Every tradition is a vast expanse and I am vast, vast as the ocean!"

He smiled and rubbed the top of my head with his hand.

"You're crazy!"

"Well, like your father says: *It takes one to know one*." He laughed again. "And anyway, I am a very bad Muslim. Instead of praying five times a day to the *Kabba*, I meditate when I get up in the morning and just before I go to bed at night. I don't fast during Ramadan. Now I fast the Essene way, only at the full and new moons. Yes, I give to the poor when the opportunity presents itself, but I still haven't been to Mecca to touch the Kaaba. But then *The Qur'an* says this is not obligatory, just a request."

"Seems like there's a lot of things you have to do. I wouldn't be able to pray even once a day!"

He laughed. "You'd have to, if you came from a strict Muslim family like I did. But you know as well as I do where the real truth is."

"*An al Haq!*" I said.

"Yes! *An al Haq*! I am the Truth! Well done, Zeke. You have a beautiful memory, but do you have a great one? Who said it?"

"Mansur Hallaj."

He sat up. "Very good! You see. Just like Montaigne. He looked within. Mansur Hallaj had no other business but with himself. He was not a this or a that religion:

My heart has become capable of every form:
it is a pasture for gazelles and a convent for Christian monks,
And a temple for idols and the pilgrim's Kaaba and the tables of the Torah and the book of The Qur'an.
I follow the religion of Love: whatever way Love's camels take,
that is my religion and my faith.

He placed his right hand over his heart. "Mecca is in here, in my heart. That's where I visit when I need to go to Mecca."

"Are you ever going to go, Yusuf?"

"I don't know. Let's see if it is written."

He lay back down on the hay and we looked up at the branches and leaves of the plane trees moving by above our heads.

THE TREE OF LIFE

I was sitting waiting for the dawn on the northwestern end of the Mount Carmel mountain range in Israel. It was July 16th, 1946 the feast day of Our Lady of Mount Carmel. In Hebrew they call those mountains *Har ha Karmell,* God's vineyard. Below me birds were singing in the oak, pine, laurel and olive trees. I looked out towards the Jezreel Valley still in darkness, the darkness just before the sun's light comes up to illuminate everything. Nothing was moving.

I thought of the *Isa Upanishad* as I waited to sing *The Tree of Life*:

O life-giving sun, off-spring of the Lord of creation, solitary seer of heaven!
Spread thy light and withdraw thy blinding splendor that I may behold thy radiant form:
that Spirit far away within thee is my own inmost Spirit.

Then I remembered Krishna's words in the *Bhagavad Gita*:

There is a tree, the tree of Transmigration, the Asvattha tree everlasting.
Its roots are above in the Highest, and its branches are here below.
Its leaves are sacred songs, and he who knows them knows the Vedas.

I thought of Dad because I'd just finished reading an article about a newly found gospel, *The Gospel of Thomas*, the night before. The *Gospel* had been found in Egypt in December of 1945. I smiled. Dad would have anticipated reading a living gospel with as much joy as me, as opposed to an interpretation of one. He used to always tell me he didn't interpret the sayings of Jesus as *The Bible* does. Instead, he felt them. You can only feel the truth, he often said, you can't tell someone how to understand it, how to interpret it.

I know the kinds of questions he would have asked about *The Gospel*'s discovery. He would have asked me, did I think it a coincidence and luck that it had been found in the month in which the world celebrates the birth of Jesus, after the end of another horrific World War? Or whether it was *unusual* when Muhammed edh-Dhib broke the sealed jar with his mattock, after finding it at the foot of the Jabal al-Tarif, that an indescribable golden substance flew out of it and disappeared into the air? Oh yes, of course, Dad would have teased, it was probably just the papyrus fragments glistening in the sun! Nothing magical or alchemical! No, there's nothing mystical or alchemical under the sun!

Of course, before the arrival of *The Gospel of Thomas* only scattered statements from the church fathers referred to something of that name. Over seventy years on, I have read and re-read the various texts and translations of the *Gospel*, and can say that not only is *The Bible*'s interpretation of Jesus' sayings weak and misleading, but they pale in comparison to the wonderful *Gospel of Thomas* and its lack of intense fear-mongering and apocalyptic proclamations. In *Thomas*' gospel there are no end times, only the transformation of time by acknowledging right now, this moment. It is a Jesus that tries to wake us up to that reality by any means possible, and it's beautiful.

Why would the Church want to control the interpretation of Jesus' sayings? And another question: isn't it a bit insane that the *earliest* records of the Passion of Jesus, *The Gospel of Mark*, dates from 40 years after the event? If I were a journalist today, and an editor for a reputable newspaper, say *The New York Times*, wanted me to report on a crucifixion in downtown Jerusalem from 40 years ago, and I tried to write an article about it based on memory and hearsay, would they publish it? Even the *Pseudo-Ezekiel* scroll wasn't published until 2001. Why? Sixty years to translate something? Also, why is Thomas' account two hundred years older than the other scrolls?

Dad taught me to think like this, with awareness, but what he also taught me was about all the places associated with the *Tree of Life*. He told me how that mountain in Israel, Carmel, had been a sacred mountain to us, the Essene, for millennia. How Dad would have loved to visit Carmel. I took out the piece of brown scapular in a leather pouch worn around my neck which Dad had given me when I was twenty-one, a relic which has been passed down in our family for centuries because it came from Mary Magdalene's red robe. I hid it in our barn before leaving for the war and told Dad where it was. He wrote to his brother Gabriel in Ireland telling him where to find it, if we didn't come back from the war. It was still there when I went back to read Thérèse's letters. Like Dad, when it is time, I too will entrust it to one of my family initiated into the *Tree of Life*.

Dad initiated me into the *Tree of Life* at the age of seven by the stream that ran though our farm.

"The *Tree of Life* is like this tree, Zeke," he said and placed his hand on the huge olive tree we sat under. "Its roots stretch into the ground beneath us, into Mother Earth, and its leaves reach for the stars. It draws its source from these two things, its Mother life-giver below us and its Mother Father creator above us. Do you understand?"

"Yes. You've told me this already, Dad."

He smiled. "I know, I know. I just want to make sure you understand. It is important to understand things deeply, not to just learn them off. Learning off is not knowledge. That is intellect, being an intellectual. Real intelligence is when you *know* deep inside you."

"You've told me all that before too, Dad."

He laughed. "Yes. Okay! It's just that what I am about to tell you is something my father taught me when I was your age and his father taught him and his father taught him. It is a tradition and it is sacred to our family. Try to listen to what I say. If you don't completely understand me, don't worry. We have a lifetime to talk about it."

He lit one of his roll-ups and smiled. "We are a family that was seeded from a great Essene family in Mount Carmel in Israel many, many centuries ago, Zeke. Later you will read of an Essene settlement at Qumran in the works of Pliny the Elder, Josephus, and Philo, but we were not them. What everyone misunderstands about the Essenes is that we were many different communities. Our community was no way as distant to the outside world as those at Qumran, but that's not what's important. What is important is that you know your ancestors. They shared everything they had. They had no slaves, lived by a solar calendar not a lunar one like their contemporaries. Above all, they had very deep spiritual teachings and initiations like the one we are about to enact, one which Jesus, as an Essene teacher, taught others too. All initiations are to open your own inner Christ, your own inner Buddha nature. When Peter's Christianity came, our teachings and rituals were threatened. We were ostracized because we didn't follow his way, the way of the Church."

"What's ostracism, Dad?"

"When someone is different than the general populace, they try to put them in a box, they try to imprison them with a label so that they can throw them out of the community."

"Like Judas?"

"Exactly!"

He grabbed my shoulders in both his hands. "Yes, exactly like our Judas! You are a very smart boy! You make me very proud."

"Why? What is so smart?"

"Because your intuition told you the truth. Your intuition, the teacher from within you, told you that it was just like Judas. I gave Judas his name out of affection, not malice, because he always escapes."

"What's malice?"

"When you are mean to someone else. A lot of people have felt malicious to Judas because he is so different. And this is because he is the most different ram we have. All the other rams gang up on him. Right?"

"Yes, he's crazy. He's always escaping."

"Exactly. So, our family was like Judas. We kept escaping from the rest of the sheep, from the religions of the world. We lived by our own religion, one that comes from inside, from your connection as God, to the presence of God all around us. The church doesn't like this because it means we do not believe in a God that controls us. We do not trust that God. We trust ourselves. Do you understand, Zeke?"

"Yes. God is in everything. I am God. You are God. Judas is God. This tree is God."

He smiled and cupped his hand on my cheek. "You are a far brighter child than I ever was, you know that?"

He closed his eyes and then opened them again slowly. "You cannot tell anyone what I am going to tell you, Zeke. This tradition is a secret. It has to stay in our family. Otherwise people, priests, neighbors, everyone, will treat you the way Monsieur Ducon treated Judas."

"What, they'll hit me?"

"No, that's not what I meant. No, they will try to hurt you. They will try to put you in a pen like the one Monsieur Ducon said Judas should be in."

"But that's why we let him run around the farm, Dad. Because he will escape again anyway. And he always jumps back in to be with the other sheep when he wants to play with them!"

Dad started to laugh out loud. He laughed for a long time, tears falling onto his cheeks. "How observant you are! Do you know that the *serv* in observe comes from minding sheep?"

"No."

"You have me going off on tangents now. Anyway it does. *Serv* means to mind sheep. Judas is a sheep."

"What's a tangent, Dad?"

"Something that has nothing to do with what a person was saying before."

"What you said had nothing to do with what you said before?"

"Yes, no. Oh, Lord. This was a lot easier for my father."

"Why?"

"Because I didn't ask so many questions!"

"Is asking questions bad?"

"No! Yes." He shook his head. "Jesus, what kind of a life are you going to have? I've never met anyone like you, Zeke. You know that?"

"And I've never met anyone like you, Dad."

He smiled again. "Amazing. Simply amazing. What I wouldn't give to see what you get up to in the distant future." He shook his head again from side to side.

"So, first we have to give thanks." He closed his eyes again. "Close your eyes and in your mind, the heart of your mind, give thanks for what I am about to give you."

I closed my eyes and concentrated and gave thanks as Dad had asked. When I opened my eyes he was looking deep into them. Then he reached down into the stream and ladled some water in his hands. He closed his eyes for a moment until a shiver went through his body. He opened his eyes and standing over me he put his hands on the crown of my head.

"Now, you have to ask me to pass on the tradition to you. This is your choice, Zeke. If you don't want me to pass it on to you, then say it now and we can stop all this and go back to our apple-picking. It's your choice."

"No. I want to do it, Dad." I closed my eyes. "Please give it to me."

Water trickled onto the top of my head and Dad spoke. "These are the garments of the King. May they help you see the many names and faces of the King."

A sensation went from the crown of my head all the way to the base of my spine. In my mind's eye I could see a white circular light.

"These are the roots of the world. These roots run into the sky, their leaves running down into the earth."

He lifted his hands and then put them back on the crown of my head. "This is *Keter*, the unqualified absolute, the grace of the present time, the crown of God, where he manifests, no identity, undefined, the vanishing point of heaven and earth."

He placed his hands on my forehead. "This is *Binah* and *Hokhmah*, the Divine mother, where the energy of the Divine forms before form, the womb and the wisdom, the path to service."

His hands moved down to my throat, rested for a moment there and then moved to my arms. "This is *Gevurah* and *Hesed*, the arms of balance, the purified energy of judgment and love and mercy."

He moved his hands down to the center of my chest, one on my back, the other on my front. "This is *Tif'eret*, the heart, the trunk of the tree, the sound of creation, the marriage of compassion and forgiveness, the Divine position of love."

His hands descended to either side of my solar plexus. "This is *Hod* and *Nezah*, legs of prophesy, the energy of individuality, the majesty and endurance of the Divine, the shining jewel of your city."

He took a deep breath and guided his hands down either side of my navel. "This is *Yesod*, the force of the Divine, the Righteous One, the foundation of Her special abode, the host of God."

He inhaled long and deep and placed his hands on either side of my hips. "This is *Shekhinah*, our community, our roots, the Goddess that balances Yesod, the Rose, the Garden of Eden, the Moon, the earth Herself, the all as one."

For a few moments he stood in front of me with his hands closed in front of his heart much like Rodin's *Cathedral*. Then he inhaled and led his hands back to the crown of my head and after a time said: "Whoever discovers the interpretation of these truths will not taste death. And so it is. So be it."

For the next year Dad would bring me to the olive tree beside the stream every Saturday and go through the *Tree of Life* with me. Then, on my eighth birthday, it was my turn. I had sat down under the tree expecting him to bless me with water from the stream again, but he didn't.

"This time it is you who must bless me, Zeke."

I leant down into the stream and cupped up some water into my little hands and blessed him the way he had taught me.

Years later, I taught the same *Tree of Life* tradition to my daughters under the same olive tree when they were seven. The devastating winter of 1956 had killed all the olive trees in Aramon except that ancient tree beside the stream. Still, my daughter's hearts and mine were not present. I was too obsessed with being the perfect doctor to pay proper attention to what was needed on those days of initiation. Later, I tried to make up for it. When Daniel was seven, I went to my daughter Celine's house to ask her if I could bring him to the tree to continue the tradition. She closed the door in my face. The following week I went back to ask her again. Again she slammed the door. The third time I tried to call her. She hung up. Maybe someday Daniel, or his children, will start the tradition again. Maybe someday they'll read these words and be inspired to speak their truth to the truth that surrounds us all.

When I was fourteen, Dad and I sat under the same olive tree for another *Tree of Life* initiation, but whereas before it was to welcome me into the tribe of the Essene, this was to welcome me into the tribe of men.

I lay on the ground and recited the *Tree of Life* seven times, laying my hands on the areas of my body each part related to. When I was finished, I washed my whole body in the cold stream with an ointment Dad had made of Camargue salt and olive oil harvested from the tree we were under. After drying myself I sealed each area on my body with apple cider vinegar made from the apples on our *mas*.

When I had finished and dressed, Dad anointed my feet and head with the ointment. Then he moved his hands slowly down my body as he spoke. "You are now no longer a child of seven days. You are no longer half a man of seven years. Seven times the body will change, every seven years until you are that man you should be completely." I could feel energy, heat, flowing into me from his hands even though he wasn't touching me. "You are now a man who stands on fourteen years, anointed. Many of the first will be last and will become a single one." He smiled and kissed me on the forehead. "It's done. What's done cannot be undone. Go in peace to love and serve!"

The sun started to come up on the horizon beyond Mount Carmel. I closed my eyes and sang the *Tree of Life.* The first time I recited it as a prayer for all of the Jews I'd met in the camps, all the ones who never left and for all the people who'd died in the war: Dad, Alphonse from the café, Maurice, all those killed. The second time I sang it, I prayed for Mathias and that wonderful friendship we'd shared. The third time I sang for Thérèse and Julie and Nausicaa for confirming all that is beautiful about love to me. The fourth time I sang it for all the people who love the Divine, the Sufis, Yusuf, Tara, Jesus, all the Buddhas. The fifth time I sang it for all the people who changed the world in some good way, Gandhi, Martin Luther King. The sixth time I sang it for all the priests and holy people who are of service in truth, honoring those they serve with love and compassion, not power and delusion. And finally, the seventh time I sang the *Tree of Life,* I sang it for everything that is, for the present moment, for the moment I sang it, this very moment, now.

When I opened my eyes the sun was sitting on the horizon, smiling.

THE HIMALAYAS

We were meditating when it came up and into me in an all-consuming fire. The faces of the people I'd killed. Hermann Schmidt. The officers. The others. They raced across my mind's eye in a rage, a riot of emotion. Then, the Capos and fore-men. Finally, the Gestapo. Their faces. Their smiles. The hatred and enjoyment they took in pushing my head down into that water. The heat inside me felt like it was burning me alive. The pain was beyond pain, cataclysmic, incandescent.

Tara knew, even though she still had her eyes closed. Had it been my breathing? My *dhoti* drenched in sweat? No. I knew better than that by then.

She rested her hand gently on my knee and said, "It is time to release it, Ezekiel. It is time."

I opened my eyes. The anger and hatred, I was drowning in it.

"Close your eyes, Ezekiel. Meditate on it. Go into it."

Dad came into my head, the time he told me about my mother, what she had gone through, about forgiveness. His smiling face appeared in front of me. His words came to me again, *Forgiveness is far more powerful than any jail. It is a part of the hidden power within humans. Pain can be turned into something meaningful with forgiveness. Punishment never gets a person to grow, forgiveness does.* I found myself praying. I sat there praying that the anger and hatred would leave me. I prayed for the joy of my childhood to return. For days, with my eyes closed and my heart open, I prayed inside myself to forgive. I thought the *baignoire* had been painful? Sitting there that day, meditating for eight hours, and in the days that followed were more painful than anything I endured at the hands of the Nazis. The pain was deep inside me, but the more I watched it and witnessed it and accepted it in my body, the more it started to fade. Like a snowflake on a hot plate my hatred and anger evaporated. My prayers started to be answered.

What I have taken with me from India is not Tara's wisdom and words but her presence and practice, that practice that allowed me to heal. Her presence, meditating, was wonderfully powerful. There are *sādhus* and there are *sādhus.* As she said to me once when the other three *sādhakas* were gardening:

"As the Buddha said: *Someone may recite much of the texts, but if he does not practice them, such a heedless person is like the herdsman who only counts the cows of others: he does not enjoy the rewards of the life of a truth seeker.* Religions are sectarian, Ezekiel. They are the clouds in the sky, cyclical, coming and going. The technique of meditation is universal. It is the sky, the uncreated that your religions say their God created. When God created the world was there sky? If there was no space, then where did he create the world, to put somewhere? It would be ridiculous to say God created space when he would need space to exist in the first place. Space comes before God."

She closed her deep blue eyes, smiled, and then opened them again. "You in the West look to the clouds. We in the East look to the sky. We do this by being mindful, by meditating. Others call it *zazen.* It is like the yoga postures of Patanjali, it is a method. It is the Kriya yoga I have taught you from Mahavatar Babaji. It is scientific, not belief based. Distrust beliefs. This is why it works and why religions do not. Religions create the wheel of suffering. The only religious science is meditation. It gives you results. These results are based on your own personal experience of meditating. The peace you receive after you meditate releases you from the illusion, the madness of the ego, the I, which wants you to continue negative reactions to others and the world around you. It teaches positive action, responding with a balanced mind that observes sensations without craving or aversion.

Being alone is very different from being lonely. Being alone is positive, a restorative state of mind. Loneliness is to crave to be with another. This relationship I have with you Ezekiel, it brings me happiness. We are alone together, multiplying that positive energy, not merely adding it together. Loneliness is the opposite, negatively multiplying craving. If I were to feel out of balance in this relationship, I would meditate and return to you fresh, alive, balanced. But then even this is not true. I used myself as an example, but I'm not a good example. People hate others but I cannot hate anymore. I don't love people the way you do. I am love. Everything around me is love. It is natural, like breathing. So I don't need to meditate to return to balance. I cannot hate anymore. I cannot even hate your devil. It is not a question of a devil. I simply cannot hate. It has disappeared..."

I had woken up in a ditch three months earlier in the Valley of Flowers. I'd been robbed, beaten and left for dead in that ditch while searching what seemed the whole mountain range for my teacher, a woman who has been called Mataji, Annai and Tara. My leg was a mess but I was still able to walk, and I vowed I was going to walk all the way back to France if I had to. India, I had let go of the whole enterprise.

A month before I had arrived in Badrinath in the western Himalayas, in the northern part of India called Uttarakhand, the Land of Gods, or as it was known then, Uttaranchal. I'd walked everywhere. Vasudhara Falls, Vyasa Gufa, Neelakantan Peak, Badrinath Temple, the hot springs bathing ghat.

It happened when I was walking back from unsuccessfully trying to find Santopanth Tal, a wonderful green lake surrounded by mountains on all sides an American had told me about. I was hit from behind. I know for a fact that it wasn't anyone local. The Mongolian villagers of Mana, not far from Badrinath, were not the kind of people to rob tourists. Anyway, whoever it was, that blow to the back of my head was the best thing that ever happened to me. It made me give up and, as Tara would say to me later, it is only by giving up that we can give in.

India was a crazy place in the forties. After over-eating in Italy, I under-ate in India. I had no choice. Dreaming of a Roman *gelata*, I had made the mistake of trying to reinvent the same experience in demonically hot Jaipur. I needed something to cool me down. I would have been better off trying to eat some of the explosives the Turks blew the Parthenon up with. I was in bed for ten days, deluded out of my brain, my body releasing stuff I had never put into it. Pascale, who lives in the woods the next village above mine, used to go to India every third winter. She says it's still as crazy today. Eleven-hour waits for a train that has people sitting on the roofs and chickens in the carriages. Queues of two days to get your passport stamped. Sacred cows eating plastic in the street, getting in the way of the manic traffic. Naked Jaina monks. Children constantly begging for money. Horns honking. Scooters buzzing. Music blaring. And people, people everywhere. Everywhere. The place is mayhem.

I started my walk to find somewhere I could get my bank to wire me money. I was going home. As I walked the dusty path back towards a village, any village, dejected and exhausted, I heard quick steps behind me. For a moment I thought I was going to get mugged again, but then I let go of that too. Frankly I didn't care. What more could they rob from me anyway? The only thing I had left was my passport and the clothes on my back, literally. Before they left me in the ditch they'd even taken my shoes and socks.

The steps caught up with me and then I spotted him, a little boy I'd talked to weeks before outside Badrinath Temple. He pulled at my trousers. I stopped. What? I said in English, expecting him to ask me for money.

"My master, she want talk to you."

"Your master? You mean your mother?"

"No. She not my mother, but yes she my Mother too. She the Master you look for."

After three months of talking to the natives I'd had enough, even if this kid seemed like a legitimate human being. I kept walking.

Again, the pulling on my trousers.

"Sir, this is truth. She said you would not want come."

I stopped again. "And what else did your master say?"

"When the student is ready, the master will appear."

I nearly hit the kid. How many times had I heard that one. "Any more clichés for me?"

"She said, when he get angry with 'master will appear' response tell him there is nothing original under the sun, and that clichés are only clichés because they tell truth."

His words made me sit down on the dirt road. Now I'd heard it all. I looked at him smiling above me, the sun behind his back setting between two mountains.

"How far?"

"One hour as walking."

"Fine," I said. What had I got to lose except my sanity, not that I'd been very fond of that back then anyway.

"You come?"

"Yes. I come."

He was already walking. I limped along and tried to keep up with him. He might have been eight or so but he walked faster than any eight-year old I'd ever met. That hour was all uphill, climbing.

"What, does she live in a cave?" I said, half way up a cliff face, my damaged leg killing me.

"Yes, sir, underground cave, but most times in cave near to ground when she giving of *darshan* and teachings."

Great, I thought, they'll kill me and throw me to any one of the endangered animals of the Valley of Flowers, an Asiatic black bear, a snow leopard, maybe even a brown bear.

"Does it have electricity this cave?"

"Electricity, sir?"

Conversation now futile, I endured the pain and climbed the rest of the cliff not daring to look back down.

Three hours later, when we finally got to the top, I was

destroyed. I collapsed about a hundred yards from the edge, spread out on my back in a human cross. It was like being in the camps again, my energy depleted, striving to breathe. I found myself asking myself the question, Why? Why are you at the top of this godforsaken mountain when you could be back in France with your electricity and indoor plumbing and water that doesn't make you sick in bed for ten days?

"Welcome," she said, her palms together in that Indian way, a greeting I later learnt is a gesture to the person being welcomed, the God in the welcomer, welcoming the God within the welcomed.

I opened my eyes wider. She was standing facing east, at the entrance to her cave. A white cotton shawl that extended to her feet covered her head. On her feet were shoes made of cloth interwoven with indigo seisel on the bottom, much like the *espradrilles* we wore back in Provence. She seemed to be about thirty-five, but she could have been a lot older or younger. I had no idea. There was this lovely glow around her which I thought was because of the sun, but as I found out later it had nothing to do with the sun. I began to feel lighter, happier, just lying there looking at her. The only time I have ever felt that same presence is around people just before they die, or when I went to see the Dalai Lama in Toulouse. I asked her about it a week after being there.

"Are you enlightened, Tara?" She was weeding her small garden.

"Why do you ask?"

"Because everyone here says you are. They all call you master and teacher, and saint. I never thought of an enlightened person as weeding gardens or cleaning caves or putting poultices on injured legs like you did for me that first day."

She sat up and put the weeds in her hand on the ground beside her. "I will tell you a story. Maybe it will help you?"

"Okay."

"There was once a man who came to find a very famous Zen monk in China. This monk was enlightened and the man wanted to be enlightened too. So he went to the mountain where the monk lived and when he arrived he met an old man carrying a bucket of water from the stream. He said to the old man 'I have come to find the enlightened monk who lives on this mountain. Can you tell me where he is?' The monk put down his bucket and told the man that he was the monk. The man laughed. He couldn't believe him. So he went up the mountain to the monastery and he met more monks and he asked them where their master was. They pointed to the old man carrying the water up the hill into the monastery. The man still couldn't believe it. So, he ran after the old man with his buckets of water and said to him: 'How can you be enlightened? Masters do not carry buckets of water from the stream!" The old man smiled and said: 'Before enlightenment I carried my buckets of water from the stream. After enlightenment I carry my buckets from the stream.'"

She started to weed her tomatoes again. "It is a beautiful story, is it not?" she said.

"Yes. So you're saying the teaching, the master, is in the actions, what St. Thérèse of Avila calls our 'works'?"

She sat up again. "Yes and no. I do not talk of saints. Your churches make saints of people. I do not make saints. Your St. Thérèse was a holy woman with beautiful things to say, but I do not say beautiful things. I do not teach you anything. I am no sage or saint. We teach each other. We are all each other's teachers. We are all lessons to each other. Everyone in your life is a lesson."

She smiled. "I will tell you another story, Ezekiel." She put down her weeds again and rested her upturned hands on top of one another. "The Buddha had spent many years visiting saints and sages, fasting and doing yoga and many other things. He had grown very frail. One day he was trying to cross the Niranjana, a shallow river, and because he was so weak he couldn't do it. He had to grab the root of a tree to save himself. Holding onto that root he came to a great realization. He realized he had been wasting his time with sages and saints. There he was in a shallow river about to die because of all that he had been taught. After a long time, he eventually pulled himself out of the river and sat underneath a tree. That night he slept so well. He had given up all effort. No yoga postures, no sages or saints or priests to meet the next day. For the first time in many years he was free and the next morning as the last star faded in the full moon sky Siddhartha disappeared and the Buddha appeared." She started to weed her tomatoes again.

"But if that's how the Buddha became enlightened, then that means there's no need for Buddhist monks and priests? Then is there a use for religion and exercises and rituals and prayers and teachers? Why practice a religion just so that you can let go of it all to realize yourself?"

Tara sat up, her face radiant. "Exactly!" she said. She put her palms together over her chest and bowed to me. "Now, now you are seeing things as they are."

She started to weed again. As I stood watching her, I thought of Thérèse and Mathias and all that I'd learned from them, all the lessons and talks about religion and books and meaning. How I wished they had been there to meet and listen to Tara. How they would have loved the experience. Then I remembered I wouldn't have been in Tara's garden if I hadn't gone to the Himalayas because of what had happened to them. They'd planned on going to the Himalayas for their honeymoon after Mathias' first exhibition had shown in Heidelberg. Again they had helped me without my knowing it, helping me find myself when I didn't know what the truth was anymore, when I was still looking for it, when I was still lost, when *I was living and partly living,* and oh, how I wanted to start living again.

The first day I went to sit with Tara she was down beside the little river the other side of the cave. She smiled at me. Just as she was about to say something to me, a bird started singing in the neem tree above us. When the bird rested, she looked at me and said: "That is our talk for today." And that was when I understood I had to open my ears to everything around me as I'd done in the camps. I had to open my ears to the song of everything around me and be grateful and joyful for it all. I remembered what Thérèse had said about the Garden of Eden and how it was Nature as corruption. When I really started to listen to the songs of the birds again, I realized I wasn't cut off from the source of all life at all. It was right there all the time.

Just before Mathias married Thérèse he invited me to India with them. Maybe he didn't want me to feel left out. No. He was too enthusiastic and generous. He really just wanted to share the experience with us both, with Thérèse and me.

"Let's go to India, Zeke. They know how to live there. They're more alive than anywhere else on the planet. All the books say it. There's no meaning to life here as we've been force-fed it, like Henri's *gave* geese. Let's go live and really have fun! The Himalayas, now that would be an experience, the real experience of being alive! It'll be wonderful!"

Wonderful. I wanted things to be wonder-full again. I wanted my friend back like nothing I'd ever wanted in this life. In the camps another thing that had kept me alive was the image of us sitting in some French café again, outside Avignon, drinking cheap wine and talking about Shakespeare and Marcus Aurelius and how horrible brothels are.

Now I really know why I left. Not because of Mathias. No. I left to try to understand my suffering. I wanted to open my mind to the great loneliness of the sages of the caves of the Himalayas, and evolve and dance again, not theologize all that I'd been through. I wanted to grow, to evolve.

"Can't we live without suffering, Tara?"

She put down the knife she was chopping a tomato with. "Suffering is always here, Ezekiel. The tomato suffers when I cut it. Everything suffers. If we cannot accept the suffering in our lives, then we are not living. Joy is the other side of suffering. They are one. There is no secret here. The Buddha told us Life is suffering. Jesus said it too. Blessed is the man who has suffered; he has found life. This is not religion. These are the words of enlightened beings. Jesus and the Buddha are well known examples of the East and West and they say the same thing. There have been many Buddhas before and after Gutama and Jesus. Accept suffering into your life and you accept joy into it too, like they did. This is something to meditate on. Meditate on your suffering and you will become a real saint, not one of these saints who are poster people for suffering. Real saints never show their suffering because they have meditated upon it and gone beyond it into a blissful joy, a lightness in their soul, away from the complaining mind. Why complain? Everyone else is suffering too. They do not need to hear about your suffering as well. They are caught in the suffering of pleasure and happiness when they could discover the truth, *sat*, your eternal reality and the light of consciousness and go even deeper inside to *anand*, bliss."

She smiled and picked up the knife to continue chopping.

Three months later I brought Tara Psalm 23. A friend, another Auschwitz survivor, had made this copy for me after the War. The one Dad had given me had been taken from me in the POW camp. The friend was one of my many patients from the camp. I had taught him the psalm.

"Ah, Psalm 23." She raised her hands laughing. "Ah, yes, this one is beautiful, very beautiful."

"You know it?"

"As the Americans say, does a bear shit in the woods?"

I laughed. Then I told her about the story of the platoon of soldiers.

"Why of course. It is spiritual logic. It is a mantra. It is a mantra of protection that is far older than your Judeo-Christian traditions. It actually comes out of the Egyptian tradition. It is the most irreligious psalm there is. That is why it is so beautiful. It is about connection, to your soul, your higher soul."

"How?"

"This," she tapped the paper gently with her spindly fingers, "is not a prayer to something outside of you. It is a prayer to another dimension of you, which is outside your idea of time and space, a magical place, alchemical, what some would call the fifth dimension. You can be there right now of course. It is not necessary to die. That is the beautiful thing of this psalm. It is a great shift."

She smiled and handed the psalm back to me. "Sing it for me. Chant it, Ezekiel."

'What, now?"

"Is there a better time?"

She waited, silently.

And so, unconfident, tentative to begin, I did what she asked and, as I chanted, I gradually lost myself in the beauty and the mystery of the words of the psalm, coming back to consciousness again only at the end. At the closing line. *And I shall dwell in the house of the Lord forever.*

"There, Ezekiel," she said eventually, "don't you see, in this moment you *are* home. You have come home to yourself, and this house is forever. Your higher soul is forever." She put her palms together in front of her heart and smiled. "I am very happy you brought this to me today, Ezekiel. I am very grateful. It is very beautiful. Where did you get it?"

"My father gave it to me."

"Ah, he must have been a man of intuition. This is good. Now, meditation."

We closed our eyes.

Three weeks later we were sitting outside the entrance of her cave.

"How old are you, Master?"

She hit me on the knee with her long stick.

"Sorry. I am my own master."

"Yes, yes, yes. This is better. The master is within. You me him her. They are not masters. You are master of your own person." She laughed. "You are already a Buddha. You are already what you are looking for."

"How old are you, Tara?"

"You would not believe me."

"Yes I would."

"I am older than this tree. Now, meditation."

I looked up at the huge Neem tree and guessed it to be at least two hundred years old. I closed my eyes and tried to meditate, but couldn't. I had to ask her.

"Don't you ever want to make love, Tara?"

She laughed again. "Oh, you men. Always talking of foolish things like sex. Me have sex now? How ridiculous. Love is heaven and hell. Love is all feelings, the center of all feelings, negative and positive. I will give you a response Krishna gave to Arjuna in *The Bhagavad Gita*. Maybe this will help you. *Even as all the waters flow into the ocean, but the ocean never overflows, even so the sage feels desires, but he is ever one in his infinite peace.* Does this answer your question?"

"Yes."

"There is something else here too. You must understand this, because there is a connection with your addiction to philosophy. You fall in love with me and you are falling in love with yourself. You rise in love with me and you rise in Love with me. Falling on the ground, you hurt yourself. Rising up you are growing. If you want to continue to grow, to evolve from desires, making love, having big automobiles and power over others, then you have to realize that the answer to all your questions, all your to be or not to be's that you are always asking, is that being and not being are of the mind. Emptiness is the Mind. Don't bother with questions such as your Aristotle and your Shakespeare pose. Philosophy, religion and science want everything explained. This is not possible. Life is a mystery, not duality. Duality is ideas. Mathematicians create new ideas. God is an idea. They are all made-up, ideas. That which is life gives life, not that which is unreal."

A bird landed on the branch of the neem tree above our heads. She looked up at it. "If that bird and others like it had ideas, then their God would be a bird. It definitely wouldn't be a man. Have you seen how frightened the birds are of people? People are not in harmony with Nature. The birds know this. They sense it. And the other types of birds, the eagles would have their own idea of God, just like different races of humans have created their own idea of God. But why invent? All these hypotheses of God. There's no need. Religions and science and philosophy try to replace the mystery all around us with ideas. They want you to be helpless. Be like the birds instead, be free from hypotheses and ideas. The holes, the mystery, they try to fill them in with ideas and hypotheses and Aristotelian methods."

"But why is Aristotle wrong? Isn't contemplating a blade of grass the same as what you do when you close your eyes?"

"No. Aristotle was a scientist. He looks at the leaf with the eyes of science. I look at its mystery. I meditate on a blade of grass, he contemplates on it, analyses it, dissects it. He believes in the religion of science, I trust the mystery of the leaf. There is no criterion, only the mystery. Meditation is awareness of the leaf, contemplation is belief in what man presumes the leaf to be. As the writer Wilde once wrote, *Who can calculate the orbit of a soul?* The moon, the stars, you could try to map them all, but in the end you will always be with the mystery, the mystery of you."

She smiled. "Be a witness to a different perspective, Ezekiel. Go to the question of your own heart, your heart of hearts. There lies the emptiness that defeats all questions. There lies freedom. Freedom from evaluation. Postponement is desire and desire is the trap and you fall into it every time. Everybody does. This is desire's trick. It doesn't want you to transform. It doesn't want your transformation. It is all that your mind has to hold onto. If you postpone your transformation, with to be or not to bes and wanting to make love to people and all the other desires, then you will always be or not be, you will postpone, you will not be empty, and you will keep asking questions. Just drop the questions. You don't need them. You don't need anything, anything but this moment." She closed her eyes. "Now meditation. To be is to be here, in meditation, to be in harmony."

I thought of Thérèse, what she'd said about transformation all those years ago in her bedroom. I was filled up with such an intense joy. Energy started to move up and down my body, and I lost complete track of time, where I was.

For two years I lived in the Valley of Flowers. I would have stayed there for the rest of my life but Tara told me it was time to go. I asked her why I had to leave and she simply said, "It is time. You need to help people." When I asked her how I was supposed to help people she smiled. "You will know when the time comes."

"Have you tired of all my questions, Tara?"

She smiled. "There is an old Chinese proverb: *He who asks is a fool for five minutes. He who doesn't ask remains a fool forever.* There are no foolish questions, Ezekiel."

In Arles years later, another disciple, an Indian friend, visited me to tell me personally how Tara had entered *Mahasamādhi* on September 26th, 1966. She turned her body around seven times, he said, faced south, and said "Watch this! Now is the time. Watch this! Now is the time. Now is the time." Then she left her body. Her body sat in the exact same position for seven days.

JULIE

When I got back from India, I knew I wanted to help people in the way I had in the camps. It took going from Germany to India to realize the simple fact that I should continue what I'd *already* started in the camps, serving others through medicine. This time though, instead of stealing a dead man's passport, I went and got an actual qualification. After many years, I finally got my degree from the same place Nostradamus failed to get his, the University of Montpellier, not far from where I grew up outside Avignon. Thankfully, I wasn't kicked out like Nostradamus, although I came close at certain points. Getting a medical degree in France is not the same as elsewhere. First, it's very difficult to get into a course and second, the courses are incredibly competitive when you do get in. At the end of first year they fail anywhere from eighty-five to ninety percent of the students and, when you get to the last year, you face the final dreaded *concours* to qualify. Fortunately, because of my gift for remembering things, I didn't have as much trouble as the other students.

When I finished in Montpellier, I set up a practice with three other young doctors near Aramon, in the small town of Remoulins, continuing my daily routine of Kriya yoga, and meditating in the mornings and evenings as I'd done since I was a child. I kept my yoga to myself. It wasn't until much later that I realized that what I had learned could be of benefit to my patients, although I could never see myself teaching them things like *Khecarī Mudrā.* I could just picture the reactions of octogenarians from Aramon and housewives from Montfrin when I told them to touch their tongues to their uvula, or to place it in their nasal cavities behind the uvula. Imagine what they would have thought if I started telling them about the divine life-current that draws the *prana* from the senses into the spine, bringing it up through the *chakras* to the Universal spirit, *Vaishvanara.* This unites the consciousness with spirit, I'd tell them. They'd say, I'm never coming into this crazy person's office again.

During my final year of exams, I met Julie. I was exhausted from all the study and went out one Saturday night with some of the other students to do anything other than study. We were in a café drinking, something I'd stopped doing, when Julie introduced herself from the adjoining table. She seemed happy and fun, at the very least outgoing and forward, almost like Thérèse. She talked of traveling and I told her about the places I'd been after the war. She was the first person I'd ever really mentioned my travels to. She was shocked and impressed, hungry for all the details. The farthest she'd ever been was northern Italy and Ajaccio in Corsica. Her enthusiasm for travel took me out of the world of medicine, allowing me to escape for a few hours from the sterile years of study and isolation. I started to fall for her smile. The more drunk we became, talking about all the places we wanted to see, the further I fell.

Two weeks later, in the same café, she told me she had missed her period. She was sure she was pregnant. She said she was keeping the child and wanted to know what I was going to do. Was I going to be like her father, and leave her? Later, I found out more about her father. How he left her and her little brother when she was five, moving back to Morocco, saying there was no work for North Africans in France. After he left, her mother slept through the rest of their childhood, cleaning offices, at night, leaving Julie to mind her brother, and herself.

I should have noted the almost vicious anger in her question but I was blinded by the shock of the situation, in addition to the fact that my final *concours* was only a few months ahead. I agreed. We would keep the child. It was during the following weeks I discovered Julie was a practicing Catholic, another shock. She asked me was I going to marry her, or was she going to have to find a different husband? I told her there was no reason to be married and she asked me did I want to bring a bastard into the world. I told her I didn't care what people called my child, as long as it felt loved. She gave me an ultimatum, either I marry her and do it *her* way, or it was all over. She refused to discuss my role in my child's life, no matter how many times I tried to present my ideas, feelings, hopes. As with her own family, she was a single parent, all over again. I was to play the role of absent father, like her own father, irrespective of my refusal to leave, something she felt I was going to do at any moment. The fact that I could be present and love my children enraged her, threatened her control, insulted the system she had created inside her own head on how a family should be. Later, when she opened her practice as a psychiatrist, my attempts at asserting any positive, engaged role as a father became even more futile. What did I know about relationships? She was the expert on relationships, not me.

We married in the *mairie* of Montpellier six months before Celine was born. Our best man, a friend of Julie's since childhood, became one of her future lovers, and the witness, one of my friends from university, died in a car crash ten days later. It's easy to look back on it all now and see that our relationship was cursed from the beginning, Julie treating me like a child, exactly the same way she had treated her brother. Celine's arrival into the world wasn't just harrowing because Julie was in labor for so long, but because her postpartum depression was like living with a dictatorial psychopath. I allowed her to ridicule me and say things I should never have accepted. I allowed her to throw things at me and abuse me because I didn't meet her erratic, arbitrary and impossible demands. Frequently, she hit me.

Her depression and the stress of having a newborn in the house stopped me from reacting. Instead, I kept my mouth shut and concentrated on setting up a practice and providing for a family I had never planned on having. I am still very grateful for my accidental family because of the wonderful experience of watching my girls grow up. However, to say I was fully present during their formative years would be a lie. Ironically, I became the very person I assessed my father as being, a man who worked all the time so that he wouldn't have to be in the house with his abusive wife.

ST. THÉRÈSE AND THE HEALER

With the years, my practice grew into a mammoth thing, becoming more and more stressful with each year. At the time I was aware of alternative remedies from my experience with our old neighbor and friend, Yvette, but I never had the time to research them because I was always so busy in my allopathic practice. I continued handing out prescriptions for illnesses instead of helping my patients understand the importance of doing as much as they could themselves to keep their health. I should have been telling them that health care is about health promotion, not the alleviation or quelling of disease symptoms. Indeed, this is what modern, allopathic medicine means, to work *against* a disease and its symptoms, to be different from the suffering. The homeopathic method however is to treat patients with remedies that are *similar* to disease symptoms, or as Hippocrates once said: *Through the like, disease is produced and through the application of the like it is cured.*

It was Yvette who introduced me to homeopathy. Homeopathy works at the energy level, Zeke, she once told me, not at the level of matter, just as acupuncture and the movement of energy, *ch'i*, does along what the Chinese call *meridians*.

One morning Yvette came into my surgery with her eleven-year-old granddaughter. The girl refused to take Yvette's natural remedies, remedies I'd forgotten I used to take when I was her age. She had her arms crossed, even refusing the bonbon I offered her. Her grandmother sighed.

"She'll have nothing. She's like you when you were a boy, stubborn. If it hadn't been for your father, you would never have taken anything I offered you."

I stood up and we went over to the examination table. Yvette lifted the little girl with her crossed arms onto the table.

"So, what's your name?"

"Thérèse."

I dropped my stethoscope on the floor. Yvette looked at me, worried. "Are you alright, Zeke?" she said.

"What?" I picked up the stethoscope and grabbed a wipe to clean it.

Another sign. Thérèse. What, this time?

"What a lovely name," I said. "And where did you get such a lovely name?"

I checked her chest with the stethoscope.

"I was born on Sainte Thérèse's day."

I checked her neck and asked her to stick her tongue out.

"How lucky you are."

I checked her ears.

"What's lucky?" she said. "Father says saints are masochists."

Yvette sighed again.

"Do you know who St. Thérèse was?" I said.

"No."

"She was a very magical girl when she was your age. She witnessed miracles every day."

"Miracles. Father says miracles..."

"The miracle is right now," I said. "And the miracles St. Thérèse witnessed were when she did little things, the little things she did for people in her life without telling them or looking for recognition."

"I don't understand," she said.

Yvette sat down. I checked Thérèse's chest again from her back. "Take your grandmother for example. She brings you in here when your parents are working. She makes you your meals and picks you up from school because they have to drive back here from Avignon every evening."

"So?"

"Does she ever complain about it?

I never heard Yvette complain about anything. She might sigh, but she never complained, either about a person or situation. She did what she had to do because it was there to be done.

"No."

"Does she ever tell you how it tires her to have to do that?"

Yvette moved in her chair, her brow slightly knitted.

"No."

"Well, then she's like St. Thérèse, saintly. You see, Sainte Thérèse became saintly when people didn't notice her doing things for them. That was her way of being a wonderful young girl and then a great, great woman."

She looked at me, her brow like her grandmother's and her little brown eyes staring through me.

"Where did she come from?"

"France, the north, a place called Lisieux. They've built a beautiful cathedral there named after her."

"I want to go there."

Yvette moved back in her chair, shocked.

"Well, maybe you will some day." I went back behind my desk and started scribbling a prescription. "It's nothing, Yvette. Her glands are swollen, but it hasn't gone into her chest."

The little girl got down off the table and sat in front of me, still staring through me.

"I think one of your herbal infusions would work just as well as this, if not better," I handed Yvette the prescription, "because I know they did for me when I was her age."

She got up and gave me a huge hug and *bisous* as they left.

"Thank you, Zeke."

I didn't understand then why she was smiling so much at me and had no time to think about it because my next patient was already coming in the door. It was only at the end of the day, when I was seeing my second to last patient that I understood.

Yvette came back into my office and, after excusing herself to the local priest I was talking to, she handed me the *Organon of Medicine* by Samuel Hahnemann.

"Thank you. That's very generous, Yvette," I said. "Did Thérèse take the medicine? How's she doing?"

"Yes, she took medicine and she's doing better than you know." And she closed my door, leaving me perplexed for a moment as I tried to remember what I had been saying to Father Muller about his migraines.

That night I read Hahnemann's book all through the night, finishing it during my lunch break the next day, and reread it again the following night. I was amazed, completely inspired by it.

Two weeks later, I met Yvette on the street during my lunch break.

"You know, I didn't want to say it in front of your patient, but she took my remedy instead of the medicine you prescribed."

"And did it work?"

"Yes."

"Of course it did."

"You know, Zeke, you have a gift."

"Oh, I don't know about that. Giving out prescriptions all day doesn't feel like much of a gift. Samuel Hahnemann was a doctor. I feel more like a machine than a doctor. There's no time to sit and talk with people like I did with you and Thérèse."

"Why?"

"Because that's the way of a doctor today. Get them in and get them out. People don't have the patience to listen."

"Then why did you spend more time with us?"

"Because you ... you're like family to me. Indeed, you're one of the only ones left from my old life."

"Do you have to move so fast? Couldn't you spend more time with your patients?"

I laughed. "Yes, maybe, if there was a different type of medicine."

"Well, maybe there is. Did you read the book I gave you?"

"I've read it a number of times."

"I thought you might like it."

"You knew I'd like it."

"Like Yusuf used to say," she said. "Some things are written."

I felt sad to have to leave her. "I'm sorry, Yvette, I have to get back to the surgery."

She smiled at me and gave me *bisous*. Walking away, she turned around. "You know, Aramon is not very far from Remoulins, Zeke. My door is always open."

THE MACHINE

I started to visit Yvette every week after that, excited to drive out to Aramon every Friday.

It was the Saturday evening after my first visit to see her that I experienced an important epiphany. My girls and Julie were asleep. I was reading Darwin's autobiography. It came to me as I was reading this passage: *formerly pictures gave me considerable, and music very great delight. But now for many years I cannot endure to read a line of poetry: I have tried lately to read Shakespeare, and found it so intolerably dull that it nauseated me. I also lost any taste for pictures or music ... My mind seems to have become a kind of machine for grinding general laws out of large collections of facts, but why this should have caused an atrophy of that part of the brain alone, on which the higher tastes depend, I cannot conceive ... if I had my life again I would have made a rule to read some poetry and listen to some music at least once a week ... The loss of these tastes is a loss of happiness, and may possibly be injurious to the intellect, and more probably to the moral character, by enfeebling the emotional part of our nature.*

I was the same. The more I had educated myself in allopathic medicine the more my brain had, as Darwin put it, atrophied. I had stopped reading poetry since returning from India, lost in trying to excel in *le concours* because if you didn't excel, getting in the top forty or so, then you couldn't choose to be a surgeon, for example, and below that score you would have to choose something you didn't want to do, such as dentistry or physical therapy. I read only medical studies. I barely played my alto and I hadn't listened to Bach's *Well-Tempered Clavier* in nearly five years. I had become a machine, unable to listen to and read the things that made me feel alive. My ego had tried to destroy my emotions with facts and information, but you cannot destroy emotion. If you try, the machine will break down. Mine did when I had my heart attack. I was forty-seven years old. A patient found me flat on my face on my desk.

It was during the months of recovery that I started to really study homeopathy. I read everything Samuel Hahnemann had ever written, from his *Dissertation on the Causes and Treatment of Cramps* to the sixth edition of his *The Organon of the Healing Art.* His *"like cures like"*, became a simple but powerful epiphany for me as a doctor. In the years that followed, I started to write papers on Hahnemann's *drug-dynamization.* I also started to study and write about *vital force*, referring all the way back to Hippocrates, to his *four temperaments* in the West, and to *prana* and *qi* in the East. Today the Chinese have proven the existence of *qi*. Of course, the reductionism of modern allopathic medicine will always refute the existence of our own energy force because it undermines the earning power of treating symptoms with man-made drugs rather than the illness itself with what Nature gives us.

Yvette came to see me every day in the hospital. She kept her silence as she knitted, simply asking me the question, "Why?" Again and again she asked it, until I finally figured it out.

I got it on a Friday, a very overcast, gray Friday. Of course I'd gotten a heart attack. My heart was broken. My heart was broken because I couldn't take care of people the way I wanted to. It was as obvious as the rain outside my window, but it took a heart attack for me to understand it. I told Yvette and she smiled. She didn't come the next day. I wondered if she was alright. When I called her, she said, "Why, of course I'm not coming. You're better now. You have your why answer."

My heart attack forced me to understand that my feelings,

emotions, the joy I had had when I was younger, had slid into a deep dark place inside me. Instead of transforming my experiences into joy, I let them disappear into my unconscious "modern" way of thinking, thinking, thinking. My head had taken over and the head kills the heart, turning it into a ghostly machine. I was less alive than I had ever been before, even in the camps. In the camps, I wasn't lost in studies and journals and footnotes to endnotes to footnotes. Imprisoned inside my own head, I had lost all touch with joy, with reality, confined by abstractions, abstractions that didn't even cure my patients. I was trying to treat symptoms, not the actual illnesses.

I made a decision. In my old age I wasn't going to feel the same way Darwin did. I started re-reading Shakespeare and Blake and Auden and Issa and so many others. At the same time, I was reading Paracelsus, Hildegard of Bingen, Hahnemann and others. The poetry became my medicine, connecting me with memories of Mathias and Thérèse, of poets Yusuf and Dad loved, of beautiful moments of joy. My mind started to breathe again because my heart could. After two months of reading and understanding, I returned from the hospital a changed man. I now knew that what I had felt intuitively all those years of practicing medicine was true: biology is biography, and a body can be healed by healing it spiritually, or in the words of Hippocrates: *Our natures are the physicians of our diseases.*

I began to spend more time with my patients, asking them about their problems. I tried to talk to my partners about my new discoveries, about the simple psychological epiphanies I was having. They said nothing in response. I talked a lot about why I thought people felt lost today. They said nothing. They just smiled at me as they ate their salads and sandwiches. I talked to them about the immense modern generation gap. *Metiers* don't exist anymore, I said. When you were seven, you started learning to be a carpenter or mason, using your hands and learning. By the end of seven years you had a craft and were perhaps even married. They nodded.

Today the children continue to be educated until their early twenties and then when they come out of the educational system, they don't know what to do with themselves because they are so full of ideas with no practical skills. They nodded and ate their food.

Don't you see it, though? I asked. Because of this, young men and women get bored then depressed living on unemployment benefits, and they smoke hash and snort cocaine to deal with it. I urged my partners to try to help their young patients by encouraging them to learn physical skills in addition to their intellectual ones, to have a more balanced life.

I suggested we teach them how to meditate. I tried to hold meditation sessions with them before and after work but not one of my colleagues ever turned up. I told them that medicine and meditation come from the same root, one helping us physically, the other spiritually. Their apathy turned into advice. They told me it was up to the government to change the educational system, to teach the youth, and that the best thing for me to do was to keep my head down and do my work. In the end I realized they thought I was crazy. Then again, they were too busy getting their patients in and out to listen to what they called my "theories." They were using the same psychology as the jails: their patients need this for that. This youth needs this punishment sentence for using this drug. I began to feel that the doctors I worked with were punishing their patients instead of treating them. Someone addicted to hash or cocaine or other drugs needs to be treated, not punished.

I read more and more books, anything I could get my hands on, about the emotional component of disease. Because I didn't have a degree or diploma in any of it, I didn't feel comfortable advising my patients on alternative remedies. It got to the stage where I hated going into work and thought about leaving medicine altogether. When I told Julie I wanted to leave allopathic medicine and set up my own practice as a homeopath she nearly killed me, literally. I tried to explain to her how disgusted I was by the dubious methods of modern medicine, much like Hahnemann and Paracelsus before me. She stared at me without saying a word. I tried to explain to her my reasons, even giving her medicine's abominable history of leeching, cupping, blood-letting, cathartics, emetics and how most of the time these remedies killed the patients. I told her about the foolishness of Galen and how it was considered heresy in medieval Christianity to go against his methods, which were the complete opposite of Hippocrates' belief that a doctor should help the body to heal itself. I was trying to tell her how, even with the advent of Descartes' rationalism, the Church still outlawed dissection. Her response? She told me to shut up. She said homeopathy was for fools who believed in placebos. I gave her examples from history.

Hahnemann and his homeopathy had saved 179 of Napoleon's defeated troops at the Battle of Leipzig in 1813 from dying of typhus, and twenty years later he received the same results when he treated cholera patients. Then there were the three percent of homeopathic patients who died during the cholera epidemic of 1849 in Cincinnati, as opposed to the seventy percent of patients who died using allopathic treatments. She screamed at me to shut up again and I asked her why, whereupon she hurled a vase at me. It glanced off my head and into the wall, leaving me with bandages on my head the next day at work. I said it was the result of yet another "fall."

Of course, my marriage had been falling apart well before this, but my desire to leave medicine was unbearable to her, the end. I couldn't blame her. I was doing long hours at the office only to return home to voraciously read books about "alternative" medicine. One night I was at the table with the family reading Paracelsus' *The Archidoxes of Magic* when she finally lost it.

"Can't you see we're eating dinner? Is it not enough that you go to see that old witch every Friday and any other chance you get? When are you going to realize you have a family? Look at your daughters! They're growing up around you like weeds."

I looked at Rose and Celine, then fourteen and fifteen years old.

"They're young women for Christ's sake, and all you can do is keep your head in your books, play your infernal alto, give too much time to your patients, and visit that old hag out in Aramon! Are you having some kind of sick affair with her or something? What about us? What about your family? If I were to diagnose you, I'd say you were a narcissistic pedant who barely knows his family exists!"

"Can't we talk about this in private, Julie?"

"Private? When? Where? If you're not in your office, you're in

Aramon. And when you're here you're not here, you're in alternative medicine world."

"Maman, please. Can't we...?"

"Don't parrot your father. Someone has to take care of this family. Families don't exist on autopilot, you know. Jesus Christ, I'm a psychiatrist. I hear this shit every day in my office and now I have to come home to it too?"

She stood up and flung her plate into the middle of the table, her food running onto the floral table cloth, the red sauce drenching through the old wood underneath. "When's the last time you made a meal? Well? They call this the sixties, the emancipation of women and I, even though I work long hours too, have to come home every night to make you your meals! When's the last time you cleared your plate from the table? Well?"

"Julie, I..."

"Don't *Julie* me. I'm finished with all this, all this shit!"

She picked up her wine glass and flung it across the table at me. I raised my hand just in time to stop it hitting my face. It smashed into my hand, a large piece of glass puncturing my palm, the rest falling to pieces into my meal.

She grabbed her car keys and coat as she left. We didn't see her for two days. When she returned, we all slipped into a system of apologies and forgiveness, vowing to go into counseling, which we never did, and promising we would never do anything like that again in front of the children, which we didn't. From then on, we fought in our bedroom or in car parks or on the beach, anywhere nobody else could hear us, or so we thought.

THE ANGEL AND THE FRYING PAN

I didn't leave my girls and Julie until she put me in hospital. She had knocked me unconscious with a cast iron frying pan, leaving me with ten stitches in the side of my head. Not even the Capos in Auschwitz had hit me as hard as she had.

When I regained consciousness, the nurse went to get the doctor. He came in soon after.

"Monsieur Moran, can you see this?"

He moved his finger in front of my face from left to right. I followed it.

"Ah, good."

He sat down on my bed. He seemed like a kind man, older, with what looked like a cancerous mole on his left cheek I wanted to warn him about. "How are you feeling, Monsieur Moran?"

"Good."

"You got a very nasty concussion there." He massaged his beard in a thoughtful way. "You know, another centimeter or so, and I wouldn't be talking to you right now."

I tried to smile, but it didn't happen.

"Do you recall what happened, Monsieur Moran? Your wife said she found you on the kitchen floor."

I remembered the frying pan flying for my head.

"You wouldn't believe me." This time I managed to smile.

"I've seen a lot of crazy things, Monsieur Moran. I was in the war too you know."

It was his turn to smile. I understood his smile. He was one of us, one of the survivors, like me he probably became a doctor to be of service to the world, to create something positive out of his second chance at life.

"My wife. She hits me," I said.

He continued to smile compassionately at me as the tears fell down my face. For the first time I had admitted it to another human being. Then it all came on me like some kind of emotional avalanche, the why. My ego, my conditioning from my parent's marriage, my sense of duty, like Dad's, as opposed to a relationship based on love. I was the brave soldier, the RAF trainee who worked for the secret services in London, the Free French resistance fighter, the prisoner of the Gestapo, the concentration camp survivor, the man, the successful man, the top of his class in medicine. No, I wasn't abused. No. That wasn't me. I was a hero. I'd killed men with my bare hands. I'd escaped POW camps. I'd...

He handed me some tissues from the night side table. I wiped the tears from my eyes.

After a few seconds he massaged his beard again. "Well, what are you going to do about it..." and he looked at my chart again "... Ezekiel? That's a wonderful name you have."

I remembered the time Thérèse had used the same words. "What a wonderful name you have, Ezekiel!" How it had changed my whole concept of myself at the time. How it had made me stronger in myself. She seemed to be calling to me now from some other time.

"Monsieur Moran?"

"Yes?"

"Do you mind me calling you Ezekiel?"

"No."

"You never answered my question."

"Oh, yes, what am I going to do? I don't know. I really don't know. I have two daughters."

"I have two sons and a daughter." He picked a pen out of the front of his white coat and begun to write. "This is the number of a friend of mine. He's a lawyer in Avignon. When my wife left me for her boss, he helped me a lot. You tell him I sent you. My name is Doctor Rondelet..."

"Oh, but I could never leave them. Doctor..."

"You can call me Mathias."

And now Mathias? The two of them in the same conversation.

He put the number on the night side table under the water jug.

"Thank you, Mathias."

He smiled again. "You're welcome." He left the room. I never saw him again, another one of those angels we mistake for humans.

DANCING IN THE STREET

The next day, an indigo one, I was strong enough to meet with Dr. Rondelet's friend in Montpellier, M. Serge Klarsfeld, a balding man with spectacles and a Spartan smile, wearing expensive clothes sloppily put together.

M. Klarsfeld told me I had no case for my girls. In France, the children go to the mother, he said. The mother, my wife, had no prior convictions and short of her being a drug addict, I had no chance of winning. Also, when I blurted out that I was being abused by Julie he looked at me and said, No, that won't work. The judge'll think you're either a liar or mad. He said he'd had another husband in the same position three years before. The man had multiple facial injuries and cried for fifteen minutes in the same chair I was sitting in because of the same problem, and again there was nothing to be done about it. You have to remember that judges are people, he said, and if you start giving them information that is outside the ordinary, they get suspicious. He asked me to imagine the situation if he came into this office and told me: I'm being beaten by my wife. What's your immediate reaction? he said. That it's strange, I said. My point exactly, he said. And that was the end of that. Reality out the window.

He said mine was a very positive case because I'd come to see him early on. My only recourse would be to look at my situation in a positive light. He said I was indebted to Dr. Rondelet for sending me so soon. This way he, my lawyer, could set me straight from the outset. I would have no false expectations and thus not do things that would have turned out negative for my case, like trying to fight it with the truth! At that point in the conversation he laughed, but I can't say I did the same. To him, the most important thing was to help me safeguard my finances. This would be the first thing she would come after as soon as she found out I was leaving her. But she has a very successful career, I told him. She makes more than me, I said. He frowned and I knew why. She was successful and I was not. What judge wouldn't favor her over me? Man leaves his wife and two children for no apparent reason, and then asks to have custody of his children when he earns less money than his wife. Who's going to look better from behind the bench? And what if you get a female judge? he asked. I didn't respond, too depressed to even ponder that position.

When he said the words "leaving her", I felt like being sick, but then felt instantly relieved at the same time. I sighed audibly and he smiled, having obviously seen it many times before.

He also told me my history in the war would serve me well so long as I wasn't up before a Vichy judge. He would make sure to try and find one who was sympathetic. I looked at him, shocked, never having realized in all my years of blinded study and workaholicism that those who were a part of Vichy France had any positions of power after the war. How wrong I was. How amazing it is that it's only when tragedy hits us that we become more aware of the reality surrounding us.

We shook hands, and I left him to prepare my "case".

Although emotionally exhausted as I walked away from Serge Klarsfeld's office, I realized the ever present pain in my back was no longer there. From the first days of our marriage I had had back pains, especially around my shoulders. For days at a time I would be sporadically driven to bed, unable to move. Acupuncturists, massage therapists and doctors couldn't help me. I would lie in our bed and listen to Julie ridicule me. She would tell me there was nothing wrong with me because none of the doctors or specialists could find anything scientifically wrong with me. The spasms would pass after two or three days and I would return to work, slowly building up my momentum so as not to relapse.

Again, another epiphany. I had found out what I was breaking my back over – trying to stay in an abusive marriage. No amount of Kriya Yoga could have helped this, until I realized what my problem really was. It wasn't my workaholic nature or the stress of long hours that had done my back in. It was my marriage. For the first time in years I stood up straight as the people flowed by me on rue Bernard Délicieux, named after the Franciscan monk who died in prison in 1319 after defending the Cathars for years. Thinking of Délicieux, I realized I was free again. Like the Cathars, I would be able to live again.

How many times in a life do we have to escape from cages we create ourselves? Yes, this one I had created myself. I had escaped Oflag II D, survived Auschwitz, but my longest captivity had been with Julie. When we had married in my last year of medical school, she in her final year of psychiatry, I never thought I was entering into another prison. We'd accidentally fallen in love and never made the effort to rise in love afterwards. In fact, we'd fallen in love with the delusion that the pregnancy was fate's way of bringing us together, two professionals trying to be "successful" in the world, creating careers and a family that conformed with society's ideas of normality. It was only natural that we fell out of love. We had created our own prison of love without even being aware of it.

Oh, how good it felt to be free. I felt as if my ribcage was about to explode. I danced on the street. People stopped to look at me, obviously thinking I was insane, but I didn't care. I danced and danced all the way to the Promenade du Peyrou and finally sat down on the stone steps below the statue of another dancer, the Sun King, Louis XIV of France. I was breathing heavily and exhilarated, happier than I'd been in over a decade and proud, proud to have finally escaped the prison of my own making.

I had failed Julie and our children. I'd let my enthusiasm for helping others allow me to forget the people I should have been caring for the most, my own family. However, I'd failed myself the most, by not being aware of the situation I had put myself in. I tried to make peace with Julie later on, after all the paperwork was started, but it wasn't to be. Soon after my meeting with my lawyer she left me for her lover, a colleague at work. I didn't blame her, only myself, but the fact we'd grown apart, as seems to happen so often nowadays judging by the number of divorces, didn't have to mean she had to treat me even worse than she had before.

During the weeks of the divorce she actually accused me of having an affair with a woman in Avignon, her lawyer citing the fact that I left work early every Friday, as most people in France do I might add, to spend the bulk of Friday in Aramon. That was all the lady judge needed to hear. Her suspicion had been aroused and, because Yvette was sick in bed all that week, there was nobody to come to my defense in court. Julie got full custody of Celine and Rose. Later she brought me to court to restrain me from seeing them more than once a month due to the constant abuse I hurled at her and her lover in front of my girls. Of course, this was another lie.

I moved out of Provence completely, settling in Carcassonne, establishing a little practice at the top of the Rue Verdun facing a wonderful *boulangerie* where I used to buy my bread every day. The office has since been turned into a driving school that doles out obligatory driving lessons to pass the *permis*, an ordeal that can only be called a form of state torture. Still, I was not to know any of all that sitting on my park bench, panting and smiling. I remember a sparrow flew down and parked itself at the other end of my bench and started to sing and I almost felt like crying. It was a wonderful day, a wonderful, wonderful day.

PART EIGHT
VIOLET

TUESDAY, JANUARY 10TH, 2017

THE BLACK MOUNTAINS, FRANCE

ORDAINED

My particular irony, or the irony of my story, is that I have held nothing back, spoken my truth every time, and lived in truth with everyone I have come in touch with in the most compassionate way I could. When I say truth, I don't mean I didn't lie about my identity at times. What I mean is that I said what I felt and then backed it up with action. This, I am sure, kept me alive during all those selections in the camps. It's probably why Julie hit me with that frying pan. Julie, like a lot of people, can't bear too much of the truth. I didn't always tell the whole truth, but when I did I said things that were true. I think that's what saved me, allowing fate or *karma* to work its design, *for we carry our fate with us – and it carries us.* Now, though, after all these years, I finally see my greatest flaw: I never told my story to anyone when I returned from the war and my travels. This is the greatest truth, to give to others our experience so they can learn from it. I am not judging those survivors who do not tell their stories, I'm just saying that for me, now, I feel guilty that I kept my silence for so long.

I really feel now that not voicing the truth of our experiences in the world kills the soul. I am the problem. I am the world problem, if I do not use my voice. I kill my soul by not expressing myself. I think of all the women in the world whose voices were, and still are, taken from them by patriarchal mores and I feel guilty for keeping my silence for so long. I look at Pétain and Pilot and all the others washing their hands of injustice and I feel guilty for keeping my silence so long. Yes, history has a silent drama that has played out because the minorities have been wiped out, or just never had the opportunity to speak out. There are so many books that have parts of my story: the camps, the France of the forties and before and after, the New Age movement in naturopathy and homeopathy, but not many have had the opportunity to tie them all together as I can. When I think of the fact that not once have I talked to my daughters, even Julie, or now Daniel, of my experiences I feel only shame.

But, and this is the big but, shame can disappear. Silence can be transformed. And this is the great realization I came to as I wrote the last few entries into this journal. I am talking. I am speaking. This book is me speaking to my family, friends, acquaintances and all the patients I never spoke to about suffering when I could have used my example, my own experience, as a way to alleviate their pain. Yes, I realize now that this is my calling. I am calling back my soul from the past to write this all down, to tell what happened to me. It is my specific destiny, something decided even before I was born. God does not shape the future, we do. Our choice depends on which of the many paths offered to us we will take. I could have chosen to run into the wire and die. I didn't. I could have chosen to die from another heart attack. I didn't. They were the turns in the road, the choices of a different path, the times to be aware of where I was going astray.

For years I'd been searching for the answers to the many mysteries I've encountered. How one person heals and another doesn't. How one man twice the size of another died in the camps. Why? Why did Mathias die? Why did we three meet at all? Why did Thérèse have to die? Why am I still alive, even after everything I've been through, at 99 years of age? What did they do wrong to not live, or what have I done wrong to continue living? I had no idea that these questions, my consistent seeking of the truth, would finally give me an answer as I slept.

A couple of weeks ago I woke and remembered. I remembered Thérèse in the barn telling me I had an important book to write. Oh, Thérèse, if you are watching me writing this right now, Thank you. Thank you from the center of my heart. My whole experience with sick patients has led me to this one truth: if they become aware of themselves, not their sickness, they will heal. If they become aware of their purpose on this planet, they will heal. For me it was coming to the awareness that this is the book I was supposed to write. Recently, when I started thinking about what I was going to write, the pain from the cancer in my throat started to subside. My depression from the war, from my divorce, all disappeared. The depression lifted when the hatred and anger were accepted, replaced by forgiveness, much as it had been when I meditated in India with Tara.

Now I understand why they died and I didn't. Now I understand why I am spending my days in this little room above the Orbiel river writing down the story of my life. What I am writing right now is the book Thérèse talked about all those years ago, not the homeopathic books. No. The real book of healing is this book, the one I am writing right now. This book is my book to the world. This is the book I have come onto this planet to write. Nothing else but this. No wonder I am still alive. I haven't finished what I came here to do! Now I see it all so clearly. I was ordained to do this. If I don't, the Essene tradition my father has passed on to me will die with me. All the things that have happened to me, all my many crazy and frightening experiences, were experienced to write this book.

Hafiz did not
Of his choice wear
This wine-soaked cloak;
O puritan Sheikh, beware!
He is helpless;
It was thus ordained!

Now I know when it is finished I will be finished and grateful to be too. By writing it all down, I can pass on all the things I have never said and should have. I will have passed on the tradition of my family, *The Tree of Life*. In her anger, my daughter Celine wouldn't allow me to pass it on to Daniel. But now, now I have, by writing about it. Perhaps now, something of what I have put down will help and even empower the Daniels of my family to learn from my mistakes. Now I can also pass on where I went for those years after the war. Nobody knows what happened to me in India and Italy and Greece. They didn't even know I went to those places. They only know I disappeared for years.

How right it all seems to me now, what Tara used to call Right Livelihood. It is through writing that I have become a vessel for divine energy, not through poultices and medicine and wise words of advice over a desk. An ordained priest, a master, a doctor can feel the appreciation from those around them for what they do. That is why they come onto the planet. It is their gift to others and so their gift to themselves. Just as Mohammad's gift was to write his *surahs* on palm leaves, as was the Sybil's of Cumae in her cage writing her predictions on leaves. I'm not saying that what I have written are revelations to the world. What's important is that they are important to me. Each leaf is a prophesy to *Recite! Recite! Recite!* It is a call from the cave of the Mind to prepare for *The Recital* of our soul, to honor what it is we've been put on this planet to do.

This morning, when I finally realized this truth, a fire rose from deep inside me above my intestine and below my solar plexus. It grew stronger and stronger until I started to sweat. A joy I have only ever experienced when making love to Thérèse the last time, or sitting in front of Tara in the Himalayas, for an hour, filled my soul.

Peace can only come when divine reasoning is our reasoning and this can only happen when we embrace what it is we are really ordained to do while here. For me, right now, it's to write. I'm beginning to feel liberated. Liberated for the first time, not by some army of Russians, but by myself, by the words I am allowing myself to write here, right now! I have been happy to sit on the sidelines while others more eloquent than I, like Hessel, spoke for me, but now I understand that this is a ridiculous position to hold when young people are apathetic. I am merely writing my own truth as best I can so that the memory of my father and all our family doesn't disappear from the world. If Daniel and my daughters were to read these words, I would be content, but then if they don't, I am still content, because it is the act of writing all this down, the process, not the finished product, which is important.

Thérèse used to say the past as a concept is an unnatural construct in the divine design. She used to call it a graveyard and used to always ask, Do you want to live in a graveyard or do you want to be alive? Right now, in the very moment I am writing this, unhappiness is impossible. The past simply doesn't exist anymore. It is only in the past that unhappiness exists.

My story is ending and I am happy and grateful it is. I remember one of Thérèse's many favorite quotations from *The Story of a Soul*: *What an interesting study the world is when we are ready to leave it!* Yes, with this book I can rest in peace, whenever it comes, commending my spirit into the hands of something greater than me, in gratitude, appreciation and loving kindness. As I write, I am not writing. What I am doing right now is the same thing Thérèse did when she channeled the Archangel Ezekiel. I am being present in the right now, what Tara called *herenow*, to receive guidance. This is inspiration, as Thérèse said, *in spirito*, when spirit is inside us. My spirit is now stronger than my body. These constant, ecstatic moments I am experiencing now are a side-effect of this. I can "hear" things so clearly now. Now I understand why I have been growing weak these last nine months. It's a natural progression. It took nine months for me to come into the world; it has to take nine months for me to go out of it.

PASCALE

Pascale opens my old front door. She never knocks. She has her own key. As I no longer have a car, Pascale had very generously got used to fetching my groceries every week when she travelled down the mountain to Carcassonne. But since they've now banned her from driving, the mayor of her village, a communist who idolizes her, does the shopping for the pair of us.

"So, are you dead yet, Ezekiel?"

"No, not yet."

"I need to use the toilet. I know, it's not a very French thing to ask, but we live beyond what our society demands, eh, Ezekiel?"

I laughed, and she went into the toilet. She was right. In France, there are certain things that are frowned upon. One, never clean the dishes after your hosts have made you a meal and two, never ask to use your hosts' toilet. Perhaps this explains why you find so many men in our country on the sides of the road, outside fields, in parking lots, even outside friends' houses, urinating. Absurd, I know, but then every country has its absurdities. When someone creates thoughtless customs, people will always find a way around them or, as my friend Jean Vialette used to say, a way of pissing all over them.

I had just sat down to write the next section and, ordinarily, I would simply have kept moving along with my words, but Pascale's arrival reminded me of my appointment with a specialist in Carcassonne. What would I do without Pascale? For years she's cared for me as a daughter does an elderly father, even though she's the same age as me. I put down my pen and paper and tried to find my *carte vitale.*

Like the Cathars who were persecuted in these same mountains, Pascale, too, has been ostracized and persecuted. It is undeserving treatment for such a generous and overwhelmingly intelligent woman. But then isn't this our way? We punish all the outcasts of this world, the Gallileos and the spiritual agitators like Jesus, or the Jews, the gay community, the artists, anyone different.

I found my coat in the garden of all places and continued to look for my *carte vitale.*

Pascale lives in a house we built of wood from her own forest. I bought her those fifteen hectares of *garrigue* when I sold my *patrimoine*, the half-share of my mother's house in Beaucaire. She uses the water that runs from the *source* on her land. She's completely off the grid and because of this she is seen as crazy. Behind her back the locals call her *Pascale la Folle.* I have even heard them call her *gay.* If you ask her, she'll tell you she's asexual. The thing is, though, Pascale is anything but crazy. In fact, she is so smart that it is oftentimes hard to keep up with her. On her land she has twenty *ruches* of bees. Her bees' honey supplies the money she needs to buy such foodstuffs as Germalevure, flour, and milk from the farmer up in Pradelles. Other than that, she has her own hens for eggs, her bees for honey and propolis, her *potager* for vegetables which she preserves in the summer for winter, the nuts from her walnut, chestnut, hazelnut and almond trees, and fruit from her peach, apple, pear, plum and nectarine trees. She makes her own soap, bread, jam, wine, liquors, tisanes and cheeses and can build anything she needs for her house or property with her own tools. All this from a woman who spent most of her life as a history teacher in the public school system in Arles.

I sat down at my table again to try and remember where I'd left my card, but all I could think of was Pascale and how kind she has been to me all these years.

Pascale's real name is Anna. She has never told me her true family name. That life doesn't exist for her any more. The only thing she's ever let me know is that she was born in Poland and was studying French at the University of Lodz when the war started. I know that she, like Yusuf, lost everyone. The only other time she talked about Poland to me was to describe how she was one of only three people to crawl out of a Nazi death pit before she walked to France to fight with Raimond and the *Résistance*.

She came out of the toilet rubbing her face vigorously. "Well! What are you writing, another homeopathic article, or maybe *the* book?"

Pascale has been telling me for years to write the book of my life. Of course, I had always thought of it as secondary to writing about the healing power of homeopathy and herbs.

She walked into my small kitchen, rubbing her head in circles with her hands, finally yawning and stretching them up and out to the ceiling.

"Yes, I've been writing my book."

"Super!" she cried with great enthusiasm. "*En fin*! You have started it!"

"Yes. In fact, I think I might be finished it soon."

"What? But I saw you barely a week ago?"

"Yes, that's when I started it."

"Ezekiel, your life story would take years to write!"

"Not if it flows from you like a stream."

"Beautiful. How many pages is it?"

"I don't know yet, but I'd say I've written about two hundred and fifty typed pages. It's hard to know. You know I only use computers for music."

"Two hundred and fifty pages in seven days? *Mais, c'est pas possible!*"

"*Mais, tout est possible*," I said, "*C'est la France!*"

She laughed out loud. "But how? Have you slept?"

"Yes. I've been going to bed at midnight, not nine as I usually do."

"Why, this is fabulous! You must be inspired. Tell me at least that you've left the house to sit in this wonderful January sun."

"No, I've been sleeping and writing, writing and sleeping."

"But you have to take care of yourself, Ezekiel! I would rather have Ezekiel than *The Book of Ezekiel* and a dead Ezekiel!"

"Oh, don't worry about me. I've been through worse."

"I know," she said, "and that's why you shouldn't have to endure any more of it."

"But it isn't painful. Yes, there's depression as I write, but then there's joy too, discovery."

"Okay, okay!"

"Where's your grand-niece?"

"She never came. She had to finish doing some research in Paris first."

"But she *is* coming, *non*?"

"Soon."

She rubbed her face with her hands again, as if trying to wake herself up from a long sleep.

"So, are you ready to make the odyssey to the church of commercialism and the *rendez-vous* with *Monsieur le grande spécialiste*?"

"Yes to the *rendez-vous*, no to the *hypermarché*. I haven't been eating much lately. No desire."

"And you a *gourmand*? Are you sure you're alright?"

"Yes, I just have no desire. Would you like a *verveine* before we go?"

Pascale never refuses a drink, especially if it's made with herbs. It isn't that she drinks too much, she just loves eating and drinking, like most French people.

"The *tincture* you make? I'd be mad not to!"

She sat down at the table with her immense coat still on. I brought the bottle out from my bag, where I keep all my private concoctions. Over the years I have shown Pascale nearly everything I know about homeopathic and herbal remedies, everything Yvette has passed on to me and everything I've learned along the way. It has been a joy to share the information with her as she is always so grateful and fastidious about keeping notes, which I never was. Well, I suppose I never needed to. I remember everything, everything except where I left my *carte vitale.* It's good to know she has kept records and that one day she wants Daniel to publish a book with all the recipes in it.

I put an empty glass on the white plastic table and filled it.

"Are you not going to have one too?"

"No, like I said, I haven't the *envie.*"

"Would you like me to do some *magnetism* work on you?"

Pascale is also what Yvette was, a *magnetiser* who *prends le feu*. But where Yvette read people and their energy by the colors of their organs and aura, Pascale reads books and essays, anything she can get her hands on. She's the consummate autodidact. She works a lot with Bert Hillinger's family constellations and *movements of the soul*, and of course everything I know about naturopathy and homeopathy. She's also deeply influenced by anything of a numinous nature.

"No, thank you, Pascale. That's generous. I think I'm just working through something. My whole energy started to change about seven days ago. It's very unusual."

"*A votre santé!*" She lifted her glass and drank some of the *tincture*. "Did you know that the magnetic pole has changed and that in certain airports they've had to repaint the runways?"

"What?"

"Yes, even the Inuits are lost. They can't hunt properly anymore because they don't know how to get home. The stars are in the wrong place and the sun is setting in the wrong place. Their whole landscape has changed. That *Inconvenient Truth* movie was good and so was that *Inside Job* one, but someone has to start joining all the dots! It's not global warming we'll be dealing with soon, it's another Ice Age. Did you know that the man who invented the microwave in England has said that, if we don't change things drastically by 2050, Europe will be a desert? And that's a fact. It's simple science. There's no arguing with it. *Mais*, it doesn't matter, does it, Ezekiel? If we blow the whole planet up, it'll just start all over again on its own, without us."

"You don't know that."

"It will. Look at Chernobyl. Everyone says it was a complete and utter disaster. Yes, it was, but only for humans. If you go there now, you'll be visiting one of the most diverse areas of new plant life on the planet. No. Mother Earth, Gaia, will be fine. It's just us idiots that won't!"

She drank the rest of her tincture and I went to pour her another. She put her hand over the top of the glass and stood up. "No, we have to get you to your *rendez-vous* on time! It's bad enough I no longer have a license, but being over the limit too?"

I stood up and remembered where I'd left my *carte vitale*, the inside pocket of my coat. I put on my coat and followed Pascale out the door.

"It's not Gaia that has to worry, it's us." She closed my door behind us. "She's been through all this before. There's proof of nuclear explosions on the planet from thousands and thousands of years ago. You only have to go looking for dendrite, the stuff left over after a nuclear explosion. And they've found it. Look it up. We're what came after those explosions. If we blow it all up, the earth will just start all over again."

She walked down the white corridor in front of me, turning back occasionally as she continued to talk and wave her arms in front of her. "Only yesterday I was thinking about it. I was walking in my woods and two metaphors came to me, like that!" She clicked her fingers. "The first is that the whole of humankind is like micro-organisms living on the skin of the world. We have this immense density below the skin, organs, emotions, everything. And if the greater organism starts to smell, and degrade, well then it simply cleans itself. And you know, humankind is starting to stink! The second one, the fish bowl, is the same. Mother Earth doesn't mind if we swim around in our fish bowl like goldfish, forgetting everything we did three seconds back, never cleaning out our bowl. When the bowl gets too dirty, She'll simply throw the fish and the water out and start all over again with new fish, as happened with the Lemureans and Atlanteans or whoever came before us. The bowl always stays the same!"

"So what do you think is going to happen then?"

"Who knows? If one tenth of the one percent who own around ninety percent of everything in the world have their way, they'll just keep on going to the bitter end until they've squeezed every last cent out of their industrial revolution. Or at least until all the oil runs out. And do you imagine they'll stop even then?"

We had arrived at the car-park, and I waited while she scrabbled about in her bag for the keys to her car. It was a white Peugeot 205 GR, and it hadn't had a clean in a long while.

"You really think it's that bad, Pascale?"

"I don't think. I go by what scientists are saying, ones who are not *funded* by the big corporations." She folded her skinny arms together over the roof of her car, sighing as she leaned her thin chin on them. "People say it will end when oil ends. But do you think that's going to make Rockefeller, de Rothschild and Ford and all the rest of them stop rolling out their conveyor belts of toxicity? No! They'll drain it dry, and then they'll start pushing all the water and hydrogen and electricity-based cars which they've already bought the patents for. Or more like Tesla, killed for."

"They can't all think like that? Not every rich person is rotten."

She banged a fist on the roof of her car. "Of course they are, Ezekiel! It's logical. You were brought up on a farm. You have your own vegetable garden. You love gardening. These people were brought up in a totally different way. They get helicoptered in to their homes on the tops of mountain ranges they own along with other dynasties to swim in their Olympic sized swimming pools made of gold!"

"That can't be true."

"Oh, it's worse than that!" She bent down and got into her car. I opened the passenger door and got in. "Look at the Saudis. What about the man who has his silver Audis made out of real silver? You should see the pictures of his waterfront home. It stretches further than the whole of the Cité of Carcassonne!"

She took in a deep breath and started up the car. "These people don't care about the planet, Ezekiel! They're not like the Gautama Buddha. They're not going to leave their palaces to heal the planet.

They're going to rape Her and then try and rebuild Her the same way they do countries after obliterating them in their wars..."

"Hold on a second, though, Pascale. Are you sure about driving? Sure there are no gendarmes about?"

"Yes." She lit up a roll-up.

"Maybe we should get a taxi?"

She put the 205 into gear and reversed like a rally driver into the road, fast and loud. "Look at Iraq and what the Bush dynasty did there only recently. How many million more Iraqi civilians need to be killed before the United States leaves?" She shifted into first gear and almost immediately into second, breaking the thirty kilometer an hour speed limit in a matter of seconds. "They only destroy so that *they* can rebuild, for profit. You, and I, we create. We grow our own vegetables. We put our hands in Mother Earth and we feel Her. We feel a connection to Her. Do they? They put their hands in their pockets for their checkbook. All they know is how to buy things. But they can't buy that connection, can they, Ezekiel!" She tapped me on the side of the arm gently and smiled as she careened around the ninety-degree corner opposite the *boulangerie*, barely missing an octogenarian cyclist.

"That's true," I conceded. "It's the same with medicine. The big drug companies have basically blocked homeopathic medicine for decades in the United States. Do you know that an ayurvedic doctor can't practice medicine in the United States unless they have a degree in allopathic medicine first? It's ridiculous."

"Yes, but to be fair, it's not just America. Ezekiel. It's the same in France." She tapped some ash into the open tray as she drove. "You know that. You have to have a degree in medicine here to practice homeopathy. Six thousand years of accumulated medical knowledge against what – two hundred years of so-called scientific doctoring in the West? It's retarded!"

"Watch out, Pascale! That pigeon!"

"Don't worry about the pigeon. You couldn't hit them if you tried." She tapped some more ash, and went on. "And who knows anything these days about those *sixty centuries* of learning today? I was a history teacher for years, remember, I know what we feed our children. We feed them rubbish. Human civilization started when we learned to write, is that the sum of it? With the Sumerians of 3600 BC? Gobekli Tepe was discovered in the 1990's, and it's at least 11,000 years old! As for the recent past, you're aware what has happened to the French Revolution…?"

"Huh? How do you mean, the French Revolution?"

She put her cigarette out. "They've taken it out of the history books, just as the Americans did with the Native American Indians. They've reduced the Revolution to a paragraph!"

"They can't do that."

"They did."

We were already nearing Conques-sur-Orbiel when Pascale said this, her speed increasing with each new thought or fact.

"That was just one part of their strategy," she said bitterly. "Sarkozy and his marionettes didn't want us manifesting anymore. They wanted to dilute the revolutionary spirit of our country, Ezekiel. They wanted us to stay on our couches in front of the TV watching shows of people on couches watching TV and advertisements of the products they want us to eat and drink and stick in our air-conditioned nightmare! Do you remember how he called *us* a *racaille*, when we manifested and then wanted us to accept his disgusting policies on race and immigration? Why can't we be like the Spanish government and integrate the Roma population? He wanted us to re-elect him when he'd already pushed through his new immigration rules and deported the Roma gypsies…?"

The Roma people. 1935. The Nuremberg laws stripped them of their German citizenship, allowing the Nazis to imprison them and later commit genocide by sending them to death camps such as Belzec. Germany's allies, the Independent State of Croatia, Romania and Hungary did exactly the same.

"Maybe aliens will come down and save us from ourselves soon?" I said, trying to lighten Pascale's anger and frustration, as well as the lead in her foot as she stamped on the accelerator each time a new atrocity rose in her mind.

"If you were an alien, would you land on this planet?" Pascale asked. "I wouldn't! The one percent would lock me up in isolation and try to patent my spaceship so they could make more spaceships to make war with all the other friendly aliens out there."

I laughed.

"You may laugh, Ezekiel, but think about it. Given all those stars out there in the sky, more than we could ever so much as count, each star a possible sun for another galaxy of planets like ours, how can we still think we're alone? We can't imagine otherwise? That's folly! Human arrogance! No wonder they haven't landed, if they believe that is our mentality. Only an inferior, unimaginative species could ever think that. If I was an alien out there, I'd certainly be thinking that. And just pass on by."

She pushed in the car's overflowing ashtray. "Look at it this way, it's the *exact* same perspective our own world has of all the remaining uncontacted peoples in South America. We feel that going into their communities and introducing ourselves to them would blow their minds, destroy their cultures, give them diseases they've never encountered before and that they'd have a mass nervous breakdown! Look what we've done to the Matis of Brazil, the Jarawa in the Andaman Islands in India and all the other uncontacted peoples. Most well-meaning human beings want to leave them alone. Why wouldn't it be the same with aliens? It's logical. The aliens are the same. They are non-interventionist. It makes perfect sense."

"I'd never thought about it that way."

"Look, I know you don't like the Internet, Ezekiel, and that you don't read newspapers, but you do know that NASA said they've found an organism on Earth that needs arsenic to live, the very thing we've been taught to see as contrary to life?"

"No, I didn't know." I thought of what Thérèse's angel had said over sixty years before. "Where do you get all this information?"

"You remember Jean-Marc, my neighbor, the one who was always protesting against Sarkozy? He may be studying politics in Paris, but he's still open to reality!" She smiled. "He e-mails me this stuff every week."

"So, what's the solution, Pascale? What do you say to the world?"

She shifted into fifth gear as we made our way by the outskirts of Conques-sur-Orbiel. "You have to ask the question: how do I create my home? Ecology is how. People need to literally get up off their *culs* and start growing gardens like we do, instead of wasting water on a green lawn out the front of their house that serves no purpose! Get up off their knees and stop praying and begging things of God, thinking he's going to give them a miracle! Synchronicity only happens when you get up off your *cul* and knees and get out there to do creative things with people who are on the same wavelength."

I smiled at her.

"Isn't that what's happened with you and me. I created that synchronicity, and so did you. You moved from Provence because you wanted peace. And now look what I have! A font of medical knowledge that you won't find in books and one of the dearest friendships of my life! And you have this crazy hermit who does your shopping for you and makes sure you're not dead. That's co-creation! Creative intention! Only that can give you creative power, only that can move the world. Only that can change the world. *And* give birth to a new planet in the process!

I smiled at her once more. She started to search for her lighter as we passed the *gendarmerie*. She had already rolled a cigarette, which lay untouched in her lap. I thought what a gift it was to have this amazing woman in my life.

"God, that *tincture* was good. Where did you get the *verveine*? It's got..."

"My garden, of course."

She smiled. "Of course... There's something you're not telling me!"

"Well, I did put some thyme flowers in that particular bottle."

"I knew it! It's got thyme in it! I'll have to try it. How much did you use?"

"About one eighth of a cup to the regular mixture."

"Got it." She put the cigarette her hand had finally found into her mouth. "Now, are you sure you don't need any groceries, because I won't be back down again until this time next week as I have to prune fruit trees. I never got around to it in November, but then it didn't matter, it's been so hot this winter."

"No, I'm sure. Thank you, Pascale."

When we arrived at the Clinique Montreal she got out of the car and we gave each other *bisous*. Pascale looked at me with tears in her eyes and hugged me.

"Thanks for bringing me, Pascale."

"It's nothing. Now, are you sure you don't need any groceries?"

"Yes. Be careful the police don't stop you."

"I'll be back in an hour then." She got into her 205 and sped off, barely missing a Mercedes coming out of its parking spot.

When I got inside, I looked out the window of the waiting room at a murder of crows landing on the telephone wires, thinking about what Pascale had said. I couldn't help thinking that right now we are at the brink of something, of what Aquinas once called *a great deep*. This deep is not below us though, it's inside us. We humans are a great deep, inside, not outside. We are beyond our own comprehension, and it is this truth which makes us fear taking the leap into the unknown, ourselves. Yes, we might blow ourselves up and it'll be the end of us or maybe even the planet too, but it won't be the end of the universe. The sun has bigger explosions happening on it all the time, the universe growing even bigger again in their wake!

Looking at the crows fighting for their places on the wires I couldn't help but wonder whether we have really grown as a species. Yes, we have modern, technical advantages. When I was a child, there were no sinks or toilets or washing machines. In the Black Mountains alone it wasn't until 1958 that running water was connected to the houses. The washing machine alone was a *benediction* for women. No longer did they have to trudge outdoors to the *lavoir* and break the ice to wash their clothes. Also, today, you won't see so many children's headstones or crosses in the graveyards.

A sudden gale hit the birds outside. They flew back and up into the cloudy sky in one black, cooperative movement, in an utterly reasonable and natural flow of movement. And then they were gone, as quickly as they'd appeared.

Yes, we have to return to Nature. Life on this planet is a brotherhood, not just with us humans, but with the birds on the wires and the trees and the animals of the sea. God is not separate from Nature. We are not the masters of this world, we are a part of it, literally. The hand writing that thought down came out of the Earth. I, just as you are, was born out of the earth. We are the Earth, its fingers writing this, its eyes reading this, its consciousness understanding this right now, as the birds outside our window, the rest of us, sing.

We need to be aware of this consciousness. That is the only morality that is needed, awareness. The only sin is a willful lack of awareness. In our wonderful French language, we are unique. We do not divide our awareness into *conscience* and *consciousness*, as in English and in most other languages. We do not give consciousness a conscience. In French we are conscious, but not moral about it. We do not have consciences, we have consciousness! Conscience is what society gives us. Consciousness is Nature, the reality of the all around *us.* If I were to fly in an orbit around our planet and look back at the Earth, would I see Ireland and India and France? No. Would I see all the things that divide us? No. Reason alone will tell us: There is only one country, Earth. Reason alone will only tell us: There is only one people, the people of Earth. Us.

A MIRACLE

My specialist, a man with a great degree of belief in his own powers, looked at the tests, shaking his head from side to side. Who was I to judge him? Hadn't I thought I knew everything when I got my degree?

He kept moving the paperwork of my file around with his impeccably clean fingers, as if his movements would somehow make the results agree with his education. "But this isn't possible."

I remembered Dad's words and paraphrased them to him. "Everything is possible, doctor. Anything impossible is just an imagining or illness of the minds of men."

I knew before he spoke to me what he was going to say, so I told him first.

"It's gone."

He merely shook his head up and down and stared at me. I stood up and then bent over to shake his hand goodbye.

"But, but this is a miracle. Throat cancer doesn't just disappear in a few weeks by itself," he said.

I thought of Thérèse, of what she'd said all those years ago, how miracles are the most natural things on the planet and it's because of fools like us that they don't happen. It's mankind that's unnatural. We disallow miracles from happening every day.

"Yes," I said. "Miracles are the most natural things in the world. It's only when they don't happen that something's wrong."

"What?"

I asked him had he read Marianne Williamson's book *A Return to Love* or Hahnemann's *Organon of Medicine.* He said no. I wrote down the names and titles and left after shaking his hand.

Walking out the main door to meet Pascale in the car park, I wondered whether the doctor would read the books or whether, like me, it would take a heart attack before he realized something was wrong.

CREATION

Thérèse often used to quote Blake's *I must create a system, or be enslav'd by another man's.* For me, the next line of the same poem is just as significant: *I will not reason or compare: my business is to create.* This is my business too, to create. Whether it's in my lab proving another remedy or planting a vegetable or flower or writing, I create. I trust this completely.

Creation is not just painting, writing, arts and crafts. I'm talking about creating life. A nihilist like Hitler destroys life. The *Résistance* created life out of his ashes. That was what a creative mind was to me back then, *resistance*, not the destructive, mad, creative mind of a Hitler or his accomplices.

Think of what Hitler turned to once he stopped painting. How many creative people (artists, musicians, writers), and how many who were different (intellectuals, homosexuals, dwarves), did he kill after he stopped being an artist, stopped being a positively creative individual? How many books did he burn? Hitler destroyed art. Why? Because, for whatever reason, he could no longer create from a positive perspective. It was easier, more satisfying, to destroy. Love is an effort, hate is simple, its aim destruction. When St. Augustine was asked to simplify Jesus' message he said, Love, and everything else follows. We destroy ourselves without love, the most creative of feelings. We destroy the people and things around us with our lack of love, with our hatred. This is creation grown cancerous, grown awry.

Hitler was not the first dictator to indulge the power of creative destruction. The Mohammedan emperor, Aurangzeb, or as he called himself: the "Conqueror of the World," was another of his kind. I choose Aurangzeb because, in history, he represents the suppression of the creative form I love most: music. Aurangzeb banned all music. And why? Because he believed it was contrary to his religion: unholy for all believers, and perhaps especially for beautiful women. He issued a decree that any of his subjects found playing music were to be beheaded.

Music and death have formed a strangely intimate connection in my life too, for I was to meet many musicians in my time in the camps. We were the lucky ones. We got to survive by playing our music in accompaniment to Nazi orgies. I hid food and cigarettes inside my alto when the Germans were too drunk to notice. We stole cigarettes because we could trade them with the capos for food and simple privileges. Those nights spent playing the alto, they were like flying for me. The music I played kept the Germans happy but, more importantly, it re-created for me a whole symphony of memories from growing up in Aramon, the trees, the stream, the birds, Yusuf, Dad, Mathias and especially Thérèse. This was something the Germans never grasped.

Every time they dragged me and other musicians out of the camp to play for them, they were giving us the greatest gift there is, creation. They thought they were punishing us by making us watch them enjoy their feasts of food and alcohol and their orgies with prostitutes. Oh, how wrong they were. All right, they had stripped us of everything. They had made us into the "pigs" they never fed, waiting for us to die, but then, because of their lack of awareness, they gave us the power to create beauty. They actually *forced* us to do it. Those nights I would go back to my bed of boards, squeezed up against the other skeletons, floating in happiness, not because of the stolen food and cigarettes, but because of the joy of creation, the bliss of creating music, and doing so right in front of their faces. Yes, they had burned our books. Yes, they had tried to wipe us off the face of the planet, but there is one thing they could not take from us, from any human being, and that is the power to create, a power stronger than any other I have come to know.

As human beings we aren't given a road map on how to live our lives. We don't just pick up our sense of purpose or meaning off the ground like lost money. The search for purpose is itself an act of creation, but it is not ultimate creation. Creation does not lie out there somewhere, waiting for us to chance by. We must search for it inside ourselves, in the music we play, the song we sing, the car we mend, the surfboard on which we float across the wave. Call it what you will - God, Truth, harmony, simplicity – what is important is to give birth to something, a prayer, a new business, a book, a cake even, a new idea. It doesn't have to be extraordinary, just extraordinary to us, to its creator.

Every single one of us is extraordinary because each of us is a manifestation of the mysterious. Every creative act is something that penetrates from that mystery into this field of reality. If we wait for meaning to come to us as we sit on a couch in our living room, we'll be waiting until the day we die, still asking the question the mind loves most, *What does it mean?* Ask a flower what the meaning of itself is. Will it answer? The flower doesn't see itself as anything. It just is, a flower. How can it be anything else? In the same way, people are who they are, but they will not, they cannot fully realize their natures if they do not create. A flower doesn't sit on a couch. It grows. It gives. It creates, it blooms, and everything else enjoys its beauty.

My mind often turns these days to Carl Jung on his island in the middle of a lake, building and rebuilding his tower over the years as he wrote his books. He built his tower, stone by stone. He carved it. He painted it. He created that space for himself, his sacred retreat. And what came from his labor? Did this one man not completely change the face of psychology? I have created my own sacred retreats, the garden outside my door and my little homeopathic laboratory inside this house. Twenty-five years ago, when I bought this house and moved here from Carcassonne to clean out my consciousness, there was nothing out there on that hectare of land but briars.

Now thirty-three olive trees, fruit trees like the old varieties we had on our *mas*, a vegetable garden in the summer, walls I built out of stone from the mountain mixed with *chaux*, and every type of herb I could find, cover that hectare. Wildflowers and birds and bees from my *ruches* surround these creations. My lab was merely the biggest room in the house, initially an empty one. In there I now have every tincture Hahnemann wrote about, lined up in alphabetical rows which fill that once empty room, in addition to many Hahnemann never wrote about. In there I must have ten different types of mortar and pestle for grinding and trituration, hundreds of glass bottles for potentization and succussion. This is what I have created over the years and now, when I need to meditate, I go out into the garden and breathe in the smell of lavender and rosemary and take in the sound of birdsong. I don't care how small my little house is. What matters to me is that I continue to create on that one hectare of land and in that room. To see, to watch all that creation in my lab or outside my little window right now brings a great joy to my heart as I write this.

The flower in my garden there, just beside the lavender, creates without asking and gives me moments of beauty, every day opening more, creating more, offering more and more beauty. Each moment can be an artistic event, an epiphany, a moment of becoming, a fishing rod launching its line out onto a body of water, the hook just about to hit the water, the lady just about to pick the flower. Those are moments of creation, where something is about to happen or an individual is about to try and capture them in paint or music or on video.

As Pascale so often says, we are co-creators in reality. We create our own reality, our own synchronicity, by getting up and out into the world, by standing up and being heard, by acting creatively with intention. It is this creative potential that makes us a powerfully positive species. Our creative potency will always defeat the Hitlers of this world. Blaming the upper class, or blaming our parents, as was the case with Freud and as I myself have done, gets us nowhere. Man is, as Thérèse said so many times, a being living a human experience. We beat Hitler. Finding a way out of potential failure. We beat Mussolini. Out of another potential failure. And how did we do it? We became creative. We created resistance networks, an Allied invasion. A new French state. We created the United Nations. We created. We stopped the destruction. We used our creative potentiality and changed the direction of the world.

The perspectives of all those around me who resisted have made this feeling even stronger inside me as I've aged. Thérèse resisted anything that suppressed the human soul. Mathias did the same when he deserted. Dad, every time he defended outsiders. Yusuf, in not allowing the deaths of everyone he knew to create that which is the most destructive: reactive anger. Yusuf responded by forgiving those who murdered his family. It was this same form of creative resistance that saved me in the camps.

Dad used to say there are two types of people in the world: those who want to live a comfortable life, looking for death, and the others who are living creatively, looking for life. The first are waiting for a comfortable grave, the second are the risk takers who embrace difficulty to enjoy the life they have right now. These people play. These people create life.

Had World War II not happened, I would never have left our farm in Provence. I would never have seen as much of the world as I have. Might it have been a good thing if I'd stayed on the farm? No. Looking back on my life now, even after all I've endured, I can see it was of enormous benefit to me. Although I was in a creative environment on the *mas*, surrounded by love and the natural progression of sowing and reaping our crops, I know I would not have evolved into the man I am now, had I stayed there. Yes, I would be 'living a happy life', save the tempests of my mother's alcoholism and the odd anti-Semitic sneer, but would I have truly grown to be happy?

I see the tragedy of the war, even the camps, and the wandering years before I married as creative and positive. I was forced to change and grow. All that moving about, being pushed and pulled by the waves of life, was what caused me to change, for doesn't change only occur with movement? Yes, I would rather be in this world of an old man with his garden and experiences looking back on the worlds which changed around me, than be sitting in Aramon stuck in an old world, and afraid to enter a new.

The meaning of all my experiences, from 1939 until my release from Auschwitz, from my odyssey from Ireland to India and back to France, from lover to doctor to husband to old man, was to create something that resisted the destructive actions of a man like Hitler or, today, the mega-corporations, the pharmaceutical companies which want doctors like me to be their vendors, not healers. Yes, any true meaning I have gleaned from this life is that we need to create, not destroy, and that we can only creatively heal within the families and communities that surround us. I resist destruction. I resist anything that destroys the creativity of any person or the potential for the individual to create their own healing. I resist the Hitlers of this world, and his subtler contemporary acolytes, who urge us to give up all creative purpose and allow them to take care of things.

The forms of creative resistance are simple, and they are all around us. What, for example, can be more powerfully creative than a smile? If we can create nothing other than a smile, well then, have we not created as much as any protest or political action? Thérèse nearly always had a smile for me, even in her hardest times. Dad smiled more than any one person I have ever met. Yusuf had a smile, even after telling me what had happened to his family. Emil and Hermann had smiles on their faces as they passed away in front of me. If we can create a smile, then everyone benefits. Yes, to smile is probably the most creative thing we can do.

I have given simple examples, but they are very powerful. They undermine the subtle dictatorial manipulation that loves our apathy, our indifference and lack of community. Creation is power. Creating empowers us to not only do things that give us joy, but at the same time to benefit from that creation so that those *in power* have less of it. As we found out in the *Résistance*, if only a few of us have the will to create a different world, then look at what can happen. Imagine the momentous power for change if every one of us on the planet were able to realize, in action, our creative potential. What a world of change we would have in every day.

I continue to trust in my own personal truth, one I feel is universal: I have to find a way to live my life creatively, in joy and happiness. True, realised happiness, not *the pursuit of happiness* as the American Declaration of Independence has it. How can we *pursue* happiness? Happiness simply … happens. Any moment of happiness I have ever experienced has only ever happened when I *wasn't* looking for it. This is why I live every day now in appreciation and gratitude for my potential to create a reality that abounds in freedom.

The human race has to choose to be free. We do not live inside the world of *Waiting for Godot.* We are not consigned to waiting all our life to be free. We in the *Résistance* fought for that freedom many years ago. People are still fighting for their freedom now, every day. Choose resistance, choose freedom. Choose to be a humanist, not an apathist.

Every seed must die before a new tree grows. The pain of dying is natural, and what a miracle it is to watch that seed turn into a tree which then towers over us in the sky. Choose to plant the seed and live creatively. Choose to live. Take courage, take heart. Even death is a friend when we are creative, and our only enemy then is fear.

THE DARK NIGHT OF THE SOUL

Seven days ago, instead of trying, instead of making an effort to search, instead of struggling to seek, I stopped. I gave up creating my ego, the process and demands of my ego. So, it collapsed. All that I could think, I had thought. And that was when I started writing. I had no more expectation, and my voice became one with the Truth. That day the intense pain in my throat disappeared. That day I knew the cancer had gone, the day I expressed a divine Will, my reason for being here, to write of my experiences and life and how they had transformed me. In doing so I have saved myself from experiencing the lesson of a long and painful illness.

In the weeks before, I had become bored. My boredom had grown and grown, becoming more and more intense, and it was seven days ago that this incredible boredom with everything around me, shopping for food, answering the telephone, going for a walk in the village below, even attending to my precious garden, became stultifying. I felt suffocated, overwhelmed by it.

That day was the beginning of a transformation. For ninety-nine years I had thought it was so very far away, and it was here all the time. A new energy started to surround me as I wrote, coming from nowhere, but everywhere, from the birds, the leaves, the rocks, the very air. By searching I had lost myself, looking into the distance, into the vanishing point. I had stopped the first ego goal of the worldly, money, power, prestige. I thought I was on the correct path, but my ego had simply replaced it with another goal, that which is not of this world, the search for enlightenment, God.

Seven days ago, I let go of letting go.

My ego couldn't survive anymore. Its wall came down because the ego is the seed's wall. Inside is the plant. The wall needs to gradually break down, to die, so that the plant can be born. My ego started to break down because I gave it no fuel, no desire to cling to. I just wrote and did what I had to do each day. I was completely in the present, no future, just writing from my heart. The wall broke down the more I wrote.

An even better way to describe it would be to say that seven days ago the searching, the seeking, stopped. I did not stop desire. It stopped. The search stopped and I started to write to merely document what has happened to me.

That first day, even though I didn't write it down, I felt helpless. I felt no hope. It was total. This is not negative. There was simply no hope. It was a positive presence, though, the "I am Not", my tremendous surrender. The second day, I felt the same way. And for these seven days I have only felt hopelessness.

But at that moment when my hopelessness started, this new energy began happening. Suddenly, all of existence started to rush into me, enter me. Matsuo Bashō wrote of this rush:

The old pond
A frog jumps in
Plop

Today, though, just this morning, a totally new energy overcame me. I almost couldn't bear it. It was a joy, an ocean of bliss. Everything started to disappear for me like the sea into the sand on a summer's day. Things shattered. Everything was disappearing. My whole personal history. My mind was fading away, and there was no desire to cling onto it or my past or anything. My factual memory bank stayed, but my psychological memory bank was obliterated, annihilated.

This is the problem for everyone: psychological memories, stored on an energetic computer, outside the brain. You are not this brain. You are the being looking and connecting to the database of memories inside your external biological computer. These memory files are what create fictions, content, "facts," when the real fact is seeing life as it is. These psychological memory files are what create the ego, the "I." The fictions of my previous psychological memory bank are gone. The database has been wiped clean. The computer is still there, but all the data has been removed.

The mirror is gone, now there is only the mirror of Nature.

These last seven days I have been staying up until sometime between midnight and 1 a.m. to write. I was alert as a child waking in the morning. But today, all I wanted to do was sleep. And the pain, it grew. It became very difficult to withstand, what I can only imagine it is like to give birth. I felt as if I was going to die, that dark night of the soul I had read of somewhere I couldn't remember where. For once, I couldn't remember something! What a blessing! I suppose I should have understood this earlier when I couldn't remember where I'd left my *carte vitale*.

Then the pain came again, and a feeling that something was going to happen. I couldn't keep my eyes open any longer, though. I went to sleep but I was still awake. Only my body was asleep. It was a meeting. I was aware, but I was asleep.

I slept until two in the morning, until my eyes opened like a baby's does in the morning, immediately, as if involuntarily. And then I felt Her. I didn't see Her, I only felt a deeply feminine presence, one of extreme abundant light, a joy. It was extreme unction as birth. The time Thérèse and I last made love together was a drop in the Ocean of Her light. It was the love all the Sufis sang of, the human soul searching for God and by Her grace She falls on you, like the dove from heaven, and you are annihilated, *fana,* in Her, forgetting *Ishq-e-Majazi*, illusory love, this dying of love and crossing the bridge to *Ishq-e-Haqiqi*, true love, love itself, God, to dwell there in the Eternal existence and consciousness of God, *baqa*. This joyous violet light surrounded me, involved me, devoured me in ecstasy, joy and light, everything becoming unreal, my house, my bed, my body. The *Gita* says it better:

> *By love he knows me in truth, who I am and what I am.*
> *And when he knows me in truth he enters into my Being.*

I couldn't handle it anymore. It was as if I was being smothered. I had to get out! I got out of my bed and went out through the terrace doors of my little living room into my beautiful garden of herbs and olive trees. As soon as I was in nature, under the sky, the smothering sensation fell away. I needed the sky. I needed everything to be open. As I walked, I felt like I was walking on the air, as if I was flying, floating. I felt as if I was being carried away.

I looked around me. Everything was alive and full of light. I could see the movement of energy in the air, in the sap in the grass.

I walked, glided over to the old olive tree at the end of the garden, as if guided there. When I sat down, I could see the sap in its leaves over my head flowing through the branches and back down into the trunk of the tree. As soon as I leaned against its trunk, I took a deep breath and things started to resolve and everything, everything, became eternity, virgin, timeless.

For four or maybe five hours I sat underneath the olive tree. As I write this, it is just turning seven o'clock in the morning. I can hear the bell sounding the hour from the Mairie in the valley below me.

There is just one more thing I would like to write and it is this: I am so grateful to all the people I have loved and known in this life, my parents, my friends, everyone that has touched me. To Thérèse and Julie and Yvette and even Nausicaa, I am so grateful. They broke my heart, but in the breaking opened it. Thanks to those heart-opening experiences of love, thanks to my peace and sanity being wrecked by love, I was able to leave love behind me and have the opportunity of experiencing Divine Love.

I am driven crazy by this different Love! By the song of birds. By the rush of the wind through the trees and the clouds through the sky. It all makes me feel as if my soul is going to explode out of the cage of my heart. This is the song, these are the chords of the world. This is the song of God. It wants you to play its chords, and oh how happy it makes you when you do. Every moment is an opportunity to sing its song, this song of life, this joy and bliss, this appreciation, this gratitude for all that we receive and perceive every moment of every day, each one an inhale and exhale of the universe into song. *The Song of Songs* is the song of creation, the lover, human, falling in love with the Beloved, God, after having lived through the experience of lover and beloved. It is the music of the universe, the *Elast.*

"*Elastu Bi Rabbikum?*" Do you not recognize your Lord? Yes! Oh, Yes, I do! I have drunk the *Ma'rifat*, the *gnosis*, real Knowledge, the God within, awakened through love, divine love, *bhakti*, a gift given, a grace, a blessing, a mercy, a beauty, a loving kindness! Oh, how I am blessed and graced!

The past is dead to me now. I no longer see the present through the eyes of the past. To tell the truth it never existed anyway except in the people and places I remained attached to. That is over now. My life force is flowing through me as at no other time. There is no death, only life. I remember Tara, *We will all die. It is natural to be fearful. Accept the fear and then the fear will have no hold on you. Accept the fear and death becomes a fiction and life becomes freedom. If we accept this beauty then we can live, truly live. The natural world shows us again and again every day of the year, in a flower, a bird, that home is here, within us. Go along the path in. Go in to your home. Yes. This is it. Go in.* And Marcus Aurelius, who advised us to accept *death in a cheerful spirit, as nothing but the dissolution of the elements from which each living thing is composed. If it doesn't hurt the individual elements to change constantly into one another, why are people afraid of all of them changing and separating? It's a natural thing. And nothing natural is evil.*

Now I am really home. Oh, now I understand! All our houses and towns and villages are not homes. They are an illusion, *maya*. Yes, before I knew the word *maya* meant illusion, but now, now I am *aware* of it because of my experience today. I had created an unreal world, as everyone does because there are as many worlds as there are people. As Heraclitus said, the waking have one world in common, sleepers have each a private world of their own. I am no longer reality and *maya*. I am reality without ego now. The mirror is gone. Home is not a place; it's an experience. Now I am no longer who I was before. Last night I became empty, a positive emptiness, *shunya*. And now I am full. I died, and now I am reborn. Nothing of that man I was exists anymore. Everything in the story of my life has been for this day. I accept all the choices and things that have happened to be because they could not have been otherwise. I see it all now. This day, I died. Another being exists now.

During the night a door opened. What it is called doesn't matter to me anymore, Tao, God, Allah, Dhamma, Truth, Goddess. What matters is the experience, this experience, this experience I have continued to experience, of not being in my body anymore, of floating around it, so powerful and yet so fragile, like a rose in the morning sun, creative, giving, precious as a dewdrop about to fall, beautiful, a miracle.

And tomorrow, will this miracle continue? I don't know. I am content in today, in the miracle of now.

PART NINE
THE BLACK MOUNTAINS
FRANCE

WEDNESDAY, JANUARY 11TH, 2017

A BEAUTIFUL MEETING

Pascale picks up Ezekiel's "Loi de Travail: NON!" T-shirt, the words scrawled across the white cotton in red paint. She folds it, rests it on the couch below Mathias' painting of Thérèse.

"I'm going to the toilet, Daniel. I'll be back in a moment."

"Hey, I'm not going anywhere." He continues to read his book.

There is a knock at the main door. Daniel gets up from the couch and walks down the hallway to answer it.

A tall, well-dressed woman, with short, highlighted hair and bright blue eyes, stands in front of him.

"Yes?"

"Hello. My name is Thérèse, Thérèse Sanador. Ezekiel told me to come. This is Ezekiel Moran's house, yes?"

"Yes, it is. When did he ask you to come?"

"A few weeks ago."

"He never mentioned you."

"Here's a printout of the e-mail."

"He e-mailed you? I didn't know Pepe had an e-mail address." He reads the e-mail, his other hand still on the door. "Yes, this is Pepe. But ... Come on in."

She walks in. Daniel closes the big wooden door. "You'll have to wait though. He's meditating. He'll stop soon, but not for long, so as to talk to Pascale."

"Pascale?"

"A very close friend of his."

"Ah, I see." Thérèse points into the biggest room in Ezekiel's house. "What's that room in there?"

"It's Pepe's lab, where he potentizes his homeopathic remedies and writes down his provings. Homeopaths come from all over the world to visit that lab."

"Pepe?"

"It's what we call our grandparents in French, although Pepe's my great-grandfather. Your accent, it's American. Where in America are you from?"

"New York."

He bends down to pick up his copy of *1984* from the floor. "New York. I've always wanted to go there some day. Here, sit down." He points at an armchair in front of the couch. He slumps onto the couch.

Thérèse looks at the walls. They are covered in old photos. Men with guns standing beside what looks like a version of Daniel, only in black and white. Ezekiel, she guesses. Other men, who look as if they had been in a concentration camp. A beautiful woman in a white wedding dress stands on a beach beside a really tall, handsome man with curly black hair and a curious smile. A photo of an Indian woman in white robes sits with her legs crossed in the lotus position. She has an immense smile on her face. There's also a floor to ceiling painting of the same beautiful woman from the wedding looking out a window.

"Where is Ezekiel?"

"In his bedroom. He sits in there in lotus position all day. I'm beginning to get worried about him. He doesn't move. He's gotten so thin."

"When do you think he'll be finished?"

"Soon. He used to meditate in the mornings and evenings. Now he does it all day. The only thing he said to me when I got here from the hospital was: *Daniel, I am very happy to have you here*. Usually we sit and talk about stuff, music."

"You were in the hospital?"

"Yes. I was in a coma."

"Are you OK now?"

"That's debatable. Well, I'm walking. My head's not completely there yet, but I'm walking and talking. What was I telling you? Oh yes, Pepe, music. He has me listen to music a lot. Do you play music?"

"No."

"Anyway, last time he wanted to know what I thought of Glass' opera *Akhnaten* and *Bartok's Viola Concerto, Sz. 120* which, he said, was written at the very end of World War II when Bartok was dying of leukemia. Pepe is a mad man about music. He has his two altos, a violin, sitar, an accordion and a mandolin."

With an arm extended he points behind him. "They're all on the shelves over his bed. He used to give me lessons, which I loved. He used to have four altos but he gave me one of them, and my mother stole it. He didn't mind. He just lets me play one of his when I come here. Last time I was here he taught me a lot of Strauss' *Don Quixote* and the times before that some of Mozart's quintets and a lot of his *Sinfonia Concertante in E-flat Major, K. 364*. His favorite piece for the alto is the last movement of Handel's *Harpsichord Suite in G minor*. It's a *passacaglia* arranged by Halvorsen for violin and alto. We listen to Itzhak Perlman and Pinchas Zukerman's amazing versions all the time. I like the one they did in 1977, but Pepe prefers the one they did in 1997."

Thérèse looks at Daniel, trying to work out whether he's finished.

"Pepe doesn't like computers at all, but when I showed him how I use Spotify on my iPhone he got Pascale to get him a computer. He never uses the Internet, but he uses Spotify alright. You can ask Pepe anything about music and he'll know it. Like me he's got this crazy memory. He even listens to stuff I listen to. He has one of those photographic memories. He can tell you dates and album names and the record label and everything about the musicians, who they married, what made them write a song."

"So he hasn't eaten in how long?"

"Days. I asked him did he want me to make him a *tisane* or something when I got in from the hospital and he said no, but that I was welcome to eat or drink whatever I wanted. Pepe's mad about *tisanes*, so I thought that was a bit weird that he didn't want one. The weirdest thing though was when I went to get something to eat there was nothing in his fridge except some dried out vegetables. I asked him whether I could get him some food in the store, and he reminded me there were no stores in these mountain villages. I'd have to wait for the *épicerie* truck the next day, he said. I didn't mind. I'm used to not eating for long periods."

Daniel lifts his glass of water from the wooden coffee table beside the couch. "Did you want some water, a cup of tea, a *tisane*?"

"No. No thanks." Thérèse looks about the room.

"I know what you're thinking. You Americans have TVs in every room. Well, Pepe has no TV. He doesn't even have a radio. The only thing he has lots of are books. They're everywhere. You can't see one of the walls he has so many books, all piled up on top of one another to the ceiling. If you stayed in this place too long you'd probably turn into a book." Daniel starts laughing and spills some water on his brown corduroys.

"Can I be candid with you, what was your name again?"

"Thérèse."

"Thérèse. I can be candid with you, Thérèse, yes?"

"Sure."

"You must be important if Pepe invited you here. OK, I'm very proud of my Pepe. He's changed my whole life. Never mind what he's done. You'll have to read his journal. Jesus Christ, that'll blow your head right off. I read it when I started to regain my consciousness. Pepe had been in there with me for a week until I woke. Didn't move. Not once. Pauline, my nurse, said he slept in that room. The man is a miracle. Can you imagine? He's nearly a hundred years old and he sat in that armchair for a week in the same clothes until I woke up. This man." Daniel shakes his head from side to side. "This man. Because of him I now know what my problem was. I had no elder to help me like the Indians and the Celts, or the Essenes of our family. TV and iPhones and all that doesn't help you on a spiritual path. They say spiritual paths are for weirdos and crazies and New Age hippies. Way I see it TV and the rest of it is what makes you crazy. TV stops you on your path. It makes you nuts. Like, who goes out killing people after watching a meditation video? They do when they watch the *normal* TV right?"

Thérèse smiles. "Yes, you're right."

Daniel leans over and picks up a black journal. On the front of it there's one word printed on a piece of cloth with a red Camargue cross stitched onto it, "EZEKIEL." He hands the journal to Thérèse.

"What is this?"

"You'll have to read it and find out."

"What, now?"

"If you like."

"Why do you want me to read it?"

"Pepe wouldn't have invited you here, if you weren't meant to read that."

She opens it. "It's hand written. So, it's his journal?"

"Yes, you could call it that. When I finished it, I had all these questions for him. He smiled at me. He's always smiling, Pepe. He smiled and then asked me was it going to be my birthday soon. Yes, I said. I was 21 the day I finished reading that journal. He asked me whether I thought that was a coincidence. I said no. That's a very important age in our family. As ever, perfect timing, he said. What age are you, Thérèse?"

"I'm 79."

"And when are you 80?"

"In a day or two actually."

"See! It's happening again! I'm sure it's another important age in our family. From what I remember him telling me, this is when you become less attached to the world. You become more accepting of people. It's when you think a lot about death."

Thérèse smiles at him, not knowing what to say.

"I know. You think I'm high. Well, for once I'm not. My head's a bit out of it because I was in a coma, but I've never been clearer about all this. You'll understand too, when you read it. You'll see. It's all in there."

He smiles at her. "Yes, you don't want to do that right now. I know. So, who are you? Why does Pepe want you here, when he barely wants to see me or Pascale?"

"I reached out to Ezekiel. He didn't know I existed until a month ago. He told me a lot about you, in e-mails. He wanted me to meet you as much as he wanted me to meet him."

"What?"

"He said you might like to go to the States."

"How?"

"He jokingly suggested that I adopt you."

"What? Now you're messing with my head." He rubs his forehead and long black hair with all his fingers at once, back and forward for about ten seconds. "How did you find, Pepe?"

"Let's just say I have a few friends."

"What do you mean, friends?"

"I'll be honest with you, Daniel, as you seem to distrust me. I have some friends in the French government."

"What? Whatever. Let's just put that to one side for a second, even though that's already not good." He rubs his eyes with the palms of his hands. "Why didn't you search for Pepe earlier?"

"As I said already, I only just found out." She sits forward. "Your parents seem very ... unhealthy."

"What? Did you find that out from your friends too?"

"Yes. And Ezekiel. How is your mother?"

"Oh, where do you start with her. Every time I start to talk about her I feel like people start judging me as crazy just because I'm talking about her craziness. The drugs. That's been fun. Right now she's in trouble because she took a lot of money from the state, pretending to be not working when she was. Also claimed she had no husband when my father was there a lot of the time. She owes a lot of money to CAF."

"CAF?"

"The government." He rubs his temples. "My father's in prison. They both live in the courts or prison when they're not high."

Pascale walks into the room, confused.

"Where have you been, Pascale?"

"I ... I don't know. One second I was in the toilet, the next I was lost. I had no idea where I was. It seems to be happening a bit more often than it used to."

"Well, this is Thérèse. Thérèse, this is Pascale, Pepe's best friend."

Thérèse stands up. "Pleased to meet you."

"Pleased to meet you too."

"Are you American?"

"Yes. Is my accent that bad?"

"No. I can tell an American accent pretty quickly. I used to know a lot of Americans at one time, a long time ago."

"Pepe's been e-mailing her. He asked her to come here."

"Really. Daniel, did you not get her a coffee or tea?"

"I offered her some water."

"It's cold outside. She probably wants something warm. Does Zeke have coffee?"

"Yes, I bought some from the *épicerie* yesterday. It's awful stuff, though."

"It doesn't matter. Coffee is always terrible in France. We have the greatest cuisine in the world and the worst coffee. Make a pot, please."

"Yes, sir!"

Daniel jumps up and walks down the hallway into the kitchen.

"He's a bit off right now. He just got out of hospital."

"What caused the coma?"

"Oh, so he told you already?"

"Not the cause."

"He was beaten. Hit his head off the side of the sidewalk. The other victim was OK though. He had a slight concussion."

"There were two of them?"

"Yes, and five or six Maghrebians. I can tell you about it another time. Would you like me to see if Zeke is finished meditating?"

"Please."

Pascale opens the door into Ezekiel's bedroom and closes it behind her. After a few minutes she comes back out, as Daniel puts teacups on the coffee table in the center of the room.

"He says you can come in. Bear in mind that he's pretty weak."

"I will." She follows Pascale and Daniel into the room. They sit on two old chairs at the end of the bed.

Ezekiel is on the bed in the lotus position, his body covered in a white wool blanket.

"My name is Thérèse Sanador," she says, nervous, excited, but calm at the same time.

"Sanador?" Ezekiel says as if returning from the fog of dream.

"Yes. You probably remember my other name better, Kreutzmann?"

"Kreutzmann? Ahhhh..." Ezekiel smiles. "Finally ... we meet!" He takes one of her hands in both of his. "Sit down. Please." She sits on the side of his bed. "I tried to find you, many years ago, after I came back from India. You would have been about five then."

"I doubt anyone would have been able to find me back then. My grandfather had moved us into hiding in South America."

"Ahhh..."

She moves closer on the bed. "I've been searching for you for a long time."

"So your grandmother told you about me then?"

"No. It was much later on. It was when I was going through her things that I found your letters to my mother hidden inside the back cover of their wedding album."

"Mathias' and Thérèse's daughter. What a wonderful, wonderful gift this is!"

She smiles. "No."

Ezekiel looks confused. "I don't understand."

She takes a letter out of her bag and opens it. "Can I read this to you? It was a letter my mother never had the chance to send to you. I found it with the rest of the letters in the back of their wedding album."

"Yes, of course."

"Dear Zeke, I know now for sure that you have gone to war because I haven't had a letter from you in such a long time. I do hope the ones I have sent you will be there for you when you get back. This will be a short one as I have been very ill. Our beautiful little girl was born only two days ago and she is a gift, a blessing! But I have not been myself at all and today I feel weaker than ever. I have not told Mathias this but I don't think I am going to be here much longer. I've had visions, such wonderful visions, transformative visions! I'm not afraid to die. I have accepted it. But this is not why I am writing this. I am writing to tell you something I should have told you before now but didn't have the courage to. Do you remember that night when I refused your proposal and we made such wonderful love? Well, what I'm trying to say is that Thérèse is your daughter, not Mathias'. I was due my period the day after and it never came, and Mathias and I didn't have sex for weeks after that night. We were so busy trying to plan the wedding and honeymoon in Collioure and where we were going to live and he was painting and discovering himself that way. Oh, Zeke, can you forgive me having waited nearly a year to tell you this? I know you will. You were always a far nobler person than I could ever be. I must end this now as the pain is starting again. I'll send it to you tomorrow if I can. Please forgive me! Please! Until we meet again, Love Love Love, Your Thérèse."

She folds the letter. She puts it back inside the envelope. She is crying.

Ezekiel takes both her hands again in his and smiles at her.

He lifts his right hand and points to the front of his journal on her lap. "She stitched that Camargue cross onto my handkerchief before I left for the war." He smiles. "Everything I have to say about your mother is in here." He pats the journal. "I'm so grateful to have written it all down now. What a blessing. Now that I am going, you will be able to profit from it. It is written."

Daniel smiles. "It is written."

"You really are her daughter, Thérèse. I can see it in your face."

"I'm yours too."

"I know. And I am so very grateful to meet you. It is a great honor."

She touches his head with her right hand, worried. "You know, your aura is a very pale yellow and your chakras are all dark." She caresses his face.

"Ah, so you're a synesthete too! Daniel here is one too. He has a fantastic memory for things he loves, computer coding, music."

"Yes, but I see people's energy. Depending on the color around them, or the colors of their organs I can say what is making them sick."

"How wonderful. You're a synesthetic medical intuitive then."

She laughs. "Yes, I'd never thought about it like that before, but you're right." She takes her right hand off the journal, places it on top of his. "Can I hold you?"

"Can a father refuse his daughter's love?"

She leans forward and surrounds him with her arms. After a few moments she releases him. Ezekiel slowly takes the leather necklace with the brown scapular on it from around his neck. "This is for you to pass on. It is sacred to our family." He puts it over her head and rests the scapular near her heart. He lays his hand on his journal. "Read this, and you'll understand."

She kneels down beside the bed and lays her head on his lap. Ezekiel smiles. He sings quietly to her, *Her Mantle So Green.*

When he finishes she raises her head. Ezekiel's breathing seems to disappear. His eyes are closed. After a while, he opens his eyes.

"It's time." Daniel and Pascale move nearer to him on the bed. "It's time to leave things behind, time to go home."

"But you can't be dying, Pepe?"

"I'm not, I'm entering into life, Daniel!" He reaches his hand out into Daniel's and puts his other hand into Thérèse's hands. He looks directly into Pascale's eyes. "Pascale..."

"Yes, Zeke, I know."

They both smile at the same time.

"You can't go, Pepe!"

"Existence decides its timing, Daniel."

"But we've only just met."

"And what a beautiful meeting, Thérèse."

He smiles, closes his eyes. "May all beings be free ... free as the wind."

YOU CAN MAKE A BIG DIFFERENCE

Reviews are the most powerful tool a writer has when it comes to getting attention for books.

Honest reviews of John's books help bring them to the attention of other readers. If you've enjoyed this book John would be very grateful if you could spend just a minute leaving a review (it can be as short as you like) on the book's Amazon page.

Thank you.

ABOUT LA MUSE BOOKS

La Muse Books is a small independent publisher based in France.

We believe in the power of ideas and art. One of the best ways to empower ideas and art? Books.

We publish the community of artists and writers who create at La Muse, (lamuseretreat.com) our artists and writers retreat in the south of France.

Thank you for reading our books.

Connect with La Muse Books:

contact@lamusebooks.com
Facebook: lamusebooks
Twitter: @lamusebooks
Instagram: @lamusebooks

We occasionally send newsletters with details on new releases, special offers and other bits of news relating to our writers and books. If you sign up to our mailing list we'll send you six books **for free**, when you sign up on our website:

lamusebooks.com

ACKNOWLEDGMENTS

I would like to thank Gabrielle, for inspiring me to write this book. Ezekiel's story is loosely based on the story of her amazing father.

Thank you, John Clanchy. Your critical eye, good humor, and unfailing solidarity, helped me to return again and again to *Ezekiel*.

I'd also like to thank Nancy Collins-Warner and Sarah Sullivan for their support and help.

Of course, the most important acknowledgement is to Kerry, my wife. If she had not obliged me to retreat from our retreat to write in the first place, *Ezekiel* would never have appeared. Thank you Kerry for your love, support and constant encouragement.

ABOUT THE AUTHOR

John Fanning was born in Ireland. After university he managed bars in Dublin and London, until he went to New York where he met his wife, Kerry, while working in a coffee shop in the East Village. They got married six months later, and moved to Alaska.

When he's not writing, John runs La Muse artists and writers retreat, in the south of France. His last job before co-founding La Muse was as a researcher/reporter at *Vanity Fair* in New York.

He is presently writing two novels, some of the characters having previously appeared in his novel, *Ezekiel.*

John lives in France with Kerry and their three children.

Get an automatic email when John's next book is released, visit: johnfanning.me.

Follow John:
Instagram: @johnfanning_
Facebook: @johnfanningwriter
Twitter: @fanning_j

CPSIA information can be obtained
at www.ICGtesting.com
Printed in the USA
BVHW031342151118
533140BV00022B/38/P